The Lads From The Pleasant 'B-Team'

E

Tom Wheeler

Foreword

On Friday 2nd April 1982 the Argentine forces invaded the Falkland Islands in the South Atlantic Ocean, followed the next day by the invasion of nearby South Georgia and the South Sandwich Island. These islands were British overseas dependencies but disputed by Argentina who knew them in Spanish as "Islas Malvinas". This was an attempt for them to establish sovereignty.

Shortly after the invasion the British Government sent a naval task force eight thousand miles to retake the islands. The war/conflict lasted seventy-four days, just over ten weeks, with the surrender of the Argentine forces on 14th June 1982. This was with a great cost of lives – Argentina six hundred and forty-nine military personnel, two hundred and twenty-five British military personnel and three Falkland Islanders.

After the British general election, the following year in 1983, it was announced by the then British Prime Minister Margaret Thatcher that an airbase would be built on the East Falkland Islands approximately forty miles west of the capital, Stanley, near a mountain called Mount Pleasant. This would commence later that year.

The following story is a fact-fiction account of the time during that project.

Chapter 1

The Start

December 1983

"The last time I saw a place like this a man was saying, 'this is one step for a man, one giant leap for mankind.'"

Two men who were sat at the breakfast table looking out of the ship's window at the island they were passing turned together to see the young twenty-year-old, short in height, black-haired Liverpudlian waiter, Joe, who had come into the restaurant to clear their plates away.

"Piss off, scouse," Colin replied as they turned to look at the brown rolling hills of the island go past.

"Oh, come on, lads, look at it, it's a real shithole, I am only glad we are sailing back to Cape Town tonight and not staying here. You must admit, it does look like the moon."

"Yeah, fourteen months here," put in Bob English, the thirty-three-year-old, dark-haired, slim, medium height Londoner as he pulled on one of his duty-free cigarettes looking out of the window again. "Daresay we will be around the twist by the time we go on leave in seven months' time."

"I think you're all mad anyway," said Joe as he cleared the table. "I mean coming eight thousand fucking miles to work in a place like this..." He turned to walk away with his trayful of plates, then stopped and looked at them again. "And on top of all that the Argies could come back and blow the crap out of you any day. I mean Liverpool is total shit these days, but all in all I think I would just about put up with going back there than staying here." He turned and left.

The ship's restaurant had been almost empty when Bob and Colin Watson, another thirty-three-year-old, a stocky built, fair-haired, five-foot-ten-inch-tall man also from London, had come in at ten minutes past seven that morning. But now at eight fifteen it was almost full of other workers who had made the two-week trip on the MV *Kenya*. The ship had previously been a North Sea ferry but had been brought out of mothballs to ship workers from South Africa to the Falkland Islands. Around two hundred workers had been flown from London's Heathrow Airport to Cape Town before boarding the ship to make the fourteen-day journey.

The ship was making its way into West Cove, an inlet on the islands, where a few weeks before the *Merchant Adventurer* cargo ship had docked and was converted into a bridgehead to act as a floating jetty for the duration of this very one-off contract.

The vessel had been secured by using specially designed struts and anchors with a Bailey bridge in place for access to the island. It had taken thirty-two days for the *Adventurer,* a thirteen-thousand-ton vessel with four thousand tons of materials and the twenty-four male personnel, which would rise up to around a two thousand two hundred strong workforce, to get there after leaving Avonmouth, England.

"I won't be sorry to get off this old rust bucket," said Colin.

"No, you have not had a good trip, have you?" replied his friend. "Been sick a few times?"

"Yeah, but it's been a bit rough, hasn't it?"

"No," said the waiter clearing the last of the plates. "It's been good, I know it's December and only eight days until Christmas, but it's summer here. Wait till you go on leave in June or July, you will see some rough seas then. Get hit by some of those big waves and this old thing would soon turn over, and forget the lifeboats and lifejackets, if they tell you to put one of those jackets on bend over, put your head between your legs and kiss your arse goodbye, as out there in those seas it would be as much use as a parachute. See you later, lads." He picked up the full tray, turned and walked away.

Bob and Colin looked at each other for a moment. "Well," said Bob, "if we do ever have to go over the side I hope he's not in charge of our lifeboat."

"Yeah," said Colin, "he would have us all jumping in after five minutes."

"We shall be docking at West Cove in about ten minutes," the speaker above their heads burst into life. "Jim Morrison, the contracts project manager, will be joining us on board, and a briefing with him will be held in the bow bar, that's the pointy end to you landlubbers, at zero nine hundred hours. All workforce must attend," came the order from the ship's radio operator. "Oh,

3

and by the way, lads, there's no way I'd stay in a shithole like that. It looks awful. Have fun, boys!" he laughed as he turned off the microphone. Bill and Colin looked at each other morosely.

"Shall we go on deck and watch the docking and get a better look at the shithole, Col?"

"Yeah, let's go," came the reply from his long-time friend and colleague. The two men both from West London got up and walked through the restaurant's large glass double doors then up the main staircase that led them to the upper deck. They had worked together on different building sites as carpenters for about five years but had been friends a lot longer. Their wives had become friends sometime before and they would all often go out together as a foursome.

They had only filled the application forms out for a laugh when they had been given them by a mate in a pub and said, "they would only go to the interview to find out how much the money is being offered," as there was no pissing way they would ever go to the other side of the world to earn a few bob! "Then the next thing I knew," Colin told a co-worker one drunken night at the ship's bar, "I was on this fucking thing bobbing up and down and puking my guts up every five minutes."

At eight thirty-seven on Saturday 17th December 1983, about eighteen months after war had raged on these small islands in the South Atlantic Ocean, the MV *Kenya* crashed into the side of the *Merchant Adventurer* to almost flatten the very large inflatable rubber buffers that hung from it.

"Nice soft landing," laughed one of the ship's crew as he passed a group of five workers who had been standing on the outside deck and had almost all fallen over when the ship had docked but for hanging onto posts and handrails.

Almost all of the crew took great fun in taking the mickey out of the workforce who had found it hard coming to terms with life at sea. On top of this they had enjoyed spreading rumours regarding how they should expect life to be when they got to the island. Stories had been going around that most of the first twenty-four pioneers to this new land had resigned their jobs as life was so bad on the island, and would be returning on the *Kenya* that evening. Or that they had run out of food and were now living on baked beans. The most up to date one that was doing the rounds was that the enemy had re-declared war and attacked the islands the night before with a loss of life. Fortunately, most of the workforce had been around a fair bit and were not easily taken in by this latest wind-up.

*

Morrison, a six-foot-two-inch-tall, dark-haired Scotsman in his early forties was from Fort William which stood on Loch Linnhe at the base of Ben Nevis in the West of Scotland. He had gone south to England as a young man to study as a civil engineer, and being possessed of sharp intelligence it had not been long before he was supervising his own contracts and moving on to run some of the UK's larger projects. A very respected man in the industry, he had been chosen to start a contract of this magnitude because of his calmness under pressure and the strength others drew from him. As he now stood on the small stage in the bow bar of the *Kenya* he was about to face one of the biggest challenges of his life. He had tried to choose men he knew he could rely on when he needed to. One of them had now joined him on the stage. Mike Collins was a very old friend, who he had worked with many times over the years. Mike had been the party leader during the trip on board the ship, but would be running the vast office complex when the contract got underway. He was a tall, slim, grey-haired man in his early sixties who had been looking forward to a few quiet years working in the head office in London before his retirement until he was given the option of the Falklands for at least fourteen months or taking early retirement. He was pondering both options when his friend Jim Morrison called and said it was he who had requested Collins' expertise. That and the fact Collins wasn't quite ready for retirement made the decision for him.

As the two men talked together on the platform they were joined by an army officer by the name of Colonel Anthony Warren who had just flown in by helicopter from the islands' capital, Stanley, which was about forty miles from the very isolated area that they now found themselves. Colin and Bob were among the last to enter the bar and take their seats. When all were settled Collins and Warren departed the stage to take their own seats near the front as Morrison was left on his own to address the captive audience.

"Good morning, gentlemen, and welcome to the Falkland Islands," the broad Scottish accent boomed across the now silent room in the very confident manner that its owner had. "I don't want to take up too much of your time this morning as there is much to do.

"You will soon be disembarking from the *Kenya* and will be able to find your way around the pioneer camp we have set here for you. I just want to tell you briefly of what is happening here. As I am sure you are all well aware that for this one-off contract three very large construction companies have come together, Johnston, Lewis and Butler to form a joint venture, and from now on our employers will be known as JLB." Morrison shifted his weight from his left leg to his right.

"We are here to construct an airfield which will be at Mount Pleasant, which is approximately seven miles from here at West Cove, and will be our base camp. The airfield will be used by the British military to defend these islands. It will be at the base of Mount Pleasant, a high and flat area of land. Twenty-four of us have been here just over a month now as a pioneer crew to this new land; you men are also pioneering. A base camp has been set up here of transportable cabins each of which will house eight men. There are also toilet and shower units in that area. You will be eating for the time being on the *Merchant Adventurer* which we have moored as a bridgehead. There is also a bar on her which you may use." This last comment brought a loud cheer from the audience. "I thought that would make you happy," smiled Morrison, "but while we are on the subject of drink, there will be no carry-outs. When you purchase a can of beer at the bar the barman will pull its ring there and then. Gentlemen, there will be no drinking in the cabins." His voice grew loud and harsh as he gave out this news, and in return was greeted with a low groan from the men.

"We have driven a haul road up to an area just before where the airfield will be. This will be the site of the contractors' camp which you men will start building. Yesterday we completed our small airstrip, which is about half a mile from here. It has been stripped of peat, which makes up most of the top layer of this island, down to rock and levelled off so that the small Islander aeroplane can now land here, and among other things this will bring us all mail from the UK." This brought a large cheer from the workforce. "We need this airstrip as we are forty miles from the capital. Between us and it is open land with the odd homestead. There are four roads, if one could call them that, as they are in fact little more than dirt tracks. They all go in different directions and

6

depending on the weather conditions they can be impassable. Last week it took one of our Land Rovers almost eight hours to get there. So, gentlemen, at the risk of being a scaremonger, we are to all intents and purposes cut off here." Morrison stopped at this point not only to take breath, but also to let this thought sink in. Looking around he could see it had its desired effect. "This is a very barren land, wander off and you will be lost in no time, and with all the landscape all looking the same it would be very hard to find your way back, and as the weather conditions can change very fast and dramatically in this part of the world – even in summer – survival time could be very short. Part of our contract is to build a new road to the capital." Morrison turned to a small table beside him and picked up a glass of water, took two sips and returned the glass and looked back at the men.

"Sorry, gentlemen, very dry."

"Was that vodka?" called out a voice from the rear of the bar.

"No, sir," came the reply from the stage. "Gin, I only drink gin at nine o'clock on a Saturday morning." This comment was met by guffaws and clapping from the audience.

"Where was I? Yes, I just want to tell you about overtime payments then I will hand you over to Colonel Warren of the Royal Engineers who will talk to you regarding safety of the land. I digress, in your contracts it states that you shall work a basic sixty-hour week and any overtime needed to be worked by you will be worked in lieu of time off. The men here in the past month or so have already worked many extra hours to get us where we are today ready for you men. So, our head office in London, very wisely in my opinion, has now decided to pay everyone all of their overtime at the end of their contracts." This again brought a large cheer from the men.

"Right, Colonel… Oh, sorry, one last thing. If you walk along the beach about one mile," he pointed, "you will find Westland Beach, which is home of many penguins and at this time of year the babies are hatching. I would truly recommend it for you to go and have a look as it is a wonder to see, but please, I would ask you not to interfere with them."

This brought a roar of laugher from the men and one wag shouted, "We haven't been here that long yet, Jim!"

Realising what he had said he thumped his forehead with the palm of his hand and with a broad smile said, "Gentlemen, I will rephrase that. Please do not get too close or disturb them. By all means take your photographs, but these animals are not used to humans."

"Who said we are human?" another called out from the rear.

"Well some of us may be, sir," smiled the project manager again. "Gentlemen, I give you Colonel Warren." Morrison left the stage to a round of applause and took up the vacant seat next to Mike Collins. The man who replaced him on the platform was in full uniform. Not one of the tallest soldiers in the armed forces at five-feet-seven inches, but very confident and sophisticated mainly brought about by his Oxford University education and his upper-class Berkshire upbringing. In his soft but firm tone he began to address the audience.

"Good morning, men, I am Colonel Anthony Warren of Her Majesty's Royal Engineers. I've been asked to talk to you regarding your personal safety and the possible dangers of the island – mainly landmines." There was a hush in the room as the officer had their full attention. "When the enemy were in occupation here they planted many landmines, but unfortunately for us did not keep records, make plans or keep maps of these areas. Of course, this is against the rules of engagement, but shaking the rule book at them will not help us now. All the areas in which you will be working have been cleared by the Royal Engineers, but there are a lot of areas that have not been cleared. Most of these have been fenced off, but of course there will be some that have not." He paused to let the men take this in. "Gentlemen, if you see this," he held up a metal plate six inches high by twelve inches wide. The side he showed them had white skull and crossbones on it with a red background, "hanging on a barbed wire fence, do not enter this field under any circumstances as it is mined. If you see this," he turned the plate around with his fingers and held it high for all to see a plain silver side, "as they would say, you have shit it, as you would be in the middle of a minefield. Just hope that someone sees you and calls us and we will try to get you out. But I cannot say strongly enough, should this happen DO NOT MOVE as it may be the last thing you do. At least with all your parts that is." The Colonel then held up a picture of a leg that ended at the kneecap. "This is what an antipersonnel mine can do to a person." He took another photograph from under his arm and held it up. This time it was a hand that had no fingers and a stump that used to be a thumb. "This is what happened to a construction worker over in Stanley. Gentleman, most of his hand

8

was blown off." At this point the Colonel had told fellow officers in their mess that night it was obvious that a very high percentage of the workforce unbeknown to them were now sat on their hands as if it would stop anything happening to their own.

"He said later he wanted to take home a souvenir with him to show his friends. Well I think we may all agree he's done that alright. These are not toys and can do real damage that will be with you for the rest of your lives. Men, I beg you, should you find anything like this laying around please report it to your supervisor who in turn will report it to us and my men will come and safely remove them.

"Gentlemen, please keep safe and enjoy your stay here. Thank you very much for your attention." He left the stage to a small round of applause, mainly from those who were not still sat on their hands or others who were not too stunned to clap.

Colonel Warren was replaced on the stage by Mike Collins with whom it was obvious from the beginning did not have the gift for public speaking that the two before him had. Looking nervous with his head bowed low he read from a piece of paper he held in his hand. "Outside the bar," he pointed without looking up, "are lists of cabins that each of you will be staying in. In the canteen on the *Adventurer* at teatime tonight will be a list where each man will be working and where to report to on Monday morning, meaning contrary to rumours doing the rounds on the *Kenya*, there will be no work tomorrow with-it being Sunday." This last bit of news brought a cheer from the workers, but pressing on without looking up Collins continued. "However, there are other things that need to be done. A briefing will be held for each section that a person will be working on. This will give you some idea of what one will be doing. Also, each of you will need to collect your work gear, coats, boots, gloves etc, from the hold of the *Adventurer*. There will be a list up in the canteen at breakfast tomorrow saying what time each cabin will do this."

"They like their lists here," Bob told his friend next to him who smiled his reply but said nothing.

Still without looking up Collins finished his speech with a, "Thank you for your time, gents." He then left the stage like a little boy who had been found with his hand in the cookie jar and could not get out of there any faster.

*

9

It was just turned twelve midday when Bob and Colin left the ship that had been their home for the past two weeks to find their new one. It was a bright sunny summer's day in this southern part of the world, but with a strong wind blowing from the Antarctic the wind chill factor made it feel very cold.

Cases and bags were put onto the back of a trailer being towed by a tractor for the two hundred yards uphill journey to their new home. Colin and Bob would be sharing the same cabin, as persons were able to put their names on lists on the *Kenya* so that friends could be in the same accommodation. They were the first of the eight to arrive and so therefore had the choice of bunk beds. The portable unit was forty feet long and ten feet wide with a central entrance door. There were four sets of bunk beds with their heads against the far wall facing the door, these were separated between each other by two wardrobes for each set of bunks. There was also a wooden fold-up chair for each person. The two friends chose the beds at the far end of the room to the left-hand side of the door next to a two-foot by three-foot window. Bob chose the bottom bunk with his friend taking the one above him.

It was not long before their six roommates started to arrive. They all welcomed each other and made their introductions as they went about the task of unpacking.

"Does anyone know what time dinner is tonight?" asked Jim Wotton a medium height, slim twenty-six-year-old Northern Irish lad who had not long left the Royal Navy and was going to work as one of the boat crew in the cove. Small boats would be used around the *Adventurer* when it was being unloaded in case anyone fell in the sea as life expectancy in these cold waters could be very short, and also used for other short work trips. Jim was now at the other end of the cabin from Colin and Bob and was about to take the top bunk at that end.

"About five on a Saturday night," shouted Colin from the opposite end. "Shall we all go together?"

"That's a good idea," said Eric Stamp, a very fit muscular, black young man from the York area of England. He was in his mid-twenties and was in the middle of unpacking.

"Where the hell did that come from?" asked Bill Terry, the thirty-three-year-old six-foot-two digger driver from Birmingham. His ginger, shoulder-length hair and bushy beard made him look just right for the possible cold weather and wild land that lay

10

ahead. Bill also wore thick dark-rimmed glasses. He would be taking the bunk below Jim.

"He's putting his things away," answered his bunk mate from his wardrobe door. "I think it could be time to have a bit of fun," said Jim in a mischievous voice, as he turned quickly towards the middle of the cabin where Eric was in his wardrobe, picking up a folding chair as he went. Within seconds Jim shut the double wardrobe doors with Eric inside then propped the chair under the handles so that it wouldn't open.

"Now, you silly fuckers," said the northern voice from inside, "it might just be best if you open the doors before I kick them off."

"Do that and you'll lose the eight hundred pounds retention we have got to pay according to the contract," put in Phil Thomas, the thirty-year-old Welsh bunk mate of Eric as he jumped from his top bunk and made towards the wardrobe as it started to rock backwards and forwards with the force of its captive pushing from inside. "For God's sake," said the prisoner's rescuer as he tried to open the doors, "give me a chance and I'll get you out." With that all went still inside as Phil opened the doors.

"I will kill whoever done that," promised Eric.

"Well," his bunkmate put in, "far be it for me to drop anyone in it, but what I can say is that the perpetrator of this crime has a Northern Irish accent."

"Bollocks!" shouted the voice from the far end of the cabin. "It wasn't me." Colin walked from his end of the cabin to the centre.

"What's that smell?" he asked, as Eric walked past him to Jim's end of the cabin.

"That's the finest African weed, my man," said Ron Dobson, the spectacle wearing man from Darlington in his late twenties who had almost straight shoulder-length black hair that parted in the middle of his head. He was sat on the edge of the bottom bunk under Andy Ryman, the twenty-eight-year-old slim Mancunian who seemed to be taking in all the smoke sent up his way by the marijuana joint from the bunk below.

"Would you like a pull?" Ron offered the joint to Colin with a smile on his face.

"No thanks, I don't."

"No doubt you will in time here," came the reply.

As the talk was ongoing, screams from Jim could be heard coming from the far end of the room, but none of the others seemed to take any notice of this.

11

"Has anyone ever told you, you look like Hack Woodfield, the rock star?" asked Colin to Ron.

"No," replied Ron.

"Well you do," Colin continued.

"He does, doesn't he?" remarked Andy who was now hanging his head over the side of the bunk looking at Ron through the thick smoke of the joint.

"That's it then, from now on you're Hack," said Colin. "Okay?"

"That's fine, man, I can live with that. I've been called far worse."

"I hear we are being called the 'B-Team'," put in Andy from above.

"How's that?" asked Colin.

"It's the lot who came down here first," the voice from above continued. "They said they are the A-Team after the TV show cause, they were picked first. They think they are the best, and one told me on the way to the cabins that we're the B-Team."

"Again, I can put up with that," smiled a more stoned Ron.

"So, we are the B-Team," said Colin.

"How about a walk around the place before teatime?" said Bob who had walked into the middle to join them.

"Sounds like a good idea," said Bill, who had also joined them to get away from the very one-sided fight that was taking place at his end of the cabin. They all made for the door together when a cry came out from Jim.

"What about me?" They all looked together to see Jim hanging upside down with his legs tied to the top bunk with belts. Bill and Bob went to his aid as the others made their way out.

They all made their way down towards the *Adventurer* then turned right just before the Bailey bridge to walk about one hundred yards to what was now known as the "Lay Down Area". This had been made the same as the haul roads and airstrip, stripped of peat, down to rock, but in the case of this area no crushed rock had been put on it and rolled to compact it like had been done on the roads which of course would get more use.

This area was to be used as an open-air store which was loaded out almost as far the eye could see with mechanical plant. This was the first delivery of what would be over a thousand pieces of equipment. It had been said that what was now standing beside the sea at West Cove had cost around five million pounds. This had come the week before on the first cargo ship of approximately thirty that it would take to feed the workers' needs. Appropriately this had been called Cargo 1, and it was planned for one a month to arrive in the cove for unloading in as fast a time as possible.

The equipment was all brand new and mainly yellow in colour. The lads now joined by other newcomers wandered between the rows of equipment that was made up of diggers of all shapes and sizes, the same with cranes. The dump trucks were all the same with very large open rear bodies, and the tail gates which were in place to stop any of the load falling out had been removed, the idea of this being to speed the operation of dumping the loads so that the lorry driver did not have to get out of his cab to remove the pins that held the gate in place. Of course, this could be a very dangerous practice and would be illegal in any other part of the UK, but as the workforce would soon find out the only law in this far outback would be JLB law. They had already changed the clocks to suit their needs when they first landed at West Cove so that the working parties could go ashore in the small boats with the tides before the *Adventurer* had been moored.

"First time I've gone to bed at midnight and the sun is still shining high in the sky," one of the workers had reported to his workmates.

One workmate had replied, "We're not on Greenwich mean time, it's JLB time." That was the first but by no means the last time that the company would change rules, laws or anything else for that matter at the drop of a hat or in this case at the drop of a safety helmet if they thought that it would progress or advance the contract in any way.

*

"I suppose this is what they meant by changeable weather?" asked Bob as he walked about with his hands in his green anorak pockets. His head was bent down low covered by the hood as the rain was driving in on him. He and five others had been dropped off by a Land Rover in the middle of nowhere beside the haul road. The Land Rover had left them there and had returned to the base camp to pick up co-workers who would be working with Bob and the others building and laying culverts under the haul roads. These would be made up of metal sections that would be bolted together to make up a large round tube six feet in diameter and thirty feet long. The haul road would then be dug up by a machine, the pipe then laid under the road and covered again with a few feet of compacted crushed rock. This operation was carried out in areas of the road that were near water or ponds that it was thought may flood the roads in heavy rain and make them impassable, and then in turn stopping work on the airfield. It was hoped that the culverts would divert water away from the roads leaving them flood free.

"We must be mad," a voice came from behind Bob. He turned to see a very large Irishman in his mid-thirties who was wearing an anorak that had been issued to him the day before on the *Adventurer* which seemed to be about two sizes too small for him.

"Sorry, Jerry?" asked Bob.

"I mean, sweet Jesus, look at us," came the reply. "Not only is it six days before Christmas, not only are we eight thousand fucking miles from home, not only have we been dropped off in the middle of nowhere in what could be a fucking minefield, it's pissing down with rain, I've been given a coat..." He held both his arms out sideways, "...that would not fit my little boy and leaks like a sieve."

"So, what is it you're trying to say, Paddy?" said Cliff, the tall Yorkshireman who had just come over to join them. "Is it that you're not a very happy man?" They all laughed at this comment.

"Well," came the reply from the Irishman with a grin on his face, "you could say that, lad."

"Things could be worse," said Bob. "We could be sat down having another meal cooked by the fair hands of Eastham's Catering."

"God," replied Cliff, "what was that slop last night?"

"Well," Bob came back, "I heard it was supposed to be steak and kidney pie, but shit would be a better description."

"Well thing is," reported Cliff "it takes the human body twenty-four hours to turn food into shit, yet Eastham's cooks manage do it in five minutes." The group all laughed at this.

"And you couldn't get a potato without its jacket on," said Jerry.

"The lads who have been here a while reckon that you get jacket spuds every night. It's the easiest and quickest way for them to do them," answered Bob.

"I heard," said Jerry, "that the potatoes were going to take their jackets off when the weather gets better." This brought another round of laugher from the men.

14

"That will be some time to wait in this place," sighed Bob, walking away with his head bent low. He stopped and turned to look at the group of workers. "I mean, if this is meant to be mid-bloody summer, what's the fucking winter going to be like?" He cried out as he took a few steps backwards. "ARGH!" he screamed as he fell up to his knees into a concealed brook which ran up the side of the haul road then turned just before it met the road.

"I think Bob has just found our day's work, the stream we are going to divert under the road," smiled Cliff.

"Yeah, and on top of that," laughed Jerry as his workmate climbed out of the freezing water, "if you wanted to jack it all in and go home on the next boat, it's a month away!"

"Good to see a happy workforce, bonny lads," said George Connors as he climbed out of the passenger seat of the Land Rover that had just pulled up at the side of the road. George needed to use two hands, one on the handle in the ceiling, the other on the side by the open door to pull the five-foot-two inches, and almost as round fifty-eight-year-old body out of the vehicle. "You'll need to be able to laugh in a godforsaken hellhole like this," said the red-faced, ginger-haired foreman. "George Connors is the name, from Newcastle, but spent the last twenty-odd years in Africa, the most beautiful place on this earth. I am your foreman, men." He walked around shaking hands with all the men, when Bob walked over to him.

"And what happened to you, bonny lad?" he asked looking down at Bob's wet legs and boots.

"Just fell into that little stream over there," he pointed.

"Do you know if you were in Africa," came the reply, "you'd be dry in no time, bonny lad, but in this place, you're just going to be wet all day." He turned and walked away.

"Wanker," Bob mouthed to his back as George walked away.

"Did you come on the *Kenya* with us?" Cliff asked his new boss, as other workers got out of the Land Rover and joined the group.

"Came down on the *Adventurer*, bonny lad. They pulled me off a smashing job in Uganda to come to this rotten hole. We sailed along the African coast on the way down here for a few days, great it was, just like being home. When I was in Kenya…" At this point Bob turned and walked towards the Land Rover as he had seen who the driver was. It was his cabin mate, Eric. Bob went over to the open driver's window.

15

"Alright, mate, what you doing here?"

"I am George's driver," came the reply.

"Oh, who's a lucky boy then?"

"Not me, I've had him burning my ears for the seven miles from the camp."

"Don't tell me, Africa?"

"You've met him then?" smiled Eric.

"Yeah. Anyway, why doesn't he drive himself?"

"Well, I'd say because he's too fat to get behind the wheel." They both laughed at this comment. "But his story is because he hasn't had to drive for twenty years and he's forgot how to, always had a black to drive him in Africa." Bob gave his friend a sharp look at this comment. "His words not mine, and of course he has got another now!"

"God, I hate people like him, and the ginger-haired, red-faced bastard didn't let me go back to the camp to change. I fell in that bloody stream," he pointed, then they both looked down at Bob's soaking legs.

Eric smiled and said, "It would have been really funny had it been little Jim."

"He's not right that lad, I think he's around the bend," came the reply from Bob.

"Thinks he's Cato out of the Pink Panther films. Wants to jump out and beat me up all the time."

"Don't think he's going to win there very often is he, Muscles?" Bob squeezed Eric's biceps through the vehicle's open window.

"Watch out for this." Eric turned to see a very large low-loader lorry coming towards him. He quickly moved the Land Rover out of the lorry's path. As the truck went past the two lads could see two large metal containers on the back. They each had an end cut off, they had then been welded together to make one long unit, and an opening had been cut in the centre to act as a doorway. This was access for the workers to climb inside. As there were not enough Land Rovers to go around this would be their mode of transport until buses arrived on a later cargo ship. The joiners had made wooden benches, which were very uncomfortable for the seven-mile journey to the new campsite. Every bump could be felt up through the lorry into the seats, then into the workers who were sat on them. It was lucky it was wet as on a dry day the dust would fill the inside choking all of its occupants. This vehicle would soon be named by the lads as the "Cattle Truck".

A lorry pulled up behind Eric's Land Rover. It had the sections of pipes on it that would be used to make up the culvert; they would be lifted off the lorry by the mechanical crane that was fitted on its back. The road was now getting very busy with plant moving up towards the new camp and the airfield. The road ran up the side of a not too high rock face. This had the road carved in its side and had been named "April Ridge" by the workers when they had started it in late November as one of the lads had said, "It will take until April to dig this." In fact it had been just over two weeks. From the top of the ridge the land became flatter, and it was just over a mile from here that the contractors' camp would be built and another mile or so from there would be the airfield, but some of the plant and lorries would be going on for a further three miles to where the quarry would be formed. From there stone would be blasted out of the rock then taken to a production area that would be built. It would then be crushed and made into sand and aggregate which would be used to make the concrete that would be needed on the contract. The cement would be imported from the UK; together they would bring something that this part of the world had never seen before – pollution!

A small production area had already been set up to feed the batching plants that would make the concrete to use on the building of the contractors' camp. Next to the main production area would be the office compound and stores area.

Bob and his new workmates spent most of that first ten hours that made up their work day in driving rain as George sat watching them from the cab of the Land Rover shouting out the odd instruction to them – of which they took very little notice. The rest of the time he spent driving Eric mad with stories of Africa.

*

"Is there anywhere in Africa that he has not been?" Bob asked Eric as they walked back to their cabin that evening.

"No, I don't think so. He hasn't called me 'boy' yet, but I am waiting for it," came the reply from his newfound workmate and friend. Bob was not only soaking wet but was now covered from head to toe in tar. This had covered the outside of the metal sections they had been working on. They had made the journey south on the deck of the *Adventurer*, and as they had sailed through the tropics the tar had melted in the sun and as they had been stacked inside each other they were now all stuck together, so when the boys had parted them to work on the tar had gone all over the workers.

Their other cabin mates were already back when the two entered their accommodation. "What's this then?" asked Bob as he and Eric stood at the doorway to the cabin looking around. Two lines of red and white bunting tape ran the whole length and each end of the cabin. This was hanging from the ceiling, the official use for this being to fence off work areas, holes or other hazardous spots.

"They are called Christmas decorations," said Ron as he sat on his bunk with a very large smile on his face, as he pulled on an equally large joint of grass. "Little Jim found it on the ship and put it up to cheer us all up, put us in the Christmas mood I guess."

"So where is the little shit?" asked Eric as he looked around as if he expected Jim to jump out of thin air.

"Don't know," said Andy from his bunk above Ron, getting high just on the smoke blowing around him. "He was here just now."

"CATO!" was the shout from Jim as he threw himself from his hiding place under blankets on top of Ron and Andy's wardrobe onto Eric's back so they both crashed to the floor.

"Okay," said Bob as he looked at the two rolling on the floor with total contempt. "I am changing, then going to have that shit they call dinner." He walked to his part of the cabin.

His friend Colin was laying on the bunk above his smoking. "How's your day been?"

"Well," came the reply from Colin, "as I am a carpenter and craftsman and spent five years severing my time as one they have put me to good use. Spending all day freezing my nuts off being a banksman to lorries is not too bad, pointing to them which way to go."

"Ah, you big bastard," came the Irish voice from the floor not far from them.

"Mine hasn't been much better," replied Bob.

"Piss off, Eric, that hurt," came another cry from the floor.

"Do you know what I heard today?" Colin asked Bob.

"I am going to get you when you're asleep," came the Irish voice again.

"Not if I kill you first," came the reply.

"Ah!"

"Can you make less noise or take him outside and kill him please?" asked Bob.

"Okay," came the reply. Eric opened the door with one hand, the other holding Jim by the neck he threw him outside and went out after him slamming the door as he went.

"That's better. What did you say, Col?"

"Some of the lads up at the new camp said that the manager told them we would get paid any overtime over the basic sixty hours, but if we lose any time because of the weather or any other reason apart from having a sick note the hours will be deducted out of any overtime we have earned!"

"Bollocks! I don't believe it," said Bob.

"I am only saying what I heard."

"It's a rumour, the lads who have been here a while say they go on all the time."

"Well," said Bill, the tall ginger-haired Brummie who had just walked over to join them, "I heard the same." He picked up Bob's cigarettes off the chair and passed one to each of the others. "The thing is no one knows what the weather is going to do when the winter gets here."

"Thanks for one of my fags, but I know what you mean," said Bob. "Look at it now, and this is meant to be summer."

"Right," Bill carried on. "I've heard that it's their idea to tell us that we will get paid our overtime so that we will work a load of extra hours in the good months, then say if we lose a lot of time because of snow, rain or whatever in the winter, they will then take back the hours we have lost, meaning they have got loads of extra work done for no extra cost."

"Bloody bastards," spat Colin. "That's not fair, we've got to fight this."

"Well actually," added Bill, "I don't think we should work the overtime if we are not going to be guaranteed to be paid it."

"Hold on," said Bob, "let's find out if this is true to start with before we do anything rash only to find out later that it's from Rumour Control. Then, if it's true, we can do something about it. In the meantime, I'm going to get changed for dinner... no I'm not. Let's go now. Who's coming?"

"Yeah," both Bill and Colin said together. They all made for the door to leave as it opened for Eric to walk in.

19

"We're going to dinner, Muscles," Bill told him. As the three men left the cabin they did not see behind them that the pole which had a washing line suspended from it had Jim tied to it with a towel around his mouth as a gag.

"I saw a notice in the canteen this morning," Bill told Bob. "They want the lads to form a workers committee so they can take any problems to them and sort them out. They want people to put their names forward for it."

"What about you, Bob?" Colin asked his friend. "You would be good at that."

"No way," came the reply, "it's bad enough just being here let alone having all the aggro of being on a committee as well."

"Well," said Bill as they got nearer the Bailey bridge, "not only would you be very good, but it would be very handy having someone in our cabin on it. You could get things done for us."

"Yeah," said Colin, "it would be really good to get extra things and all."

"Piss off, I am not going on it!" Footsteps could be heard behind them. They turned to see Eric running to catch up with them, the other lads from their cabin could be seen behind him with the exception of Jim.

"Where's Jim, Muscles?" asked Bob.

"Oh, he's not coming. He's tied up for the night."

*

"Oh God, my arse is red raw," moaned Bob as he took a small bottle out of his wardrobe. It contained a white and cream mixture which made up the kaolin and morphine that he had been given by the doctor that morning to stop the diarrhoea he had along with most of the workforce who seemed to have had it since dinnertime the night before.

"This is going to be some New Year's Eve this is," said his friend Colin from the bunk above him. "We've all got the bloody shits."

"Apart from me," shouted Eric.

"Yeah, we know you don't eat meat at all, and all of us who had the pork last night are dying, and even if we could drink there's no bloody beer as all the pissheads in that new bar they opened, Huggies, have bloody drunk it," said Colin.

20

"Well at least you got rid of that silly rule of the barmen pulling the rings on the beer cans since you have been on the committee," said Bill to Bob as once again he joined them from the other end of the cabin to talk to his friends. "I knew it would come in handy if you joined, Bob."

"Oh my God," groaned Jim as he ran from his end of the cabin towards the door holding his stomach, passing Eric on his way. The Yorkshireman put out a foot to trip Jim as he went making him stumble as he left by the door.

"I did hear," said Bill, "that four Land Rovers had been sent to Stanley this morning to get beer for tonight. Don't know if they have got back yet."

"Here, forget the beer and try some of this, man," said Ron, who had walked over to them and held out a joint of cannabis.

"Not for me thanks," said Bob as he took another sip of medicine.

"Well sod it," said Colin as he reached out from his top bunk for the joint. He then laid back as he pulled on it a few times. "Thanks, Hack," he said as he passed it back to Ron, "but I don't think it's done anything."

"Relax, man," came the reply, "lay back, relax and let it wash over yer."

"Here," said Bill putting out his hand, "I've chased penguins in the last few weeks, pulled my meat for the first time since I was at school, had Christmas dinner in the hold of a cargo ship, so what the hell, I might as well smoke dope on New Year's Eve." He stood with a cigarette in one hand and the joint in the other. He then leant back on Colin's wardrobe pulling alternatively on each of them. "Do you want to know what I heard today?" he asked the others.

"I suppose you are going to tell us even if we don't want to know," laughed Bob.

"After that uncalled-for interruption," said Bill as he pulled on the joint again, "I shall be telling you anyway. Let's try this again, without the interruptions please. Guess what I heard today?"

"What did you hear today, Bill?" the others all asked in unison.

"Well, I heard that some of the Eastham's lads said that they found a refrigerated container full of food, but it had been turned off for God only knows how long, and because we are running short of food they were told to turn it back on and that's where the pork came from that they fed us last night."

"So, we HAVE been food poisoned!" said Bob. "And it's not something in the water like Doctor Death has been telling everyone."

"He does work for Eastham's," said Andy who had just joined them and took the joint off Bill to smoke it. "Well," he continued after he took a few pulls, "he's not going to tell us that the company that employs him are killing us all, he wouldn't be here long if he did that, would he?"

"I suppose that means we're all going to die then," said Colin from his smoked-filled top bunk, as he burst out laughing.

"We're doomed, we're all doomed, Captain Mainwaring," laughed out Ron. This brought a round of laughter from all, Ron's comment about Private Frazer's saying from the TV comedy series *Dad's Army*.

"Oh, here you go," said Bob, "give us a go on that thing then." The joint was passed on to him.

"Don't forget you lads are in a five-a-side football final tomorrow," said Eric who had also now joined them.

"Do you want some muscles?" asked Bob.

"No thanks," came the reply, "you know I don't smoke anything!"

"Don't drink, don't smoke, what do you do?" Colin sang out some of the words from the Adam Ant hit song.

"Two shoes, two shoes, goody two shoes," the others all sang out then all laughed together.

"No, I just look after my body," smiled Eric, "and that's more than I can say for you lot."

"How in God's name did you lot get into the final anyway?" asked Ron. "And who gave you the name the 'Skid Marks'?"

"Well as it goes the Skid Marks is about right for us just now," said Bill. The door opened and Jim came in.

"It was Jimmy who went and paid the money and gave us the name," Eric said.

"I didn't know we had to give a name, it was the first thing that came to mind, we could not have entered without one." He shut the door then ran up to Eric who had his back to him. "Cato!" he shouted as he jumped onto Eric's back wrapping his arms and legs around his friend's body. Eric stepped backwards away from everybody, turned sideways then ran backwards crashing Jim between himself and the wall. The arms and legs that had encased him for just a few moments went limp as Jim gave out a cry, then slid to the floor in a heap. Eric very calmly walked back to the others.

"And we got to the final because we won the first match on penalties after a goalless draw, we then got a bye in the semi-finals because the other team wouldn't play another game on that pitch."

"Pitch?" laughed Colin. "I nearly broke my leg on it, it's all rock, all they did was strip the peat down to the rock. It's so uneven it's unreal."

"Still," said Bob, "we have got at least twenty-five quid to come now, and fifty if we win!"

"I can't see us winning," said Colin as he pulled on the second joint that Ron had lit up and was now passing around. "They are a good team the Quarrymen."

"I heard," Bill said, "that they had been hand picked to win it. Two ex-pros and a semi-pro in the team I also heard," he carried on.

"You've always, 'I've heard'," said Bob. There was a silence between the two for a moment, then Bill came back with a laugh.

"I listen a lot." This brought laughter from everyone.

"Anyway," asked Andy, "what time are we going to the bar? It's nine o'clock now."

"It's what?" asked Eric.

"It's nine," came the reply.

"Nine, and we're three hours behind the UK, so it's midnight there now."

"So, what?" asked Colin.

"Well," added Eric, "it just happens to be New Year in England now."

"Happy New Year!" shouted Jim from the floor.

"Happy New Year!" was the shout from all the lads in the cabin as they all shook hands.

"Oh, come on," said Bill as he crossed arms for the others to hold and form a circle, as they all held hands and started to sing,

"Should auld acquaintance be forgot…"

At this point Colin who was hanging from the top bunk holding hands with the others fell off and crashed to the floor. The song was finished with him lying on the floor, so along with the fall and the intake of cannabis Colin didn't seem to know where he was. All the lads went around shaking hands again and some hugging each other. "I think I'm going to cry," Bob said to Bill.

"Piss off, you soft southern bugger. Do that and you'll start me off," came the reply to the comment.

"Come on," said Phil the Welshman who had also come to join in the singing, "let's go to the bar, and by the way, Eric, it's New Year in Wales as well as England you know, boyo."

"Sorry," came the reply.

"Yeah, and Northern Ireland, you big Yorkshire pudding!" shouted Jim.

"You can shut up," came the reply from Eric.

"Make me!"

The lads saw the two of them sometime later in Huggies Bar as Eric chased Jim out of the door. Huggies Bar was two portable cabins joined together end to end and sited at the far end of the camp next to an area where a new canteen was now under erection for the next ship that would be docking in the next few weeks with another intake of workers. This ship would mainly be made up with Erect-A-Com personnel from the Hull area of England. They would be building the new camp from prefabricated wooden panels. These would be erected on concrete base pads with RSJs (Rolled Steel Joists) sat on them to take the weight and span the bases. The concrete bases for the first block had already been cast by the crews working there.

The bar was quite full when the lads got there, stocked with beer from the NAAFI (Navy, Army and Air Force Institutes) in Stanley. As the group had got into the New Year spirit early, at ten o'clock they celebrated New Year and sang "Auld Lang Syne" for South Africa. At eleven o'clock Bill decided it must be New Year in Wiger, Wiger Land, "wherever that is," he said. By the time midnight came around most of them were too drunk to do it again, but try they did.

*

The £75.00 combined winnings were mostly drunk between the two teams the following day after the five-a-side football final. The match was meant to start at midday, but as none of the players were fit to play it was agreed to put it back to six in the evening. With Bob in goal and the wind blowing a gale into his face in the second half, he looked a picture with kneepads, padded red gloves, safety goggles and wearing Eric's grey tracksuit trousers. But as well as he played he could not stop two well taken late goals to give the Quarrymen a 2-1 victory after Jim had given the Skid Marks a well-deserved first half lead from a very good through ball from his good friend Eric.

It was a rather morose group of hungover workers who sat in the rear of the Land Rover that second day of January at six thirty am waiting for George to join them. A pin could be heard to drop as the red-faced foreman opened the door and dragged himself in. "Good morning, bonny lads. Happy New Year and a happy 1984 to all of you." He turned in his passenger seat to face the workers who lined each side of the rear of the vehicle. "Do you know what, bonny lads? We'd be having the day off today if we were in Africa!"

Chapter 2

The Start of a New Dawn

On 30th December 1983, the Commander of the British Forces in this part of the world, Major General John Wilson OBE, performed the turf cutting ceremony at the airfield site. The access road had gone nine kilometres from West Cove and reached the perimeter of the airfield by mid-December and had continued from east and west so that runway works and construction on the main contractors' camp could commence. After the ceremony the Major General had praised the contractors, "for the amazing progress achieved thus far, and for commencing on time." In fact it had been one day early.

By mid-January work was in full swing on the new camp and many areas had now been cleared for the arrival of the Erect-A-Com materials. The prefabricated wooden sections had been transported there and these would make up the many criss-crossing corridors, each with eight rooms on either side with toilets showers and drying rooms (rooms for leaving clothes in lockers to dry at night) at each end.

Also made from these sections would be the three large canteens, two for the workforce and one for supervisors and management. The same amount would make up the bars; alongside them would be games rooms – snooker, table tennis and video rooms – outside these would be a telephone area. A medical centre and post office would make up the camp which when finished with by the contractors would be handed over to the army for their use. Also, by mid-January the MV *Kenya* had left Cape Town and was on its way back to the island with the next intake of workforce.

All the different gangs of men working on the camp had metal containers which they had fitted out to use as mess huts and changing rooms. Containers had also been used as stores, all of which had been positioned just north of the camp surrounding the two batching plants that had been erected there to produce concrete for the camp. The concrete was then taken from there on small dumper trucks to construct the bases and floor slabs that would be needed for the erection to begin.

Cement had been shipped from the UK in one-ton fabric sacks. These were loaded out beside the hopper that with the aid of hydraulics would tip aggregates and cement into the mixer drum. The first component was put into the hopper with the aid of a mechanical shovel operated by a man, but the cement was loaded by a non-mechanical shovel with a man on the end of it. Given the very windy climate this made for a very dusty environment in this area most of the time. Workers doing the loading looked more like outlaws from the old Wild West in the US as no dust masks had arrived yet. They all had handkerchiefs tied around their mouths most of the time to stop them from choking on the cement dust, and also to cut down on the intake into their bodies.

Work had progressed well on the culverts and all were now in place at the required intervals and areas of potential road flooding.

The gang Bob had been working in had now been split up, and as he himself had found out the night before he would now be working with his friend Colin at the new camp. Colin had now been made up to chargehand joiner by George who had gone up there the week before.

"I really did not think it was this bad," moaned Bob as he sat on the wooden bench next to Colin in the Cattle Truck on their way to work. "This is ridiculous," he said as the lorry hit yet another rut in the rocky road.

"It jars you right up the spine when that happens," replied his friend.

"God, with the dust and smoke in here it's hard to breathe."

"That's why most people who get in here put their heads down for the seven miles," said the voice of Terry, the twenty-eight-year-old from Hartlepool on the north east coast of England.

"You're moaning now," said another voice, "and this is your first day. We've had this shit for weeks!"

"So why don't you do something about it?" said another voice from the gloom. "You're on the workers committee, aren't you?"

"Yes, I am, and I'll hold my hands up and say that I didn't realise it was this bad. Look, there's a meeting this afternoon, I'll bring it up then."

"And what about the overtime?" asked another. "What are you going to do about that?"

"It's on the list for this afternoon," he replied, now wishing that he had never moaned in the first place, which had started all of this and also wished he had not been talked into going on the committee by Bill and Colin.

"And what about the food?" asked Terry from beside him. "It's inedible some nights."

"Most fucking nights," put in another voice from the darkened truck.

"I suppose that's on the list as well?" asked another.

"Yes," came the reply from Bob, now with an edge of irritation in his voice. "Along with the freezing and sometimes no water some nights at the camp."

"And what about the thunder boxes we have to use up here to have a crap?" asked Reg Kane, the tall, thickset, balding, grey-haired, fifty-year-old machine driver from Derby, half turning his head from the row in front of Bob. "You'll be finding out all about them today. You will not be able to get the Land Rover back to the ship for a shit or lunch like you lot on the culvert gang have been doing with George. No, you'll have to be sat in a wooden box on a toilet seat that is fixed to two planks of wood over a hole in the ground that is full of shit and flies, and when you are finished dumping if you don't get the lid down in time the wind blows up so fast the bog paper will stick to the ceiling."

"I was waiting outside one last week," put in Colin, "when the lad came out and went past me he had bog paper stuck to the back of his jacket."

"Agh," came the collective sigh from around him.

"And I didn't have the heart to tell him."

"And wait until you have a doggy bag for tea and lunch," said Billy, the four-eyed Mancunian with such a big red nose and black-rimmed glasses that it made him look as if he was wearing a false nose and glasses that one can buy in a joke shop. "A plastic bag with a corned beef roll and a year out of date fruit cake," he continued.

"I didn't eat corned beef for over a year," said Terry, "because of the war here as it came from Argentina. Our whole family boycotted it altogether, none of us ate it, then I come here where the bloody war was fought and what do I get the first day in the rolls? Bloody corned beef." This statement brought a ripple of laughter from around him.

28

"And if you don't eat it you'll starve," said Colin, "because that's all you get here, every fucking day. "By the time the truck pulled up at the camp and Bob climbed down the wooden steps not only was his spine hurting, his back aching and his feet tingling because of the journey, but also his head was spinning with everything that had been fired at him during the seven-mile trip. He was now asking himself just what had he done by "not only joining the three-man workers committee, but worse still allowing them to vote him in as chairman."

*

"I heard tonight," said Bill as he and Ron stood at Bob and Colin's bunk beds in their nightly get-together and put the world to right session, "that if you didn't sort out the Cattle Truck thing at the meeting this afternoon, the lads would refuse to get on it tomorrow."

"Well that's no good," said Bob. "That's refusing to work and it says in the contract."

"Con-trick, don't you mean?" put in Ron.

"As I was saying, HACK! That we would be playing into their hands if we do that. It's not going to work."

"So, what did they say about the Cattle Truck?" asked Colin.

"They said that we would have to put up with it for another week as Cargo 2 will be here then, and it's got four single-deck buses on it."

"Well," said Bill, "if Cargo 2 has got everything on it that has been said is on it, then it will have to be five fucking miles long." This brought a round of laughter from everyone.

"When the pointy end gets here," said Colin from his top bunk, "the blunt end will just be passing Cape Town." This brought another round of laughter, but only to be interrupted by a knock on the cabin door. The door opened and the tall, thin crane driver, Scott, from London who had been working on the camp with Bob came in.

"Hello, lads," he said as he walked over to them. "Didn't know you lived in here, Bob."

"Yeah, what are you after, Scott?"

"I am looking for someone called Hack. Is he here?"

"Why do you want Hack?" questioned Bob.

"Heard I could score some dope off him."

29

"I don't know," said Bob turning to Ron. "Is Hack about?"

"He might be," came the reply. He then turned to Scott and said, "Come with me, my good man, and we shall see if we can find him." Scott followed Ron to his part of the cabin.

"He'll get caught the way he's going," said Bob. "Mark my words."

"He's supplying the best part of the camp at the moment," said Colin.

"He can't have much left?" Bob questioned.

"I heard he's got a big supply coming from one of the crew on the *Kenya* this Sunday when it docks," said Bill.

"Knowing Hack, he will have a containerful coming on Cargo 2," replied Bob. This brought another round of laughter from them all. The door opened and Eric came in, he was wearing shorts, trainers and a vest. He was sweating profusely.

"How far did you run tonight you musclebound bastard?" asked Bill.

"About three miles past West Cove International Airport to the cattle grid. I suppose about eight miles in all. I am going for a shower." He went and sat on his bunk to take his trainers off. "Oh, you little bastard!" he shouted as Jim grabbed him from his hiding place under Eric's bunk.

As Jim grabbed his legs he shouted his war cry of, "CATO!"

"Wondered where he had gone to when he came in," said Colin.

Eric got free from where Jim was holding his legs then proceeded to throw trainers, shoes, flip flops and anything else that came to hand under the bunk at him amid cries of, "Oh, fuck off, you big bastard. Oh, piss off, Muscles, that hurt," and other cries of protest.

"He's lost it that lad," said Bob, "he's not right in the head."

"Yeah," said Bill, "he's been drinking a lot of late. Bloody fell on me last night trying to get in his bunk."

There was still the odd cry of a Northern Irish accent that came from under Eric's bunk, as Eric was now stripping for his shower and kicking Jim with his foot every time he tried to escape from under the bunk. When he had changed to a towel around his waist with a pair of flip flops on his feet and holding his wash bag he kicked Jim once more before telling him, "I'll see you later." He then turned and left the cabin for the shower block.

"Shall we put money on Jim to be going on the ship on Sunday? I think he's going into a depression, he's been like it since the *Kenya* left Cape Town, I think he has got ship fever," said Colin. The term "ship fever" is a nickname used on the project. It is when workers know that the ship is on its way from Cape Town and they are feeling down and think of breaching their contract and going home. Once it has left West Cove they are okay until they know it is on the way back then it can start again. It gets worse for some the nearer the ship gets to the island.

"I've got a pound in the sweepstake where I've just started work at the hangar site that there will be twenty-one sackers, jackers and medivacers on the ship when it leaves here Sunday," Bill told his friends.

Jim had managed to get out from under Eric's bunk and made his way out of the cabin past Ron and his new friend Scott who were now sat on the former's bunk concluding their deal, with money and drugs changing hands.

"What's medivacers?" Colin asked.

"It's short for medical evacuation," Bob answered for Bill. "Someone who is medically unfit to stay, and the best of it is that they get paid up their bonus, overtime and retention. If they jack or get sacked they are stopped all monies owed to pay for the fare home."

"I reckon Jim could get that," replied Colin. "Well you know, mentally unfit to carry on," he laughed.

"We brought it up at the meeting today, and also about losing overtime pay if you can't work for one reason or another."

"How did we get on?" asked Colin.

"Well I think the short answer," came the reply from the committeeman, "was bollocks!"

"Is that the technical term?" asked Bill with a smile.

"Yeah." Bob thought about it. "And possibly with a fuck off thrown in for good measure."

"There's no way they are going to give in," said Colin. "If they can save money they don't give a damn about us at all. What they think is if you don't like it here there's a boat going home on Sunday, so get on it."

"I think you're right," put in Bill.

The door opened and Jim came running in with Eric's towel and flip flops in his hands. The men stopped talking to look down

31

the room at him as he disappeared past Eric's wardrobe and towards the same person's bunk.

"Has he done what I think he has?" asked Bill.

"He's got a death wish that lad, he wants to die," reported Colin from his vantage point on the top bunk.

At this point there was a lot of noise coming from Eric's area and an opening and shutting of wardrobe doors.

"What the hell are you up to?" asked Ron walking along to see what his cabin mate was doing.

"Getting my own back," came the reply.

"I should hurry up then," came the voice from the top bunk. "I can see out of the back window a wet, naked, sore footed, and very angry-looking Yorkshireman coming this way."

"Right, lads, I'm off out for the night. See you later," came the reply to Colin's news. Jim then ran along the cabin and with one jump leapt up onto his top bunk at the end of the room, opened the top section of the large window, then head first disappeared out of sight as the door opened.

"Where is the little Paddy bastard?" asked the naked wet man who stood in the middle of the cabin.

"Who's a big boy then?" asked Bill with a laugh.

"Don't let that Eastham's cook see you like that," called out Colin.

"Yeah, if he was about and there was a tenner on the floor you would have to weigh up if it was worth chancing bending over for it," said Bob.

"I'd chance it for a tenner," added the Brummie machine driver.

"So, where is he?" asked the dripping Eric.

"Just slipped out," smiled Ron.

"I'll have him later," he said as he bent over to pick up his towel. He then sat on his bottom bunk to dry himself. "Arrrh!" came the cry as he sat on his mattress only to find Jim had removed all the wooden slats that supported the mattress from his bed so that Eric would fall through to the floor below as soon as he put his body weight on it. All the lads came around to see what all the noise was about. None could contain their laughter at what they saw, Eric's naked body hanging on the side of the bunk and his head and back laying on the floor.

"Well you must admit he got you this time, Muscles," smiled Bill to him as he climbed out.

32

Even Eric could not stop himself from smiling. "No, I must say the little wanker put a bit more thought into it this time. Where's he put my slats?" he asked walking around.

"I heard your wardrobe door opening and shutting," said Bob. "Have a look in there and put some bloody clothes on." He turned to walk away. "You're putting us all to bloody shame."

"Revenge is a dish best served cold. I'm not going to do anything about it tonight because by the time he gets in from the bar it would be far too easy and noisy. No, I'll think about this a little." He pulled a pair of shorts from the wardrobe and put them on. He then pulled out a needle and cotton from the wardrobe, looked at it, smiled and said, "Yes." He then walked to Jim's end of the cabin.

*

"Jim, Jim, come on, you'll be late for work again. You've overslept."

"Oh, aha!"

"JIM!" Bill shouted as he shook his logger. "Come on, Jim, you said yourself you'll be going on the *Kenya* if you're late again."

"Oh, piss off, I'm dying." He rolled to face the opposite window that he had jumped out of the night before, which now had the early morning summer sun shining through it.

"Okay, if that's the way it's got to be. I'm only doing this for your own good, Jim lad, and of course your wife, baby, and mortgage that has to be paid this month." Bill then pulled back the bedcovers to expose the thin, lily-white, curled up body clad only in a once white pair of underpants that was overdue a good washing.

"Fuck off," came the reply from the hungover body as it tried to pull back the covers.

"No you don't," said Bill as he grabbed Jim's legs, pulling the half dead body off the top bunk letting him crash to the floor in a heap. Bill then bent over and picked him up and propped him against the bunk. "Come on, put your cloths on, Jim."

"Okay, okay, I'm getting ready. Oh shit, my head aches." He then went to the chair that he had thrown his work clothes on the night before. He picked up his trousers and put his leg into the right leg of the garment only to find that his foot would not come

33

out of the other end as Eric had sewn it up the night before. "Shit!" was the cry as he hopped on one leg trying to keep his balance only to once more crash to the floor, only this time hitting his head on the cabin wall as he went down.

This brought cheers from the others as Jim looked up to see his cabin mates who had all come to see his suffering, and bring comments like:

"That will teach you, making a noise every night when we are asleep."

"Yeah, noisy little sod."

"What's it like to be stitched up, Jim?" shouted Eric. This brought laughter from all.

"Time, we went to work," said Bill as he stepped over the body. "See you later, Jim lad."

"Go fuck yourself," came the reply from the floor. The rest of the lads all left the cabin together to go to work leaving Jim to try and get his head through the neck of his green army jumper that had also been sewn shut.

*

Bob, Colin and Eric walked together to the far end of the pioneer camp near the Lay Down Area that was used as parking for the Cattle Truck and Land Rovers overnight.

"I see," said Eric as they neared the parking area, "that there's a folk night on in the hold bar on Saturday night. Shall we go?"

"Might as well," said Bob. "I was going to have a weekend in the South of France, but how could I refuse an invite like that?" he laughed.

"What's going on?" asked Colin as they got nearer the pick-up point to see a large group of workers standing beside the Cattle Truck talking to George and Arran Jones, a Welshman in his mid-forties with black curly hair. He was the section manager on the new camp. Jim Morrison joined the group at about the same time as the three lads.

"Good morning, gentlemen, and what seems to be the problem?" asked Morrison.

Reg Kane was the first to speak up. "Well, Jim, it's a total joke travelling on the back of that lorry, you can feel every bump in the road through the lorry's flatbed, the benches are sawn timber and rough on your arse, there's a bit of rag as a door that lets in dust so

34

that you are choking, the driver can't go fast or he'll throw us all over the place. It takes three quarters of an hour each way, and as it says in our con-trick that we don't get travelling time, we don't start getting paid until we get there, so not only is it the rottenest trip you could think of, it's also taking up to two hours a day. And it's our time, Jim."

The little speech from Reg brought a few yeah's and moans of agreement from the gathered crowd.

"Well," Jim said, "I must admit I did not realise it was that bad, but the thing is that until Cargo 2 gets here with the buses it's the only way we can move a large amount of men."

"Why can't we go up in Land Rovers like the managers and foremen do?" asked a voice from the back.

"Well, as I am sure you are aware at this moment, we only have a few Land Rovers and most of these go to other work areas. Again, there are more coming on Cargo 2, and even if we could use them all we have to ship you men up to the camp and it would take hours to get you all up there. I really don't like saying this but there is very little I can do about it until next week." He came across very understanding but at the same time like an unmoveable object, Bob thought to himself.

"What about some extra money for travelling while this is going on?" another voice called out from the back.

"I am unable to do that, sir," came the reply from the project manager.

"Have you ever used the thunder boxes up there?" asked another.

"No, I have not, sir, and I do believe they are not very pleasant, but this time next week we will have portable toilets off the cargo ship set up there for your use."

"So just how long is this bloody ship, Jim?" called out another. This brought about a small round of much needed laughter, and even brought a smile to Jim's face.

After the laughter died down Jim said, "Yes, gents, I know everything in the world seems to be on it, but the fact is there are very much needed supplies aboard her, and you should be pleased to know that I got a telex this morning to say that she is making good progress and will be here next Thursday."

"That's another twelve or fourteen trips away," said Reg.

"There's very little I can do about it," came the reply.

"It's alright for George and his little mate and those other chosen few who travel in the Land Rover," said a Scottish accent from the right-hand side of Jim.

"And he comes back for meal breaks and to have a shit on the *Adventurer*," shouted another.

"Is that right, George?" Jones asked him.

"Well," came the reply from a redder in the face than usual George, "maybe sometimes."

"I don't mind going up on the truck," said Eric coming forward, "if someone else wants to drive the Land Rover."

"When's George going to travel up in the truck?" shouted a northern voice. This comment brought a round of, "yes," and "good idea," from the crowd.

"He's going to travel in it from now on," said Arran Jones.

"What!" came the very sharp reply from the short, fat foreman.

"Can we just have a minute please, gentlemen?" Jim asked the workers, then motioned Arran and George away without waiting for a reply. The three management members walked about ten yards away from the discontented workforce.

"I think Arran has a good point, George. From now on I want everyone who has been travelling up to the camp in Land Rovers to go in the Cattle Truck from now on, and, George, that includes you." Jim took time to look around at the almost silent watching crowd then continued. "Also, I want you to stay up there all day, I want you to eat doggy bags with the men and I want you to shit in the hole like the rest of them."

"I don't think that's fair, Jim. I am a twenty-year man with Lewis Construction, I do not expect to be treated like this."

"It's because you're a twenty-year man that I expect you to help us through this by leading by example. To show the men there is no us and them. Arran," he turned to the section manager away from a very unhappy-looking George, "I want you to draw up a rota for the men who have not travelled in the Land Rovers to take turns until the buses are here. It's early days here at the moment and morale is not very high. It hasn't been for a few weeks now, and I don't want any confrontation over this. The overtime issue is being brought up more and more at our workers committee meetings, and word is going around about an overtime ban." Arran Jones nodded his head in agreement. "That would be the last thing we would want, gentleman, so I don't want to infuriate the situation. Something like this could tip things over the edge. Also,

36

remember there's the *Kenya* docking here on Sunday and if we had a big jacking party going on it would be made very hard for those of us left here." There was silence between the three men as Jim let this news sink in. Then Arran spoke.

"Jim, what about if we try to get as many men away from here as possible on Sunday?"

"Go on," came the reply.

"Well, what if we make as many Land Rovers available as possible for the day so that they could go on a trip? They could go to Hampton, there is a social club there and I believe the beer is very cheap."

"I could talk to Eastham's camp manager to make up packed lunches for them," replied the project manager.

"I don't think that will go down very well if they are anything like the doggy bags," put in George.

"Well," said Jim, "I'll make sure that they put some effort into them."

"Also," said Arran, "we could give them two cans of beer each to take with them."

"I think that's going too far," sighed George. "If we were in Africa we wouldn't do anything like this!"

"The point is we are not in Africa, George," came the snap reply from Jim. He then turned to Arran. "Good idea, Arran, I will tell Eastham's. It won't hurt them as I think they buy the beer for ten pence a can and charge fifty pence so they make plenty. They can give a little bit back. If they play up too much I will pay them what they pay for each can. Okay, I'm happy with our little package. Another thing, we could give each man a ticket for a free beer when they go in the folk night on Saturday. We'll tell them all this now as a little sweetener."

It took about ten minutes for Jim to explain everything. On the whole it went down alright. There were a few moans and groans as Jim gave his little speech, but mainly the workers realised it was a no-win situation that they had got into, and this way neither of them would lose and both sides would come away with something, apart from George who was very unhappy at what he had just heard. It was a very loud cheer that greeted him as he pulled his round body into the Cattle Truck.

*

"Butch."

"Yes, boss?"

"I want a word with you."

"Okay, boss." George and Butch Dickens, the concrete batcher chargehand in his early fifties, tall and thin with grey hair also from Newcastle, walked away together after leaving the Cattle Truck and out of earshot of everyone.

"Yes, boss, what can I do for you?"

"We've known each other a few years now, haven't we?"

"Yes, boss."

"I've always looked after you, haven't I, bonny lad?"

"You have, boss."

"I need a little favour, but I want you to keep it between us, Butch."

"Of course, boss, anything."

"Right, I'm sending you a new lad today, young Eric."

"Isn't he your driver, boss?"

"Was, bonny lad, just done himself out of a job shooting his mouth off and saying he'd travel on the Cattle Truck. Got the ball rolling and put ideas into people's heads. So, bonny lad, I want you to put him shovelling cement into the hopper."

"Well we all take turns, boss, it's too bad a job for one person to do all the time."

"You don't take turns anymore, bonny lad, there's only one person who does it from now on. I don't want to see anyone else on it from now on, just him, and I want to see his back bent all day. I want you to work the balls off him, I want to see him covered in cement from head to foot, I want him looking like one of those little graded flower graders on the telly."

"Boss, that's not fair, and he's the only black lad here. It won't look good, boss."

"I don't care what it looks like, and him being black has nothing to do with it. I gave him a good driving job and he dropped me in it, and life's not fair, bonny lad. Now you and me run things up here, I tell you what to do, you tell the lads what to do, that's the way of things. Now you're a clever lad and I am sure you don't want to be going on a little boat trip on Sunday night to Cape Town, do you, bonny lad?"

"No, boss."

"That's good. If only we were in Africa, I'd have the little bastard pushed down a mine shaft or something."

"Yes, boss."

38

"Guess what?" Bill asked as he walked into Colin and Bob's end of the cabin.

"What?" Colin asked from his laying position on his top bunk blowing smoke from his cigarette into the air.

"Well I heard from Eastham's camp manager that there are nineteen sackers, jackers and medivacers going on the *Kenya* up until now. Two more by tomorrow afternoon and I win the sweep. It's thirty-five quid."

"That could be up to twenty at least the way that little fat George bastard has been treating Muscles," reported Colin.

"Can you not do anything about it, Bob, being on the committee and all?" Bill asked.

"I asked him and he said no, that he was going to outlast him. I mean it's unreal what he's got that lad doing in this day and age. Men walked on the moon well over ten years ago and that fat wanker has got poor Eric shovelling cement out of a ton bag in a gale every day."

"The state of him when he comes in of a night is unbelievable," commented Colin.

"Where are they all anyway?" asked Bill.

"Gone to folk night early so that they could get to the front was the answer I got," said Bob.

"When are we going?" asked Bill.

"Just as soon as I get the football results off the radio from the World Service," replied the Londoner.

"Oh, I miss all that," sighed his friend from the bunk above him.

"Yeah," said the man from Birmingham, "getting home from seeing the Brum get beat, then ham, egg and chips."

"Out down the pub with the boys and get pissed," said Bob.

"Then home to get the leg over," put in Colin.

"A lay in Sunday morning with a roaring headache," said Bill.

"Get the leg over," said Colin.

"A few pints down the pub on Sunday dinner time," replied Bob.

"Then home for Sunday roast," said Bill. "And if you say then get the leg over," he pointed up at Colin, "I'll thump you."

"What are Sunday afternoons for if not for getting the leg over?" he asked the other two.

"God, that's all you ever think of," said Bob as he jumped off his bottom bunk. "Come on, let's go, we can get the football results in the top bar on the ship then go down to the hold bar for the show."

There were two ways to access the main hold of the *Adventurer* which had been converted to double up as bar and canteen. One of these was a wooden walkway on the starboard side which had been built from the top deck down the outside of the ship until it came to a purpose made doorway for entry. The other route which the three men had taken was from the deck down through the inside of the ship. They had stopped off at the top bar at deck level for a couple of beers and the football results. Bill was right, Birmingham had lost.

They stopped off at the video room which was just outside the hold bar, which was showing as usual a Saturday night "blue" film. They stayed a few minutes, but not only had they already seen it, but there was standing room only as the area was packed with open-mouthed men.

By the time they arrived the show was well underway. They entered from the bow end down a port side staircase, via the video room of course. An area at the starboard side of the hold in front of what would normally have been the food serving counter had been blocked off and a small stage had been erected there. The three lads had picked up their free beer tickets from one of the welfare officers at the door on the way in and then made their way to the stern end which housed the bar that had been built on the trip down from Avonmouth by some of the joiners on board. It seemed that everyone on site was there, apart from those diehards who had been watching the "blue" film, and for the first time in a long while there seemed to be a very happy workforce.

"What's it like?" shouted Bob to Reg who stood just a short distance from him at the bar as he had a drink with his mate Stan. He had to raise his voice to make himself heard above the din.

"Fucking crap, Bob, but everyone's enjoying themselves and getting well pissed. It's the best crack the lads have had for a long time," came the reply.

"It's a woman," cried Colin.

"Where? Where?" asked Bill as they all turned to look at the stage though the crowd. Overweight she may have been, as Bill

40

pointed out a bit later, but nevertheless a person of the female gender with long blond hair had come onto the platform to a very loud roar. She sat on a chair with crossed legs and a guitar on her lap and soon won the audience over as she started to sing "American Pie" with them all joining in the chorus.

"She can't sing," said Colin, "but those are the biggest tits I've seen for a while."

"They are the only bloody tits you've seen for a while," shouted his mate Bob.

"Well you know what I mean."

Taking in the drunken scene all around them Bill commented to the others, "It's starting to look more like a Wild West saloon." He thought about this to himself for a minute then said, "Or in this case should I say a Wild South saloon." This brought a laugh from the others.

The three stood in the bar area talking, drinking and at times almost hearing the music over the roar of the crowd. It was not much longer before most of the workforce were drunk; beer was flowing very freely, most of it onto the metal deck. The folk group was made up of four men and two women working in the capital for the government, all of which had come across from the UK for this purpose. One of the locals had brought them in a Land Rover on a good track and the forty miles had only taken four hours, which was some kind of record.

The bar staff had given up trying to pull the rings on the beer cans as they had been told to again that night as the demand for the beer was so great they were just handing over the cans and in some cases armfuls. Most of the staff were not even checking the money. If they had been told that it was the right amount they just put it into a shoe box at the rear of the bar area that was their cash till.

When the bearded faced singer on stage started to sing the ever-popular song "Sailing", most of the deck was awash with beer and now resembled a skating rink. Almost everyone in the bar held their arms in the air and swayed from side to side as they sang along with the Rod Stewart hit. Unfortunately for most of the night the noise in the bar area was so loud that it was hard to make out a lot of the professional singing. But also, this did bring about some good comments on the evening, one being when one of the male singers asked the audience when he was about to start a song? "I am sorry if I am fucking interrupting you."

The loudest roar of the night came when a Glaswegian woman called Jane came on and said into the microphone, "Okay, I like this song, so if you do not shut the fuck up I will come around and put the heed on each and every one of you."

After the laugher and cheering had died down and Jane was about to start, one of the workers shouted out, "Get them off!" Jane, a quick-witted lady and also a veteran performer of some seedy clubs, was quick to return with, "No, you get them off and we'll all have a fucking laugh." The crowd erupted again adding a smile to the faces of the folk group and also a much-needed calm, which was helped by her first song "The Wild Rover" a singalong, known to much of the workforce which many of them joined in with.

"Hi, Hack," Colin said as the three were joined by their other cabin mates at the bar. "Tomorrow's a big day for you then?"

"Why?"

"Well you've got your grass coming in. You're almost, out aren't you?"

"Jesus, man." Ron almost spat in his face. "Shut the fuck up will you. You don't know who's listening." Then gave Colin a shove in the chest.

"No one's listening, everyone's pissed, look around you."

"Well let's not chance it anyway," came the reply, but now in a calmer voice.

"No, you're right," said Colin. "I'm sorry, Hack."

"It's okay, man, forget it." The two cabin mates shook hands.

Being thrown together miles from home had encouraged a lot of new friendships to form. However, it had also created the opposite effect too, and some of those who had their differences were now in close proximity to each other, and with that tongues had been lubricated by the drink.

"Watch out," snapped Bob as he was shoved in the back spilling most of his drink. The group of friends all turned together to see a young Irishman, Declan, who Bob knew from working at the camp being pushed by an ex-paratrooper, Barry. The two of them had an ongoing thing regarding the Irish issue, which had started one drunken night in the bar of the *Kenya* on the trip down. Barry had served there a few times and words had been spoken between them on a few occasions since that night. But this time the contest was of more than just words; the powerfully built Barry had taken a shove in the chest from Declan when words had

42

overheated. Barry had then pushed away the slightly-built Irishman with the flat of his hand, this was when he had bumped into Bob. The ex-serviceman had only done this to give himself time to put his can of beer on the bar and to line Declan up for what was to follow. That was a frightening display of speed, strength and power. As Declan straightened up from the push, Barry slammed his large right fist into the left-hand side of his victim's jaw, followed very quickly by a straight left hand that was later deemed to have done most of the damage as it smashed into his upper lip and nose bringing blood spurting in all directions. It was said later that Declan was unconscious before the third and final blow hit him, but hit him it did, and at this point his legs buckled under him as he fell backwards onto the metal deck and with a loud bang as his head hit.

There was a lot of confusion as to what happened next. Some people, namely Bob and Bill, went to the aid of Declan, some of the Irishman's friends went for Barry, and it did not take long for the area in front of the bar to become a mass of brawling bodies on the floor. Colin looked upon this as a good opportunity to take some action photographs, so he backed off a few yards, picked up a turned over chair, stood on it and started snapping away.

*

"Oh God, what a night that was," moaned Bill.

"Yeah, I feel like shit," sighed Bob.

"Well you will drink beer all night," put in Ron. "I have great nights and no hangovers," he laughed.

"Whatever turns you on, Hack," was the reply from Bob.

"What turns me on is out there on that ship." He pointed out into West Cove. Ron along with Bill and Bob were lined up the on the side of the *Adventurer* with many other workers looking across the cove at the large white bulk of the *Kenya* which had sailed into the cove about one hundred yards away from the jetty ship, turned to face the open sea then powered itself so that it stopped with the bow only being a few feet behind the *Adventurer*'s. Then it started to move in towards its mooring for the rest of the day.

Most of the workforce had taken the opportunity to go on the trip to Hampton. Now only the three from their cabin stood on the bridgehead waiting for the *Kenya* to dock.

43

"Alright, Bill?" He turned to see the short fat Cumbrian Eddie who worked on the new hangar site, but more important to Bill the man who ran the sweep and held the money on their section for the sackers, jackers and medivacers that Bill had entered into.

"Hello, Eddie, how's it going?"

"Fine, and it will continue to be if we can get onto the *Kenya* and get some decent food for a change."

"Yeah, that will not be a bad idea," said Bob looking at his watch. "It's three now so they will be serving tea in a couple of hours. We may get some food that can be eaten for a change."

"I suppose you've got some money for me?" Bill said to Eddie. "In fact, I would say thirty-five quid."

"No, well not yet anyway."

"I know what you mean, you've got to wait until tonight before you pay me out just in case there's any more to go on the ship."

"Well," came the reply, "you would not win unless one more was on the boat, and in any case the shutoff time was when the *Kenya* came into the cove, so sorry, Bill, you lost."

"No," said Bill with an angry look building on his face, "there was nineteen yesterday. Barry and Declan have been sacked this morning, when I went to school that would have made twenty-one."

"But that was in Birmingham, remember," laughed Bob.

"Piss off, Bob," came the reply. "It's not funny."

"Sorry, Bill."

Eddie replied, "You can't count Declan."

"Why not?"

"Firstly, he is still unconscious, and secondly he will be kept in sick bay until he is well enough to go home, so he won't be going on the *Kenya* today."

"Hold on, let's get this all straight. What's being un-fucking-conscious got to do with anything?"

"Well," Eddie held out his hands to jester, "he doesn't know he's been sacked."

"I don't give a shit if he knows. The rest of us all know he's sacked, don't we, lads?" He turned to his friends who all nodded their agreement. "Mark Lord the Eastham's camp boss knows, he told me he has been told to make up his bunk for one of the new arrivals. So, everyone bloody knows."

"Declan doesn't know, and he will not know until he wakes up, so technically in his mind he still works for JLB."

44

"Technically my balls. I don't give a fuck if he knows or not. He's sacked and that's all there is to it." The anger was now starting to show in Bill's voice as well as his face. "And if it's only about him knowing, I'll go and wake the bastard up myself."

"Look, Bill, I'm sorry but the sweep committee made a decision on it this morning and it's final."

"Who the fuck is in the sweep committee?" barked Bill.

"Well it's me and Ken Chadwick."

"He's your bunk mate, isn't he?" asked Bob.

"Well, yeah."

"What a load of shit," claimed Bill.

"Well that's it," said Eddie as he turned to walk away.

"So, who's got twenty?" Bob called out to him.

He stopped and turned back towards them. "Aha aha, it's Ken." He then turned and walked off.

"Bill, ever had the feeling you're being ripped off?" asked Bob.

"Yeah, too right I know. Hey, hold on, Eddie, I am not finished with you yet," shouted Bill running off after the stakeholder.

"There's a woman… look, look, there's a woman," cried Ron. He had been using Bob's binoculars to watch the ship move in towards them while Bill's row was going on, mainly to see if he could spot his supplier, which he had just done. Bob in his haste to see the woman grabbed the binoculars even though the cord was still around Ron's neck, which meant he dragged Ron to him at the same time.

"Let's see, Hack."

"Hold on," came the reply, "let's get them off."

"Cor, I wish she'd get them off," said Bob as he focused on the ship's new nurse. When they had come down on the *Kenya* there had been a male nurse, but things were now looking up as Bob was fast to tell Ron. "And I must say that she's a sweet-looking thing at that," Bob continued, not taking the binoculars from his eyes as he talked. "That's three women we have seen in two days, can't be bad. Bloody hell, I think I am getting a 'lazy lob' on."

As the MV *Kenya* got nearer docking with the *Adventurer* the shouting at the incoming ship increased. The sun was shining brightly and the sea was calm. Of course, the always relentless wind was still blowing as the ship docked.

Lining the deck of the incoming ship were the new workforce, members of the ship's crew, and the new nurse who was standing alongside the captain, John England, a sixty-year-old long serving seafaring man. As the ship got nearer the calls from the jetty head could be heard more clearly:

"Get them off!"

"What you doing tonight, love?"

"Do you want to come in my cabin?"

"Fancy a shag?" So much abuse was shouted at the twenty-eight-year-old nurse, Mary Williams from Sydney, Australia, that Captain England at one stage produced a pair of ear defenders and put them on the very red-faced nurse's ears to loud roars and applause from the watching crowd.

When the gangplank was lowered between the ships, Morrison, Jones and Collins went aboard to meet Kim Benjamin the new project coordinator, who from now on would have full control of the contract on the island.

*

It was some time before all the formalities were completed of briefings, passport checks and the new workforce leaving the *Kenya*, however, within minutes of the dismemberment of the ship a loudhailer announced that, "anyone wishing to come aboard for evening dinner is more than welcome to do so." The three lads boarded the ship along with many others. Ron was met by Chinese John as he was known, his crew friend who would be supplying him with drugs. They shook hands, then within a flash of the eye they disappeared below decks.

Bob and Bill sat in the *Kenya*'s restaurant enjoying the best food they had been served since last being on her, which now seemed at least a lifetime ago. When Ron came in carrying a carrier bag and joined them at their table, the wide grin on his face not only told them that the deal had been successful, but also that he had sampled some of the shipment.

While everyone was enjoying the hospitality of the ship, the three cabin mates filled up carrier bags with any food and fruit they could get their hands on. Not many yards away in the captain's cabin a meeting had begun between Benjamin and the three senior management members who had joined him.

Benjamin, a tall and slim thirty-nine-year-old, once of King's College, Cambridge, who then had a long spell as an army officer before taking a very senior post in the construction industry, mainly as a trouble-shooter to start with on a dam in Africa that was experiencing labour problems. Benjamin made a name for

46

himself in no time as he turned the ailing project around very fast, albeit with some very harsh and hard tactics. After that it was onwards and upwards very fast as he went on to some of the world's largest contracts. He was a no-nonsense man who would never take no for an answer when he wanted to hear yes.

"Right." He looked at the others from the large leather armchair in which he sat. The three were on two two-seater settees, that along with a coffee table that furnished the cabin. "I believe there have been a few problems of late concerning overtime and travel amongst others?"

"Well," started Morrison, "on the travel we have come to a compromise with the workforce, and with the overtime…"

"Let me stop you there, Jim." Benjamin got out of his armchair and stood in front of his subordinates. "That is the last time I want to hear the word 'compromise' on this contract." He then started to pace around the cabin. "Gentlemen, we are not here to compromise, we are here to build a two hundred million pound plus airfield for the British Government – and on time. In early 1985 an aeroplane WILL land on the runway, and come hell or high water, gentlemen, it will be done, and what's more it will be done our way." There were looks between the others as Benjamin looked out of a porthole as he gave the comments time to sink in. He then turned to address his audience again.

"On the last major contract in the UK, the barrier, the workforce was allowed to get on top to the point that it did not only go way over time and budget because of the extra bonuses that had to be paid, it got to the point that the workers were all but running it." His voice rose and his face reddened as he spat out, "I am here to tell you that there is no way on God's earth that it will happen here." He stopped and walked around again, then in a calmer voice said, "We don't want to lose too many employees, but if we have to we will, and if we have to bring more people out here we will. Gentlemen, there are over three million unemployed in the UK at the present time, and if I have to bring each and every one of them out here I will. I am a great believer in the fact that if you have a very large rock and keep hitting it with a large hammer in time that rock will crack."

Benjamin walked back to the coffee table and picked up a cup of black coffee and took a sip. "So, gentlemen, we are here to crack that rock with us firmly holding the handle of that hammer. And let's make it very clear to all the workforce that anyone who does not go along with that reasoning, then the MV *Kenya* will dock here once a month and there will be a cabin waiting for them on it."

The new project coordinator then moved to the cabin's door, then with his hand on the handle he turned to the others and said, "Jim, I want you to bring the next workers committee meeting forward to this coming Wednesday. Pleased to meet you, gentlemen." He then opened the door and left the room leaving a shocked silence in his wake.

Chapter 3

Wave Them Goodbye

The midnight moon shone high and bright in the night sky lighting up the calm waters of West Cove. Suddenly the still was broken as the small Beaver boat raced across the waters. Four main beam headlights blazed out in front of the twelve-foot blue cabinless motorboat as it twisted and turned inside the inlet. High laughter and music could be heard coming from it. It headed for the high seas of the South Atlantic, then rounded the small island that was about half a mile out from the cove then headed back towards the *Merchant Adventurer*. It was about twenty yards off the bridgehead when two arc lights, one from the *Adventurer* and the other from Cargo 2, the *Orion*, that was docked beside her, shone brightly onto the small boat, lighting it up in the dead of night.

"Pull over and stop the boat now," came the instruction from the loudhailer on the *Adventurer*. The boat stopped in the water for a few moments then roared into life again and headed towards a small floating metal jetty that was moored about one hundred yards from the bridgehead, which was used for access to the small boats such as the Beaver and others. It stopped alongside the floating metal deck as one person jumped onto the platform holding a rope then tied the boat up, before the engine was killed and five others left the boat and ran off into the night and the cover of the pioneer camp.

*

"We know you were driving the boat, Jim, now we need to know who was with you," Morrison said as he sat next to Benjamin at a dining table in the officer's mess on the upper deck of the *Adventurer*, which was used by JLB as a meeting and conference room. Jim and Bob, who the Ulsterman had asked along as his representative, sat facing the two senior management officials across the long, wide polished table.

"Well," said the young Irishman in his gallic tone, "where I come from you don't rat on your mates. Besides, that could end up a very dangerous thing to do, so I'm not going to start now regardless of where I am in the world."

"The thing is, Jim, if you tell–" Morrison was cut off in mid-sentence by Benjamin who stood up and moved away from the table.

"The thing is we have wasted far too much time already, so this is what we will do, young man. You will be fined £50 to be taken out of your next payment, and you will give a list of the others joyriding with you in the boat and they will be fined also, or you will be dismissed from last Saturday, charged £20 a day for food and accommodation until the next time the *Kenya* gets here, and another £475 for your return fare to the UK."

"I don't think that's fair," put in Bob.

"That's what you may think," came the reply, "but that's how it will be. You have until tomorrow morning. Good evening, gentlemen." The project coordinator turned and left.

The others sat in silence for a moment only broken by the Irishman when he commented, "He's a fucking wanker." This brought smiles to the faces of the other two, albeit a small one in the case of Jim Morrison.

"Jim, I would like to protest this decision," said Bob.

"I'm sure you would, Bob," came the reply as Morrison got up and walked to the door. "But it won't do any good." He held the door open for the others. "I think that's the meeting ended, gentlemen."

*

The two men walked back from the ship to the new field canteen that had been set up at the end of the pioneer camp that overlooked the *Adventurer*. This had a very large kitchen and serving area that led though a double opening that was joined by a closed in walkway to a canteen that when full would seat about one hundred and eighty persons.

Jim and Bob joined their cabin mates at an eight-seater table for their Monday evening meal and to repeat to them what had been said at the meeting. All of their friends had finished their meals when the two joined them.

"I'll tell you what," said Bob as he sipped his soup, "you won't get much out of that Benjamin, I don't think he's here to give anything away." He looked at the soup. "Does anyone know what this soup is meant to be?"

"Says tomato on the board," said Colin who was sat to his right.

"Tomato?" he replied as he poured the liquid back into the bowl. "It's clear!"

"It's tomato without any tomato," laughed Andy.

"Yeah," put in Eric, "Eastham's forgot to put them in." Bob pushed the bowl away from him with a disgusted look on his face.

"I heard," said Bill, "that the rest of the boxing team from the folk night were up today and they all got sacked, all eight of them."

"Just as well for you, Bill, that they did not get sacked before the *Kenya* went or you would not have won the sweep," said Colin.

"I'm just lucky I suppose."

"Luck has got nothing to do with it," said Bob now starting on his dinner. "He didn't really win it with twenty-one."

"Just a little bit of persuasive talk, my friend."

"Oh, I see, that's what it's called in Birmingham is it? Holding someone off the ground by their throat with a ten-inch spanner hovering above their nose. Where I come from it's called threatening behaviour with menaces!" replied the committeeman.

"I suppose that if you wanted to get technical you could call it that as well, but when all's said and done it got me my thirty-five quid."

"You're lucky not to be going on the boat with the rest of the fighters," Bob said as he picked at what he thought was a sorry excuse for a meal in front of him.

"So, what are you going to do, Jim, can you afford to take the sack?" asked Phil.

"Not really, no."

"Well," said Andy, "it's okay to tell them I was on it. You shouldn't have to take the blame yourself."

"Thanks, mate, it's just that Benjamin really pissed me off."

"Look, apart from Bill and Bob," said Colin, "we were all on it, so if it costs us all fifty quid each I think it's worth it to save Jim's job."

"I don't," said Ron. "That could buy a lot of dope."

51

"DO WHAT!" snapped Colin in a very loud voice. "It was your fucking idea."

"Had you going there," smiled the Hack Woodfield lookalike as he pointed across the table at Colin.

"Well I'm not telling them," said Jim.

"Okay," said Colin, "we'll go and own up."

"That's up to you, I can't stop you doing that, but I'm not ratting on anyone!"

"That's cool," said Eric. "We'll go up and see Benjamin before you get fined, you go in and get your fine and it's all over."

"Well if you all agree," said Jim, "it's up to you."

"That's it," said Eric. "Then we'll take him back to the cabin and kick the crap out of the little Paddy shit."

"I can't eat any more of this," said Jim as he pushed the plate away. He then brought his right foot up under the table and kicked Eric in the shin with his size seven steel toecap boot. He then leaped up nearly tipping the table over and ran from the canteen with the muscular one in hot pursuit, and in turn almost knocking over two co-workers who had just come into the eating area holding their dinner trays.

"Good to see the children are happy again," laughed Bill.

"Yeah," agreed Bob, "you wouldn't want any of them getting sacked, would you? I mean the place just wouldn't be the same."

"So, what's happening with Muscles over the cement, Bob?" asked Phil as he handed cigarettes around the table. "You've got involved now, haven't you?"

"Yeah, we have got a meeting at the batcher tomorrow with George and Jack Hudson the safety officer at nine."

"He's a bloody waste of time," said Andy. "He doesn't give a damn what they make us do as long as we are wearing a safety helmet when we do it."

"Well he's all we've got," said Bob as he pushed his half-eaten meal away. "I can't eat this crap."

"If it's at all possible," put in Bill, "I reckon the food has got worse since the last ship got here, and it's all because Eastham's haven't sent any more staff out here when there's been a lot more men sent out to deal with."

"Well everything has got worse since that last boat got in," put in Ron. "More freezing water when there is any, and queuing for everything now! Queue for dinner, queue for post, queue for the shop, shower and shit."

"Well then," said Bob, "talking of all those," he stood up and moved away from the table, "that's what I am going to do. Buy some fags, dive under the shower then have a bloody good tip out." The rest all got up together and left.

*

Jack Hudson had his own Land Rover for moving around the island. He was one of the few who had this privilege, but it was the only perk he did have. He was beginning to think he was very put on. He was starting to feel he was only out here as a figurehead for the safety unit. As he drove along the main access road towards the contractors' camp and his nine o'clock meeting, he pulled on his pipe. The fifty-eight-year-old Surrey man recalled in his mind his first conversation with Kim Benjamin less than one hour ago. Jack, a safetyman for the last twenty-seven years and a construction man all his life, was happy to be seconded to this job and was full of ideas that he wanted to put in place here on what would be a one-off job, with none other in the world ever being like this again.

He had drawn up the project safety plan on the *Kenya*, that was between very bad bouts of seasickness. He had also made up a league table for each section to compete against the others, gaining points for the length of time they had gone without an accident, the winner at the end of each month getting some sort of prize that he was going to ask Kim to donate. But now he was not so sure.

Kim had allowed him to talk for a short while before he broke in on him. "Jack, we are pioneers in a new land, and because of that there are bound to be casualties. I mean, we didn't ask to have twelve coffins put on Cargo 2 for no reason. Construction can be a very dangerous business at the best of times, when risks have to be taken, when sometimes we will have to do things that…" Benjamin stopped to think, "…let's say things that we would not always want to do, or maybe things we would not want to do at home, but to make progress to push on to achieve our goals let's say have to turn a blind eye to things."

"I really want things to go well here, Kim, I really do, but safety is of paramount importance. That is the reason I have come, to get things right for us to do things safely. Safety must come first, Kim."

"Jack," Kim walked across the office and put his arm around Jack's shoulder. "Look, I have been looking at your file. It was

53

Butler who gave you your break in safety, wasn't it?" Jack never got the chance to reply. "So maybe it's now a very good chance for you to pay a fine company back a little? Now, I believe you are going to the new camp to sort out a problem this morning. In three weeks' time another ship will be here with a lot more men. We need that accommodation ready so that we can move men from the pioneer camp up there to free up beds down here for the new intake." He walked the safety man towards the door. "We wouldn't want to put that ship back now, would we?" Jack again didn't get the chance to reply as Kim held open the door for him and said while looking him in the eyes, "I do make myself clear, don't I, Jack? Good, I will see you later, old chap."

It was all Jack could do to get through the door without being shut in it. Even to his own amazement Jack found himself saying to the door, "Oh, of course, Kim, no problem."

Jack pulled up outside Arran and George's office feeling very angry with himself for not putting his foot down and nipping all of this in the bud, but Benjamin was very hard to say no to, and besides that he had very high backing in the UK and Jack did not want to rock the boat.

"Come in, bonny lad, we'll have a few minutes then go and sort that troublemaking Yorkshire bastard out. Do you know what I've had in Africa? With the wind, dust and salt blowing, you could not see your hand in front of your face. What these boys have got here is a picnic compared with what we had to put up with."

"Well, George, I don't suppose it's very nice for them out there, not from what I've heard anyway." This brought a very pained look to George's face.

"Has Kim had a word with you, Jack?"

"Yes, he has, George."

"Good, there shouldn't be any problems then. Fine man that Benjamin, worked for me in Africa when he was a young slip of a lad. Knows how to get work done, not like some we have here, so if he's had words with you let's go and sort the fuckers out," he barked, then pulsed for a second. "Bonny lad."

*

"It's inhumane having to put up with this, Jack. I mean the lad is choking on cement all day. It's in his eyes, there's no dust masks, he's covered from head to toe in it." Bob was stating Eric's case for him as the four stood near the offending cement bag. There

54

were also onlookers of the rest of the batching crew and other workers from the camp.

"I know it's not nice but the work has to be done," said Jack, "now I've seen that personal protection equipment is on Cargo 2."

"Along with everything else in the world on Cargo 2," shouted one of the watching batcher crew.

"So, when will the container with that gear in it be unloaded?" asked Bob.

"Well, it was one of the first on, so it will be a few days yet I am told."

"Let's stop work on here until that happens," said Eric.

"What are you saying, bonny lad?"

"No," jumped in Jack in a loud voice. "We can't stop the job."

"Does men's safety not come first?" asked Bob.

"Of course, it does, that goes without saying."

"It's easy then," the committeeman replied to the safety officer. "Stop work on here until we get the gear for the lads. And by the way, Jack, you do know that Eric is the only one doing the shovelling these days because he upset George?"

"Is that right, George?" Jack turned to look at the foreman as he asked the question.

"Well as he's a fit young lad I thought it would be best all round."

"George, you are joking. You can't have one man on that all the time, it was always meant to be rotated. Right, the first thing we do is to go back to the rotation. Is that understood, George?"

"Okay," came the sheepish reply.

"Look, if you lads can carry on for today, I'll see if there's any way I can get into the hold of Cargo 2 to find the container. It's the best I can do."

"What about making that fat bastard do some shovelling?" Eric snapped pointing at the foreman.

"Right!" a shouted reply came back. "You're getting a written warning for that, bonny lad." Eric walked over to George and put his face right up to his. The foreman backed off in fear.

"Do you know what? I don't give a fuck, 'bonny lad'." Eric then turned and walked away as the watching workers roared their approval.

*

"So, it was right in his face?" asked Colin from his high point on top of the bunk beds.

"Yes," came the reply from Bob as he reported the news to his friends who had gathered for the nightly meeting at his and Colin's end of the cabin. Bill and Ron were also in attendance.

"I heard," said Bill, "that everyone thought he was going to nut him."

"We did," said Bob.

"I was talking to him," said Colin as he pulled on a joint that Ron had passed around. "And I really don't think he cares anymore."

"So, did he get a written warning then?" asked Ron.

"Yeah," replied the committee chairman. "He has pinned it up on the wall beside his bunk."

"What does it say?" asked Ron.

"Go and have a look, Hack," Colin suggested from his high point. He was now high in more ways than one.

"Where is he then?"

"Went out," came the reply from Colin.

"Okay then." Ron left the lads and passed the wardrobes into the next bunk area. The written warning was pinned to the wall at the other side of Eric's bottom bunk, so Ron had to lie on the bunk to read it. This he started to do, then after a moment he said, "Bloody hell, look at this!" As Ron had laid on the bunk he had looked up to see on the underside of the bunk above that Eric had on the slats six photographs of his girlfriend, who just happened to be topless in all of them. "It's his bit of stuff, pictures of her topless, only got her knickers on, showing her tits in all of them." The remaining three workers made a mad scramble towards Eric's bunk to have a look. The four men were all fighting for a view of the semi-naked young lady between the two bunk beds when the door opened and Eric walked into the cabin and stopped to look at what was taking place on his bunk.

"What the hell's going on?" Bodies fell from the bunk at the sound of the Yorkshireman's voice as the four tried to escape the scene.

"We were only reading your warning," moaned Colin from the bottom of the pile of human flesh, now on the floor in front of Eric's feet.

"Wouldn't have anything to do with the photos of my Anne would it?" He smiled as he looked down at them.

56

"No, no," came the collective cries from the lino floor below him.

"Cramp, cramp," came a cry of a Northern Irish voice from inside Eric's wardrobe. Those lying on the floor had now all gone quiet as they looked at the talking wardrobe. "Shit, my leg's gone dead," was the next scream from within as the wardrobe doors burst open and Jim fell out holding a length of rubber hosepipe which also fell to the floor.

"What were you doing in there?" asked a very surprised Bill.

"I was going to jump out on Muscles and do him with the hosepipe, but he took so long to get here that I got cramp." Eric took the hose from the floor and started to hit him with it.

"Oh, oh, fuck off," he cried. "I've been sacked, leave me alone."

The noise in the cabin died as Bill asked, "What did you say?"

"I've been sacked," came the reply from the aching ex-sailor who was sprawled out on the floor rubbing his parts.

"I thought it was all sorted," said Bill as they all started to get to their feet. "The boys owned up, took the fines and you're in the clear."

"Well I had to see Benjamin after the lads had been up to see him and he said I was still sacked as I didn't tell him. They owned up by themselves. The deal was for me to grass them up."

"That Benjamin is a real wanker," Colin told everyone as he bent and rubbed his own aching legs.

"He said I can carry on working till the *Kenya* gets here so that I can pay for my board and lodge, but he's still going to stop me £475 for my fare home."

"Oh, that's sodding big of him," said Ron. By this time everyone was on their feet and moving towards the meeting point which also doubled up as Colin and Bob's living area.

"Well," said Colin, "we've got to do something about this," as he jumped onto his beloved top bunk.

"What can we do?" asked Eric.

"Stop working?" suggested Ron.

"That won't work," said Bob, "we'll be breaking the contract and they can just sack all of us which
will get us nowhere."

"They won't sack the whole workforce, will they? I mean, they can't," answered Ron.

"No, they won't, but there's no way you will get everyone to stop work, then they will just pick off everyone who does stop work," Bob replied.

"What do the lads you work with on the *Adventurer* think?" asked Bill.

"It seems they are pissed off about it. I think so anyway."

"Right, that's it then," said Bob. "If they can just say they will stop work on Cargo 2 and it will then not be unloaded on time it will go into demurrage. The extra charge required of them as compensation would be so great they would just not go there. Jim, I will go around with you tonight and we will try and drum up support for you from the ship workers."

"What about if the rest of us go around the cabins with a paper tonight and get a petition together and get everyone to sign it?" asked Bill.

"That's great," said Bob. "Let's go and get some food and we will get cracking."

"Food? Is that what we are calling it these days?" asked Bill.

"Okay then," came the reply. "On reflection I will say let's go and eat whatever shit they are dishing up tonight, then we'll get cracking."

"That's better," said the Brummie with a big smile on his face.

It was a very busy evening all round for the members of cabin 4C. All the occupants got involved going around the cabins piling up lists of names. Bob and Jim talked to nearly all the ship's crew and stevedores in the bars and cabins, and was assured that he would be given full support the next morning. Heaps of paper lay on Bob's bottom bunk when that was all finished at about ten forty-five that night.

*

Bob and Jim walked onto the deck of the *Adventurer* at seven am that Wednesday morning in late January. It was a bright sunny summer's morning in that part of the southern hemisphere. There was still a breeze but not so cold as the wind was blowing from the north. All of the ship's workers had gathered on the deck and Bailey bridge and it had only taken a very short meeting to decide that all work would stop on unloading Cargo 2 until the very popular Northern Irishman was reinstated. It was not long after the starting hour of seven o'clock that the foreman came to find out why no work was being carried out. When given the reason he was fast to report the news to senior management. Within a short while of him entering the office high above the deck Morrison came down and asked Bob to join him and Benjamin in the conference room.

"You do realise that you are all in breach of contract?" Benjamin pointed towards the office window which overlooked the ship's main deck. "And you do realise you could be dismissed and returned to the UK on the next MV *Kenya*?"

"That would be an option for you." Bob held out his hands at arm's length where he sat opposite the two senior managers. "But it will not get Cargo 2 unloaded, will it, Kim? In fact, it will go into demurrage in a few days, it will then cost JLB a lot of money, will it not?"

"Let me tell you now, mister." Benjamin sat up straight in his seat and all at once there was venom in his voice that made the other two take the same posture as himself. "If it costs us money it will cost us money, but there is no way on God's earth that I will be held to ransom because a load of drunken yobs went out for a joyride on a very important piece of equipment and could have cost lives, and the fact that we have taken action over this has upset the workforce. I am sorry but that is the way it will be."

"Excuse me for one minute please, gentlemen." Morrison got up to leave the room and in doing so he passed the large window overlooking the main deck and glanced out. "What the hell?" He was quickly joined by the other two at the window to see that four single-deck red buses that had been unloaded a few days earlier had pulled up in front of the ship full of workers from the camp, airfield and hangar sites and were now leaving the vehicles to join the other protestors.

"I think you will be writing out a lot of dismissal notices, Kim," smiled Bob.

"Well if you think for one moment that this will make us back down you could not be further from the truth," Benjamin barked.

"I will be back in a minute," said Morrison as he left the room and headed down the corridor to the radio room. As he got there the door opened and he was met by a radio operator who held a telex in his hand.

"Think this is what you are after, Jim," said the radioman as he handed over the paper.

"Thanks, Mike." Morrison walked back to the office reading as he went. Bob was leaving as he got to the office.

"I think we're all sacked," said Bob as he passed Morrison.

"Oh look, Bob, just wait here a moment could you and I'll be right back." Morrison entered the office as Benjamin was pouring coffee.

"I've given them one hour to return to work or they will all be dismissed, lose their overtime payments, retention, bonuses, pay for their keep, then their fare home!"

"I think you had best read this first, Kim," said Morrison as he handed over the paper to the project coordinator. Benjamin's face grew red as he read the message from the London head office that was a reply to Morrison's earlier telex to them which Kim knew nothing about, telling him that he must reinstate the boat worker without further ado and return the project to normality.

"Who gave you the right to contact the office over this?"

"I thought it would be for the best if things didn't work out, Kim."

Benjamin stood and sipped his black coffee as he collected his thoughts. Then, finally, he said in a now calmer voice, "Well, I suppose you had better give them the news then." Morrison made for the door and as he was about to open it Kim said, "Oh, Jim."

"Yes?"

"That will be the one and only time you will go over my head. Do you understand?" Jim just nodded his reply and Benjamin could not be sure if he saw a faint smile on his project manager's face as he left to give the news to Bob. Even with the windows closed in the office, Benjamin could hear the cheers from the workforce on the deck below as they got the news.

While the celebrating was going on, no one really noticed Jack Hudson pass the crowd after leaving the hold of the moored cargo ship. No one heard him mumble to himself, "Safety helmets, just hundreds more safety fucking helmets!"

*

When Jack arrived at the outskirts of the camp worksite he parked up to walk around the surrounding area in the morning sunshine. The wind was still keen and he had his donkey jacket completely done up, but he did at times get to feel the sun on his face which was not for the first time this year, but this time he was enjoying it.

He pulled on his pipe as he went and was happy to have a little bit of free time to himself, a bit of time to reflect on what had been happening and to take a little time out.

He strolled past a series of newly built manholes at the bottom of which sewer pipes ran. There was an urgent need for these as the idea was for men to move up before the next *Kenya* came in at the end of the month with more workers on, who in turn would move into the pioneer camp. The manholes would take sewage away from the first block of rooms that had been built, from there it would run in the pipes some distance from the camp into a temporary cesspit. This was a large metal container which had been lowered into a hole that had been dug for it. A small section three-foot square at one end on the top had been cut out of it so that concrete could be poured in to make a level smooth floor, also to fit the incoming four-inch pipe near the top. A cover would be fixed over the hole and only removed when the tank needed to be pumped out and tipped on the other side of the island.

Since Erect-A-Com had started onsite work had progressed very fast at the camp. Jack could see the camp was now starting to take shape and had now moved out of the ground as only the foundations could be seen before. He had a good drive around all the work areas that morning, mainly, as he would admit to himself, because he was in no rush to get to the batching plant with the news that the listed safety equipment he had found in the container in the hold of Cargo 2 was just safety helmets, not a glove, mask, goggles or overalls in sight. "Just fucking safety helmets." He was in no rush that bright morning.

He had parked up at the hangar that would in time have the large jet aeroplanes parked in it for maintenance, but was now just a very large hole in the ground waiting for work on the foundations to begin. He walked onto the start of the airfield where many diggers were busy filling the fleets of dump trucks that would then be driven to Long Pond almost two miles away. This was a massive tidal salt water lake that in time would be filled with spoils from the airfield dig and other areas, the water in turn finding its way back to the sea. The filled pond would be left for wildlife of which there was much in this part of the world for them to live and feed off.

On each side of the runway digging for storm water drainage was underway. Away from the construction areas in the quiet of the virgin land which was soon to be ripped up he saw wildlife in its rawness. Even though he was part of the team that would change the island forever, he was thinking to himself, what a shame, is there nothing that is sacred anymore?

*

"I don't believe they have only sent safety helmets," said Butch the batcher chargehand. "Me and the lads are dying here each day, choking to death, and we get bloody safety helmets."

"I'm sorry," said Jack. "I did put in an order before I left the UK for safety equipment, but for some reason it did not get sent."

"I bet the management got what they put in for," said one of the north easterners, Kevin, who was with the gathered batching gang along with George and Bob.

"Oh, bonny lad, don't be like that. I'm sure it was only a mistake."

"Some mistake," put in Eric. "We've got to choke for another month until Cargo 3 gets here, and that's if they get around to putting the gear on that one." He looked around the crowd for support and got it with the moans and groans that he heard.

"I really think this has gone on for long enough," said Bob. "If we were in the UK this would not be allowed to happen. The Health and Safety Executive would be called in and the job would be stopped, and no doubt you lot would get a big fine." He pointed at Jack and George who were stood together.

"Well that's the whole point, bonny lad, we're not in the UK, we're in a wild part of God's earth with a job to do. Now if we were in Africa I could get fifty locals here in the morning who would only be too pleased to do this job, and I might add for a small part of the money you lot are getting!"

"I'm sure this might have been mentioned to you before, George?" smiled Eric. "We are not in FUCKING AFRICA!" he shouted. "AND WE'RE NOT FUCKING LOCALS!" This brought a cheer from the others who were watching.

The red-faced foreman pointed a finger at Eric and said, "You're already on sticky ground, bonny lad."

"Good," came the reply.

"Look, let's forget the arguing," said Bob. "What are you going to do about it?"

"There's nothing we can do," said Jack.

"I'm sorry, lads," said Bob turning to face the workers. "There's not much more I can do here. Bonny lad don't give a fuck about you, and the safety officer is only here to make things look good and keep management happy." He held out his arms to them then turned to leave.

"BOB!" shouted Jack. "I resent that."

Bob stopped and before turning back to face them smiled to himself then walked back. "Resent as much as you like, Jack, but it's true. For a man who has dedicated his life to the safety of others, you are now letting everything you have stood and worked for over the years go by the board, just because we are on the other side of the world. These men can get damaged lungs out here as well as anywhere. It's like we have gone backwards fifty years, and the truth is none of you give a damn, and if we say anything you don't like we are on the next ship home! Jack, you're here so they can say they have a safety officer. You know as well as I do that they won't let you change anything if it would slow up progress. For what good you are going to do for us you might just as well sit in your cabin all day long." There was no cheering from the men this time, just a silence, one that could be cut with a knife, or in this case a shovel.

"Right," said Jack after thinking for a few moments. "I won't say you are right on all counts, but there is a case to sort here, and I will agree conditions are poor."

"Be careful what you are saying, bonny lad Jack," said the red-faced person beside him in a quiet voice.

"What do you intend to do about it?" asked Bob.

"I'll tell you what I intend to do. For each day until you get the proper safety equipment George will put an extra two hours on your timesheets for each man working on this batcher. I will go and see Kim Benjamin now with a list of what we need and will have it air bridged down here in the next few days." Air bridge is a form of travel from the UK where a transport aeroplane would fly about halfway down to the Ascension Islands in the Atlantic Ocean, stop there for as long as it took to refuel, then continue on to the southern islands. Mainly it was used for army personnel, senior management, post and medivacs. It was a very uncomfortable trip and noisy, but could be done in about fifteen to twenty hours as opposed to over two weeks by sea and air.

George pulled Jack to one side and said, "Bonny lad Jack, you can't give them extra hours just like that, not without talking to

Kim first. And as for the air bridge, I am not sure he will agree to that either. It's very expensive you know."

"You're right, George, I can't give them extra hours, but what I can do is stop work on the batcher until the next cargo ship gets here. Is that what you want? No, so get the men back to work and I will sort the rest out."

"Kim will not like you doing this off your own back, I can tell you that for nothing, bonny lad," he said as he turned and walked back to the workers.

*

"Let me get this straight, Jack. You are telling me that on behalf of myself and JLB that you've agreed, without consulting me first I might add, to pay each man two hours overtime per day, and we will pay for this equipment," he held a sheet of paper in his hand as he sat across the polished office table from Jack, "to be air bridged here, at the great expense that it is?"

"Well the truth is, Kim, if I am here to uphold safety, it's one thing chasing men regarding wearing safety helmets, but in this case, it is us who are in breach of safety standards, and I really didn't think that you would have a problem over cost if it made the job safe."

"Jack, of course you're right," Benjamin said after thinking about this for a little while. "And to prove this I will get these items sent out on the next flight from the UK. We don't want to be paying extra hours for too long, do we?" He laughed.

"No, not at all, Kim. I knew you would understand."

"Okay then." He picked up the internal phone on the table, pressed one button then talked. "I've a list here I want to order from the UK and have it sent urgently." He held his hand over the mouthpiece of the phone. "That will be all now. Thanks, Jack."

"Oh, okay." He was a bit surprised at the speed of his dismissal from the office, but got up and left the room. When the door shut Benjamin talked into the telephone once more.

"There's one other thing I want you to telex the London office about if you could come down here for a moment please." He replaced the phone then sat back in his chair and rubbed his chin with his hand and said to himself, "I will stop these people going over my head if it is the last thing I do!"

"I heard today," said Bill as he leant on Bob's wardrobe for the nightly gossip and meeting, "that the quarry is in the wrong place, about two miles out. The stone they have blasted there is too soft, and after a shedload of tests the lab boys have said it has got to be moved. It's not in the right area."

"Someone has dropped a bollock then," added Colin, who was sat on his top bunk with his legs hanging over.

"Yes, I've heard heads could well roll over this," said Bill as he pulled on his cigarette.

"I've just heard on the radio," said Ron as he joined them, "that the Islander plane is in at West Cove International Airport tomorrow."

"Great, we might get some post. It's been a while," said Bob.

"Word is," put in Colin, "that there is a load of things running out."

"No crisps in the bar last night," shouted Jim, as he changed from his work clothes at his end of the cabin.

"No sweets in the shop," called out Eric from his bunk.

"Can't remember last time they had dirty mags in the shop," said Colin.

"Might have known you'd come up with that one," said Bob.

"Well," came the reply, "men without women need these things."

"You read them at home and you have got a woman there," came back Bob.

"Oh, that's different," said the voice from above him.

"At least we got the safety gear," said Eric who had come to join them wearing just a pair of shorts.

"Yeah," said Bill. "You lads did really well there, standing your ground and all."

"Even if you all look like a load of bananas in the bright yellow suits," laughed Bob. The overalls they had been given were made of a bright yellow rubber. They were all in one waterproof suits with a zip up the front and a hood.

"They are okay," said Eric who had not seen Jim creep up behind him. "They keep you clean and keep off that bloody wind that's blowing all the time. AAHHH!" he shouted as Jim pulled down his shorts from behind revealing his naked body. He made a grab to pull them up, but as he bent to do so Jim put his foot on to Eric's backside and shoved him over onto the floor.

"See you later," shouted Jim as he fled the cabin before any retribution could befall him from the Yorkshireman.

"He is mad that lad," said Bob as Eric got to his feet and pulled up his shorts.

"Go, Muscles, go kill," laughed Bill.

"I really can't be bothered. I'm not in the mood. I'll do it later."

"Did anyone see the notice up in the canteen tonight?" asked Colin. "It is about them wanting volunteers to move up to the new camp. They are going to have a block of sixteen rooms ready before the next ship gets here. It will be two sharing a room and you can choose who you move in with."

"I heard that," said Bill.

"Would have been very disappointed had you not," smiled Bob.

"Yeah, okay, smart arse, but the thing is you'd have to come down here on the bus for dinner, and you know it's seven miles each way."

"Okay," said Bob, "but we are working down there and have to make the trip twice a day anyway, so it would just be at a different time. In a way it could be better as we could get a lay in, not having to rush for the bus and all."

"Also," put in Ron, "we could all get rooms near each other if we all went up together."

"I think it's a good idea," said Bob. "We are going to have to move up there soon anyway, so let's do it when it suits us."

"But our con-trick says we will have single accommodation, not sharing," returned the Brummie.

"We'll get that later," said the committeeman, "we won't get a room to ourselves at the moment. They are under pressure for bed space. There's another ship full of men on the way and nowhere to put them. Besides, we'll only get sent up there later and maybe get no choice who we share with, we could get any wanker we don't want to be with. You could end up with Jim." They all laughed at this.

"Oh well," said Bill, "maybe it's not such a bad idea after all, but at the moment it's Saturday night, the bar's open, and the Brum lost again. I think that's a good reason to go and get pissed!"

*

66

"I don't believe it, I don't fucking believe it," snapped Bob. He had just returned to the cabin after his Sunday morning visit to the shower block, only Eric was not in the cabin. He had gone to the ship for breakfast while the remaining occupants of the cabin were still in bed. "Who the fuck would do this?" He stood in front of Colin's bunk holding up a pair of long white socks of his that he had put on the washing line outside the cabin the night before to dry after he had washed them. The feet on both of them had been cut off. Colin rolled over on his top bunk and looked at the sight before him and laughed.

"Colin, there's an old saying."

"What?" came the reply from the bleary-eyed top bunk occupant.

"He who laughs last laughs longest."

"What the fuck are you on about?"

"They cut your only two pairs of long pants in half, I mean right up the middle. You now own four legs." Bob himself now laughed at this.

"What? The bastards," Colin snapped as he sat upright in bed, then jumped off the top bunk onto the floor and run out of the hut in just his underpants.

"Andy, you've had the arms cut off your jumper," Bob shouted.

"Well," came the reply, "the way I feel, it will take a lot more than that to make me jump out of bed, I can tell you."

"It's happened to everyone in the camp, every washing line has been done," said Eric who had come in holding a white envelope that he had just collected from his pigeonhole in the canteen.

"Bastards," Colin growled as he re-entered the cabin holding two legs of pants in each hand. "I'll kill the wankers if I get my hands on them."

"I heard a lot of noise late last night," called out Ron from his bunk.

"I didn't hear anything," Andy moaned.

"No, neither did I," said Bob.

"No," returned Ron, "you were all pissed out of your brains apart from Eric. I was the only one not pissed in here last night!"

"No, Hack, that's because you were off your head on dope," shouted Bill from the far end of the cabin.

67

"Can someone help me?" shouted Jim from his top bunk bed above Bill. Bob walked down to their end of the cabin to see what the problem was. When he got there, he found Eric had bound a very deep sleeping, drunk Jim to his bunk with rolls of masking tape.

"Stay there for a while," laughed Bob. "It's a good chance of a lay in."

"Well that's it," said Eric as he sat on his bunk reading the letter. "I've been sacked, they have finished me for being unsuitable inside the first three months trial period as the con-trick says they can. I'm going on the *Kenya* tomorrow morning."

"Let's have a look at that," said Bob as he took the letter out of Eric's hands.

"It's that bastard George," shouted Colin, by which time the others had started to gather around Eric's bunk.

"Can't we do something about it?" Bill asked Bob as he stood next to him in just his underpants.

"The truth is," came the reply from the Londoner, "I don't think there is much we can do as they are within their rights to the letter of the con-trick."

"Well," said Andy from his top bunk, "we should do something!"

"No," said Eric. "I don't want you to. Thanks anyway. I'm really sick and tired of it, I'm going home. I've been thinking about it a lot lately. George is out to get me, even if I got away with it this time it would soon be another thing. No, I think it's time for me to go."

Nothing was said among the cabin members for a moment or two as the words sank in. This was only broken by Bill who said, "Well if that's the case we know you don't drink you muscly bugger, but I think today is the day to start." This was greeted with a large cheer from the others.

"Before you do that," came the Irish voice from the end of the cabin, "could someone untie me please? I need a pee."

Eric never did break his own non-drinking rule that day, but he did go out with the lads who got drunk for him. But everyone in the cabin was up early the next day for two reasons: one to see their friend Eric off, and the other was to start packing as they had all agreed with welfare to move up to the new camp that morning before the ship docked to make the whole cabin available for the new workforce. That was apart from Jim who was told he could stay in a cabin on the *Adventurer* as he worked there. The remaining six would make their way up to the new camp, along with another twenty-six co-workers who would make up the first corridor of residents in the new contractors' camp.

*

Eric had said his goodbyes to his roommates by giving them each something to remember him by. He gave Bob his needles and Colin some cotton so that they could repair their socks and pants. He gave Jim some shit-stoppers tablets, as he called them, that his mother had sent to him. He shared his pegs for the washing line between Phil, Andy and Bill. The only one he spent money on was Ron. He bought some cigarette papers off a lad in another cabin as they had run out in the shop. "Here, Hack, you can carry on rolling your dope up." There were damp eyes in the cabin as the lads left for work that morning.

As Eric made his way towards the *Adventurer* with his suitcases for the last time, he never noticed the two passengers in the Land Rover that passed him on their way to the capital, with their own suitcases for air bridge back to the UK after their dismissal. It was Jim Morrison and Jack Hudson.

Chapter 4

An Ill Wind Blows Tin Sheets

It was a very hot midsummer's night. Bob's wife Jane had gone to "slip into something more comfortable" while Colin had run the bath after opening a bottle of vintage red wine. He then took off all of his clothing and got into the deep warm water. Because it was so hot he had set up a fan near the bath to blow cool air towards them. The cooling breeze was now blowing across his face. He looked towards the door as it opened and his best friend's wife walked in and came across the room and looked down on him as she stood beside the bath. She wore a pure silk dressing gown, only kept together by the belt that was tied around her slender waist. Colin could not keep his eyes from her as he looked at the beautiful long blond-haired woman in front of him. He knew as he looked that she wore nothing under the gown by the way it clung to her slim body. She gave him a long loving smile, then with both hands pulled on each side of the belt until it came open exposing the fullness of her naked voluptuous body beneath the robe. Colin could not have forced his eyes from her even had he wanted to, they were glued to the sight before him.

He knew this was all wrong with his lifelong best friend's wife, but at this moment in time that mattered not. He just needed the beauty in front of him. Jane bent over him, her naked breasts almost touching his face, and then with both hands she cupped the warm water from the bath and started to pour it on his face. She then whispered in his ear, "Colin, I love you. Colin, I love you. Oh, Colin, I really, really love you. Colin, will you fucking wake up!"

His eyes shot open to see Bob's face above him on the top bunk. "Colin, wake up will you, the roof has blown off!" Trying to comprehend what was going on, he rubbed his eyes with both hands then focused first at Bob's face, then beyond him to see the night sky. A gale was howling and rain was pouring in on them.

"I was dreaming, I was at home, I was about to have sex with... the wife."

"Well you can say we have been fucked alright, but not the way you are thinking. Now get yourself up, we have got to move." As soon as Colin took the cover off himself he could feel the cold of the night on him, and this was compounded by the freezing rain hitting his all but for a small pair of underpants.

"Didn't you hear the bloody roof come off?" Bob shouted above the noise of the storm as they both got their clothes out of their wardrobes in the twenty-foot square room that they now lived in at the main contractors' camp.

"Didn't hear a thing until you shouted in my face. I was having a lovely dream, I was in the bath and about to shag your, I mean, my wife."

"What did you say? I can't hear a bloody thing with this wind roaring."

"Good," came the reply as Colin bent to tie his bootlaces. "I was about to shag your Jean," he said in a soft voice.

"Speak up will you," said Bob, as he pulled his coat on. "I can't hear you." Colin stood up and moved closer to Bob's face.

"I was about to shag Jean, my wife."

"Oh, that's okay." Bob walked to the door. "I thought for a minute you said you were about to shag my Jean!" He opened the door onto the corridor that they occupied. They had the end room facing Ron and Andy. On one side of their room was the shower and toilet block, on the other side was the room that Pete and Dusty lived in. On the opposite side Ron and Andy had a changing room to their left and Bill and Phil to the right.

Most of the workforce that lived at the camp were now out in the corridor now the entire double-sheeted roof with thick fibreglass insulation between them had blown off. There was still a section of about twenty-five feet of roofing at the far end of the corridor from Bob and Colin's room that was still there. But even this had parted company with its fixings and was now lifting up and down in the wind onto the wooden sections that made up the dwelling.

"What the hell are we going to do?" asked Colin as they all met in the corridor. The rain was now pouring straight down and was starting to flood the area in which they stood. Another gust of high wind lifted some of the remaining roof sections as there were still some fixings holding it to the structure. When the wind eased it came crashing back down onto the timber frame which sent the workers running in all directions of the corridor like headless chickens.

"We can't stay in here," said Bob. "If one of those sheets hits us it would cut our fucking heads off." As the last of Bob's words left his mouth a metal sheet parted company with what was left of the roof and went flying high into the night sky spinning as it went. They all stood and watched in amazement as it flew high.

"If that comes down one end first," said Bill, "it would split you in half like a carrot."

"It's gone," said Bob as they watched it disappear from view, "but we do need to get away from here and any other flying debris."

"Come on," shouted Ron above the noise of the wind. "Let's get out of here." They made their way past the toilets and changing rooms, turned right and through the single door to the outside. By the time the group had made its way outside most of the other sections of roof were being ripped from their fixings and the air was now alive with flying sheets.

Phil was the last to appear as he had returned to his room to put his shoes on. The lads all stood some distance from their residence, as Phil made his way towards them bent forward to protect his face from the driving wind and rain, which was pouring out of the darkness. It was said later by Bill himself that had he not shouted a warning to Phil the flying sheet may have glanced off the back or top of his head, but in the split second he heard the Birmingham voice shout, "Watch out, Phil!" he straightened up and lifted his head to see what was happening. The flying metal object hit him across the back of the head, about half an inch above his ears. Phil hit the ground face first from the impact of the blow and did not move as he lay on the ground. In that moment the flying sheets mattered not as his friends ran to his aid and fended off the other flying missiles. He was picked up in seconds by his workmates, still face down, by arms and legs they then ran with him to what was considered to be a safe area. Blood was pouring from the head wound as he lay unconscious on the wet stoned parking area that was used by the buses to collect passengers and to turn around.

"What the fuck do we do?" asked Ron as they looked over the prostrate body. They then rolled him on to his back to expose closed eyes.

"We have got to get him to the ship and the doctor," said Bob. "He's losing a lot of blood."

"He could die if we move him," said Colin.

"He could fucking die if we don't move him," came the reply from his roommate who was now kneeling beside the injured worker.

"We haven't got any transport anyway," put in Bill. "They keep the bus down at the ship."

"What about a lorry from the camp?" asked Andy.

"No," replied Bill. "They keep the keys down at the ship at night to stop any joyriders."

"Well we can't leave him here," said Bob, "and we really should try to stop the bleeding."

"Here," said Andy as he took off his jacket and navy-blue company issued jumper to expose a "I love New York" T-shirt. The lads all stared at it. "Just don't say a fucking word, okay?" He took it off and started to rip it up.

"Best thing for that," put in the Brummie. Makeshift bandages from the shirt were placed around Phil's head to stem the bleeding, others took off their coats to put under his head and to cover his body to keep him warm and dry.

"God," said Bob as he looked closely at him in the darkness, "he's gone very pale. I really think we have got to take a chance and get him down to the ship."

"It's seven miles," said Andy. "We couldn't carry him that far!"

"Why not," replied Bob, "or are we going to leave him here to die?"

"No, I didn't mean that."

"Whatever we are going to do," said Bill, "I think we should do it quick."

"Right, that's it then. We carry him to the ship. Now!" said Bob in a very firm voice that made everyone realise that this was what was going to happen and there would be no going back. "We will make a stretcher out of all this gear." He pointed at all the rubbish laying around them. "We can get all the lads together to help, then take it in turns to carry him." He looked at everyone then said, "Boys, if Phil is going to make it, I really don't think there's any choice. We have got to do it to save him, we all came here together, we are the B-Team!" No more was said. If they would do it or not, the talk was all of how to make the stretcher and what to use. In not many minutes it had been constructed. Two sections of sheeting that were still fixed together with insulation between them had two long lengths of four-inch by two-inch timbers jammed down each side so that they protruded at each end, to be used as handles to carry Phil on the lifesaving dash to the ship.

Phil was laid on the makeshift stretcher with the coats over his body and under his head. Belts and bootlaces were used to secure him to it so he could not fall off. Before the lifesaving journey began Bob tried for a pulse on the only exposed part of the injured person that held one, which was Phil's neck.

"He has still got one, but it's faint," he told those stood waiting to start the long trip.

"Well let's get him down there then," said Reg Kane who had made his way to the front to take first turn on the run down to the *Adventurer*. All of the thirty-one remaining men set off together to take turns to carry Phil into the storm of the night at one fifteen that Sunday morning. A handheld flashlight had been found which was also being taken in turns to be carried out in front to watch out for potholes, ruts and to keep to the road. They did not run as such, but the pace was fast to start with. They never stopped to hand over the stretcher, it would be handed over in mid-stream.

The gale if possible was getting worse, and as most of the lads had given up their coats they were now soaked to the skin and feeling very cold. It had seemed like a month since they left the camp, but it was in fact one hour fifty minutes when the lights of the pioneer camp and the ship came into sight. Donald Hartley, a slim, six-foot-two inch, twenty-nine-year-old, ginger-haired ex-paratrooper, who could be seen each night pounding the haul roads on his nightly run, said in a loud voice, "I'm off for help," then ran off towards the ship as if he had come no distance at all.

"Fuck, how can he do that?" asked Bob who had just finished a turn on a handle. "I'm about to drop," he panted.

"You're not kidding," said Colin. "We are all done in." The pace had slowed a lot as the miles had gone by and fatigue had started to set in. He looked back to the volunteers strung out behind them. Most of the heads were held low.

"We are nearly there," said Bill who had just taken his turn on a handle. "Hang in there, mate," he said to Phil, whose eyes were still shut and the white bandages around his head were now completely red with blood.

74

"Colin?" Bob said as he and his roommate, who were now walking together, were out of earshot of the others.

"Yes, Bob?"

"When we were back in the room tonight, I mean when we first got up, I think you did say you were dreaming about shagging Jane."

"I did not," came a very firm reply.

"Look, if it's just a dream I don't mind. I mean, it is really no big deal… if it's just a dream that is. I suppose in some ways it's a backhanded compliment. I'll be the first to admit my wife is very tasty, I know a lot of men fancy her, and I know I'm not the best-looking painting on the gallery wall, but what I do know is I can trust her one hundred percent."

"That's a load of bollocks," shouted Bill. "No one knows that. I think I can trust my missus as much as anyone can, but you just don't know, do you? I mean your two wives go out together and they are only human, they have been without a man for a while now. You know they are out having a few drinks, good-looking girls and all, they get chatted up. For all you know they could be getting done right now, the both of them."

"So, could yours," snapped Colin spinning around to face him.

"I know, that's what I'm saying. None of us know what's happening while we are out here."

"Oh, piss off, Bill," shouted Bob. The way Bob had intervened it was taken by all that the conversation was to end now, and so it was and no other words were spoken as they pressed on in the storm towards the ship and help for Phil.

They passed the eight-foot by four sign that read, WEST COVE INTERNATIONAL AIRPORT that was in front of the two hundred yards of stripped peat that made the airfield for the Islander aeroplane.

The group were quiet as they passed the sign at the start of the pioneer camp that read, CARDBOARD CITY. As they rounded the first cabin the lights of a Land Rover that had been converted into an ambulance could be seen. It pulled up in front of them. Dr McKenzie, Jack, the tall, slim, thirty-five-year-old medic and Donald all jumped out and went to Phil, who had now been put down.

"Okay," said the doctor, "get him in the back, fast." Phil was laid on the bed in the back of the ambulance and the doctor and medic got in with him. "He's not breathing," said the doctor as he examined him.

"Mind out, Doc," said the medic. "I'll give him mouth to mouth." Jack leant over Phil and did this for a while then the doctor examined him again.

"Nothing." Jack sighed before he continued. Donald told the lads that they had left the radio operator calling the army in the capital for a helicopter.

"I'm going to give him CPR," said Jack as he got up on top of Phil with a leg each side of his body. The silent crowd of would-be lifesavers looked in from the open rear door of the ambulance, but with the rain still coming down in torrents it was hard to tell on most of the faces if it was rain or tears.

"Come on, Phil," said Bob in a soft almost sobbing voice. "Don't leave us, mate, hang in there. You can do it!"

Joe Cooney, the large framed and dark-haired Irish concreter, who had done a large amount of the carrying gently put his hands together and looked towards the sky and said, "Well, big fellow, I've never asked many favours, but we could really do with one right now." Not a sound could be heard as Jack worked at pumping Phil's chest. After what seemed an age he stopped and the doctor checked again.

"I've got a pulse, man!" shouted the doctor. "I've got a pulse." This was greeted with a loud cheer from Phil's watching workmates.

Joe looked back up to the sky and muttered, "Oh, God, thank you, God." The doctor put an oxygen mask on Phil's face and turned on the tap of the large bottle and turned to the now jubilant workers.

"He is in a very bad way, he needs more treatment then I can give him, he has lost a lot of blood and needs a transfusion. We have got to get him over to the capital as soon as possible."

"Someone is coming," said Andy as he pointed towards the lights of a Land Rover making its way towards them in the dark and pouring rain. In no time it pulled up in front of them. The radio operator jumped out and ran to join the group.

"The army say they can't put up a chopper in this. It's too rough," he panted to them.

"Shit," replied the doctor. "This man will as sure as anything die if we do not get him to a hospital soon!"

76

"I know," came the answer from the operator. "I put out a Mayday call and it seems that there's a Royal Navy frigate a few miles from here just off the coast."

"Hope it is British," smiled Bill. Totally ignoring that comment, the radio operator carried on.

"The captain knows West Cove and says the entrance is far too tight to risk coming in with the weather how it is, but if there was some way for us to get him out to them, they would take him to the army hospital in Stanley."

"How are we supposed to get him out there?" asked the doctor.

"Jim," shouted Bob, "we'll get him up and he can take us out there in the Beaver boat."

"You're joking," said Colin. "That small little boat will get washed away in no time in those seas!"

"Well," said the doctor, "I can, assure you that if you don't, your friend will die."

As noisy as it was, the silence could be heard as all of the group looked at each other. Then Bill said, "I am up for it, Bob, I'll go with you."

"Count me in," said Andy.

"Oh shit," snapped Colin. "I'll go, but you know we are all going to fucking die, you realise that don't you?"

"Well," said Bob as he put his arm around his friend and led him away, "that will teach to dream about shagging my wife!"

*

"He'll be pissed, that's why he can't hear us. He'll be laying on his bunk pissed out of his brains," Bill told the others as they stood outside Jim's cabin banging on the door, which they had now been doing for some time.

"What's all the bloody noise about?" asked a voice. The lads turned to see the massive figure of the bearded ship worker Kevin Williams from the next cabin stood at his doorway in his vest and underpants. The lads quickly told him what had happened. "Mind out the way then." Kevin positioned himself in front of Jim's door, he then lifted his right bare foot and with one mighty blow to the door with the flat of his foot the offending object swung in.

"Jim, get up!" shouted Bob as he bent over the drunken Jim as he laid in his bunk. "We need you to drive the Beaver boat. Get up!"

"Can't... Can't..." came the drunken reply. "Get the sack... Can't..." All this was said by Jim without him opening his eyes.

"You've got to. Phil's dying," pleaded Bob.

"Can't... Can't... Get the sack..." he repeated as he rolled over in his bunk.

"Right," said Bill as he came forward. "Get him up and dressed. Let's do it." Jim was lifted out of his bunk and helped into his clothes and waterproofs, still not really knowing what was going on. The others also put on waterproofs that had been given to them by the ship's workers, who had now woken up and had come to help. Within minutes Jim was driving the small boat towards the metal jetty where the ambulance was waiting with the unconscious Phil. The boat was loaded with the injured worker, then it backed away from the jetty, turned, and headed for the open sea. The waters within the sheltered cove were not so rough, but as the small boat neared the opening it was starting to bounce about a lot. Jim may not have known what he was doing, but he was awake enough to tell the others to fasten the lifelines that hung from their waterproof suits to the small anchor points on the boat so that they could not be washed overboard. Yellow life jackets had also been given to all of them before they set off.

As they left the cove and headed out to sea the lights on the boat picked out the large outline of the grey Royal Navel frigate now moored in front of the small uninhabited island a few hundred yards from the mouth of West Cove. Already a round see-through container about seven feet long was hanging from the side of the ship, still high above the waterline with a rope dangling from each end.

Jim's first attempt to navigate the boat in was a near disaster as he mistimed his turn in front of the ship and almost crashed head on, only turning at the last moment sending his crew falling over and holding on for dear life. On the second attempt he aborted as he started his turn far too soon and missed by a long way, again sending his crew falling.

"Third time lucky, Jim boy," Bill whispered in his old roommate's ear. The boat was now lined up for another go. Jim wiped the rain from his face. "Steady as you go, lad, you can do it," Bill said from behind him.

"I'm not even sure if this is for real. The last thing I remember was being in Huggies Bar, and now I am here on the boat. It must be a dream."

"It might be a dream but fuck this up and we could all be doing a lot of sleeping," answered Bill.

Jim straightened up as if to steel himself. He once again cleared his face of the pouring rain, then pulled back on the hand throttle beside him and headed off towards the naval ship. This time it was perfect. He turned and slowed at just the right moment so that they stopped right under the lifesaving capsule, with just a small thump on the side of the ship. Long boat hooks were then used to grab the hanging ropes, and on the command of signals to the watching ship's crew it was lowered onto the boat's deck. The container was opened and Phil was lifted inside before it was fastened again. On another signal from the boat the capsule was winched up with Bill and Bob holding one rope, and Colin and Andy holding the other to stop it crashing into the ship's side.

There were cheers and clapping from the large assembled crowd of workers on the deck of the *Adventurer* as the five climbed up the rope ladder to join them. Dawn was starting to break but there was still heavy rain as Bill asked Jim, "What's it like to be a hero?"

"I don't know," came the reply. "I still think I am dreaming." Kim Benjamin made his way through the crowd to the front.

"Well done, gentlemen, we have been watching from the bridge. What you have done tonight to save a workmate is one of the bravest things I have ever witnessed." He shook all their hands in turn, finishing with Jim. "And as for you, young man, the incident the other week will be taken off your record. You will have a clean slate and your fine money returned."

Jim turned to Bill and said, "Now I know I'm fucking dreaming."

*

"So, what's the big surprise?" asked Bill as he came into Bob and Colin's room. The roof to the accommodation block had been replaced by Erect-A-Com the same day as the storm as soon as it had died down, and reinforced at the same time. The brown carpet that lined the rooms and corridors had been replaced, as had all the bedding. Kim Benjamin had instructed that the block be made liveable at once, as with another ship full of workers about to dock the next day there was a chance of a very real problem of lack of sleeping space.

Colin and Bob now had two armchairs and a coffee table, all of which had been acquired by Bob one afternoon as he passed a container that had been left open full of such items that had arrived for the staff block when it was finished. Running to find his roommate the pair had soon liberated the furniture and had asked their cleaner not to tell anyone.

"The surprise is," said Bob jumping off his bottom bunk, "we have got an element."

"An elephant?" said the visitor, as he sat in one of the armchairs and helped himself to one of Bob's cigarettes from the coffee table. "What in hell's name are we going to do with an elephant? More to the point where are we going to keep him? I didn't know they lived in this part of the world."

"An E-L-E-M-E-N-T," Bob replied slowly. He then moved across the room to his wardrobe, opened it and took out the small copper coil with a round plate on the bottom which had an electric cable in the top with a 13 amp plug on it, which when placed in a cold cup of water and switched on would bring it to boiling point in a very short time. "We have removed cups and teabags from the canteen," as he explained he took them from their hiding place and put them on the coffee table, "so when we have our nightly meeting we can have a cuppa." He walked over to the wash hand basin at the window wall at the end of the bunk beds and filled four cups. "We can nick the milk out of the canteen each night. I am not sure how to acquire the coffee yet as they make that in the urn unlike the tea."

"How did you get it?" asked Bill.

"The wife sent it. Saw it in a shop. She knew we could not get tea at night, so she sent it out."

"Now that's what I call a clever girl. But be careful," Bill warned. "Don't let the cleaners see it as you know they have to report anything like that as we are not allowed to have those sorts of things."

"Bob is going to keep it locked in his wardrobe," said the voice from the top bunk.

"Excellent," smiled Bill. "I'll get biscuits from the shop tomorrow night. Any news on Phil tonight?"

The voice from above replied, "Not yet. It was Ron's turn to go to welfare tonight, they have just set up an office for an hour each night in the next corridor. They are using a room next to the breakfast room. He should be back soon."

"Well it's been over a week now," said Bob. "It's a long time to be out cold."

"It's been known for some people to be out for years, then come around as if nothing has happened," said Bill as he pulled on his cigarette.

"Well at least he is back home in England now. They took him back on the air ambulance," came the voice from the heavens.

"Albeit in intensive care. At least his wife and family can be with him," put in Bob.

"Yeah, it's good that they are with him," said Bill as he sat up to see how the tea making was coming on. "Has that elephant boiled yet?"

"Nearly, nearly," said Bob as he carried on with the tea operation. "Shit, that's hot," he said as the steam scalded his hand. This was interrupted by a knock on the door.

"Come in," shouted Bill.

"We must be in the wrong room, Bob," Colin told his roommate.

"Yeah," came the reply. "Shit, that was hot," he said now blowing his hand as Ron entered the room and stood at the door.

"What's the news then?" asked Bill.

"He took a deep breath. "Well, lads, I don't know how to tell you this, but Phil passed away at eight thirty this morning. His wife, mum and dad were with him at the end."

There was a long silence in the room only broken by Bob when he said, "Shit." He then blew his hand again.

"I am really gutted," put in a very sad-looking Colin.

"Fuck," was Bill's contribution.

"Cheer up, lads," smiled Ron. "I am only joking. He came around this morning. He is going to be fine." Ron only just managed to shut the door in front of him as Colin's pillow hit the door followed by other objects from the others.

"Wanker!" shouted Colin.

"You could be the one to die if you come back in here," called out Bill.

"Okay, but can I come back in now?" said the voice from behind the door.

"Yes, you can," said Bob as he went back to making the tea, still blowing his hand. "You're a sick bastard."

Ron entered the room, closed the door behind him, and sat in the armchair next to Bill. "Look, you were all pissed off, now I've cheered you up with some good news."

"You have only cheered us up as you pissed us off in the first place," snapped Colin.

"It was only a little joke."

"Anyway," said Bob, "at least he is at home and the lad is okay."

"And he has not got to come back," said Ron. "They have offered him a medivac and they are going to pay up his con-trick in full. And he has accepted it."

"Probably so he does not hit them for compensation and all the bad press that goes with that," remarked Bill.

"Blimey," said the voice from above, "we should all get compo for what we went through that night!"

"It's a thing none of us will forget in a hurry," said Ron.

"I'm just pleased he is okay," said Bob. "I'm sorry I won't see the lad again, but at least he has got out of this shithole and done okay for money into the bargain."

"Well," put in Bill picking up his teacup and then standing up. "I think the first cup of tea made here with the elephant should be dedicated to our mate Phil."

"And," said Colin, "when he's better in the near future, may he have every wicked pleasure of the flesh I can think of."

They all stood together and held their cups up high and as one said, "To Phil."

Chapter 5

No Pay, No Work

The latter part of February saw a significant amount of rainfall on the islands. Existing roads and new ones which were now criss-crossing the various work areas that were opening up had been cutting up badly with the continuing rain and heavy traffic. Maintenance teams, known by the lads as West Cove County Council, were working twelve-hour shifts around the clock so that they could be kept open.

Two more corridors of rooms had opened at the camp for the last ship that had arrived. Work had progressed very well at the contractors' camp. Large concrete floor slabs which would house the canteens had been completed and work had started on the facilities and recreation areas. There had been a hold up on the work because of the quarry situation. The stone they had been using from the first quarry that had been blasted and formed had been found to be too soft, so after many rushed tests the quarry had been moved about five miles to a smaller mountain range which had been found to hold a much better stone that could be used on the contract as a whole.

The production area saw a large improvement at that time; the concrete and tarmac batching plants had arrived on the last cargo ship, along with other heavy equipment that would be used for crushing the rock that would produce the aggregates and sand that would be needed.

Work on the airfield was progressing, but the digging of the storm water drains and service trenches, which ran the length at each side of the runway, had hit many layers of rock. It had been found that the diggers and breakers that had been shipped out for that task were making little progress, so it was now being discussed at senior management level regarding using the quarrymen to blast the rock for the pipes to be laid so as not to fall behind.

There was growing unrest amongst the workforce regarding the overtime issue. It had been brought up at most committee meetings with management, but the workers' representatives had been told in no uncertain terms that they would not be guaranteed overtime worked, and if for any reason they were unable to work, apart from sick time with a doctor's certificate, these hours would be deducted from any overtime they may have accumulated.

At a Sunday morning meeting of the workforce in the field canteen at the pioneer camp it was voted to ban all overtime until such a time as payment was guaranteed. The fact that they were now in breach of their contracts by refusing to work the extra hours when asked did not worry the men as it was considered that they were unable to dismiss the whole workforce.

A friend of Kim Benjamin had replaced Jim Morrison. His name was Roger Clifford and he had worked with Benjamin in different parts of the world for many years. A Welshman from North Wales, he had a lot of the corners knocked off his accent from his worldwide work travels. A man in his mid-forties of average height and build with greying black hair, Roger was a veteran of global wide construction, from highways in the Sudan to dams in China, hotels on the beach in Barbados to army camps in Iran. It had been over twenty years since he'd last worked in the UK when he was setting out as a young engineer. He was not as uncompromising as Benjamin, but a man who knew how to get the job done and would let nothing stand in his way. Clifford attended his first management-workers committee meeting along with Benjamin and Arran Jones just a few days after he landed via the air bridge. The three senior members of JLB sat across the polished table from Bob, Reg – who had now joined the committee after another member had resigned – and Dave Newby, the third member of the workers committee.

Dave, a pipe layer, a short but stocky man in his early thirties, came from Swindon in Wiltshire and talked with a very heavy West Country accent, which most of his workmates took the mickey for, with them giving out a lot of "Ooh arrs" when Dave was about, all of which he took very much in his stride as he let very little upset him.

The meeting looked at many issues that were raised that afternoon, among which was an emergency vehicle that would be kept at the camp each night with a member of management staying up there as a keyholder. The issue of fire was raised regarding both the pioneer camp and the main contractors' camp. A converted Land Rover had arrived and was being used as a fire engine, but as there was only the one it was at the moment spending nights in different locations, one at the ship, the next at the main camp, and so on. It was pointed out by Dave that "should fire break out the fire tender not being there would be a very big problem."

"There's another on the next cargo ship," came the reply from Benjamin.

"Oh, another five-mile ship," put in Reg. This brought a round of smiles from everyone apart from the project coordinator. No answer or reason was given when Bob asked the question why a D8 bulldozer was now kept at the main camp all the time but never used and again the key being kept with the keyholder.

The problem of poor food was mentioned. They were told that more Eastham's employees would be coming on the next *Kenya,* and these would include the first intake of females. "The lads will be pleased to hear that," smiled Dave.

"A new corridor that is to be opened next week will be blocked off at one end and used only by the women," said Jones.

"So long as it does not break any fire and safety regulations," said Bob.

"I am sure," said Clifford, "that everything will be within safety regulations."

"Well, we will be checking it out," said Bob. Overtime was the last issue to be raised. It was asked by Bob if JLB would reconsider its stance on this issue, and not only guarantee the payments but also pay the overtime one month in arrears, as they had been asked by the men at the Sunday meeting. This way no money could then be stopped.

"This will never happen," said Benjamin. "In the contract you all signed you agreed to work overtime for time off in lieu."

"In our con-trick," said Reg – this brought a smile to the face of the newly arrived Clifford – "it says we will work a reasonable amount of overtime. I don't think asking some men to work two hours plus each night and every Sunday reasonable. The hours some of these men have worked, if it was for time off in lieu, means they would have the last six months of their time off." This brought another smile from the newcomer.

"As long as a person has no time off, other than illness verified by the medical staff, they will be paid the overtime which they have worked," reported Benjamin.

"But if it's a bad winter we could lose all the overtime we have worked for," returned Bob in a firm but controlled manner.

"Well then," replied the project coordinator, "we'd better all hope for a good winter then."

"Well," snapped Bob, "we are here to tell you that it was voted at the last workers meeting that no more hours past the basic sixty-hour week will be worked by any of the workforce until we are paid our overtime at the end of each following month."

"You do realise that this action will put each and every one of you in breach of their contracts which means that you could all be dismissed?"

"Okay," the workers chairman replied. "In that case you had better get a lot of passports and air tickets together, I'd say it's around three hundred at the moment, and of course if that is the case the press in the UK would be alerted to be at Heathrow for our side of the story when we return."

"What if we telex that request to the London office and we could give the reply later today?" put in Clifford.

A long pause followed this suggestion, and then Benjamin said, "Very well, we'll do just that and will let you know as soon as we hear back, gentlemen. I would say that concludes our meeting. Good day." The three committee members looked at each other and all left without any further ado.

"Shall I send the telex?" Clifford asked when the three managers were alone.

"Arran, could you give Roger and myself a moment please?"

"Of cause, Kim." Jones got up taking with him the book he had used to take the meeting's minutes. When they were alone Benjamin said, "Roger, out here is not the same as other contracts we have been on with local labour. These men will run this site if we let them get away with things now. The overtime payments will just be the start, they will want extra money for this, extra money for that, then it will be extra money for just turning up for work. No, my friend, a stand must be made on this and early in the contract is a good time to do it, so we won't be bothering London about this. We can deal with it. This will soon all blow over when they realise how much tax-free money they are losing hand over fist, the reason they have come out here. So, tell me, how are Mary and the children?"

*

"Is that elephant boiled yet?" Bill asked Bob who was making tea for his Birmingham visitor and Colin who was laying on his top bunk blowing smoke rings in the air from his cigarette.

"It might not be a bad idea for you to make it some night," came the reply.

"I am a guest in your little house," said Bill as he sat in the armchair and also blew smoke in the air. "It wouldn't be right to come in here and start sorting through your things to make tea."

"You do it with all our other things," came the voice from up high. "I mean, you go through all our newspapers, dirty mags and books, don't you?"

"Well that's different. I mean, we are almost family now!"

"Well," said Bob as he handed the tea out, "family or not, you're making it tomorrow night, oh bearded faced one from Brum."

"Okay, okay, it's a deal."

"Andy has been a long time getting the post," said Colin. "The Islander was in today according to the radio, so with a bit of luck there should have been mail."

"Well," said Bob as he sat in the armchair next to Bill with his cup of tea and lit a cigarette, "there's been no letters for over a week or so now, there should be a fair bit to sort, and you know what the queues are like on the ship when the mail is in."

"I heard today that one of the new foremen at the camp, David Anthony, has been offering the lads days off in lieu in the capital if they work overtime, and JLB will pay their £10 airfare there and back on the Islander aeroplane," commented Bill.

"Oh, he is a real conman he is," said Colin, from his high viewpoint. "The lads call him Arthur Daley on the camp after the conman on TV. He promised the lads new waterproof coats the other day if they stayed on to finish a concrete pour in a thunderstorm. They did it and when they went to him for the coats he told them they were on the next cargo ship and to put their names down for them."

"He offered our chippies a large jar of coffee each the other day if they worked late," said Bob.

"He brags all the time to the other foremen," said Colin, "that he can get the lads to work overtime."

"I heard," said Bill, "that he won a tenner off George in a bet by getting his lads to stay late and finish that concrete pour late at night."

"Well that's okay," said Bob. "If George lost money that's one up for Eric, wherever he may be now."

"I heard," said Bill, "that this David is a long-time mate of George and Benjamin, from Africa, and so is that Clifford."

"It's the African Mafia," laughed Bob. They all then stopped talking and looked at each other as a thud-thud-thud noise came from the corridor side of their room.

"What's that?" Colin asked the others, as he jumped down from his bunk. The three men all walked to the door to see where the sound had come from.

Bill open the door and went to walk outside, when a voice shouted, "Watch out!" from the far end of the corridor from Colin and Bob's room. It was their next-door neighbour, Dusty, as another thud-thud-thud was heard and Bill saw the cause of the noise. A four-inch round object went past his feet, this was followed by Dusty and his roommate Pete, who came running down the corridor with the object still moving towards the first one which had now stopped about five inches from a strip of cream-coloured masking tape, which was on the floor from wall to wall across the corridor.

"Go on, go on," cried Dusty Parker, the thirty-five-year-old, short, overweight Cornishman as he got near the ball-like object. It rolled past the other and continued on over the tape until it came to a stop, the same distance as the other from the tape but at the far side.

"What's going on?" asked Bill.

"Bowls," came the reply from Dusty.

"There's no need to be like that," came the reply. "I only asked."

"Bowls," said Pete as he passed by. "We're bowling."

"I've got it," said Dusty, as he looked down on the home-made bowling balls.

"Bollocks," came the reply from his roommate Pete Jennings, a stocky, dark-haired, forty-year-old from Reading in Berkshire, as he looked down on them also. "Mine is closer."

"No way."

"Here, lads," said Pete to the spectators. "Who's the closest? There's a tenner on this."

"Hold on," said Bob. "I've got my tape measure in the room." He then disappeared and soon returned with the metal cased instrument. He pulled out the tape and measured between the two balls three times each, then stood up and said, "The winner is, by two centimetres… could we please have a drum roll, oh bearded one from Birmingham?"

"Of course." Bill turned and made a drumming noise on the plaster boarded panelled wall of corridor.

"The winner is," Bob cleared his throat, "by two centimetres, in the red gravy-stained T-shirt, all the way from Cornwall, England, Mr Dusty Parker." At this news Dusty leapt up and down waving his arms in the air and dancing around the hallway.

"What the hell have you made them out of?" asked Colin as he went and picked one up. "Christ, they are heavy!"

"They are toilet cistern ball cocks," returned Dusty. "Pete got them, cut the ends off, filed off the seams around the middle, then filled them with sand and cement grout at work then let them go off hard."

"No wonder none of the bogs are working," said Colin as he tossed it up and down in his hand, "if you have nicked all of these out of them."

"No, I did not. I nicked them out of the new bogs in the birds' corridor," replied Pete.

"Oh, that's okay then," smiled Bob.

"Right then, where's my tenner?" asked Dusty.

"Double or quits," came the reply from his roommate Pete.

"No way, that was double or quits on the fiver I won on roll the beer can up the wall. This could go on forever until you win."

"What about for double or quits who can hold a mouthful of cigarette smoke the longest?" said Pete.

"No way, I want my money."

"Okay," said Pete as they both walked into their room together. "Or what about who can hold a lighted match in their fingers the longest?"

"Fuck off," was the answer as their door shut.

"They are well suited to live together, them two," said Bill. "They are both round the bloody twist."

"You're not wrong when you're right," said Bob.

"I've got an idea," said Colin as he held the ball. "What about if we make some skittles? We could have a bowling alley here in the corridor."

"What would we make them out of?" asked Bill.

"Timber," said Bob. "There's loads by our workshop. I could cut some down and round them off. That would do fine."

"We could have a corridor tournament," reported Bill.

"We could play pairs as a knockout competition," said Colin. "Each room could play against each other."

"Twenty quid a team," put in Bob.

"Between all the rooms down here," said Bill, "that would be... aha!" He held his fingers from both hands up.

"Sixteen rooms at twenty pounds each, that's three hundred and twenty nicker," said Bob.

"I was about to say that," replied Bill.

"Here's Andy," put in Colin. "It looks like he's got mail." Andy walked towards the three men followed by co-workers who had also just got off the bus from the ship. Andy had stayed on after dinner to queue for the mail for himself and the others.

"We're going to have a bowls competition, Andy," smiled Bob. "Better start practising."

Andy stopped and looked at his three friends and said, "No, can't," then put a pile of letters in Bob's hands, turned and disappeared into his room.

"What's up with him?" asked Colin as the three men stood looking at each other at the way the usually cheerful Andy had acted towards them.

"Don't know," said Bob, "something is not right."

"Well," said Bill, "I've got a packet of fags here that I owe him." He pulled them out of his pocket and showed the others. "I'll just pop in and see what I can find out. Put the elephant on and make the tea, I'll be back in ten minutes."

"It may be personal," said Bob. "He may not want to talk about it."

"You're right," came the reply from the tall person from Birmingham after thinking about it for a few seconds. "It may take a while longer to get it out of him. Make the tea for twenty minutes time." He turned and walked into Andy and Ron's room without knocking. "JLB suicide squad here!" he called out as he entered the room. "Anyone want to kill themselves here tonight? I've got loads of rope out here for a hanging."

Bob turned and said to Colin before they entered their room, "That lad sure has got a way with words." Bill was almost true to his word of only being twenty minutes. Well, it was in fact one hour twenty minutes when he arrived back at the room, entering without knocking of course.

"Get the elephant out and get the tea on," he said as he moved towards the armchair next to Bob who was writing a letter home to his wife and family. Bill picked up one of Bob's cigarettes off the coffee table as he went and lit it as he sat down.

"You were going to make the next one," said Colin from his usual position high up on his bunk as he read a letter.

"Well," came the reply from the ginger-haired machine driver. "I've got some really juicy gossip," he said as he pulled on the cigarette. "You get the tea made, and I'll give the news."

"I'll do it," said Bob as he got up. "This had better be good," he mumbled as he went to his wardrobe. "Anyway, I'd rather do it myself than have you poking around in my things."

"That's not very nice, what are you trying to say about people from Birmingham? We are no worse than Londoners you know!"

"I'm not saying anything about Brummies'. It's just you."

"Well," came the reply, "that's definitely not very nice!"

"Come on," said a voice from the top bunk, "what's the news?"

"The news is that Andy got an anonymous letter from home."

"Anonymous? Who was it from?" Bob laughed to himself inside his wardrobe.

"Shall I get on?" asked the impatient storyteller.

"Yes, yes," came the joint reply.

"Someone from near where he lives has sent him a letter saying his wife is having an affair with some chap."

"Oh, bloody hell," said Bob.

"She's all right her, I'd give her one," said the voice from above.

"You would give anything one as long as she had a hole between her legs," replied his roommate as he carried on with the tea making duties. Colin poked his tongue out behind his friend's back at this remark.

"He is in a bad way," said the news reporter. "Still, Hack is helping him!"

"How's that?" asked Bob as he sat down.

"He is filling him up with wacky baccy. The way they are going at it in another half an hour he won't know where he is, let alone that his wife is having an affair. In fact, he properly won't even know that he is married."

"Suppose that's one way to deal with it," suggested Colin. "Mind you, it's a long way from home to be getting news like that. Won't he be able to get a free phone call home with that kind of news?"

"He went in and asked. He saw Joe Benson at welfare and he said he needed to see the letter so he told him to get fucked."

"Good for him," said Bob.

"Bloody pervert," said Colin. "He's a real tosser that bloke."

"Can't you do anything?" Bill asked Bob. "Through the committee that is."

"Only if Andy asks me," came the reply.

"You know he's not that sort of bloke," replied Bill.

"I know, but I can't interfere if he doesn't want me to."

"Well if that's the case I'll make sure that he does want you to interfere," came the reply from the man from Brum. "Anyway, enough of this downer news. Oh, and by the way, at this point I must say that I did go on record as saying that any one of our wives could be getting shagged silly while we are here, didn't I?" This bit of information brought no response from the two London roommates so Bill carried on. "When are we having this bowling contest? I could do with winning a few bob."

*

Over the next few days pieces of wood were cut and shaped like bowling pins in the carpenter's workshop at the new camp. As the nights passed and the lads recruited more players for the competition, the sound of balls rolling down the corridor and that of falling skittles could be heard most evenings in C corridor as the practising became more intense, with the money coming in and the big day of the draw of who played who getting nearer. As all the overtime had now been banned, it was considered that a Sunday was a good day for the event to take place.

Red and white bunting tape, which had also been known to fence off deep holes and digs for safety reasons, was draped along each side of the corridor and also hung from each door. Crates of beer had been purchased from the bar the night before for re-sale at the same cost.

Bill set up guess the weight of a bucket of hard concrete at fifty pence a go, all monies going to the winner. The same amount and prize were on offer from Colin to guess how many stones were in a large lemonade bottle. And also, for fifty pence Bob had guessed the name of a large toy penguin which he had bought from the Eastham's camp shop. Dusty and Pete played their part by setting up a picture board; this was made up of photos from newspapers and magazines of the famous and not so. The person to guess the most would again get all monies paid in.

Derby Reg had been asked to be referee, organiser, draw master, umpire, master of coronaries and anything else that may have been required. The draw was made on the Saturday evening, by Reg of course, in the corridor amid much noise, hoots and cheers as each team was pulled out of the hat, or in this case the safety helmet. A carnival atmosphere was guaranteed for the big day.

*

"Oh shit, what time is it?" called out Bob as he awoke.

"What?" came the reply from the top bunk.

"No need to shout, Col. I'm dying down here you know."

"The same thing is happening up here as well."

"God, how much of the beer for today's event did we drink? Is there any left? What time did we finish?" There was a long silence then came the reply from his friend and workmate.

"Fuck off, Bob, I am in no fit state to answer all those questions the way I feel, and this early in the day."

Bob was laying in his bottom bunk facing the wall looking at the photos of his wife and family that were pinned to it. He was wishing he could be waking up with them instead of this godforsaken hole, and was also thinking he wished he had never come here. He rolled over in his bunk to the sight that greeted him. Not only was the floor covered in empty beer cans, but what appeared to be the two dead bodies of Bill and Andy, one in each armchair. "What the hell are they doing here?"

"You said they could stay," came the reply from above. "Because they could not find their way back to their rooms."

"One lives about four foot across the corridor from here, and the other, well, turn right and about eighteen foot along."

"As we could not get them a taxi it was decided they could stay here."

"Oh my God," Bob held his head. "Did we really have that much to drink?"

"We had that much and lots more besides I think," Colin replied.

"Will you two shut the fuck up and let a man sleep on a Sunday morning, or better still make yourself useful and put the elephant on," said Bill as he turned over in the chair.

"Good morning, oh bearded one from Brum. And how are you this lovely Sunday morning?" asked Bob.

"Shit, I feel like shit. My mouth is like the bottom of a bird cage, my head is pounding, I am in such need of a piss that I could do it sat here in the chair, and apart from all that I am fine." Before Bob could reply the door to their room flew open to reveal Reg standing there.

"Good morning, gentlemen, it's nine fifty-five, the bowling tournament starts in five minutes flat. Bob and Colin are on first against Les and Henry at ten o'clock." He shut the door just in time as the beer can Bill threw at him hit the door. It then re-opened and Reg carried on as if nothing had happened. "Anyone not there in five minutes for their nominated roll off time will forfeit their place in the bowling tournament and their entrance fee." The door was still open when the next beer can landed, but it was on the wall next to Reg. "Five minutes or you're out without bowling a ball, or in this case a ball cock." The door shut and he was gone.

Bob and Colin made it just before they were counted out of time for the start, but they were in no fit state to be taking part in anything that morning. They had stumbled around the room trying to get dressed, moaning at each other about the "silly bowls competition" and "who's idea was it anyway?" No one could really remember. But make it they did to much cheers and roars as they came out of their room to be greeted by Reg counting them down from "ten-nine-eight" and so on. The corridor was packed at the two ends, and at open doorways to all the rooms. Beer was on sale at the furthest end of the corridor from Bob and Colin's room from where the bowls would be bowled. The other competitions were also held in that area.

About three feet behind the skittles was a four-inch by two-inch piece of timber that had been placed between the corridor walls to stop the bowls going too far. Stood behind this was Reg, with a pen and notepad, keeping all the scores.

Each pair in each team had three bowls each to knock down as many pins as possible, which Reg counted. Each person went five times and then all scores were added together. In the semi-final and final each person had ten goes. Bob and Colin, both appearing to still be drunk from the night before, not only got beaten by Les and Henry, but got severely hammered into defeat. They not only went out in the first round but in the very first game.

The competition went on all day, with much alcohol being consumed. Bill and his new lodger as he called him, Harvey, a very large North Yorkshireman from the pretty seaside town of Scarborough, went out in the second round. Pete and Dusty were beaten in one of the semi-finals by Ron and Andy who went on to win the tournament by beating two Scotsmen, Fergus and Cameron, in a very one-sided contest. Bob was one of the first to congratulate them on their victory. "Well done, Andy," said the Londoner as he shook his hand. "I'm really pleased for you."

"Thanks, Bob. Oh, and by the way, thanks for getting me that free phone call home."

"No worries, it was the least I could do for a mate and all. How are things there anyway?"

"Put it this way, I was thinking of going on the *Kenya* when it's in tomorrow, but not now."

"No?"

"No. I had a good talk to the wife on the phone and she said that she fell out with some girls at work and reckons they sent the letter to get back at her."

"Bastards," came the reply.

"It's okay," said the Mancunian. "I can handle it. No one's going to wind me up!"

"Good, I'm pleased. So what are you going to do with the winnings?"

"I'm going to send it home."

"Oh good, that will be nice for your wife. Cheer her up and all having some extra cash to spend on the house and family."

"No, it's not going to the wife, she'd only fucking waste it. No, I am sending it to my brothers so they can find out if the bitch is shagging someone, then kick the crap out of him!"

*

The clouds that had made it an overcast start to the day were now rolling away from the land and out to sea at West Cove to leave a very bright but also very windy morning. The seagulls that were flying high above the *Adventurer* were singing out loud as the *Kenya* docked against it that Tuesday morning. It had been decided at the highest management level that the MV *Kenya* would only come in on weekdays from now on after the problems that happened when it last came in at the weekend. It should have docked on the Monday having spent the Sunday hanging back some miles out to sea, but its skipper Captain Edwards, a seaman with many years of experience in these waters, would not carry out the operation as the wind was gusting up to ninety mph, so with the entrance into the cove being narrow as well as shallow he felt it was too risky and would not put any persons on board or the ship at risk. So, the Monday was spent sat a few miles off land.

The new intake of workforce that were on the ship had quickly been nicknamed the "Boat People" by the other workers as news got around, like the Vietnamese refugees from some years earlier who had been refused entry at every port they had come to. But at eleven o' clock that day the wind had died enough to make the manoeuvre into the cove safely.

Ron had got a few hours off work on the pretence that he wanted to meet his brother who was on the ship. His real reason for being there was to collect his new consignment of marijuana for which he now had a large and growing market at the two camps and the ship. Selling drugs at UK prices and buying at South African prices was also making Ron – alias Hack – a lot of money. He was now pleased that he had the nickname as most of his customers only knew him by this name and not his real one.

Ron was one of the few non-ship workers viewing the *Kenya* coming in towards the *Adventurer* as the rest were workers on the jetty ship or senior managers. These people were let on first to do all the formalities and hold briefings. When Ron had first tried to get on board, he was told by two of Eastham's security men that he would have to wait. He decided not to make a fuss and run the chance of drawing attention to himself so he bided his time for about an hour, but when he was refused entry at the third time of asking and also told that "unless you are travelling on the *Kenya* today in which case you would need to have your travel papers and passport with you, then you will not be let on." At this point his temper got the better of him as his frustration boiled over.

As much as he argued with the two men guarding the bottom of the gangplank, and try as he did for some time, he could not get his point across that he needed to get on and give his brother some very important and personal family news that he had received on the phone from home that morning. All the security men would say was that, "everyone would be disembarking soon and they were under instruction from Kim Benjamin that no one was to be allowed on the ship that were not on official company business, and those who were had been issued with a dated pass." Because he could not tell them the real urgent reason that he needed to board the ship, and the fact that he had let this upset him so much as he always classed himself as cool under pressure, he was now starting to shout obscenities at the two men.

He was at the point of losing it, so much so that it had gone through his mind of rushing on when he saw his contact John, a lad born in Dover England twenty-eight years before to Chinese parents who stood some yards from the gangway, in an open doorway leading to the crew's quarters on the *Kenya*. He motioned to Ron with his eyes and movement of his head to move to the far end of the *Adventurer*, which with no further ado Ron did.

*

Being head of security in a place like this was going to be a tough challenge for Karl Davis, but after taking early retirement from the London Metropolitan Police Force as an inspector after thirty-two years' service, and now newly divorced, it was a challenge the fifty-three year old was looking forward to, and the fact he had been headhunted for this post made him feel very important again, a thing he had not felt for some time now. Karl knew that in this position he would always have to have his wits about him and to call on his police experience, keeping his eyes and ears open at all times which he always did but never in his wildest dreams did he think it would pay off so soon.

As he came down the gangway with suitcase in one hand and travel bag in the other he glanced between the two moored ships towards the rear. He always knew when to believe his eyes, and even at this distance it was time to believe them now. It happened quickly, but he knew what he saw, and that was two parcels passing each other in mid-air, the larger one going from the *Kenya* to the *Adventurer*, and a smaller one going the other way. He could only see one person who was on the deck of the jetty ship he was about to board. He picked up the parcel and disappeared.

"Come on, mate, you going to stand there all day?" asked the impatient male voice from behind Karl. He had not realised that his stopping to take in the sight was holding up the dismemberment and the first intake of thirty women to this part of the island.

Chapter 6

Up in Smoke

Bob, Colin, Bill and Andy sat and listened to the radio in stunned silence in the meeting room. On Bob's newly purchased wireless radio from the camp shop the local radio station was giving out the news of the hospital fire over in the capital that had occurred the previous night. Eight patients had died and also staff trying to save them. It had been a wooden structure on a concrete base very much like the one the lads lived in. It was still not known how it started but it had spread very fast, and with most of the patients asleep and a lot of them old it had proved very hard to get them out.

The army based nearby had come to help, and one young soldier was in tears as he told of a young female nurse who climbed in a back-corridor window that she smashed out with a hammer from the back of a Land Rover and brought many people out to safety. As the fire and smoke increased the soldiers had pleaded with her to give up and save herself, but she kept insisting to return "just once more" until the time she did not return. The soldiers themselves had a lucky escape as the corridor she had entered was engulfed by a giant fireball moments after she had gone back in for the last time.

Bob got up from his bunk and walked over to the radio and turned it off. "I can't listen to that anymore," as he returned and laid on his bunk.

"I know what you mean," said the voice from above him. "I'll be crying in a minute."

"That could happen to us here," said the Brummie from the armchair as he drunk tea and pulled on one of Bob's cigarettes.

"Piss off, Bill," said Andy from the armchair next to him. "That is not funny."

"No, it's true," said Bob as he got up and sat on the side of his bunk. "This place would go up in no time, it's a load of dried out timber waiting to go up."

"And there was a fire in the toilets of block F the other night," said Colin.

"Mind you," said Bob, "we were told at the committee meeting that it was an electrical fire."

"Well I heard," said Bill, "from one of Eastham's lads, that when it had been put out they found what looked like a load of papers and rags in one of the cubicles." He pulled on his cigarette. "And they were told to say nothing."

"Well," said Andy, "I was told today that an old armchair was found in one of the drying rooms the other day and someone had tried to set it alight."

"We don't know that," said Bob. "You know what rumours are like here!"

"You're starting to sound like management," came the reply from Andy. "You've been to too many meetings with them."

"That's not fair," said Colin. "There are rumours going around here all the time."

"Well you're just as bad now you're a foreman," was Andy's answer to that comment. "And have you told your roommate that you have been offered a single room in the staff block when it's finished?"

"Is this true?" asked Bob as he got off his bunk, stood up and confronted his roommate.

"I've been asked but I haven't said yes yet."

"Well thanks for telling me."

"I was going to when the time was right."

"That means I could end up getting some right old wanker."

"I'll move in with you," said Bill.

"See what I mean? It's happened already." This comment brought a laugh from all of them which helped to break the tension which had noticeably started to build.

"Well," said Bill, "you've got the elephant, the radio, the armchairs, the coffee table, yes, I could be very happy in here. All I've got is Harvey, that bloody great Yorkshire pudding. God, he has a hell of a job just getting up to the top bunk, then he's puffing, panting, blowing and farting all night. He's a fat wanker!"

"Don't sugar coat it," smiled Bob, "say what you think."

"I think what we should do is find out if someone is starting fires. It would be so hard to put out if one caught," continued Bill.

"I am not sure that would be the case," said Bob.

"How do you mean?" asked his roommate.

"Well... oh, look, I am not meant to be telling anybody."

"Come on," said Andy.

"Oh, bloody hell, I really shouldn't tell you."

"Come on," said Bill, "you've started so you'll have to finish!"

"Oh!"

"Come on," said his roommate. "You can't stop now!"

"Okay, you know the big D8 bulldozer that is parked at the camp all the time and never moves? We have asked many times now what it is for, and in the end they said they would tell us if we didn't let on to anyone."

"Yes?" said Bill.

"Well if there's a fire up here, in a corridor, there's a staff member with the key who can drive it, and he just takes out the section of corridor which is on fire and the next section it is spreading to, to stop it going further."

"And what about the men inside at the time?" asked Bill.

"Hmm, well, it would take them out as well if they didn't get out in time."

"Oh shit," came the joint reply.

"Bloody hell," said Colin, "if the fire doesn't get us, the D8 will."

"They seem to think it's the best way to cut the fire off and save lives."

"That's ridiculous," said Andy. "Can't you lot on the committee do anything about it?"

"The thing is, Erect-A-Com gave a video to JLB, and it shows what can happen if there was a fire in a corridor, and if one of the fire doors was opened at one end it would create a fireball that would travel so fast down the hallway that no man on earth could outrun it. That's how fast it would spread and they haven't got the water to stop it, so they think to take that section out is the best bet."

"Bloody hell," said Colin. "All those women have just arrived and we're going to get burnt to death or run into the ground!"

"Well," remarked Bill, as he lit another of Bob's cigarettes, "they have got all those coffins here and have not used any in anger yet, and no doubt it will happen before long!"

*

101

Bill was right about the coffins. It was just a few days after the conversation with the lads when the contract saw its first death. He was a twenty-nine-year-old steel erector, Joe Seaton, from the Coventry area of England. He fell over a hundred feet from the top of the water tower he had been erecting at the contractors' camp to feed it with water.

With the arrival of the *Kenya* came the biggest in intake of workers to date, with almost four hundred new male workers and thirty women which almost doubled the personnel on site.

JLB may have banned the overtime, and the entire new intake were told the story and were asked to join in the ban, but Erect-A-Com had no such problems as they got paid their overtime a month in arrears. They had been told they could work as many hours as they wanted to so that more accommodation could be made ready in good time, along with three new canteens, two for the workers and one for the staff, the latter to be used as a bar until they were all finished. With these open no longer did the boys have to travel back and forth to the ship for food. But the fact that Erect-A-Com were now working a lot of overtime, this upset a lot of the JLB workers.

Before the new intake had come the post office at the camp had been opened, this being the fourth on the island and the first for seventy-three years. They brought out a first day cover to celebrate the opening. Bob purchased one saying, "It could be worth a few quid one day!" A Union Jack flag was raised outside the post office each morning. The new medical centre was also opened in time for the mass intake that was about to descend upon the camp and its newly opened corridors.

More equipment was arriving on new cargo ships. It also took a massive operation to put the new intake to work; hours were spent by section managers and their foremen, working out all of their own requirements such as which tradesmen were coming, who they wanted on their section, and more to the point, who in fact they would be allowed to have. For Kim Benjamin the airfield was his main priority so they had first choice.

The first of the offices at the new compound were now open, along with the new meeting and conference rooms. The clothing stores were also opened in this area and next to them were other stores, along with workshops for the equipment and other vehicles. There was also a tyre repair area, welding repair shop, one very large workshop that was for dewatering pumps only that would hopefully keep the project dry, or at the very least stop it from disappearing underwater with the winter now less than a month away. Out of all the workforce the fitters and welders carried on working overtime as most of their work was inside and they were unlikely to lose any time. This did not go down well with the rest of the workers.

More buses, Land Rovers and other forms of transport had now arrived. The camp now had a very large area for buses to pick up workers and signs acting as bus stops with the destination of the bus reading like, Airfield North or South, Power Station, Hangar, Production Area, Office Compound, Tank Farm, Stanley Road, and so on, as the sections were popping up. Each morning from six fifteen until six forty-five am, it was a proper little Victoria, London, bus station.

Foundations had been dug at the hangar and concrete was now being poured at a very quick rate. Also, the power station was now in full swing, and with other works ongoing the production area was finding it hard to cope with the demand, and the fact that very few workers would work extra shifts because of the overtime ban, time was drawing near whereby it would soon come to a head as management had identified the fact that a lot more hours would need to be worked to keep the contract running on its very tight programme.

Work was still going well on the airfield but the drainage was still a problem, with the difficulty of breaking the very hard rock. Blasting was still an option but had not been used to date. This was among many worries Kim Benjamin had on his mind, but this was not the reason he had called a meeting at the new offices with himself, Roger Clifford, Graham Keane, Eastham's senior manager, a tall man in his mid-thirties and a native of Newcastle but now settled in the South of England with his wife Debbie, herself a Londoner. Karl Davis was also there.

After the pleasantries had finished, for the first meeting of the four men Karl told his story of what he had seen coming off the ship a few days earlier.

"So, what do you think they were exchanging?" asked Kim.

"I would say, without a doubt, it was drugs of some kind coming onto the island, and money as payment going the other way onto the ship."

"Have we got a drug problem here?" asked Kim, with much surprise in his voice.

"The few people I have talked to since I've been here say that drugs are readily available if you know who to see, but as yet I've still to find out who that is."

"Can you find out, Karl? I want whoever is responsible to be found and sent to court in the capital, then removed from here!"

"Okay," came the reply from the ex-policeman. "I will be right on it."

"There's one other thing," said Benjamin. "We have an arsonist on the camp. We have kept it under wraps up until now but the cases are growing all the time. If we don't stop it soon one night we are going to have another Stanley hospital on our hands. I was there the next day and all that was left were rows of burnt-out metal beds on burnt-out concrete slabs. It was the worst thing I have ever seen in my whole life, and to think just a few hours before those beds had been occupied by people. Gentlemen, I don't want a repeat of that here. So, Karl, I would also like you to work on that. I know the drug thing is important and I really want it stopped, but the fire thing must have top priority!"

"Of course," came the reply. "Could I maybe make a suggestion?"

"Be my guest," said the project coordinator.

"There must be many men here who are unable to work because of illness each day, but could be put on light duties."

"Go on," came the very interested reply.

"Well, unless they are very ill they could be put on fire watch duties at night like a fire warden in the war. Walk around and keep an eye on things."

"What a super idea," said Kim as he got to his feet and extended a hand out to Karl to shake. "Sir, I believe you and I are going to get on very well indeed. Roger, get the fire watch sorted out to start tonight."

"Yes, Kim."

*

Karl sat in his new office at the main compound that had been allocated to Eastham's. He had been for his evening meal, then decided to go back and look at files of men that had been brought to his new office that day from the old security office on the *Adventurer*.

104

He may have worked for Eastham's but he had to agree with what he had been hearing from the lads, and that was the food was crap. He had left most of what was meant to be a steak and kidney pie as he felt it was inedible, so he had picked up some bread, ham, cheese and fruit on the way out and was now enjoying them with a cup of tea that he had made. Being the head of security had helped him with some items already, like getting a much sought-after kettle.

He was really just flicking at the files looking at faces on each ID sheet. Maybe he might just recognise someone or a name or could find a clue. He really felt that being here tonight was a good idea because he would be in his room on his own as being classed as a senior manager, or he would be in the bar which he did not want to start doing too often. He knew Kim had asked him to work on the firebug first, and quite rightly so, but he was very much against drugs, not only as an ex-policeman, but his best friend from school Eddie Armstrong had died of a drug overdose many years before, and he had never quite got over that, so he felt he could maybe work on both fronts.

He had been looking for some time and was feeling tired when he passed a photograph, and as he went on to the next one his brain told him something. He had recognised a face. He went back and there it was looking at him. "Oh, I know that face," he said to himself. He picked out the file and looked at it on his desk. Ronald Arthur Dobson, born 28/03/1955 in Darlington, County Durham. No previous. Never been there so how do I know him? Name means nothing. Who is he? Oh, you're an old fool, you must be worn out or going around the bend, he thought to himself. "It's Hack Woodfield, the rock star, that's why I thought I knew him. He looks just like Hack. That's it, I'm off to bed!"

*

Ron was sat in the drying room a few corridors away from his own; he never sold drugs in his room, or for that matter in his corridor, and he would try not to go to the same place too often. He would set up deals at different places around the camp. His customers only knew him as Hack, a good cover. He had got a large shipment last time from John off the ship. It had not been easy as the wankers on the gangway had not let him on. He had chatted to John across the ships at the blunt end, as he would say.

105

They had both agreed to throw the money and the drugs onto the opposite ship at the same time as there seemed to be no other way to conclude their deal. Not that either of them would have ripped the other off, and when it happened it was over very fast, and more to the point Ron was happy that no one saw anything. There was a really good market here, ripe for the picking, and he was going to do the picking. Not only was Ron the only one on the camp selling the weed, but he was now starting to think he was the only one on the island doing so as some soldiers had come over from Stanley a few days before to get some. They had said they could take as much as he could get.

Oh yes, he thought to himself as he sat waiting. This could really be very easy. Hundreds of blokes away from their families and bored out of their brains. Even blokes who had never smoked it before were at it. If he could get enough gear over here and stay for two or three years he could almost retire, and that was without his wages. Oh, wasn't he a lucky boy, and the best of it was that management didn't seem to care. In fact he had sold some to a few of them. And there were no coppers here, no police to worry about, what more could he ask for? Don't get silly, cover your tracks and you can't go wrong, lad. This thought brought a large smile to his face.

He had already asked Chinese John to double up next time if he could. Money was not a problem as it was very cheap in South Africa. Oh boy, he was sitting on a goldmine. John was not charging that much over the top and he knew many people in Cape Town to make some good deals, and even if John did push the price up as time went on he would still make a fortune.

There were only two problems as Ron could see it: One, they were tightening up on security on the ship when it came in, but John had told him that as from when the next *Kenya* came in the ship's crew would be allowed to go up to the camp and use the duty-free shop that should be open by then, so if that all happened he would get the gear okay. He would just have to bunk off work for an hour or so, which would not be a problem as the lads would cover for him.

The other problem was money, not the lack of it, in fact the opposite. Most of the money he was getting was local currency which had penguins on it amongst other things and John did not like that, having to change up hundreds of pounds of "Benny money" as the lads called the locals who they felt acted like Benny

106

out of the TV series *Crossroads*. He felt that this would draw attention to himself. So, Ron was now asking his customers to pay in English currency if they could. Also, anyone coming to work or who lived near him who had just come off the ship he would target to change money. He also had some of his mates doing the same for him. As for keeping the money and the dope, he had it stashed all over the place. A little of each was kept in his room for private use for himself and Andy, who he had really come to like. The rest? Well, where wasn't it? He had thought about putting it all in one place, but if he got caught or someone found it, it would all be gone. No, it was everywhere. He had even kept a book so he knew where it all was, and he made up a code so that only he understood it. He had it in ceilings, behind sinks, in drying rooms, shower rooms, toilets, under cabins, the list was endless. No, Ron, he thought to himself as he sat pulling on a cigarette. You are a guinea's son, you have done brilliant in such a short time and I know it will only get better.

The door opened to the drying room. Ron was sat on a bench in one corner of the room behind a row of metal lockers that lined the centre of the room which made it harder for him to be seen. He had also removed a light bulb from above himself just to make it a little harder for people to see him.

"Hack? Are you there, Hack?" a voice called out from the doorway.

"Yeah," came the reply. Ron was happy until he saw two figures appear from around the end of the last locker. He knew one was Harry one of Eastham's Scottish kitchen hands, but he had never seen the other before. Ron stayed sat down and wanted to play this cool, but he was not happy as he had always made it clear to his customers that he would only meet them alone. He would tell them when and where and they must be alone. He was not a violent man but he could never be too careful, so he always carried a flick knife which had a six-inch blade with him which he had owned for some years. At this new development he slipped his right hand into the same side trouser pocket and held the weapon in his hand.

"Hi, Hack, how are you?" asked Harry as the two men approached Ron.

"Stay there, just stay there," came the reply. "What the fuck have you brought someone with you for? I told you to come alone."

"It's cool, Hack. This is my cousin Declan. He came on the last *Kenya*. He's from Ireland and he wants to score some gear from you too." Declan walked towards him with his hand out to say hello. Ron was off the bench and on his feet in one easy move, and with as much ease the knife was out of his pocket. His right thumb pressed the small button on the handle and the blade glided out, with Ron holding it at arm's length which almost poked Declan in the face.

"Back off! Back the fuck off!" came the barked order from the man with the knife. The two men did as they were told and in double quick time.

"Hey," said Harry in his Glaswegian accent. "Hack, it's cool," he put his hands in the air as if to surrender, "it's cool, man. We are not here to hurt you, we are only here to score. Deco wants some too."

"I said come alone!"

"I am sorry, it's my fault. I really didn't think you would mind. Look, Deco, wait, outside will you?"

"Okay," came the reply from the tall, ginger-haired Dubliner. He then turned and left the room shutting the door behind him.

"Look, Hack, man, I really didn't mean to spook you."

"Okay, forget it. Let's get this over with. You got the money?"

"Yes." He took a roll of notes out of his pocket and handed it to Ron who then proceeded to count them like a tiller in a bank. Ron flicked the blade of the knife back in then returned it to the trouser pocket.

"That's cool," he said, then walked along the row of garments hanging from the wall, stopped at a long camouflage coat, took a package of silver paper out of its large external pocket, then walked back and handed it to Harry who opened it with a smile, then held it to his nose.

"That's good gear, man." He rewrapped and placed it in his jacket pocket. "Look, Hack, I am really sorry about what happened, I only wanted some gear."

"Fine, it's over. Let's go."

Harry held out his right hand to shake. "No hard feelings?" Ron was not happy about shaking hands after what had just occurred but decided it was best to part on good terms. As soon as their hands met Harry squeezed his hand like a vice. It was so hard Ron thought it was about to break. The Scotsman pulled him close then snarled into his face, "Pull a fucking knife on me would you?

108

I am the last fucking person in the world to do that to. Do that again and I'll fucking kill you!" He then put more pressure on Ron's hand, this time holding it with both of his. His victim's face was screwed up with agony. "Now, for trying to fuck with me, you Geordie wanker, I'll have the money back as well." Ron's eyes opened wide and he looked at Harry.

"I am not a fucking Geordie, I am a 'Pit Yaker'."

"What?" came the surprised reply. Harry was not sure what came first. Was it Ron's right knee crashing into his testicles, or his forehead smashing into the bridge of his nose? No matter, they both brought flashes to his eyes followed closely by blinding pain to both areas of his body as he passed out on the floor. After bending down to remove the package from him, Ron kicked the unconscious man in the face and said, "I am no fucking Geordie." He went outside, took the knife out of his pocket, and flicked it open for a second time that night, and went over to Declan who was sat on the floor leaning against the wall smoking a cigarette. This time the blade did touch him, the point of it going into his chin. Fear was all over the Irishman's face. "Now fuck off, Paddy, and forget who I am if you know what's good for you." Declan was up and gone in a flash.

It was two firewatchers who found the unconscious Harry on their first patrol. They raised the alarm and he was immediately transferred to the medical centre for treatment.

*

Karl's internal line rang as he sat in his office that Saturday evening. He had spent the day looking at files again, and he had also spent some of the time on the phone to friends in the Met and JLB's head office to run some names for him on the computer to see if anything came up. He was happy with the news he just heard on the phone. He had asked to be informed as soon as the patient in the medical centre who had been admitted the night before was able to speak. Karl was convinced that Harry's assault was drug related.

Four beds were in the square room at the back of the centre. Harry was the only person in there apart from the security guard who sat by the door reading a book. Karl asked the guard to leave as he entered the room then sat in another chair beside Harry's bed. He looked in very poor health as the broken nose had blackened both his eyes and the kick in the face had puffed his mouth up, but he could still talk but not very well. Congealed blood was also around his mouth and he had lost two teeth into the bargain.

"Well then, Harry, what happened to you?"

Harry looked at him through the swollen eyes, then after a short while said, "I fell over."

"Okay, yes, and it's not going to get dark tonight, Harry, lad. I was a copper for too many years to believe that old shit."

"Well you're not a copper now, so fuck off and leave me alone!"

"I might not be in the police force anymore, but I'm here to see that these things do not occur, and should they, then the perpetrator should be brought to justice."

"Can you just leave me alone, please?"

"You know you have been sacked for this, don't you? And I've been talking to people, and I know you're here because you are deep in debt and need this job badly."

"Why have I been sacked?" Harry was now sat up and very alert.

"It's Kim Benjamin's rule that anyone involved in a fight, if they started it or not, goes home."

"That's not fair, I was..." He stopped himself before saying attacked.

"You were what, Harry?"

"Nothing."

"Look, at the moment you are sacked, your money has been stopped as of this morning. Just as soon as you are fit enough to get up you're off the island and on your way home. No more tax-free money. In fact, you will have to pay tax on the money you have earned in the past few months as you have not been out of the country a year to become tax exempt. No bonus, you'll lose your retention, pay your fare home, no, Harry lad, you will be a lot worse off than when you came here." Karl got to his feet and walked to the door. "I can save your job if you tell me who did this to you and what it was about." He looked at his watch. "It's Saturday night and I am off for a few beers. Think about it, sleep on it, and I'll see you soon. Goodnight, Harry." He turned and left the room.

*

110

It was just after nine that Saturday night when Bob, Colin, Bill and Andy walked into the newly opened bar in what later would be the staff-canteen, which had a pub-like sign hanging outside above the double entrance doors which read "The Gull & Penguin" and a very well painted picture of the two, the gull flying in the blue sky above the penguin who was stood on ice with the sea as a background. This had been painted by Jack Harris, a drain layer who was working on the airfield. A competition had been held for all the workforce to enter, to name the bar, with a crate of beer as the prize. Bob and co had entered but their offers of "The Written Warning", "The Arthur Daley" and "The Dog It Inn" had all been rejected, not to their surprise.

The bar, being the only entertainment in this part of town, was not surprisingly packed. Bob fought his way to the front and purchased four cans of lager and passed them to the others.

"Hello, Bob," said a voice from beside him. He turned to see a red-faced and drunken-looking Alf Henson, a fellow Londoner about his own age Bob had come to know. Alf was very much into football and was a Fulham supporter and had a very good knowledge of the game. Bob was a Brentford follower having been born very close to their Griffin Park ground in West London. He didn't get to see them much these days, even more so with the fact that he was eight thousand miles from there, but he enjoyed following the game as he had all his life and now on the radio with the BBC World Service, and also enjoyed chatting to fellow workers about matches, but as both their teams had lost that afternoon there wasn't much joy between them regarding football.

"Load of shit," slurred Alf in his drunken state. "We were 2-0 up at half time and then the bloody idiots go and lose 4-2. Load of shit," he repeated as he took another swig from the can, this time spilling beer down his chin and the front of the navy-blue jumper he was wearing.

Bob was thinking, What time did you start drinking to be in this state at nine o'clock? He must have come in straight from work at six. "You've had a good day then?" Bob asked his friend.

"Oh yeah," came the drunken reply, "been drinking all afternoon and listening to the football. Load of shit," he said as he put the empty can on the bar.

"What, no work?"

111

"No," came the reply from Alf as he leant on the bar to hold himself up. "I am on the sick, I've got gout." He pointed to his foot and nearly fell over at the same time. Bob held on to his shoulders to keep him upright. "Right, got to go."

"Is that the medicine the doc put you on?" Bob smiled and pointed to the empty can. "Here, I'll get you a drink before you go."

"No, no, can't do that."

"Well you haven't got to get up in the morning, Alf."

"No, I am going to work now."

"WHAT?" came the surprised response from Bob. Alf took an orange badge out of his pocket and pinned it on his jumper. Bob looked at the white letters on it which read, FIRE WARDEN.

"Got to go, mate, got fires to start. I mean stop. See you later." He then staggered off into the crowd of drinkers, bumping into most of them as he went. Bob could not help laughing to himself as he thought that all their lives were in Alf's and others like his hands. When he re-joined his group of friends he was still grinning to himself. When asked what was so funny by Andy he told the story to them which brought a roar of laugher from them all.

"Sounds about right for this place," said Colin.

"Well I heard today," said Bill, "that one of the fire wardens got caught starting a fire as there hadn't been one for a while and he was worried he would have to go back working at his old job."

"Is that the end of the fires then?" asked Colin.

"No," said Bill, "he didn't start any of the others. Anyway, he went air bridge today, but my reckoning is that there's still another fucking nutter here doing it."

"Well," smiled Bob, "talking of that, there's a lot to choose from in this place." They looked around themselves and the bar was starting to swing with most of the workforce now looking the worst for wear with drink as they went about enjoying their Saturday night out. The canteen was temporarily being used as a bar so that many drunken personnel did not travel between the base camp and the contractors' camp, where they used Huggies or the bar on the ship.

Most of the lads, The A-Team, who came down on the *Adventurer* on the first trip mainly frequented Huggies. On one drunken night all of them had their hair shaved off, and now they kept that up. Because they appeared to be very cliquey and came across as cocky, and as they had been chosen to go out first, they were generally not liked by a large number of the latter workforce.

The Erect-A-Com workers had become sworn enemies of the A-Team and had tried to take over Huggies on a few occasions. This had resulted in some minor scuffles but little more.

Since they had been on site, the Erect-A-Com workers had pulled a different stunt each Saturday night. It had been them who had cut up everyone's clothes on the washing lines at the pioneer camp. One week they all went into the bar with their clothes turned inside out, another time they wore their underpants on the outside of their trousers, and all had a paper S pinned to their T-shirts to look like Superman. Another time they turned up in orange waterproofs with all the hoods done up.

Each time they entered a bar they would start to sing what had become their anthem, the song "Old Faithful", which was the theme song for a rugby club near them at home. Bill had heard that they had planned something for tonight for the opening of the new bar, but up until now nothing had occurred.

"So, what did you hear they would do, Bill?" asked Colin.

"Don't know," came the reply. "Just heard they were going to do something to mark the opening of the new bar."

"Well," said Andy handing out cigarettes, "I am told that every night is party night in their corridor, crates of beer most nights."

"I suppose that's one way to get through this con-trick, and that's to drink your way through it," said Bill.

"I am up for that," said Andy with a smile on his face as he finished his can. "Or in Hack's case, smoke your way through it. I'm up for that also," he said with a smile. "I'll get more beer."

"Where's your roommate tonight?" asked Colin.

"Got a big deal going down."

"Where does he do it?" asked Bill.

"Don't know, don't want to know and don't care," came the reply. "Who wants another beer?" He turned and walked to the bar.

"Hack is going to get himself caught," said Bob.

"No way," said Colin, "he is too careful."

"Mark my words," said Bob, "mark my words."

"Oh, my good God," said Bill. "Look at this." They all turned and looked towards the double entry doors to the bar where there was now a clearing. Twenty Erect-A-Com men had entered the bar. They were all dressed in white long johns and they all wore

113

black Wellington boots, safety helmets and safety goggles over their eyes. Their appearance brought great roars of laughter from the gathered workforce; they had carried in their own crates of beer and stood in the area in front of the double doors drinking from them as they waited to start their show.

"After three, lads," said the one at the front of the assembled choir as he turned to face them with his hands held out as if to conduct. "One-Two-Three..."

"Old Faithful," started the twenty voices, *"in any kind of weather, when your round up days are over, and the boulevard white with clover, you old, old, faithful pal of mine."*

"Giddy up girl for the moon is yellow tonight, giddy up girl for the moon is yellow and bright, carry me back to the one I love, carry me back to the one I love, yea old, old, faithful pal of mine."

The end of the song brought loud hoots, claps, cheers and obscenities from the watching workforce. One of the new intakes, Matt Pearson, from the Midlands in England, a large framed person but also well overweight with white hair and a full beard the same colour, had staggered forwards towards the choir. Then in his drunken state he had started shouting at the top of his voice and pointing his arms at them.

"You're all a load of wankers, a load of fucking wankers," he shouted at them. "Look at you in your pants, a load of wankers!" This brought cheers from the JLB workers, and the fact that Erect-A-Com seemed lost for words made it all the better. About fifteen JLB workers got together and after a quick chat gathered just a few yards from the choir, and in the form of a football chant started singing and pointing at them:

"You're not singing, you're singing, you're not singing,
You're not singing anymore!

After this short burst from the newly formed JLB choir, Matt resumed his shouting, and he was now getting redder and redder in the face. A quick chat between the Erect-A-Com choir brought a response towards Matt of.

"Grandad, Grandad, we love you, that's what we all think of you, Grandad, Grandad!"

This brought great roars of laugher from everyone in the bar, apart from Matt who gave them the V sign and a "fuck off," before turning and walking away. The JLB choir regrouped, and after another huddle turned again to Erect-A-Com and started singing and pointing to them:

114

"You're just a bunch of blacklegs!
You're just a bunch of blacklegs!
You're just a bunch of blacklegs!"
With a sense of victory against the overtime breaking Erect-A-Com workers, great joy was in the air amongst the JLB choir, that was until the rival choir got in a huddle again and the men in the underwear stated to sing:
"We get paid our overtime, we get paid our overtime!" There was no clapping in response to this song, in fact the opposite. It was greeted by boos and jeers. Then came the reply song:
"You're just some Hully-Gully's, you're just some Hully-Gully's, you're just some Hully-Gully's."
"Hully-Gully" is a nickname for a person from Hull where all the men in the Wellington boots came from. After another chat between the goggle wearing men they all turned away from the others, bent over and exposed twenty bare backsides.

*

The roar could be heard in a corridor not far from the bar where Ron stood in a shower block doorway facing a drying room waiting to meet his arranged buyer. He had his hand firmly on his flick knife in his pocket because of what happened the other night, but a smile came to his face when he heard the noise from the bar thinking that the silly bastards from security would all soon be over there. Good cover for him. Ron saw his meet coming down the corridor towards him. He was pleased he was on his own and he also knew a lot of dope and cash was about to change hands. Ron again didn't like the idea of shaking hands when offered, but at the same time he did not want to offend his client, so he took the hand lightly in his and quickly returned it to the pocket which held the knife as they both exchanged. "Hi, man."
"Let's go in here." Ron pointed to the drying room with his other hand. They had only just entered the room and had started to discuss the deal, when from behind the lockers came a fairly short stocky man who ran with his head bent down between the two of them almost knocking them over as he left the room. "What the fuck?" asked Ron as the man disappeared out of the door.
"What's that smell?" asked Ron's buyer. They both looked behind the lockers to see on the floor a large pile of work clothes that had been set alight and were now burning profusely.

115

"Fuck," said Ron as he ran outside looking for a fire extinguisher. It was the third one he tried before he got a full one as the drunks had set the others off the night before. By the time Ron returned to the drying room his customer had disappeared and the blaze was on its way to being out of control. It took a little time but he put it out. Had he not kicked over the smouldering rags to make sure it was all out, he thought later, he would have missed the two fire wardens who turned up as he was leaving to acclaim him as a hero.

"No, lads, really, anyone would have done the same. I was just passing on my way to the bar when I smelt it."

"Well," put in Alf in a drunken slur, "I think you should be rewarded for what you did here. Give us your name and we'll see you get fixed up."

"No, it's fine," said Ron turning to leave. "It's fine, don't worry about it."

"Thought you were going to the bar?" asked Malcolm Moore, the tall southerner with Alf.

"I am."

"Well," came the reply, "the bar is the other way."

"Yes, I've got to get something from my room." He turned to walk away.

"So, what did you say your name was?" asked Malcolm.

"I didn't."

"Well can you?"

"No."

"Why don't you want to give your name?" asked Malcolm.

"No reason. I put the fire out, it's no big deal. I am going."

"If it's no big deal give it to us and you may get a reward."

"Okay, it's Hack."

"Just Hack? That's a funny name."

"Yes, it is." Ron turned and disappeared around the corner very quickly and lost himself in the maze of corridors that now made up the contractors' camp.

*

When Karl entered his office Malcolm and Bob Smith, a short, stocky Scotsman in his mid-forties who was on the security team, were sat at his desk waiting for him.

"Morning, Bob."

"Morning, boss," came the reply. Karl hated this term of phrase but never said anything. "This is Malcolm Moore, the one I told you about, boss." Karl shook hands with him.

"I've been through the files, boss, and I can't find anyone named Hack on the camp."

"Have you looked at the mugshots, Malcolm?"

"No."

"Would you mind coming in tomorrow and having a look?"

"No, not at all." Karl got up and shook hands again.

"Thank you very much, Malcolm." It was midway through the night when it came to Karl. He had been lying in bed thinking about the fire, but something was bugging him and he could not put his finger on it. It had worked putting the fire wardens on, and they had caught this chap red-handed, and he had made out he was putting the fire out. The drug dealer could wait, this was a really good early breakthrough on the arsonist. If only he could find out who this Hack was then he would have his man. The fact was that Hack was not a common name; well the truth was the only Hack he knew was Hack Woodfield the rock star. It was within seconds of that thought going through his mind that Karl sat up in bed with a big smile on his face with the picture of Ron in the file firmly in his mind. "Got you, you fire setting bastard."

*

Ron decided to stop all drug deals as soon as he realised he was being watched. It wasn't hard to spot. Ron smiled to himself as he bounced up and down in his dump truck moving away from the digger that had just loaded him with peat. No, he had been followed by professionals and had spotted them, and Eastham's security were hardly MI5, even if they thought they were. No, play it cool and it will be okay. Right, they knew he was selling drugs, so he would close down the operation until the dust settled. He had made a fair bit of money lately so it wouldn't hurt, then start up again later. He reckoned they had found the drugs he had hid in the drying room after the fire and put two and two together. Even Eastham's could do that.

He saw the Range Rover come down the road towards the tip at Long Pond where the spoils from the runway dig were being tipped. Ron had just reversed onto where he would tip with the machine waiting to one side to push and level his load into the

117

pond which eventually would be another home for some of the island's wildlife. The steep road down to the pond was not very wide and had been cut out of the hillside, so with the road blocked there was no way out for Ron as the three policemen and Eastham's head of security walked the last few yards towards him. Ron was asked to turn off his dump truck, leave the keys in it and climb down. He did as the Stanley police sergeant asked him to.

"Keep cool," he told himself as he climbed into the Range Rover, "they haven't got anything on you. Just play it cool." It was very quiet in the vehicle as it made its way back to Karl's office at the compound. Ron sat between the two PCs in the rear, with the sergeant in the front with Karl who was driving.

As Ron sat in Karl's office across the desk from Pete Windsor, the forty-two-year-old Scottish police sergeant from the highlands and Karl, he did not think he had a problem. They could not prove a thing. Okay, they had found a small amount of puff in his room as they had searched it before picking him up with a warrant, the police had got it from the court in Stanley that morning, but it was no more than they would have found in a lot of rooms on the camp had they cared to look.

It was not long into the questioning that Ron realised which way it was all going with questions like, "So how long have you been setting fires, Ron?" or "When did you become an arsonist, Ron?" or "Did you just wake up one morning and want to burn the house down?" And things like, "Were you born like this, always wanting things to go up in flames? Just come clean and tell us the truth about wanting to set everything on fire, Ron."

He sat trying to keep as cool as possible and to work it all out. He thought to himself, they think it's me setting the fires. Oh boy, this is really bad news. It's one thing getting done for selling drugs, but another for setting fires.

The questions went on for a long time with Ron pleading his innocence to the fires. What he did not want to do was drop himself in it with the drugs. He was not lying about the fires, that he had not done, but then again, he could not tell them why he was in the drying room in the first place. So now he was trying to stay calm and pick his way through the minefield that lay ahead of him. They still haven't got anything on me, he was thinking to himself when things took a surprise turn.

"Okay," said Karl, "I am fed up with this now and want to get it over with. We knew you would not own up to this, so Kim

118

Benjamin has agreed if that was the case we would terminate your contract."

"Hold on," said Ron as he sat up straight in the chair. "I've done my three months trial and you can't prove anything apart from the fact that I was there at that time. I will have a solicitor on the case as soon as I get home. You won't get away with this, I haven't set any fucking fires!"

"Let me finish please," came the calm reply. "So that you are off the island and cannot start any more fires, Kim has agreed that JLB will pay your contract up in full until it ends in January. You will be paid your bonus, any overtime you have worked, your retention and any other monies you are owed. In short, we will pay you off!"

Ron sat trying to take it all in. He would go home from this shithole, get paid up in full, and if he could manage to pick his grass up that would be a real bonus, selling all that cheap stuff at home.

"And there will not be anything on your record. We just want you out of here. There's a plane that leaves Stanley in the morning. You will be on it, my good man."

"Can I pick my gear up?"

"Yes, you can pick everything up. You will spend the night at the camp in your room, but one of my men will never be far from you. He will spend the night outside your room. So I suggest," said Karl getting to his feet, "that you get yourself packed and ready to go, HACK!"

This brought a smile to Ron's face, but it was more for the fact it was turning out to be a very good day indeed.

*

"So that's it?" asked Bob as he made tea for the assembled guests in his room. "You get a get out of jail card home?"

"Yep, in this case pass finish, collect loads of money and dope, and the most important thing, a get out of jail free card. Sell the wacky baccy, get the sacky sacky." This comment from Ron brought a laugh from everyone.

"You're a jammy bastard," said Colin from his high vantage point.

"And when they gave me my shadow for the next day it was one of Eastham's men who is a regular customer of mine, so I

119

gave him a large lump of grass and we have spent the afternoon going around all my hiding places picking up the gear and money. Even the stuff I had in the drying room I was about to sell was still there. Yes, I would say Hack has had a result today."

"Got anything you won't be taking home with you?" asked Bill from the armchair. "Anything you would like to give away?"

"God," said Andy, "don't you ever give up?"

"No, don't ask and you don't get," came the reply from the armchair.

Ron's last night on the island was mostly spent in Bob and Colin's room as it was almost like a party. Pete and Dusty came in from next door, beer was drunk and dope smoked. Ron's guard popped in every now and then to have a pull on one of the joints being passed around or to get a replacement can of beer. This had been a good job for him along with the fact that Ron had given him almost half an ounce of grass to keep an eye out for him as they went around the camp picking up his gear.

Ron was picked up early the next morning. His guard was laying outside his door more unconscious than asleep. Any number of fires could have been set that night and there was no way the guard would have woken up. Ron was taken to West Cove International Airport and was put on the Islander aeroplane to Stanley where he was put on an RAF flight heading for the UK.

*

Karl was feeling very pleased with himself that morning as he made his way to the medical centre. He had been here no time at all and he had caught the firebug and was now on his way to see Harry, who had sent him a message from his bed saying he would like to talk to him. Karl just knew it was information about the drug dealer, as he was sure that was how Harry got hurt, a fall out about drugs, and because he now wanted to save his job. Yes, things were going very well indeed. Kim had been over the moon about the firebug and now this on top. Yes, it was a good day.

Harry was looking a lot better and was sat in an armchair; the swelling was now almost gone. "You are looking a lot better today, Harry," as he pulled a chair up beside him. "What was it you wanted to talk about?"

"If I give you the name of the person dealing drugs do I keep my job?"

120

"Yes, I said you would and I'll see that you do."

"Well, the thing is where I come from it's not the done thing to rat someone up. In fact, it's not a very healthy thing to do."

"Look at it this way, Harry, you are doing it for your family. You need the money for them, and it's the right thing to do. I will never let it out where I got the info from."

"Okay, I suppose you're right, but I only know his nickname."

"That's fine. Please give me that and all you know about him."

Karl could not believe his ears when Harry spoke the word.

"Hack."

"WHO?"

"Hack, they call him Hack because he looks like Hack Woodfield, the rock star."

Karl could feel the blood draining from his face. "Are you sure?"

"Oh yes, he hides his stuff all over the place and he uses lots of different drying rooms to sell it from. When you contact him he tells you which drying room to meet him in and at what time."

It all dropped into place as Karl made his way back to his office. Of course, Hack had not been setting fires, Karl thought to himself. He was telling the truth about that, but it did come across that he was lying as he was covering his tracks regarding the drug deals, and no doubt he did put out the fire as he would not want to draw attention to himself. And I've just sent the drug dealer home fully paid up. What a fucking idiot I am, and the firebug is still here into the bargain. And just to compound that fact, a fire was found at three o'clock the next morning in one of the toilet blocks. So now Karl had to tell Kim what had happened.

Chapter 7

I'm Okay, if the Rest Are

Dusty hated being out here. In fact, he could not think of anything he had done in his life that he had disliked more, he thought to himself, as he sat in the digging machine with the heavy hydraulic breaker attached to the end of the large arm that would normally have a digging bucket on it. But a breaker had been fitted to break up the large lumps of rock that had been blown up by explosive charges that had been set off in an attempt to cut though the rock in a straight line at the side of the runway. This was to take drainage water from the airfield but also to carry many of the service cables that would be required for landing lights, radar, communications, and other important items that would be needed to run the airfield.

No, Dusty thought, apart from his two failed marriages, nine months in prison as a youngster, having to live with the in-laws, or as Dusty liked to call them the "outlaws" for eighteen months, being run over while riding his bike on the pavement by a path cleaning machine coming around the corner, spending two months in hospital and then getting no compensation as it was judged in court that it was his fault for being on the footpath and not paying attention, and having one of the biggest boils on his arse ever and not being able to sit down for about a week, and maybe a few other things he could not remember at that moment, this was the worst time of his life. Oh, of course there was the time he got shot by a local farmer while nicking sheep to sell while he was out of work once. Again, he got hit in the backside by a bit of buckshot, and it wasn't long after that the boil came up come to think of it, he almost said aloud. But this job he hated, and it wasn't even halfway through yet, and he just really hated it!

There was nothing to do here apart from drinking and smoking dope, and even the latter would not be so easy now his supplier Hack was gone. He did make up silly games with his roommate Pete. He had been a bonus. They had shared a cabin on the *Kenya* coming down and had hit it off straight away and had decided to share a room. He had met some other good lads here but Pete had been the best by far. They were both on the same wavelength.

For two pins Dusty would have jacked it all in and gone home, but with all the money he owed in unpaid maintenance for four, or was it five kids? He wasn't always sure. Plus, unpaid fines and the money he owed Eddie Stiff a local loan shark, he could not afford to go home, he was up to his eyes in debt. Mind you, on the other hand, he thought, with all those people he owed money to maybe he was in the right place eight thousand miles away!

It would not have been too bad had he fallen for a good job, but sitting in the cab of this fucking machine all day with his finger on a button to operate the breaker which on its own was driving him mad. The constant "boom-boom-boom-boom" that was never-ending, even with ear defenders on and the cab door shut, not only could he hear it all the time he was now hearing it in his sleep, but as Pete had pointed out one night as they lay on their bunks smoking dope, that if he made a fuss about being on the breaker they might put him on a job that he may have to actually work.

He had come to enjoy the rock blasting, there had not been many up until that point as it was a recent thing, but they had started to make better progress. The quarrymen had been setting the charges, but unlike up in the quarry which was miles from anywhere, and it did not matter how much rock was blown up, on the airfield it had to be controlled because of all the other operations taking place. With many co-workers around the blasting's took place at meal and tea breaks. A hooter would sound before the blast went off so the area would supposedly be clear, but the fact that the second blast had too much explosives in it, mainly due to the fact that the charge setter had an almighty hangover, rocks had blown outside the designated blast area covering the runway with pieces of rock, smashing digger machine windows and sending up dust clouds that could been seen for miles. And even more dangerous, a rock had penetrated the roof of a container being used as a canteen which was full of workers having their lunch break. The large piece of rock about the size of two footballs had crashed through, smashing a table below which workers were sat eating at. It also caused everything on the shelves to fall off. There had been very angry complaints regarding the incident and Bob's room was bombarded that night with workers wanting the committee to do something about it before someone got hurt, and to ensure it did not happen again.

Dusty was not completely sure how it happened, mainly because he was on autopilot and his mind was eight thousand miles away, but all was calm. Well, as calm as things could be with all the noise. He was breaking the large lumps of rock which had been blown up in the trench. A digger the same as his but with a bucket on was just in front of him digging out the broken rock and putting it into a large dump truck beside him, which was moving along the top of the trench as it was cleared. Four men came along behind the machines laying drainage pipes and cable ducts in fresh concrete that had just been tipped from a mixer lorry.

Dusty moved the point of the breaker to a new position which was almost under the rear of the machine in front of him. What happened next was like he'd set off a bomb. He pressed the button once to restart the breaking, but at that point the breaker hit an unseen, unexploded piece of gelignite. The large blast went mainly forward away from Dusty but under the other machine and onto the pipe layers. The blast caved in all the windows of nearby machines and lorries; it sent small bits of rock-like shrapnel flying in all directions. The men standing were all blown off their feet. Dust covered the whole area, and with the unexpected boom most of the workers along the busy construction area of the runway stopped to see what had happened.

Dusty was the first to arrive at the blast scene and apart from being covered in glass and dust he was somehow unhurt. He could not believe the sight that greeted him. Pipe layers were all laying on the ground covered in dust amongst small pieces of rock and he could see the machine driver unconscious in his cab covered in glass and bleeding from the head. Two dump truck drivers also looked badly injured in their cabs.

Dusty ran around like a headless chicken in what was almost a blind panic not knowing what to do. A Land Rover arrived soon after with one of the airfield foremen who used his radio to call the control room for help.

The Land Rover that doubled as an ambulance did not take long to arrive at the scene, by which time the injured workers were all moving apart from one. Roger Dickinson, a middle-aged man from Newcastle upon Tyne, had taken the full force of the blast and was lying face down in the trench covered in rock. Co-workers who had run from all directions of the airfield to help when it was realised what had happened were now working tirelessly in uncovering him.

First aid was being given to the wounded and bandages were soaking up blood mainly from head and face injuries. The doctor and two medics were carrying this out. As soon as the doctor had seen Roger's legs sticking out from under the rocks he had called for a helicopter to come immediately.

It was about the same time that the unconscious Roger was lifted out of the trench that the helicopter first came into sight as it appeared around Mount Sheldon and below the low laying cloud that covered most of the island that morning. It landed a few hundred yards from the accident on a cleared area of land that would soon form the runway. The fast spinning rotors lifted peat dust into the air until the pilot closed them down. Roger was taken on a stretcher in the back of the ambulance and then given over to the care of the RAF medics who would take him on a lifesaving trip to hospital in the island's capital.

The scene in the medical centre resembled something from a war film or the TV series *MASH*. All the injured had been taken by any available vehicles. He was not injured at all, but Dusty went along on the doctor's say so for a check-up, but as far as he was concerned he went for the ride so he didn't have to go back to work too soon. Another helicopter had been called for the other machine driver, Max Upton, who had come around but had passed out while walking into the medical centre, and was still unconscious when the RAF arrived with a bad head injury. Although the blast had gone under and away from him, it appeared that a piece for rock had hit the arm of the digger and had rebounded back through the windscreen and hit him on the forehead.

It was all hands-on deck in the centre; medics who were having time off in lieu had been recalled from their rooms and were tending to the vast amount of bleeding with bandages, plasters and in some cases stitches. The doctor was working his way around all the victims making notes of all injuries and giving advice to the medics on treatments. When he got to Dusty the doctor was pleased to hear him report, "Oh, I'm fine, not injured at all, took the full blast but I'm great. I had all the glass cave in on me but not a cut in sight. I was out of my machine like a greyhound out of its trap, Doc, running around helping people, getting everyone to be

125

calm. Oh, Doc, it takes more than a little blast to hurt me you know."

"That's great news, old chap," replied the doctor, "but I would like you to relax and take it easy anyway, just in case of shock."

"Shock? I wouldn't know the meaning of the word, Doc. No, I'm right as rain, a man of iron."

"Good show, old man." He patted him on the shoulder before moving on to his next patient.

It was at that time that Kim Benjamin and Roger Clifford came into the centre. They walked around and chatted to the victims for a short time, then asked the doctor to join them in the doctor's office. They were gone about five minutes and when they came out Kim asked if he could have everyone's attention.

"I have talked to the head office in London, gentlemen, and they have agreed with me that because of the nature of the accident and the limited resources we have here, you will all be returned by air bridge tomorrow to the UK for medical treatment, and because it is not known how long you will be off you will all be made medivacs. Your salary, bonuses, retention, and overtime will be paid up in full until the end of your contracts, and you will receive all the professional medical attention you each require."

It seemed the gathered workers did not want to acutely cheer, but it was very close with a lot of big smiles starting to break out on their faces. Dusty thought all his Christmases had all come at once. He could not believe it, what a bit of luck. He blows everyone up and gets away with it scot-free and gets a medivac into the bargain. A paid up con-trick he thought. Now I can get the fuck out of this shithole, pay off all my debts and I am in the clear, or on the other hand, he smiled to himself, if no one knew he was coming home he could take the money and do a runner.

The doctor said something into Benjamin's ear. "Oh, yes. Okay. Mr Parker," he called out.

"That's me," smiled Dusty as he sat back in the chair. In his mind's eye he was on a distant sun-kissed beach sipping ice-cold beer and being made a fuss of by some local girls.

"I am sorry, I almost forgot, sir, the doctor told me you were unharmed and feeling fine. I am really pleased that you stood up to it so well, and with that being the case there will be no problem for you to return to work this afternoon. Thank you all very much for your time, gentlemen, have a safe journey home and a speedy recovery to you all. Thank you again."

The medical centre's treatment room was empty when the shell-shocked Dusty finally got up and made his way very slowly with his head hung low back to his room.

*

"What a prick," Bill told his two friends in their room as he sat and had his nightly cup of tea with Bob and Colin. I can't believe Dusty blew it like that. What a wanker."

"He will hear you," said Bob in a low voice as he pointed to the wall that Pete and Dusty's room was behind as he walked over with his cup of tea to sit in the armchair next to Bill.

"Don't give a fuck," came the reply. "He had a golden opportunity to get the hell out of here, and paid up into the bargain, and he fucking blew it." He raised his voice and shouted this over his shoulder at the wall.

"Well," said Colin from his high up viewpoint of the top bunk. "I don't suppose he realised what would happen. I mean, he didn't know everyone was going to get sent home when he said he was okay. He was only telling the truth."

"That's not what I heard," came the reply from the ginger-haired Brummie. "I was told that he was bragging that he was in the middle of the blast but came out unhurt, showing off and it blew up in his face. Oh, that's a good one, blew up in his face." He laughed at his own joke, the other two just smiled. "So," shouted Bill at the wall, "the fucking idiot deserves all he gets, or in this case all he doesn't get!"

"Leave it out," said Bob. "The lad must be upset. He didn't know what was going to happen."

"Well he's still a fucking idiot," came the reply. There was a short silence in the room then Bill continued. "So, what's the latest on the overtime, Bob?"

"Well," replied the committeeman as he pulled on his cigarette, "we have a meeting tomorrow afternoon."

"And the word is on the street, or in this case on the runway," Bill laughed at his own joke again, "that the pressure is on management to settle and settle fast, to get us working the overtime as soon as possible, and in particular with all the rain we have been getting of late and with the winter almost on us, any time lost they will want to claw back."

127

"Well," said Bob who sat next to him, "in the last few meetings it has definitely seemed that they have got a bit more urgent. They seem keener than ever to sort it out."

"It's easy," said the voice from above. "If they pay the overtime each month then we'll work. I can't see the problem, can you?"

"The problem is," replied Bill, "that they don't want to pay because they will break the budget by paying extra money to us."

"Oh, believe me," came back Bob, "the money is there. In fact, it is almost an open-ended budget from Auntie Maggie and her gang, but of course if they keep it down Kim Benjamin and his mob will be sticking their chests out and get another good overseas post when it's all over."

"How could you set a price on a job like this?" asked Colin. "I mean with all the travelling, the accommodation, the food, equipment, men, it's endless. It must have been a nightmare to cost."

"I was told," said Bob, "that it was priced in London in six weeks. Two teams of twelve working twenty-four hours in two shifts, seven days a week, to do it."

"Bet they got paid their bloody overtime," moaned Bill.

"Bet they didn't," put in Colin, "not with this tight bunch of bastards."

"Believe me they did all right," countered Bob.

"Well," said Bill "I heard that–"

Bill's new story was interrupted from beyond the wall behind him by a very loud bang and a spine-chilling scream. This was followed by a shouting voice that sounded like Pete next door. "Help, someone help me!" They all looked at each other and without saying a word they all jumped out of their seats and made to the caller's aid. When Bob opened the door to his neighbour's room followed closely by his friends the sight that greeted them was very unnerving. Dusty was laid on the floor face up with Pete crouched over him. He was shaking with eyes open but rolled to the back of his head.

"What's happening?" asked Bob in a very concerned voice.

"He was on his bunk talking when he started shaking and fell off," reported Pete.

"Bloody hell," said Colin, "what shall we do? He looks awful."

"I thought he always looked awful," smiled Bill, but no one took any notice of the tasteless and untimely joke.

"He was okay then he just went all funny," said Pete.

"Well we'd better get help. It's the shock of today coming out I bet," said Bob. "I'll go and get the doctor, medic or someone." He turned and left the room as soon as he'd finished the sentence.

It seemed an age to all those gathered in Dusty's room before Bob returned with the not very happy medic. Bob explained all to his two mates back in their room after they had helped take Dusty to the medical centre. "I went to the medic centre and a notice said the doctor was away for a few days and gave the room number of the medic on call, so I went there and his roommate said he was in the bar, so I went there and he was pissed out of his brains. One of the barmen gave me one of the others' room number, so I went there and he had the right arseholes because he was in bed with one of the Eastham's birds."

"How do you know that?" asked Colin now sitting up in his bunk and taking notice.

"I could see her feet sticking out the end of the bed when he opened the door. They have got two bunk beds pushed together, and he only had a towel around him."

"Lucky bastard," replied his roommate. "What I wouldn't give for a shag tonight."

"You'd better watch out tonight, Bob, the lad's looking very horny," smiled Bill.

"Well I heard," returned Bob, "that the second thing Colin is going to do when he gets home on leave is put the suitcase down."

"That's not true," shouted Colin. "The second thing I'm going to do is shut the front door, then put the suitcase down. God, I can't wait," he said, as he laid back down on his bunk rubbing his private parts.

"Calm down, boy," smiled Bob.

"What do you think of this Dusty business then?" asked Bill as he helped himself to one of Bob's cigarettes off the coffee table.

"Oh, help yourself, Bill."

"Thanks, Bob, don't mind if I do. Now, the thing is I think he's putting it on because the others got the medivac and he didn't."

"That's bollocks," replied Colin. "We all saw him tonight and there's no way that was put on."

"That's my whole point. We did see him and I reckon there was a small grin on his face at one point."

"I don't think so, Bill," replied the committee chairman. "I know he's a bit of a toe-rag and all, but I really don't think he would put that on. They have got him in overnight now and that won't be fun, and would they have called us in if he was putting it on?"

"Of course, they would. What better way can you have than the respected chairman of the workers committee as a witness, and then have a bad night with the medics and it would all be going to plan," said Bill. "You find out what sort of night he had over there. You mark my words, he's putting this on to get out of here."

"Well," said the voice from above, "he must be pig sick that the others are going home and all. Anyway, why did they send them home just like that? It's not at all like JLB to do that sort of thing."

"Jason Benson, one of the lads, came and saw me tonight to see what I think so I went to the office to find out, and one of the things is if they take the medivac it is that it will be in lieu of any compensation, and they do have to sign to agree that."

"I could put up with that to get out of this shithole," said his roommate.

"But what happens if one of them is really bad later on and has lost his claim?" said Bill.

"I don't know," came the reply. "Would he have a case if he took it to court later on? I really don't know." Bob lit up a cigarette then continued. "I also think they will not want any of the bad publicity this might bring back home, so they are trying to be seen to be doing the right thing."

"Well I don't know if that's fair," said Bill. "I think—" He was interrupted for the second time that night, but this time it was by a knock on the door. "Come in," shouted Bill. The two lads just looked at each other. The door opened and Pete came in.

"Hi, lads, just came to say thanks for the help with Dusty."

"No problem," answered Bob. "How is he?"

"Oh, he is not good. In fact, he is in a very bad way. I was just saying to the medic he should be sent home with the others for treatment."

"I rest my case, gentlemen," Bill announced as he got out of his seat and walked to the door. As he passed Pete he said, "He went into shock alright, when he found out the others were all going home and he wasn't. See you later, lads." He left the room.

*

130

All the crushed stone haul roads which eventually would be finished with concrete and tarmac were now complete. Access to all work areas was easy, apart from the fact that the past month had seen very heavy rainfall and was making it almost impossible for the road maintenance gangs (West Cove County Council) to keep the roads open. In some areas the culverts had blocked up and were causing flooding. Other areas of road were breaking up because of the volume of traffic. The size of these gangs had been increased but only so many could work on them at any one time, so it was becoming more important than ever for them to stop the overtime ban and work longer hours.

Part of the contract was to construct a permanent tarmac road from the airfield to the capital, approximately forty miles. This had now commenced with surveyors and engineers going out in advance to plot the route. Already there had been conflict as when work commenced on the road the gang that had been chosen to carry out the construction had been told that the travelling rules that applied to the rest of contract would also apply to them, meaning that no travelling time would be paid to them regardless of the fact that each day they would be getting further and further away from the camp and could in fact take over an hour each way as time went on. When reported to Kim Benjamin at a progress meeting by the section manager Adam Cooper that the men were unhappy about this, he got the snapped reply, "I am fed up with this workforce trying to tell us how to run this contract, so, sir, you can report back to them that they will be happy or they can get the next ship back!" Adam being new to the island but an old hand at man management decided it would be prudent not to report the whole response, so instead he told them he would speak to Kim again at a later date in private, thinking this may buy him some time.

Work on the airfield was going well with the airstrip being almost three thousand metres long and very wide, and the depth it had to go down to accommodate a rolled sub base of stone on top of which would be a semi-dry mix of concrete which would also be rolled by a large road roller, then a thick layer of high-quality concrete would be laid by a machine called a concrete train. The train laid, vibrated, and levelled the concrete. The train had come on the last cargo ship but was not in use yet as it was considered it was best to let the very time-consuming preparation process get ahead so that the train would not easily catch up with that operation, so once it started it could continue without any holdups.

At the east end of the runway work had started on the cross runway which would cross the main airstrip close to the end. This would lead to concealed hangars for fighter jets that could be deployed at short notice should this ever be required.

The camp was forever growing larger with extra corridors being added at a fast rate and also the facilities taking more shape. The water tank that fed the whole camp and compound area stood high above it like a giant watchtower. The lower section of the access ladder had been removed after three drunks had been found on the top-level taking photographs. With one death already attributed to the tower there was a real fear from management that others may fall, especially if they were intoxicated. The three were also given final written warnings for their troubles.

*

It was the Sunday morning after the drainage trench accident that a ten o'clock meeting of the workers had been scheduled in the staff canteen that was still being used as the bar. In the days before the meeting feelings had been running high amongst the workforce regarding the overtime, to a point that some were saying that the messing about should stop and they should go for an all-out strike. Bob and his fellow members wanted to avoid this as they knew it would play into management's hands by breaking the contract, and there was no way Benjamin would let them get away with an all-out stoppage of work. So, it was to this tense background that they gathered in the canteen that had not yet been cleaned from the night before. There was a heavy smell of stale smoke and beer. Empty beer cans and full ashtrays covered the tables which the workers moved to one end, then took all the chairs to the other end so that they formed a semi-circle with an area left open near the wall for the three committee members, Bob, Reg and Dave. They also had a table there on which they all put their folders full of notes. Reg sat in a chair at the table taking the minutes of the meeting, while the other two stood. But it was Reg who stood up to bring the meeting to order after Bob had failed to do so. "Will you lot shut the fuck up and let Bob talk!" he shouted out at the packed canteen. He then mumbled under his breath as he sat down, "Bunch of fucking wankers."

132

Bob started the meeting by setting out what was to be discussed, which was in the main the overtime. They skipped through a few other items, one of which was the issue of the Stanley road travelling. It was quickly agreed that the road gang and the committee would talk after the meeting. Dusty and Pete were sat near the front next to Colin, Bill and Andy. It had been very noticeable in the past few days since Dusty had been released from the medical centre that he had been making a lot of strange noises and had some very strange looks on his face at times.

It seemed as if things would get out of control as many tempers were getting very heated. Bob was working hard to keep everything under control, most of all with his fellow member Reg who had taken offence at some of the comments that seemed to be aimed at the committee members, some like, "It's alright for you lot that get to sit with management drinking tea while you should be working," or "You lot have had long enough to sort this out and have got nowhere." But to Bob's pleasure this had been shouted down by the others, but it was all he could do to contain Reg who was ready to turn it into a boxing match, or at least shout insults back. Along with Dusty making noises it made for a very lively meeting.

"Order! Order!" shouted Bob as he banged his fist on the table. "Come on, everyone, roaring and shouting is getting us nowhere. Look, put your hands up and we'll deal with each point." This comment was followed by a noise and the shaking of Dusty's head which Bob totally ignored and pointed to one worker to speak.

"This has gone on for far too long," shouted the agitated man. "The only way to show them that we mean business is to stop work altogether." This comment brought a noisy response from the gathered crowd and again it took Bob a while to bring the meeting back to order.

"Now listen here, men. By us refusing to work or stopping work in any way, shape or form will be playing into their hands," the chairman told everyone. On top of trying to keep order Bob now had to contend with the cleaners who had now joined the group. The three males started throwing the used cans into black dustbin sacks, and if making that noise was not enough one of them put a face mask on and started brushing the floor with a large wide platform broom which was now sending up clouds of dust and making some of the crowd cough and choke.

"I really don't think us stopping work is going to do it. It's better to try the gentle approach," the chairman continued.

"We have tried that and it has got us nowhere," the man replied. "Now it's time for real action, they can't sack us all. Stop work for a day or so and they will soon cave in."

To Bob's surprise there seemed to be more agreement from the workers this time which he found disconcerting. The dust clouds were now growing at the rear of the workers and some were asking the cleaners to stop, which fell on deaf ears. The worker who was making his point made his way to the front. Con, a large man from the Manchester area, now stood in front of all and asked in a loud voice, "Before we all choke to death, I think it would be only fair to have a vote and see if the lads want to stop work or not."

This was interrupted by Joey, a very large machine driver from Bristol, who broke away from crowd to tell the cleaners in no uncertain terms in a very loud voice, "Now you're taking the piss. Stop it now until we are finished. It won't be long so go outside and have a smoke or I will shove them brushes up all your arses. Now fuck off outside!" This was greeted with a large cheer from the others and a shouted thank you to Joey from Bob.

"So, are we going to have a vote?" Con asked the committeemen.

"Of course," replied Bob, "if that is what is wanted."

The "yes" reply stood out from the workers much to Bob's displeasure. He asked the meeting for all those in favour of stopping work to put up their hands, then those who did not to do the same. When the count was complete it was found that, by a very small margin, the workers wanted to stop work, but it was agreed it would be one day only.

Bob was one of the last to leave the canteen after the meeting. He collected his files and had a short meeting with the Stanley road gang in which they agreed their next course of action. He refused a drink at the now open bar from workmates on his way out saying he was, "going to get lunch but did not rule out a later return." He passed the medics outside who had been called to deal with Dusty who was again rolling about on the ground making some very weird noises. Bob paid very little attention to what was going on as he made his way back to his room. He sat there alone and smoked a cigarette as he reflected on the meeting. That was when he decided that at the end of the one-day stoppage he would resign from the committee, putting it down to the fact that it was just too much hassle. He would not tell anyone until he did it, but all of a sudden, he felt a lot better, a lot calmer than he had been feeling of late. He had read an article once regarding how people who had decided to commit suicide then felt much better. He now felt he could understand that more, not that he was going that far. In fact, maybe a beer or two was not a bad idea after all.

*

It was the time that the workforce should have been getting on the buses for their work areas. Indeed, they were all at the pick-up point at the camp but no one was getting on the transport. The crowd had formed as they came out of the canteens after breakfast. When Bob and Colin joined them, the talk was that it needed the stoppage to finish the dispute once and for all. Bob tended to agree with them as he had got to know Benjamin but was thinking it may not end the way his workmates had intended, but he was keeping those thoughts to himself at the moment. It was agreed that Bob and Reg would go and tell Benjamin what was happening, but as word had already spread to the office compound by George's radio when he passed the workers, he had now been asked by Arran Jones to bring Bob and Reg to the project coordinator's office.

"Jump in, bonny lads, Kim wants a word with you," he shouted out of the driving side window as he pulled up alongside the walking committeemen. As they made their way along the muddy roads to the office compound the two did not reply to George's comments regarding the stoppage like, "You know this will get you nowhere, don't you, bonny lads? Kim is far too strong to give in to this kind of thing." With Bob sat by the window and looking out and taking no notice of the driving foreman, it gave him some more time to think. "Now that's what I call a conscientious worker," smiled George as he pointed to the diesel tanker passing them on the other side of the road. "Now that Kev puts in a lot of hours, filling up all the lorries and plant ready for the next morning." It did cross Bob's mind why the tanker was this far from the work areas and confused him even more when he saw out of the wing mirror that he had taken a turning away from where Bob felt he should be going, but at this point of the morning he really didn't care.

"Come in, gentlemen," was the greeting from Benjamin as the two entered the project coordinator's office. Arran Jones was

135

already there sat in a chair next to the large oak desk. Kim was next to a coffee making machine which appeared to have just finished making the first pot of the day. "Would you gentlemen care to join us in taking coffee?" The two newcomers looked at each other then both nodded a yes. As the drink was poured then handed out niceties were exchanged regarding the weather until Benjamin sat behind the desk. "Now, what is going on? I did think you two understood that that there was no way I would tolerate any kind of stoppage or holdup to the programme."

"Oh, we do that," said Reg, "but it went to a vote and we can't go against that."

"We don't have to tell you what action we could take over this?" Jones asked them.

"Yes, we know," said Bob, "but you are not going to sack everyone and the lads know that. No, they, like us all, are fed up to the back teeth over this and just want to sort it out. Then we can get on and earn money. That is all we are here for."

"That's is good, and we want you to earn good wages," smiled Benjamin. "Now this need not go beyond us four, but I could guarantee that you two would always get the overtime you have worked if you could get the men to realise that they will get nowhere and it's best to stop all this now."

"If you are asking us to go behind the lads' backs and do a deal just for us you are asking the wrong two people. We will stick by the lads," snapped Bob.

"And besides," put in Reg, "I could guarantee we would get our heads kicked in if they found out." This brought a smile from everyone.

"No, I would not suggest for one minute that you would go against the men. I just think that if all this did get sorted out soon and the chaps started working overtime, it would be fair for you two to get some reward for all the hard work you have put in on their behalf. It would only be right and proper. Would you not agree, Arran?"

"Would only be fair," smiled Jones, "and no one need never know."

Bob sat up in his seat. "I will walk out of here now if we carry on with this talk. We are not here for self-gain." Reg nodded his agreement.

"Fine. I did not mean to upset you, so is there any way of telling me how long this will last?"

Bob was not thinking as straight as he should have and as the words came out of his mouth he knew he had made a major mistake. "The day." He knew how fast on the uptake Benjamin was, and it would have been a lot better had he let the company think it will be ongoing until they got what they wanted. Silence filled the room as the project coordinator pondered on what he had just heard.

"Okay, gentlemen," came the reply as Benjamin rose from behind his desk, "everyone will return to work tomorrow morning or they will be in breach of their contracts and all will be dealt with accordingly. And of course, all pay has now been suspended. That will be all."

*

"I can assure you there is no way of them backing down. Benjamin just won't do it," Bob told Colin and Bill as he made them tea in his room. "And the idea of some of them carrying on until they give in is mad."

"I agree," said Colin from his top bunk, "but some of these blokes just don't give a shit, don't care if they get sacked or not. There's a few troublemakers here, you know that."

"Well," said Bill as he helped himself to Bob's cigarettes then passed them around, "I am going back to work in the morning and don't give a toss what the others say. I didn't come to the other side of the fucking world to sit in a little room and drink tea all day, as nice as the tea is."

"I could not agree more," said Bob as he sat next to Bill after handing the cups out. "I am totally pissed off with it. If they want to carry on that's up to them."

"Well I'm off out," said Colin as he jumped down from the bunk and went to the mirror above the sink, picked up a hairbrush from the small shelf, ran it though his hair a few times and told himself in a low voice, "You're a handsome bastard," then in a louder voice said, "Okay, see you two later," and made for the door.

"Where are you off to?" asked Bob in a voice that showed surprise at his roommate's announcement that he was not spending the night in.

"Going to see a video."

137

"You said there was only a load of shit on this week when they put the list up," his roommate replied.

"I've changed my mind. It's allowed you know. See you later." Colin then disappeared out the door before any more could be said.

"What happened there?" asked Bill.

"Don't know," came the puzzled reply, "he said the other day that all the films they had were rubbish and that he was not going to go to any this week."

"Don't worry, maybe he is off to shag one of the Eastham's birds." Bob did not reply to this as he knew that Bill was joking, but he also knew that if that was the case it would not be for the first time, and it once came very close to breaking Colin's marriage up. Bob had this information because Colin's wife had told his. He liked Colin's wife, Jean, and did not want to see them have problems, but at the same time he did not want to become his friend's keeper, nor would he thank him for it, so he would put it to the back of his mind for the time being, if he could do that.

"Here, Bill, fuck the tea. Do you fancy going for a beer?"

"What? You never go out midweek. What's all this about?"

"Just a bit cheesed off. Doing it once won't hurt, will it?"

"No, it won't. Come on then."

*

The situation the next morning did not go as Bob would have hoped. When people started to gather for the buses there was a hardcore of about ten workers who were trying to persuade the others to stay off until the company gave in to their demands. This had already made for some heated words. About a third of the workforce did not get on the buses for work that morning, as they thought that with that number of workers not going in that they could still force the management's hand. But little did they know this was just the opportunity Benjamin had been waiting for. He had just arrived in his office and had taken a telephone call from the London head office and was about to have his first black coffee of the day when Arran Jones came in. "Good morning, Kim," and without waiting for a reply continued, "George has just radioed me to say there is about a quarter to a third of the men not going into work. They want a meeting with you." Kim walked from the coffee making machine without saying a word, but pointed to the hot black liquid in the glass container for Arran to help himself, which he did. Jones had known Kim long enough to be quiet and to let him think it through, and that was still happening when he joined the project coordinator at his desk with his filled cup.

After almost three minutes Benjamin broke the silence. "Has Bob English the committeeman gone to work do you know?"

"Yes, I believe all of those on the committee have gone in. Apparently, there were a lot of hard words between those who wanted to work and those who did not."

"Great, this is what we needed, them falling out between themselves that is. It was always going to happen the longer it went on you know." The manager nodded his agreement but did not interrupt Kim's flow. "Okay, Arran my old friend, this is how we shall play this." He stood up with his coffee and started pacing the room. "Get hold of a pile of official final written warnings from admin, get George, David Anthony, Roger and any staff members you can find. Drive over there now, fill them out with the workers' names on them, and let them know that if they do not return to work now they will be removed from camp today and sent to Stanley tonight, and I happen to know there is a merchant ship in tomorrow to take troops back to the UK. Put them straight on it, stop their pay at once, no bonus, no overtime payments, if they have worked any that is, and tell them that they will be stopped the payment for their fare back home. Arran, sometimes we have to be brave to win the battle, and I think that time has now come. If we have to send some back now, so be it, but I'm sure it will end this overtime lark once and for all."

"Kim, I have known you a long time and trust your judgement, but I'm worried if this is the right move at this time."

"Well, I'm paid to make these decisions so I will have to stand or fall by it, but I do thank you for your concern."

"Kim, I will do it right now." He stood and turned to leave the room.

"One other thing, Arran, without a lot of people getting to know, can you get Bob over to here to see me at some point today please?"

"Of course."

Benjamin sat alone drinking his coffee and reflected on the latest happening. He felt for sure this would solve the problem in the company's favour, and no one on the site would ever know that he had taken a phone call that morning to say that if all the workforce had stayed off one more day then he was to give in to

139

their demands and pay them the overtime one month in arrears. He had been patient and his good management skills had paid off. He did not want to gloat, just move forward, but he did feel very pleased with himself. Indeed, he did.

*

The confrontation at the bus depot did not go as bad as Arran had thought it may have as he drove over there. The staff members handed out the notices when they arrived. Arran then told the gathered crowd that this was not a bluff and that they would be on their way to the capital within the hour if they did not return to work at once. When a small amount of moaning and groaning had finished, Jones made a call on his radio and as if by magic four buses turned up on cue and the men shuffled onto them. It was in the evening that Bob got his call to go and see Benjamin, by which time word had spread around and people that night started to work overtime. As Bob rode along with David Anthony who had come to pick him up, he looked out at the workers, who had decided to work overtime that evening. He was disappointed. The effort that they had put into it to have it ripped apart by a load of hotheads who could not wait until management gave in, as he was sure they would have soon, with the bad weather not far away. But then in a funny way he was pleased, not that they lost, but because it was over. He had become sick and tired of the rows and would be happy to move on. Tonight, would be a good chance to tell Benjamin he would resign from the committee.

*

"Come in, Bob, sit down. Would you like a coffee?"

"Oh, yes, that would be nice. Thank you, Kim."

"Sit down, make yourself comfortable."

"Kim, I didn't come here tonight for you to gloat, and I must admit I did think Reg and Dave would have already been here," replied Bob as he sat in one of the chairs facing Benjamin.

"Do you really think I'm the sort of person to gloat, Bob?" He passed him the cup and then sat facing him in his reclining leather chair.

"No, Kim, I don't as it goes. Thank you," he said, looking at his coffee.

140

"No, there was another reason I wanted to talk to you."

"Well," came the reply, "I was going to ask to see you about something also."

"Oh, I see. Okay, you go first."

"The thing is, Kim, I'm going to pack the committee in. I don't want to do it anymore, I am resigning."

"Why?" There was complete shock on Kim's face. He did not see this coming and could now see his plans falling apart in front of his eyes.

"Fed up with it. In fact, bloody pissed off. I didn't come here to do this, I'm a chippy, I work with wood, that's what I want to do. All this has caused me a load of hassle I really don't need. There will be others to take my place, no doubt they will do a better job than me."

"No, I do not think so. You have done a good job."

"I don't think so."

"You have done a lot for your workmates, and you have highlighted a lot of issues to us to help things run smoother here, Bob. The fact is I asked you here tonight for you to take on more of the role."

"What?" asked the puzzled committeeman.

"Bob," the project coordinator got up and walked around his desk and sat on the front of it facing Bob, "I want you to have time away from your work when needed. A Land Rover will be made available for you so that you can go and deal with problems that may crop up from time to time."

Bob could not believe what he was hearing. In fact, he did think of pinching himself at one stage in case he was dreaming. Many things were going through his mind, and the fact that he never saw this coming in a million years made it one of the biggest surprises he'd had since being out here. In fact, he could not think of a bigger one he'd had for a long time. "Look, Bob, I know this has come out of the blue, but I really want you to give this a lot of consideration as it would be a very important role. Oh, I know we have the welfare service here, but the lads won't really open up with them. I get far more feedback from you."

"There's no way I'm going to rat on any of the lads."

"I don't want you to, Bob, not at all. I know you are a man of high moral integrity. No, I want you to sort problems out for the workers, sort things out before they go too far, come to me, the other managers or welfare. We will back you up."

141

This was all too much for Bob to take in, but at the same time he did not want to show that to Benjamin as he knew far too well that a man of his intellect would take advantage of this. So, the only thing he could do was to retreat and live to fight another day.

"Look, Kim, this has been a real shock, so as you said I will take my time and then come back to you." He was almost out of his seat and had his hand out to shake Kim's as the coordinator said, "Take your time. I think you will find this a very worthwhile role. There are a lot of men who would like this opportunity, and I did think of others, but I need a man who is respected by the other workers and who I know I will get straight and true answers from." They shook hands and Bob left with Benjamin's words ringing in his ears, not really knowing if he was coming or going.

*

"So, what are you going to do?" And without giving Bob a chance to talk, Bill continued and answered it for him. "I would take it if I were you. There could be a lot of perks in a job like that you know, Bob, and that's not to mention the fact you could possibly sort problems out for old mates."

"I wondered when you would get around to that." The two sat in Bob's room on their own smoking and drinking tea.

"Where's he gone?" Bill pointed up to Colin's empty bunk.

"Oh, said he was going to watch a video."

"He seems to have been going out to a lot of videos since the women got here. I reckon he's poking one of them."

"No, he wouldn't do that," Bob said.

"You would never know what a man would do after months in a place like this. I mean, he never stops talking about shagging, does he? I think we should follow him one night, you know, find out what he is up to."

"Nooo, I couldn't do that. He has been a mate too long and it wouldn't be fair."

"Just an idea."

"Nooo!" They sat and smoked for a while in silence until Bob broke it by asking, "When are you moving in next door with Pete?"

"Tomorrow, as soon as Dusty has left for the boat. I can't believe that lucky bastard has pulled off a medivac, can you? I mean, I heard that it has all been put on, you know, all that falling

142

all over the place and having fits when there's loads of people about. They just had to give in. I mean, it's not good for the ones who are going to go around the fucking bend here. Still, I'm going to get a new room out of it, so all's well that ends well."

Bob was about to answer when there was a loud crash on the door, this followed by a lot of banging then the door swung open. In the entrance were Dusty and Pete holding each other up. As they had both grown beards in recent weeks, which had become the trend here with the winter coming on, they had both shaved half their beards and moustaches off, half of both their eyebrows and had shaved each other's hair in quarters. At this moment finding it hard to stand up because of excess alcohol, they gave the boys a rendition of the first line of the song "Sailing" before falling to the floor.

"Looks like you will be at home next door, Bill," Bob said to his friend.

Chapter 8

If it's not Nailed Down!

Bloody hell, this is cold, Bob thought to himself as he drove the Land Rover he had been allocated towards his first case as part-time workers liaison coordinator. He had refused to be called liaison officer as Benjamin had wanted to name him. He also made sure the "part-time" went in so as to let everyone know he was still doing his job, but also helping out when the lads had problems as he did not want people to think he was selling out to management. And the truth was it had gone okay up until now. He had talked it through with the other committee members. Dave had resigned as he didn't like the way the lads had turned on them at that last meeting, and his words were, "I'm not putting up with this shit." Reg was also going to pack it in but Bob talked him out of it, and he was happy with Bob's new role and Bob had insisted that they talk all cases through together, and Benjamin had agreed that should Bob feel the need to have Reg with him sometimes that would be okay.

The first of April had brought with it the first snow of winter. It had not lasted long but they were now getting snow most days at some point or another. With the winds blowing from the south the wind chill factor was the main problem because it was now feeling a lot colder than it was. Most of the lads' lips were cracking and splitting with the biting winds, Bob's included. For the first time in his life he was using a tube of lip cream he got from the camp shop to help ease the problem.

Bob was driving on the Stanley road which had now progressed a fair distance towards the capital. There had been a light snow falling since he had set off and he had been having a few problems with the conditions, but as luck would have it a large truck of some kind had gone just before him, and as the Land Rover had a wide wheel base he was just about able to keep in the tracks that the lorry had made, making his driving a bit easier. He had not caught sight of the other vehicle but was pleased it was helping him. He had been driving a while when he saw parked on the deserted road what had been making the marks in the snow. It was the diesel tanker, and the driver, Kev, was stood at the rear of it waving his arms at him to stop. Bob had hardly stopped when Kev who was a thickset lad in his early forties from the small Oxfordshire town of Wallingford jumped in with him. "Fuck, that's cold out there, lad." Kev was known around the camp as the country yokel, but he was far from a fool and very streetwise for a person who had spent most of his years in the country.

"You're not kidding, Kev, what happened to the lorry?"

"Conked out, packed up all together."

"Do you want me to radio in and get a fitter out to you?"

"No way. Nothing is working, no heat or anything, I could die waiting out here. No, I'll stick with you, then bring a fitter out later. Anyway, I could do with a break. So where are you headed, Bob?"

"I'm on my way out to the Stanley road gang. They have got a bit of a problem I have been asked to help with," he replied, as he pulled out and around the tanker that was now whiter then the dark blue it had started out as.

"Oh, I heard about your new job. How's it going?"

"I've done one or two bits and bobs, but this is really the first real one I have had to deal with to tell you the truth. So, were you on your way to diesel up for the road gang?"

"What?"

"It's just you being out here miles from anywhere. Are you going out to the Stanley road gang?"

"Oh yes, yes, me being out here, yes. I'm going out to them, yes."

That was bloody hard work, Bob thought to himself.

They did not talk much more for the remainder of the journey, mainly because Bob was finding the driving harder and harder. He had the windscreen wipers on full, and had gone some miles extra when a bus came into sight that had been parked across the road so that nothing could pass. It was an area of land that had small hills at each side of it and the road would go through the middle, the lads had nicknamed it "Elephant Canyon". No one seemed to know who came up with the idea or why, but it had stuck and now everyone knew it as that. Kev stayed in the Land Rover as the committeeman made his way through the now driving snow with his head bent over to stop it going in his eyes. "Bloody hell," he exclaimed as the folding doors shut behind him on the single-decker bus. "That is freezing out there."

"And that's just the start of it, lad," said Wolfie, the tall, slim, grey-haired and bearded Durham man in his middle-forties who greeted him at the doorway. "Mind you, when I worked in the Shetland Islands you could get worse than this every day. Yes, even in summer. Here, have a cup of tea, we brought plenty up in the flasks this morning, along with sandwiches as we knew today would be the start of THE SIEGE OF ELEPHANT CANYON." This brought a loud cheer from the other eight men in the bus.

"Thanks," said Bob as he took a cup of hot tea from one of the others then sat on one of the aisle seats at the front of the bus, and with the other hand took a cigarette from Wolfie who had lit it up for him. "Okay, lads, so far so good. Everything is okay. I got the message from Benjamin soon after start of play this morning to go and see him. I must say he was not happy, so I went through it all with him and I told him that I had already met with you all and that you were all unhappy about the amount of travelling that you have to do."

"And what did the toffee-nosed git have to say about that?" shouted one of the lads at the back.

"The thing is he was okay about it. I mean he threw in the thing about the contract saying a person would not get paid for any daily travel, but I did point out you could at one point be doing two hours each way on top of a twelve-hour day, and that if you did not get sorted out that you would all jack and go home on the next boat. Then he would have to get others to come out here each day."

"Here, lad," put in Wolfie, "we never told you to tell him we'd jack it in."

"Sometimes you have to bluff, big fellow."

"Oh, that's good, bluffing with another man's pissing job," the big man half mumbled to himself.

"Well the thing is he took it seriously. I explained that the others now living in the contractors' camp have about twenty minutes to travel to work at the most."

"So, what has been agreed?" asked Wolfie.

"He has said they will set a camp up out here for you as soon as they can. It will have a few cabins; a canteen and he will even set a bar up for you. In the meantime, he will meet you halfway with the travelling, that's paying one way." This news brought large cheers

146

from the workers on the bus. "Okay, if that's it and you're all happy, I have to dash. Can I tell him you'll go back to work?"

"Not in this fucking weather," shouted one wag from the back. This brought laughs from the others. Bob got to his feet and handed Wolfie the cup back.

"You done good, Bob lad, well done."

"Oh, by the way, Wolfie, I came across Diesel Kev the tanker driver who is on his way to you. He has broken down so I don't know when he will get here to diesel you up."

"Never."

"What?"

"Never. He never comes to us, lad, we have our own tanker with us all the time as we are so far out."

"So, what is he doing all the way out here?"

"Don't know, but when I was out in the bush in Australia, lad, this would have been no distance." At that point Bob decided he would take his chances outside and waved them all goodbye.

*

They were about to go past the tanker on the way back when Kev asked Bob to stop so he could get his cigarettes out of the tanker. Funny, Bob thought, as the cab was full of smoke when he got back in. Maybe he had run out. The Land Rover pulled up in front of the lorry; the snow had eased a reasonable amount but was still falling. While Bob was waiting he saw fresh tyre tracks going off onto a small side road which Bob thought was only used by locals. He could also see in his wing mirror an area of peat exposed as if something had been on it when it was snowing heavily. He saw at the same time Kev open the tanker's passenger door, remove something from the seat and place it in his pocket. He then returned to the Land Rover in what appeared to be a very happy mood.

"I am going to have to go back to the compound, Kev, to see Benjamin. Do you want me to drop you off at the fitter's yard?"

"Yeah, that will be just fine, my good man." If Bob could have put money on it he would have said that Kev was out there selling diesel to the locals. If he said something to him and it was not true it would make him look a real fool, but then again did he really care if he was flogging diesel to make a few extra quid? What the hell, he knew he drank a lot, and he had seen him in some of those

147

heavy-duty card schools that saw big amounts of money change hands at times, but there again he liked Kev and wouldn't have liked to have seen him sacked. But of course, there was the fact that he was now really curious to know if he was right or not, so maybe he could just test the water a little bit. That wouldn't hurt, would it?

"It looks like the boys will be getting a camp over there by Elephant Canyon soon, so that will be okay for you if you are ever there over dieseling up late. I mean you would be able to stay the night."

"No, I don't do them." Kev could have bitten his tongue off as soon as he realised what he had said, and it was just the opening Bob was looking for.

"Oh, sorry," Bob said as he put the wipers on full as the snow was falling heavily again. "I thought you said you were out there on your way to the road gang?"

"No, I had other things to do."

"What, out there?"

"What's it got to do with you anyway?"

"Nothing, nothing at all."

"Good, so let's drop it, okay?"

"Fine." Bob knew he had hit a nerve but didn't want to fall out with Kev. They drove in the deteriorating weather without another word towards the compound. They were now back on the main site roads with the snow coming down harder than ever when Kev broke the ice.

"Got any fags, Bob, I've run out?"

"Yeah, sure." Bob took a packet out of his coat pocket and handed them to his passenger. "Light me one could you please." Kev did this then passed it over. "Thanks, I thought you got yours out of the lorry?"

"For fuck's sake, what is it with the twenty fucking questions? I told you keep your nose out of my business will you."

"Kev, take it easy, I'm not getting at you."

"Right, that's it. Stop here, I'll walk back. Stop now."

"I can't let you out in this. No way."

"LET ME OUT!"

Visibility in the heavy snow was down to just a few yards and Bob had not turned his lights on. They were passing one of the turning points on the haul road that was used by the big machines

148

that kept the roads passable. They did not see until the last moment the big D8 reverse onto the road.

"BOB, WATCH OUT!" Kev cried out, but it was too late. Bob tried to brake but the Land Rover just slipped into the path of the machine that was backing across the road. On the rear of the machine was an arm with a very large curved-shaped metal tooth that was used for breaking rock. This smashed into the cab of the vehicle through the door then up through the roof. It was all Kev could do to scramble across the cab onto Bob's lap with the tooth missing him by inches. Their Land Rover was then pushed sideways across the road and then lifted up into the air, all the time the driver being unaware what had happened behind him. Bob was blowing the horn full blast, but with the noise of the machine and the fact that the driver had ear defenders on to minimise ear damage, and where they were hanging was in a blind spot meant they could have both been killed had it fallen off when it was way past the side of road with a very long drop below them. But luck was on their side as a tipper lorry was coming the other way and saw what was happening. The driver at first flashed his headlights at the D8 driver who thought he just wanted to pass. The driver stopped the lorry, jumped out and frantically waved for him to stop, which he did, and then to his horror saw what had happened. He pulled forward so the Land Rover was back on the road and then lowered the vehicle to the ground with a thump. As soon as this happened the driver's door opened and the two fell out.

The lorry driver took the two of them back to the camp where they got checked over in the medical centre leaving the battered Land Rover on the side of the road. Bob then made his way to the compound to tell the fitters what had happened. After a lot of ribbing and a much-needed cup of tea and a cigarette the foreman fitter, Tony, a tall, thin man in his mid-thirties from Newbury in Berkshire, took Bob with another fitter to collect the Land Rover in their pick-up truck. Neither Bob nor the others could believe the sight that greeted them when they arrived at the spot of the accident.

*

"What do you mean stripped?" asked Bill as he sat in the armchair waiting for Bob to make the tea.

"Just like I said. It was stripped. Word must have got around on the radios, and as you can't get Land Rover parts here for love nor money everyone and his dog must have made their way over there. You would not believe it. When we got there the first thing we saw was it was up on concrete blocks and the wheels and nuts had gone."

"Well you just can't get spare Land Rover tyres here at the moment. No one leaves them on their bonnet anymore, they all lock them in the backs of the Rovers at night because they all get nicked," put in Colin from his top bunk.

"Well that was just the start," continued Bob as he carried on making the tea. "The seats had gone, the diesel cans in the back, the bulbs out of the lights, spark plugs, the wheel jack and spanners, they even took the fucking fags I left. If it wasn't nailed down it went. In fact, even that didn't stop the thieving bastards."

"Things are getting nicked all the time now. I heard the other day that loads of lockers have been broken into to get the long camouflage coats we got when we first got here, the ones they call the pioneer coats. They don't give them out anymore so everyone's nicking them," commented Bill from the armchair as he leant forward and took the cup of tea off Bob.

"You could have got killed," put in Colin.

"I must admit as we were going up in the air after the fucking tooth had ripped through, I wondered if that was it."

"I bet a couple of new pairs of underpants were needed," smiled Bill.

"Not many. Diesel Kev was screaming and shouting as he jumped up on me."

"I don't blame him," put in Colin. "I would have been the same." He then swung his legs around so that he was sitting on the top bunk. "Okay, I'm off out." He then jumped down to the ground.

"Video is it?" asked Bill from the armchair.

"Yes."

"What's on?" asked Bob.

"Oh, I am not sure. Will just go and have a look. See you later." He then quickly looked in the mirror over the basin, plumped his hair up with his hands, turned and left the room. As soon as the door shut Bob went to his wardrobe and took out a small hand mirror and passed it to Bill who went and slightly opened the door. He then held the looking glass by the open door

150

so that he could see the reflection of Colin walking along the corridor.

"He has turned left at the end, not right."

"Okay, go, go and go!" said Bob. The two would-be private detectives left the room at speed and headed for the area that their prey had last been seen, almost knocking over one worker coming out of his room which resulted in Bob shouting, "Sorry!" over his shoulder as they fled the scene. At the far end of the corridor they turned left after passing the drying room, and with the fire door not far around the corner Bill stopped as he could see Colin walking along through the glass viewing panel. As he had stopped so abruptly Bob crashed into him making a loud noise which made the person they were following turn around, but as they both fell over he did not see them rolling on the ground behind the door. They both managed to regain their standing position in time to see Colin enter a room at the other end of the corridor which housed the women workers. Bob at seeing this shook his head and made off back towards his room without saying a word to Bill.

*

The haul roads were holding up but it was a non-stop job to keep them open, and it was taking far more crushed rock than had ever been imagined. Another crusher had now been ordered for the next cargo ship as the amount of rock needed for the roads was interfering with production needed for concrete and other materials. The fact that the overtime ban had now been lifted was seen as a great victory by the management. Kim had never wanted to lose that one, and had never conceded how close it had come, but he knew in his heart of hearts that was the turning point of the contract.

A lot of workers were now working overtime; some areas had started working twelve-hour shifts around the clock, seven days a week. The quarry was the first to go onto this to keep the project supplied with rock. The manager there had already asked for more lorries and machines to load them to keep up with the demand.

Benjamin held a meeting with all section managers to ascertain what was needed most. It came over loud and clear that it was machines – diggers, lorries and of course spare parts for these. The project coordinator was also pleased to get feedback that it seemed most of the men were pleased that the overtime ban had finished and they could now do the thing they had come to do: earn lots of tax-free money. He made a phone call to London that night to change supplies on the next cargo ship. "I don't care what you take off, food, clothes, safety gear or anything, just get me more equipment."

Mechanics, plant fitters and welders could not work spilt shifts as there was not enough of them, but they were working very long days keeping the project running. Benjamin made it clear to the managers at the meeting that now the overtime was back on that it was not a free for all for the workers to print money, and that they should monitor who was working on what and only work overtime when they wanted them to. But plant and repair workshops were ones that could work any number of hours as long as the work was there, but with their compound full of machinery which was not working for one reason or another there was little chance of the fitters not being wanted to work overtime.

Progress on the main camp was on time, and the large steel frame that was to be the recreation centre had now been covered in all around with green steel sheet cladding. The concrete floor was finished and all metal studwork inside that would form the partitions that would be covered in plasterboard. That in turn would form the different areas within there.

Two very large bars the size of football pitches were next to each other and toilet areas where the beer could be disposed of. There were two large video rooms which would have big screens in each, and there was a snooker room that would have three full-size tables and a reading room that a person could loan books and also sit and read if one so wished.

In the wide corridor that was outside the video rooms was the area put aside for ten public telephones that could be used to ring the UK or any other part of the world with the use of a phone card that could be purchased from the camp shop. Benjamin had hoped the bars and other areas would be open for the next *Kenya*'s arrival as it would then release the staff canteen that was being used as a bar for the purpose it was meant for. It would have also coincided with the Easter weekend that saw Good Friday on 20th April that year. It was hoped to open on the Saturday night as a morale boost. Large arc lights could be seen burning late into the night.

Stealing had been on the increase, not only petty pilfering but a lot of section compounds had been targeted. Cookers had been taken out of canteens and fridges had also disappeared. Machinery

152

had been taken at night and moved to other sections, and that was apart from the batteries being taken off machines, or buckets to diggers going missing. This had come to annoy the project coordinator very much, the endless taking of property that did not belong to a person. With this in mind, along with the fact that the firebug still seemed to be with them, and also the night before the camp had seen its first reported "mugging", he had asked Karl Davis to join him that morning.

"Well, Karl, I knew there would be problems here, but things seem to be getting worse and worse, and very fast at that." They were not sat at Kim's desk but in two of his Chesterfield leather armchairs, drinking coffee at one end of the office with a small table between them which held the pot and cups and a plate of biscuits.

The two had got on very well in the short time the security man had been on the island. They had talked over what had happened regarding the mistake over Hack, and to Karl's delight Kim had taken it very well and was pleased that they had got rid of the drug dealer anyway.

They seemed to have a lot in common, not least of all, politics and classical music, so it was to this theme they had spent many off-duty hours when they had then enjoyed the tapes of Mozart, Tchaikovsky, Brahms, Beethoven and many others that Benjamin had brought with him. They would drink coffee and the odd brandy as they chatted about political and world events, but this time it was only business that the project coordinator had on his mind.

"Yes, I know, Kim, I rang a friend of mine in the Met the other day, and he said the word is that with a lot of the criminals from a lot of cities that are coming here, a lot of coppers are having extra holidays!" This only brought a small smile to Kim's face as it was something he did not want to hear but was starting to believe. "And if we went through everyone's past record we would have to deport anyone who has served more than six months in prison. That is the rule of this island."

"Yes, I know, but the thing is even I know that there are times when the rules have to be bent. My good God, if we played to those rules I think you and I would have to be out there digging holes." This brought a smile and a laugh from both of them.

"I am afraid I've more bad news, Kim, and that is that in the past few nights buses have been stolen and have been used to joyride. It would seem a person has a universal key to get in and start them. They have been driving around the work areas like lunatics. I believe at one point they nearly turned one over! I say 'they' because I believe there's a few of them, and they have a party on the buses so they are in fact drunk while driving."

"Oh, my good God!" came the reply from the ashen-faced coordinator. "We must stop this at once."

"I intend to, Kim, I have people working on it now, and we will be ready for them next time I can assure you."

In fact, Karl had to wait some time before the team he had lying in wait at the bus park saw any action. They had taken over a room that overlooked the parking area and two men sat and waited each night with radios poised for the "Night Riders" as they had been nicknamed to strike. In fact, the time it did occur they almost missed it for somehow, they got on the bus without being seen at all, and it was only when the bus roared into life at midnight on a Wednesday night that the two jumped up, radioed ahead, then ran out to their Land Rover to pursue the partygoers.

The bus drove for some miles around the haul roads before the other Land Rovers that were meant to have blocked the road off could find it. From the pursuing vehicle music could be heard playing loud from the bus and it was also very obvious that alcohol was being drunk. By the time it headed back to the camp there were a lot of Karl's men waiting, and had it not been for the fact that he had so many of them the Night Riders may have got away again. As they entered the bus loading area and saw the large welcoming reception they pulled up a few hundred yards before them and made a run for it, but they were all caught before they could disappear into their rooms. They were all from Erect-A-Com and were sacked and removed from camp the next day. Their manager, Dave Waters, had gone and seen Kim Benjamin the next morning and asked him to let them off with a final warning and maybe a fine as he needed them for the amount of work he needed to complete in a short space of time. But the project coordinator had made up his mind and was not going back on it.

"Dave, there is much unruliness occurring here and I intend to stamp it out. I do understand you need these men but if I let them off it will be a clear sign to others that these things can be got away with. I have been told that the talk among the workers was these Night Riders, as they had become known, had an almost hero following. No, I am sorry, they must go, and that is the last I will say on the matter. Good day, David."

*

"What do you think of it, Bob?" asked Colin as the two friends, also Bill and Pete, sat at a very large round table in one of the newly opened large bars.

"Well with a bit of luck it won't be so packed in here, and with the next boat about to come in this should help things," replied his roommate.

"It's a bit like sitting under a motorway bridge," remarked Bill, which brought a laugh from the others and also made them look up at the high ceiling and the large concrete clad steel columns that supported it.

"Yes, it is a bit like that," put in Pete.

"There's an old tramp who lives under part of the M4 near where I live in Chiswick, London," observed Colin.

"I suppose this place could end up with a few tramps sleeping here before the night is out," remarked Bill. This brought laughter from all.

"Here you go, boys." They turned to see Andy appear at the table with a trayful of beer glasses, which he put on the table and handed around to his mates.

"Plastic glasses," remarked Bob as he took his drink. "Oh, I hate them."

"Surely it's better than drinking out of them than it is from the beer cans that we have been," put in Colin.

"Yes, I suppose so," came the reply.

"And of course, you can't hurt anyone by throwing these things around the place," remarked Bill as he looked at his glass.

"Yes, you're right," put in Pete. "If a fight started and a person stood on a table and was lobbing glass ones about you could soon have a small riot on your hands." This comment brought puzzled looks from the others. "Well, that's if a person was inclined to chuck glasses that is."

"Inclined to do what?" asked Wolfie as he joined them at the table, beer glass in hand.

"Hi, big man," said Bill. "Sit down and join us." Wolfie pulled a seat from under the table and sat down.

"Now, what did you say was going on?"

155

"Oh, Pete was just saying that if these were glass and a fight broke out they would make a mess of someone," Colin informed the newcomer.

"Cor, I would say that he is right," put in the big grey-haired man as he took a drink. "We were in a bar in Hamburg, or was it Warsaw? No, it was Hamburg. We had a good drink and we had a mouthy Londoner with us. No offence, lads."

"None taken," replied Bob, as Colin smiled.

"A bouncer came over to us and asked us to keep the noise down, which was okay as we had got a bit loud, but our southern mate told him to fuck off. Well, the thing is no matter where you are in the world 'fuck off' is pretty universal. Everyone knows it no matter what the lingo is, lads, that and Coca Cola, they are known the world over."

"What happened?" asked Bob.

"Well, this bouncer jumped up in front of him, arms and legs going all over the place, and said, 'I learnt this in Japan,' meaning kung fu. Well, the lad jumped up, picked up a big glass ashtray, and said. 'I learnt this in Hamburg,' and hit him right between the eyes with it. Down he went like a sack of shit." The others greeted this information in stunned silence. "Yes, it was Hamburg, we got deported, and from France. Paris in fact after another small riot."

"God, what happened there, Wolfie?" asked Colin.

"Oh, me and a mate of mine were going to work our way around the world for the 1970 football World Cup in Mexico." He took another drink then lit up one of Bob's cigarettes that were on the table. "We got to Paris the first night and had got fixed up with a job for the next day. That afternoon England beat France at rugby and we did manage to tell them about it a few times. The next thing you know all hell broke out. Can't take getting beat those frogs, they said we started it, chucked us in jail and sent us back to the UK the next day."

"So how long did your around the world trip last, Wolfie?" asked Bill.

"Aha, well, I suppose in fact you could say it was one day." This brought a round of laughter from everyone.

"Have you been chucked out of any other countries?" asked Andy.

"Not really, but I did get my passport stamped."

"How do you mean?" asked Bob with a puzzled look on his face.

"I was working in Poland, Warsaw in fact. Fags and booze were so cheap there in them days, well everything was, we all moved out of the camp they built for us and hired apartments. No one went to work on the bus, we all bought our own cars. Boy, the girls flocked around us. It was great."

"So, what was it with the passport?" asked Pete.

"Every time we came home we all brought back loads of cigarettes and drink. We all filled our suitcases to sell at home. The thing is customs got on to it and this time we landed at Newcastle Airport. The plane was full of us workers and they sent us to a large shed as soon as we got off and they just ripped us all apart. We had all our gear taken off us, then we got fined and had our passports stamped 'International Smuggler'. It's a fair old show off."

"I bet," said Andy.

"Oh, if you ever want to smuggle anything in just walk behind me. They will be too busy jumping all over me, it happens every time." This brought a round of laughter from all those at the table.

Two of Eastham's female employees came into the bar and headed over to the table that the lads occupied. Colin got up and greeted them, then told everyone at the table, "This is Sally." A very pretty, slim lady in her late twenties with short blond hair. She nodded her hellos to all, then introduced her friend in her Glasgow accent.

"This is Jill." A dark-haired woman about the same age as her friend.

The bar was fast becoming packed with workers wanting to enjoy the end of the working week and the new bar, and the fact that it was Easter weekend.

The mood at the table was very happy with much laughter and a large amount of canned beer being consumed. It was noticeable that Bob did not look across the table where Colin and Sally were sat together very close, and what could not be seen was that they were holding hands under the table. After a while Bob left for the toilet. He was about to leave the large empty room when Colin entered.

"Alright, Bob?"

"Yeah." He then tried to move around Colin who was near the door.

"What do you think?"

"Think of what?"

"Sally."

"She seems okay." He shrugged his shoulders.

"Is that it?"

"What do you want me to say?" Bob asked.

"Well, I want you to be okay with it. You're my best friend."

"You want me to be okay with you shagging another woman when your wife and kids are sat at home? You want me to give you my blessing or something, would that make it alright?"

"No, I just want us to be okay."

"Colin, there is no way I'm going to be happy about this, but what you get up to is up to you. I'm not your keeper."

"I mean you won't be telling anyone at home about this, will you?"

"No, I won't," he snapped.

"Still mates?" Colin held his hand out to shake. As he did this Bill walked into the toilets and Bob walked out without shaking hands.

"Everything okay, Col?" asked Bill.

"I don't know, mate. I don't think so."

*

Over the next few days things were very frosty between the two roommates and it seemed Bob tried to avoid Colin, but it was the latter that stopped eating with his regular dinner pals as he could then be seen in the canteen with Sally. But as Bob later told Bill, "He could have been knocked over by a feather," when his roommate told him he was moving in with Sally.

Before Bob knew what was happening Bill moved in with him telling him, "You never know what wanker they will put in with you." Bob only smiled at this. "And with all the nicking going on you're better off with a mate."

"I did think that about the last one!" came the reply.

Chapter 9

What Goes Around, Comes Around!

Colin stood beside the four-foot by four-foot and six-foot long silent compressor waiting for the fitter to turn up and repair it. It was a bitter cold winter's morning with the wind blowing very strongly, but so far that day the snow had kept off, which was a blessing. In his role as foreman Colin needed the machine for his men to vibrate the concrete, which would soon arrive. As he tried to keep warm he had many thoughts going through his mind. He hated this place to bits and could not wait to get out of here, with his leave now not too far off and oh boy he couldn't wait. On the other hand, he had met Sally and that had been really great. She had been so alive he had fallen for her very quickly after they met. They had sat together one night in the video room and had got chatting then Colin asked her to have a drink with him afterwards, which she agreed to. They seemed to have a lot in common and liked a lot of the same things. They met again for another video after that and then wow! it had just taken off, but Colin did regret falling out with Bob, and of course there was a chance he may mention things to his wife Jane.

"How silly am I?" he asked himself. If he was found out it could be the end of his marriage. Could Jean find out with him being eight thousand miles from home? It was really only Bob who could spill the beans, and he didn't think he would do it on purpose, but then he was very upset with him about it all. On the other hand, he was enjoying being with Sally very much and, well, the sex was out of this world, and now they were living together. Now it was every night and they had sorted a weekend away together in the capital before he went on leave. On top of that he had good tax-free money going in the bank each month, so maybe life was not so bad after all.

"You Colin?" He looked up to see a Land Rover had pulled up alongside him. A round, red-faced man in his late twenties sat behind the wheel. He had the hood of a parka coat pulled up over his head and was wearing gloves.

"Yes."

"I'm Jon Derby, the fitter. I'm here to fix the compressor."

"Oh yes, great." The fitter got out, walked over to the foreman and shook hands.

"God, it seems colder here than up at the plant compound."

"You're right, Jon, we are higher up here, and the wind just whistles around this camp. It has been a lot worse at times."

"I only came out on the last boat. You been here long?"

"Well it seems as if I was born here." The fitter smiled at this. "We came out on the boat last December, spent Christmas here and will do this year as well."

"I am hoping to swing leave for Christmas or the New Year."

"You'll be lucky. Everyone who has leave around then will want that."

"Yeah, so what's the problem with this then?" He hit the machine.

"It's not working," laughed Colin.

"I mean do you know the problem?"

"It was working this morning and just packed up."

"Look, do you want to show me how it works?"

"What?" asked Colin with disbelief in his voice.

"Well the thing is I have never worked on one of these before. In fact I have only ever seen them at the roadsides at home."

"This is a wind-up, isn't it?"

"No. Look, I'm a petrol lorry mechanic, and that's what I came here as, not a diesel plant fitter. Yes, I have been around machines since I left school, but not this sort." There was silence for a moment as Colin took the news in. This was broken only when a Land Rover pulled up beside them and George called out of the window to them.

"Have you not sorted that out yet? The concrete will be here soon."

The two men beside the compressor looked at each other and Colin said, "Yeah, almost, soon have it fixed, George. No problem."

"Well done, bonny lad. Get it done." He moved off without saying another word.

"So that's George, is it?"

"Yes, that is he."

"Seems the pig everyone says he is."

"Oh yes, he can be, bonny lad," Colin mocked. "But he has a lot of pull around here, knows people in high places and gets on well with them. He is one of the African Mafia as they call them. Upset him and you are as good as done for, yet on the other hand... Well, the thing is, we are all here to make money. Basically, get on with George and he will look after you."

"What, make people up to foreman you mean?" Colin thought about that and knew the fitter was fishing, and he was not going to bite.

"In some cases, maybe and the big pay rise that goes with it. Now, what are we going to do about this then?" He tapped the yellow compressor.

"I am really not sure. What do you think?"

"Well, it was running, then it stopped."

"Did it have a full tank of diesel fuel last night?"

"No, it was filled up this morning," reported the foreman.

"A half-empty tank will form condensation when it is as cold as it has been."

"I know what you mean. Condensation makes water, water in diesel is not good."

"Do you know where the fuel pump is?" asked Jon.

"Yes, it's around the other side." They both walked around the machine and opened the other flap to see the glass bowl below the pump half full of water. The two smiled at each other then set about fixing the problem. Within a few minutes the machine roared into life. The two exchanged a handshake before Colin invited Jon to his container for a warm up and a cup of tea.

"My good God, it is good to get out of that wind," remarked Jon.

"Yes, you're right, and it is trying to snow now," came the reply.

"It's not a very nice place here, is it?"

"No, it's not. Still, we are not here for the weather or the wildlife, are we?"

"No," replied the fitter, "but it would be nice if a person could make a few extra quid. If they could, that is."

"Well now the overtime ban is over a person could mount up a fair few extra pounds," said Colin as he passed Jon a hot cup of

161

tea, then sat down on the same bench with him in the container. "And of course, that is the case with you fitters. You can work as many hours as you like."

"There could be other ways."

"How do you mean?"

"Well," Jon looked about the container as if the walls had ears, "you must keep this to yourself."

"Of course. What?"

"Scrap."

"Scrap?" asked Colin.

"Yes, scrap metal, copper, all sorts. It's laying all over the place, heaps and heaps out there just waiting to be picked up and sold for lots of money."

"You can't just pick it up."

"Why not?" the fitter asked, and before Colin could answer he continued. "My friend Jason, Jason Copaz, he is the one who got me out here. I have known him for years, he has sorted it all out."

"There is no way that Benjamin would let us do it."

"Sorted," smiled Jon. "Jason has been and seen them and it is sorted. It's clearing up the site. As long as we do it in our own time it's okay with them."

"How could you sell it out here?"

"Jason has a mate who is working in Stanley. He can get rid of it for us. Jason drives low-loaders so we just load up containers and he takes them over there and sells them and we make loads and loads of money."

Colin sat there thinking about what he had just heard. He lit a cigarette and then asked, "Why are you telling me?"

"We need another to help collect it all."

"Why me?"

"Well, first I've taken to you and you have access to a Land Rover. Mine is full all the time and others use it, and I'm sure we could trust you. It's all set up and really needs to be done now, and we need help. What do you think?"

"Let me think about it." The two sat in silence. The container door was slightly ajar behind where Colin was sitting and Jon noticed that snow was now falling very heavily and was starting to settle outside. Colin put out his cigarette in the ashtray on the table beside them. He looked at the fitter then held out his hand to shake Jon's and said, "Okay, I'm in."

162

Jon took the offered hand. "Well done, but we must keep this to ourselves, partner."

*

"I really don't believe they are doing that," commented Bob.

"They're a bunch of wankers," reported Bill. The four lads who were all sat together at the same dinner table looked at the dark night with the rain pouring down. Andy and Pete were now roommates. Andy had moved in with Pete when Bill moved out. They all looked out of the window at the scene that was before them outside. Two long tables with chairs each side had about twelve Erect-A-Com workers sat around them. They were all dressed in orange waterproofs and two of Eastham's chefs were serving them. They had four crates of beer on the table that was going down as fast as the rain.

"When I was in New Zealand there were days when we had to stay out in weather like that." The lads turned to see Wolfie standing at the end of the table with a cup of tea in his hand. They all said their hellos.

"Do you mind if I join you, lads?"

"Sit down, big man," Bill invited the newcomer. Andy and Pete who sat across from Bill and Bob moved on towards the window so that Wolfie could sit on the end chair.

"If they had to do that day in and day out they wouldn't be laughing I can tell you." Wolfie pointed out of the window at those lit up by arc lights, and with the rain now heavier than ever all of them now had their hoods up as protection against the deluge.

"So, Wolfie," said Bill, "what do you know? Any gossip, rumours, stories, news, lies? We'll accept anything as long as it's new."

"I could give loads of lies," laughed Pete.

"Well as it goes," said Wolfie as he leant across the table and took one of Bob's cigarettes then lit it.

"Do help yourself," smiled Bob.

"Thanks. Now, where was I?"

"You were about to tell us what you have heard," snapped Bill, impatient for the news and information.

"Yes, I did hear that two twin sisters from Eastham's who have just come out are on the game." No one said a word but just looked at him. "You know, flogging their fannies."

163

"Who are they?" asked Andy.

"Don't know, but I tell you what, I have never paid for it in all my life and won't start now. Came close in Bannock once but never did."

Everyone nodded their agreement apart from Pete who said, "Don't know what's up with you all. There's no problem with paying for a shag. In a place like this it would be worth it, wouldn't it?"

"Whatever turns you on," said Bob.

"Well, your mate's lucky. Getting it for free that is. I'll pay, just point to where they are." This comment from Pete brought smiles all round, even from Bob who didn't like talking about what Colin was up to.

"Talking of your mate Colin, what is he up to? He has been seen picking up scrap all over the place," asked Wolfie.

"Don't know, I don't see much of him these days."

"He must have somewhere to flog it," said Andy. "I've heard about it. He must have tons and tons by now, he's not saving it to take on the *Kenya*, is he?" This remark brought a smile from everyone at the table apart from Bob.

"He must have told you something," said Pete.

"Why should he? I'll say it again, I'm not his keeper," snapped Bob.

"Cool, man, I only asked."

"Well don't fucking ask," snapped Bob. He got up and walked away from the table.

All was quiet with those remaining until Wolfie said, "Do you think he's upset?"

"Oh," said Bill, "his mate has really pissed him off. He just doesn't want to talk about it."

"And also," laughed Andy, "on top of all of that he's now got you as a roommate." Bill just looked at Andy in return for the comment.

"I wish I was getting it for free," said Pete.

"Look as those daft bastards," pointed Wolfie out of the window. They all turned to see one of the diners outside who was now on the table and had started to strip his clothes off.

"Hope he gets pneumonia," smiled Andy.

"Double," laughed Bill. "Let's give it to him with both lungs."

"Where did you say the twins lived?" asked Pete.

164

The whole of the camp and compound area were fed by very large generators that produced electricity. In all there were eight of these running at all times with two as standby. Each one stood approximately three-metres high by two-metres wide and five-metres long. These were all stood side by side with a three-metre gap between them on a steel reinforced concrete slab. They had all been covered by a large scaffold which in turn had been covered by tarpaulins and metal sheets with vents out of the top for exhaust fumes to escape into the open air.

At one end of the set up was a ten-metre by three-metre Portakabin which was divided into two, one being used as a workshop area and the other as an office and rest area for the two men that worked twelve hours a day each, seven days a week to maintain, fuel and keep them running in general.

It was debatable if keeping these going was in fact the most important job on the project, as with oil and fuel to be kept topped up and small repairs it was a busy time to keep them running, also a very noisy and dirty operation, but one that was liked by Gordon Johnston, a short Scotsman in his late thirties who covered the day shift. He was almost his own boss and he enjoyed being on own, but also liked people popping in to see him as Colin had done now who sat taking a cup of tea with him. But there were also other reasons he was here to see Gordon.

The generator set up was about forty metres off the main haul road between the camp and compound. A road ran up to and behind them for access, but the area behind which was hidden from view was being used as a storage area for the scrap metal. Almost every night Colin would drop a load off there and put it into a large metal container which could hold a large amount of scrap. In turn when it was full it would be picked up by Jon and Jason and taken away. Gordon had been talked into helping out by his friend Colin with a promise of a drink when they got the money.

"You have been really busy haven't you, getting all that scrap, Col? You must have sent tons and tons in the past few weeks over to Stanley. I mean they have picked it all up from here, but it is you who has done all the hard work finding it and all."

"Oh, I don't care, it has passed the time. Anyway, it is just lying around out there. It's a wonder others' have not been doing it," reflected Colin as he lay back in the armchair that Gordon had for visitors as he drank tea and enjoyed a cigarette.

"I have been into scrap over the years you know," replied the engineer. "I've done a bit of buying and selling and all that, and the truth is there's a lot of money in what you have picked up. I mean it would have been thousands."

"Yes, I know, we have got a whole lot of money to come," he smiled. "Things have got very good just lately, and I'm off for a lovely weekend break away from this shithole. Then, just after that, I will be going home and with loads of extra cash into the bargain. Take the wife and kids away for a good holiday, a few nights out with the lads, can't be bad."

"All sounds good," observed Gordon. "I just hope it all works out right for you. I mean you have fallen out with your best mate as you said."

"Oh, Bob will be fine. He's just got the arseholes, that's all. He will come around. We have got two weeks together on the ship, we will have a few beers one night, kiss and make up and everything will be fine, you wait and see. I never thought I would feel like this here, but it just goes to show you miracles do happen."

"I'm pleased for you, Colin, and I don't want to be a spoilsport, but life does have a way of coming up behind you and biting you on the arse sometimes."

"I know, Gordon, and thanks for thinking about me, but this is my time. I know life is picking up for me, I just know it."

"Well good," replied the generator maintenance man. "I'm really pleased for you. Here." He held up his plastic tea cup to Colin and they knocked them together and gave a joint, "Cheers!"

*

The mid-afternoon winter sun reflected off the sea and was beginning to set behind the twin peaked mountains that overlooked the town. Colin and Sally had just emerged from a pub after enjoying a lunch of roast beef and all the trimmings. Their weekend away from the camp together was almost over. They had spent the previous night in a bed and breakfast, but Colin had to convince the landlady they were married before she would allow them to have the key to the room.

They had spent most of the Monday morning they both had off in lieu of overtime worked wandering around the shores of the

166

town. The wind had been sharp but they did not seem to care as they walked hand in hand. They walked past Government House where they took photographs of each other outside and was told by an official whom they had started talking to how the house had been taken over during the invasion, and that bullet holes that had been sprayed in the walls by machine gun fire were always going to be left there as a reminder.

Many other photos had been taken on their morning out. Neither of them had seen a satellite dish the size of the giant one that sat back a few metres from the main road that ran though the town. This of course was the main link between the island and the rest of the world.

They got a passer-by to snap both of them under the four large whalebones that were stood up together and joined at the top to form a monument. Colin felt it may be best if that one was on Sally's camera only. That was also the case when he snapped her as she sat on a very old cannon which was near the harbour's shore. In the background was a concrete pier which ran out into the bay with a boathouse at the far end which had a sail boat moored at it.

"Can things get much better than this?" Colin asked Sally as they walked away from the pub. "This has been a great weekend. I mean, what a lovely way to finish, a fine meal, a few beers and a nice walk with a beautiful young lady." He turned swiftly in front of her and gave her a quick kiss on the lips.

"Yes, it can," the female by his side replied.

"Sorry?"

"Things could get better."

"How do you mean?"

"I felt really good yesterday when you told the landlady we were married."

"The old bag wouldn't have let us in otherwise, would she?"

"I know, but it was just nice."

"Sally, what are you trying to say?"

"Oh, I don't know. You're going home in a short time and I won't be seeing you for two months." It was at this point that she wiped a tear from eye. "I want that again, I want us to get married."

They stopped on the footpath. It was as if Colin had to take this in. After a few moments he said, "You know I can't. I am married already."

"Divorce. When you go home you will have time. File for divorce. We could be wed by this time next year." If the first comment had shocked him, this one blew him away.

"I... I can't. We are taking the kids on holiday, you know that."

"Well that's what I can't take. You're going home to enjoy yourself and I am here waiting for you to come back. I AM JUST A BIT ON THE SIDE."

As she said this her voice raised and two soldiers walking on the other side of the road looked over at them and one called out, "Are you okay, love?"

"Yes, I'm fine, thank you," she replied in her soft Scottish tone. They continued walking without talking. Sally had tears running down her red cheeks. After a few minutes of silence Colin stopped and said, "Look, I never knew you felt like this."

"How many times have you said you love me?"

"Well... loads," he replied.

"So, do you not think I feel the same?"

"I know you do. It's just..."

"It's just I am a handy shag while you're on the other side of the world. You'll get home and start bonking her and your bit on the side will be forgotten about until you come back!"

"You know that's not the case, Sally."

"Do I? Do I now? Well the fact is, Colin, I don't know!"

"Look!"

"No! No! I won't look. You have made your point. I really don't want to talk about it again!"

"Sally, we have to talk about it. Now!"

"Now? I have brought it up and blown your socks off. Well I'll tell you what, Colin Watson. GO FUCK YOURSELF!" She walked off wiping her face leaving Colin stood by himself.

On the return flight to West Cove airfield the two did not talk at all. Sally spent it looking out of the window staring as they passed over the hills, fields, lakes, and near its final destination they flew along the airfield which now had over half of the peat stripped. Colin sat next to her in the aisle seat with a fixed look on the floor.

Colin took no notice of the staff Land Rover parked in front of the bus that was waiting beside the airstrip to take them back to the camp as he walked towards it. Nor did he pass any comment on the fact that Karl Davis the security manager and section manager

168

Arran Jones were stood by the door to the bus until he went to get on. Jones nodded towards him for Karl to see.

"Colin Watson?" asked Davis as he approached him.

"Yes," came the reply.

"Could you come with us please?"

"Why?" asked a surprised Colin.

"We will explain everything once we get to the office," responded Davis. The other passengers from the flight were now standing viewing what was going on. "If you don't mind," Karl said in a now almost pleading voice so they could move away from the crowd.

"What's going on?" asked Sally as Colin started to walk to the Land Rover.

"I don't know. I will meet you back at the room soon." He was ushered into the vehicle by Karl and they were gone.

The three of them sat in Karl's office. He offered Colin a drink which he refused and said, "Can we just get on with this?"

"Okay, we have information that you have been collecting scrap metal and have been selling it," the security manager told Colin.

"Yes," the Londoner replied. "It's all above board, we have had permission from Kim Benjamin."

"You asked him?" put in Jones, the first time he had spoken.

"No, the other lads did."

"What other lads?" asked Karl.

"Jason Copaz and the fitter Jon Derby."

"Would you be surprised to know that Kim knows nothing about it? In fact, it is he who wants this sorted out. He will not have thieving," replied the security manager.

"Thieving? I have not been fucking thieving."

"Calm down, Colin," said Arran. Karl had been looking at a list in front of him since Colin had named the others.

"Colin, the two names you gave me. I thought I knew them. They resigned this morning and sailed on the *Kenya* about an hour ago." Colin sat in the chair and his mouth went so dry he thought he would be unable to speak when it was required of him. He was also unable to think straight and really didn't want to say anything until his mind was clear again.

Silence filled the air for a moment or two. Colin was about to speak when Karl passed him some paper that had been on the desk. "This is your termination of contract notice. It has been made up from this evening. Your contract will terminate with immediate effect for gross misconduct, but as you will not be able to leave until the next ship comes in a month's time you will be allowed to continue working. Should you not do so you will be billed for your bed and board for the month." When asked if there were any questions he just shook his head.

*

"I've been set up! Oh, have I been fucking set up?" Colin sat on the edge on the double bed in Sally's room smoking a cigarette. It was in fact two single beds pushed together.

"Do you really know that?" asked his girlfriend as she sat next to him, passing him a glass of beer that she had just poured.

"Thanks." He took a large sip then continued. "Yes, it all fits in now. I was just too silly to see it, or more to the point too fucking greedy." Sally put her arm around him but could feel the tension in his body.

"Do you want me to rub your back?"

"Yes, that would be nice," replied Colin. She knelt on the bed behind him and started rubbing. As a trained masseur as well as hairdresser it was not long before she had relaxed him by rubbing and kneading his shoulders. "No, the bastards have ripped me off! They would have got thousands and thousands for that lot, and it was me who had done nearly all the fucking work." Colin had to admit that with the treatment his back was getting, a cigarette in one hand and a beer in the other, things were good, apart from the fact he had just lost his job.

"Go and see Bob," Sally put in.

"Why?"

"Because he knows Benjamin. Surely if anyone could get you off the hook he could."

"No way, we have fallen out. I can't ask him."

"Even if it saves your job and you can be with me when your leave is over?"

"I don't like to. It's like creeping back to him."

"Well, my wee man, maybe there are times in life when we have to do that to make things better. For ourselves that is."

"I just don't know."

"Put that cigarette and beer down and I'll help you change your mind, darling Colin."

170

"Now that does sound like a good idea."

*

"I was sat just behind him at breakfast and he really chucked up," said Bill as he sat in the armchair in his and Bob's room drinking tea. Pete was in the other chair and Bob was laid on his bottom bunk.

"Oh, he is rotten," said Pete. "I can't believe a person would let themselves get that dirty."

"I hear he has not washed since he has been here," said Bob. "But he must be like that at home. I mean, he hasn't just done it, surely?"

"Well, if nothing else he has got himself a single room. His roommate moved out and the last person they put in moved out that night, so maybe that is why Smelly Sid is doing it," reported Bill.

"Thing is, Bob," asked Pete, "why has he not been sacked for anti-social behaviour?"

"Because," put in Bill without giving his roommate a chance to talk, "he can drive a low-loader, Arctic's and any machine you name."

"I said that without moving my lips, Pete," smiled the committee chairman. Before any response could be given by anyone there was a knock on the door.

"Come in," called out Bill, "and if you're female leave your knickers at the door."

To their surprise the door opened to see Bob's ex-roommate Colin in the doorway. Bob gave out a shocked, "Hi."

"Can we talk please, Bob?"

"Of course, we can." He sat up on his bottom bunk. "Come in."

"I'm off," said Pete as he got up from the chair and passed Colin on his way to leaving the room.

"I've been sacked," said Colin as the door shut. This was greeted with shock by the other two.

"What?" came from the surprised pair.

"They met me off the Islander plane, took me to the compound and told me I am on the next *Kenya*."

"Why?" asked Bill.

"The scrap. I thought it was all above board, but apparently not."

171

"What about the ones you were doing it with? Have they sacked them as well?" Bill replied.

"No, they have jacked and gone on the ship with all the money and laughing their fucking heads off, for finding a mug to do all the hard work and then drop him right in it."

"Sit down and I'll put the elephant on," said Bob. Their guest sat next to Bill who gave him one of Bob's cigarettes off the coffee table.

"Thanks." After the tea was made Bob sat on his bottom bunk, and Bill asked, "Did you get any money out of it?"

"No, I have been away for the weekend. We were meant to be meeting up tonight for the big split up, and the bastards are having their own share out on the *Kenya*. God, I wish I could get my hands on them," growled Colin.

"Is there anything you can do, Bob?" asked Bill. This is what Colin wanted to hear as he wasn't happy about asking himself.

"I can try, that's no problem, but you know what Benjamin is like. Once he has made his mind up over something…"

"Well you can have a go, can't you?" put in Bill.

"Could you?" asked Colin almost pleading.

"Of course, I can." Bob felt bad about it later, but he realised that he wanted to hear his friend ask. "I will go and see Kim in the morning."

"Thanks, Bob, you're a mate."

"Before you thank me, let's see what happens."

"He might bugger it up all together," laughed Bill. "And you might be the first person in the jail here, the one they have just finished."

"Oh, thanks for the confidence, Bill," commented the chairman.

"Only a little joke," smiled Bill. "You'll do well for him I'm sure."

"I hope so," Colin said almost to himself.

*

"Come in, Bob, come in." Benjamin stood up to welcome his guest who had just been shown in by his secretary, Julie. He leant across his desk and shook hands. "Coffee?"

"Oh, yes please."

172

"I'll do it," volunteered Julie, as she moved across the office to pour coffee from the percolator. The two men waited to continue their meeting until the pretty, tall and slim thirty-year-old handed the drinks out and had left.

"First off, Kim, may I thank you for seeing me at short notice like this."

"Think nothing of it, old chap. I know you would not waste my time so it is really not a problem. What can I do for you?"

"One of the workforce was sacked yesterday, Colin Watson."

"Right, yes, I do recall the case."

"I feel he may have been dismissed unfairly."

"Well as it just so happens I got the report this morning and have been going through it." He picked some papers up in front of him. "Seems pretty clear cut to me, Bob." He offered the report across the desk but the committee chairman declined by shaking his head. "In fact, when interviewed he admitted it, said he had been stealing the metals to sell for profit."

"Yes, I know that, but he thought it was all above board, and that so long as he did it in his own time it was okay, in fact helping to keep the site clear."

"We really don't believe that was the reason, do we, Bob?" smiled the project coordinator.

"No, of course not, but on the other hand that is a by-product of it, keeping the project clear and all."

"Touché, old chap, touché. Continue please."

"The thing is, Colin has been ripped off by the others, they have taken the money and have left."

"Yes, so I believe."

"He got nothing out of it himself, and he really didn't think he was doing any wrong."

"I understand all that, I really do, but as you above everyone knows how I believe the job should be run, what sort of signal would this give out? It would look as if we the management were weak."

"I can assure you, Kim, that is the last thing they will think. In fact, they will think you are fair and understanding."

"Why, may I ask, are you getting involved in this issue?"

"I think it's unjust, not fair, and he came and asked me."

"I see, and this has got nothing to do with the fact that you and Colin are best mates?"

This took Bob by surprise and there was silence between the two for a few moments. Then he said, "Yes, you are right. Then again," he thought about his words wanting to pick the right ones, "we have been friend's a long time, and our families go out together, but all that besides, I believe he has been unfairly dealt with."

"But if I let him off how will that look? I mean with you being mates and all."

"I think the lads know me by now, and know I would do it for any of them."

"What's in it for us?"

"Pardon?"

Benjamin got up from his chair and walked around his desk, then sat on the edge of it a few feet from Bob's chair. "If it were possible that we could do this for you, the only thing being that there is a chance that it may make us look weak, so I think it should be a two-way street so to speak, so that we can all benefit."

"What do you want, Kim?"

"Let's just say that if we do this for you, reinstate Watson that is, well, you will owe me one."

"What, things get tight with you and the lads and you'll want me to turn on them and back you? No way, Kim, I can't do that."

"Well that may not be the case, but I may need a favour one day, and you may be able to help."

"Only a favour. I am not going against the lads."

"No," Kim held out his hand for Bob to shake, "a favour will be fine."

As Bob walked from the office complex he was pleased that he had got his friend's job back, but at the same time couldn't help thinking he had just sold his soul to the devil.

*

"You're a mate, what can I say, you're a real mate. The fact is you have saved my job, I can't put any finer a point on it," Colin replied to Bob's news as they sat alone together in the latter's room.

"The thing is we both came out here together to get a few quid behind us. Regardless of what has happened, it is just a stroke of luck that I'm able to help out. Another time I would not be able to."

"Well this has brought it all home to me, and the fact is I have been a real prat, and I can assure you that I will change."

"Well," replied his mate, "you have to do your own thing."

"No, you wait and see. I will be a changed man, no more other women, I've already told Sally we are finished. It was getting very heavy anyway."

"Look, Col, it is really nothing to do with me, I'm just pleased you have your job back and we go home on leave soon. Let's be happy with that and get the hell out of this shithole for a month or two."

"Oh, mate, I really just can't wait. This has been the longest seven or so months of my whole life I can tell you."

"Same here, Colin, and that's the truth."

"And when we get back it will be all downhill to the finish."

"I hope so," nodded the committeeman. "I really hope so."

Chapter 10

Home. But not for Long!

"I can't believe it's all over and we are on our way back to that shithole," Bob said to Bill and Colin as they sat in the forward bar of the *Kenya* as they headed south just a day out of Cape Town, after spending the last four weeks at their respective homes in the UK. It was a Saturday in July, a cold but bright winter's afternoon in the southern hemisphere. With only a few hours of daylight left, the sun had started to set outside the large glass windows in the lounge bar to the left-hand side of where the lads were sitting, known as the port side of the ship and the western side of the world.

Bob had his feet up on the small round table that the three sat around, enjoying an after-lunch pint of beer each before the film, *An Officer and a Gentleman*, which they had come to watch. The area was starting to fill up with other workers who had the same idea.

"I have never known four weeks go so fast in all my life," commented Bill as he picked Bob's duty-free cigarettes off the table and handed them around.

"Thanks, Bill, for one of my fags."

"Quite alright, old chap, think nothing of it."

"We have left all that lovely summer sunshine behind for cold, dark winter nights in the middle of bloody July," put in Colin. "Look," he pointed out of the window, "it's nearly fucking dark now, at just after two in the afternoon."

"It's another two weeks on this ruddy rust bucket with nothing to do, that's what I can't bear the thought of," Bill remarked.

"I must admit I've got to agree," said Bob. "I am not looking forward to it very much, four weeks out of eight on this bloody thing."

"Mind you," said Colin, "it can't be too bad sat here drinking beer, watching videos and getting paid into the bargain, and there are some cracking-looking birds on here that Eastham's have taken on." Bob greeted this remark with a very sour look at Colin, who then replied, "Only looking, only looking, there's no harm in looking in the cake shop window when you are on a diet." This comment brought a smile from both his friends.

"Well," smiled Bob, as he relaxed in the armchair, "I could get used to this. Not on the way to work of course, but on a cruise or something."

"Yes, it would be okay with the old lady, or someone's old lady anyway," laughed Bill.

"I would not be able to say that," put in Colin.

"No, because you've been a bad boy," Bill replied.

"I told Jean that I would not get up to anything."

"You told her what happened?" asked Bob in a surprised voice.

"Nooo, do you think I'm mad? Nooo, I told her she was the only one in the world for me, that's about the same thing, init?"

"No, Colin," remarked Bill, "it's not the same at all. If you told her you'd been shagging another bird, now that's the same thing."

"Keep it down," said Colin motioning with his hands downward. "People will hear."

"I thought everyone knew," remarked Bill as he took a sip of his beer.

"No, no, it's time to start anew, a fresh start. Don't you think, Bob?"

"Well, I don't like living in the past and believe in moving on."

"Your mate stuck by you, Col, when things got hard," remarked Bill.

"Yes, Bill, I know, and the truth is it's time to say sorry and thanks." He stood up and held his right hand out to Bob who still had his feet on the table, but before he could put them down the ship took a sharp lurch to the right. Every person sat in the bar and lounge area fell off their seats, and beer and other drinks and ashtrays went flying onto the floor as the ship continued to do what seemed like a complete U-turn. After what seemed an age and a lot of noise, the ship continued its passage in what seemed to be a new direction.

"What the fuck was that all about?" asked Bill as they all got up covered in beer.

"There's a man overboard!" shouted one of the workers from the large glass double doors.

"What?" asked Bob.

177

"It seems one of the lads has gone over the side at the bow of the ship," answered one of the workers near the doors.

"Oh fuck," said Bill as the men made their way out of the bar and headed to the other end of the ship. As the three friends went out onto the open deck at the rear of the ship, a large crowd had gathered, all looking out to sea.

The ship had now all but stopped in the sea, which had waves of about a force six and a strong swell that meant the ship was bobbing up and down profusely. By maritime law the ship had to return as soon as possible to the area where the man overboard had first been reported, hence the fast turn.

"What's happening?" Bill asked one of the lads as they tried to see what was going on through the crowd.

"The lad who raised the alarm chucked a lifebelt in," he replied. "And the crew fired a flare into the water to mark where they thought they saw him when we got back. You can see the orange smoke. Look!" He pointed to where a plume of smoke could be seen rising out of the dark blue sea and disappearing into the darkening sky. With waves curling in the sea it was very hard to spot the bright red and white life ring which had the ship's name on it, let alone see the head of a person.

As the watching went on the crew were busy in different places. Officers were on the bridge looking out to sea and at the same time controlling a stationary ship which was being tossed about by the slightly rough waters. There were other members of the crew who had been instructed by the captain to look out on the higher decks and to fire more flares into the water should the man overboard be spotted again, and others hung a netting from the handrail which reached down to the water so that the person could get hold of it to climb up.

"How long can he last in there?" Bob asked anyone who was listening.

"Well it looks fucking cold," replied Bill.

"How did it happen?" asked Colin.

"Word is," replied their informant in front of them, "that he climbed onto the handrail and jumped."

"You're joking," said Bob in a very shocked voice.

"No, no joke about it, the young lad over there," he pointed to a man in his late twenties talking to some of the ship's officers, "said they were sat together on that bench there," he pointed. "They had

178

not talked and after a short while the other lad got up and jumped in."

"That's young Paul," reported Bob. "He comes from West Bromwich in the Midlands but now lives in the West Country. I worked with him when he first came out. Nice lad."

"Can you believe someone would jump in there?" asked Colin.

"Sounds hard to believe," replied Bill.

"Well if Paul said it, I'll believe it," said Bob.

"THERE HE IS!" A shout went up from the front of the crowd. Everybody was now looking towards the sea trying to get a glance of the man in the water and asking, "Where? Where?" At that moment another flare was fired into the sea from the bridge to mark the spot again, only this time it was nearer to the ship.

"What did you see?" Bill called out.

"He waved his arms," replied a voice from the front, "then disappeared again."

"He's still alive then," Bill told his mates.

"God, Bill, don't kill him off already," snapped Bob.

"Well I'm sure he won't last much longer in water that cold," replied the man from Birmingham in a sheepish voice. Bob just shook his head without saying any more and carried on looking out to sea. The watchers stood there looking in the water for what seemed an age. It was in fact just under an hour from the first report of, "man overboard," when for all to see, the man floated past the ship face down, then disappeared.

"Oh fuck," reported Bob, as they all now knew their workmate was dead.

"Poor bastard," Colin told those around him.

"Well," put in Bill, "if he did jump he got what he wanted."

"Bill, just, just… OH, FUCK OFF!" said Bob as he turned and walked away.

"What's up with him?" Bill asked Colin as they walked back to the lounge.

"He has just seen someone die, he is upset."

"Well so have I," came the reply. "I'm only saying it how I see it." Colin shook his head but said no more.

Shortly after the sighting the netting was pulled up and the ship set off on its way south again. The darkness came very fast, and with a cold wind blowing from the direction that they were headed it was no time to be outside. As the evening meal was being served

179

in the restaurant some people had already sat to eat when an announcement came over the ship's loudspeaker.

"This is Captain Robinson. As I'm sure you are all aware by now, I have the sad duty to tell you that we lost one of our passengers and a workmate of yours this afternoon. I would like to thank those who helped us with the search. Unfortunately, life expectancy in these waters at this time of year would not be long. At this moment in time we are unable to identify the person, so should anyone have any information on who he maybe I would ask you to come along to see us. In the meantime, it is very important for us to identify him as soon as possible, so after you have all eaten a desk has been set up outside the shop for everyone to report in so that you can be accounted for. I would like to thank you all for your cooperation in this matter. Thank you." The speaker went dead.

"Fuck," said Colin as the three sat eating dinner. "They don't know who he is."

"Must be new," put in Bill as he stuffed his face with a Yorkshire pudding. "I mean someone would have spotted a mate gone by now, surely." The pudding was followed very swiftly by mashed potatoes.

"I can't believe we watched a man die this afternoon and did nothing about it," said Bob as he was staring down at the meal in front of him.

"I don't think it was a case of doing nothing," Colin said.

"He was there in front of us," came the reply. "Why the fuck did they not put down a life raft? I mean just firing flares at him, that didn't do any fucking good, did it?"

"It was on the rough side and he could not be seen," answered Colin.

"The thing is–" Bob was interrupted.

"Do you want that?" asked Bill pointing to Bob's dinner as he pushed his empty plate away.

"What? Nooo."

"I'll have it then," Bill said, as he pulled it across the table from his workmate.

"I don't know," continued the committeeman, "it's just that he was there in front of us, as if we could just reach out and get him, and nothing happened."

"Bob," the three all looked to see Paul Ferdinand, the person who had seen the man go over. "Can I have a word please?"

180

"Of course. Where do you want to go?" He wiped his mouth with a napkin and started to get up.

"No," came the reply, "here will be fine."

"Sure," said Bob as he moved into the empty seat next to the window now facing Colin leaving the seat facing Bill for the fair-haired, five-foot-six inches tall Paul.

"I suppose you know I saw what happened."

"You saw him jump, didn't you?" asked Bill.

"Well I thought I did, but not according to the staff and officers."

"How do you mean?" asked Bob.

"I've been in the office and they have told me he was washed over, well, knocked over if you like, in the rough seas, being sick at the side and went over. They have said that although I was the only one there, the only one to see it."

"So how can they say what they didn't see?" asked Bill.

"It's the publicity, or in this case bad publicity," Bob remarked. "They won't want it getting out that one of us has jumped. There has been plenty of bad news in the papers at home already."

"But I know what I saw. He didn't get washed over, he walked to the rail, climbed up and jumped, that's all there is to it. They are making me out to be a liar."

"I suppose his family will get insurance that way," suggested Colin.

"That's a point," said Bill.

"But what does that say about me? All the lads will be saying I made it up. There's no way I would have done anything like that. You know I wouldn't do that, don't you, Bob?"

"Of course, I do, Paul," came the reply.

"Are you sure that's what you did see though?" asked Bill.

"Bill," said Bob in a surprised voice.

"I know," said Paul, "that's what they said in the office, but I know what I saw."

"Must have been terrible," put in Colin.

"I couldn't believe it. One second, he was sat next to me, then he was over the side. It all happened so fast."

"So maybe…" asked Bill, but before he could say any more Bob broke in.

"Why don't you go and have a lay down, Paul?"

"Oh, I can't sleep."

"No, just go and rest, it may do you good having a quiet half hour."

"You could be right." He got up. "But can we talk later, Bob?"

"Of course, we can." Bob got up and shook his hand. "After you have rested we can meet up in the bar tonight."

"Thanks, Bob." He turned and left.

"I was going to ask him before you rushed him off that if it did happen so fast maybe he didn't see it right. Maybe the lad did get knocked in by the rough sea being sick," said Bill.

"I know," came the reply. "That's why I sent him away. He is very upset already so that comment would not help him much, would it?"

"I think that's unfair," came the reply between mouthfuls of food. "That's what people are going to think and he'd better get used to it." The rest of the meal was taken in almost silence as Bob stared out of the window into the increasing darkness. It seemed as if he'd sat for an eternity until the loudspeaker reminded everyone to check in. The three walked together, Colin and Bill discussing the day's sports results that had come in from Britain, but it still seemed as if Bob was a million miles away. It was agreed that they would meet in the bar later for a drink as they queued for the check-in.

Bob walked very slowly around the outside deck not realising how cold it had become with the onset of night and the fact that all the time they were getting nearer the ice of the south, and that also it was still winter in this part of the world not the summer he had left in the north. They had only just started out on the trip back and his lips had started to crack and split again already.

Bob felt as low as he had ever felt since he'd first come to this place. He sat on a bench and smoked a cigarette as he looked out into the black of the night. Was it that he saw another six months ahead of him in that godforsaken place they were headed to, all that time away from his wife and two children, or was it what he had seen that afternoon? He had never seen a person die before and never wanted to see that again. At one point he closed his eyes and could see the man float past. What in hell's name made him jump? And he did believe Paul. He knew the company would be happy for it to go down as an accident. For two pins as soon as they docked he would be happy to stay on the ship and return to the UK, but he had now worked over halfway through his contract and would lose too much money, and when all was said and done that was what he was here for, to make life better for his family.

He closed his eyes but this time made himself think of his wife and children and the happy times they had just spent together in the summer sunshine at home, four weeks going out spending money on them, playing with his girls and time alone with Jane. He was thinking how much being apart had drawn him and his wife closer together. There had been times in the past when, what with the pressures of bringing up a young family and all, maybe in Bob's mind some cracks had shown, but not now. They had never spent so much time apart since they were married, and the homecoming had been great.

Bob had his birthday while on leave and their wedding anniversary the next day. His family had made a real fuss of him and he smiled to himself thinking of those happy times.

"This is where you got to," said Bill who made the committeeman jump as he had not seen him come out. "We have been looking everywhere for you, thought you went over the side as well."

"Oh, just thinking."

"Well fucking come in and think. You'll freeze to death out here, and one of them in a day is enough," laughed the man from Birmingham.

"You're right," came the reply. "Let's go and have a beer." He got up and went inside with his friend.

The two men walked together to the stern bar where Bill had agreed to meet Colin who had already arrived and was standing at an almost empty bar talking to the barman.

"I still think they could have done more to have saved him," reported Colin to the man listening to him behind the bar. "Hi, lads, two more pints of lager please, Mike." He looked into his glass which had a small amount of beer in the bottom. "Oh, make that three." He then emptied his glass.

"Do we know who he is yet?" asked Bill as the beers started to arrive.

"Didn't hear anything," came the reply from Colin. "How about you, Mike?"

"Well," the barman said as he put the glasses on the bar, "I did hear when I was below deck before coming on duty, that the reason that they did not try to get the body out of the sea was that the captain informed your party leader on board that if he had a dead body on the ship maritime law states that he has to go to the nearest port, which would have meant returning to Cape Town. So your man rang the UK and they said if they could not get him out alive to leave him as they thought many may get off and leave if we went back and of course put us three or four days behind.

"You're joking?" said Bob.

"That's what I heard this evening from the radio operator. Please don't say you got it from me, lads."

"No way," replied Bob.

"Watch out," said Mike, "officer on deck." He turned and walked to the other end of the bar to serve a newcomer. The three lads turned to see one of the ship's officers enter the bar and walk towards them.

"Good evening, gentlemen," said the tall, dark-skinned, forty-year-old officer. "Bob English isn't it?" he asked the workers committee chairman.

"Yes," replied Bob.

"Can I have a quick word please, in private."

"Of course." He looked at his two mates of which Bill pulled a face as if to say, "Oh, not us?" Bob and the officer walked to an empty area of the bar and sat at a round table with four armchairs around it. "What is it?" asked the committeeman. "Sorry, I didn't get your name."

"James, James Mayo," came the reply as they shook hands across the table. "I have been asked to talk to you regarding the incident this afternoon."

"Incident?" Bob looked shocked.

"Well, the unfortunate happening."

"Unfortunate happening? A man jumped overboard and lost his life."

"He was washed over in rough seas, Bob, probably while being sick."

"That's not what I heard, James."

"Well," James paused, "that's what you may have heard. In fact, that is part of the reason I am here." Bob looked puzzled but let the officer continue. "Mike Turner, the party leader, is tied up, very busy at the moment, that is why I have been asked to talk to you. Mike will talk to you tomorrow, but he, I and the captain had a meeting and we know that feelings are running high among the workforce over this afternoon, and Mike has been in contact with

184

Kim Benjamin on the island and he has asked you to deal with any problems the workers may have over it while we are out here."

For the second time in a few minutes Bob was shocked but gave himself time to think before answering.

"Well one thing that has been said is that the lads didn't think that an enough effort was put in getting the chap back. Why couldn't a life raft have gone out for him?"

It was James's time to think before he gave his answer. "Were you on the ship when we went into Cape Town in June?"

"Yes, I was."

"Did you see the lifeboat drill that was held one afternoon?"

"Yes, I did. It turned into a bit of a joke trying to get the boat back and all, didn't it?" As he made the comment he realised what he had just said.

"Exactly," replied the officer. He let this news sink in then said. "That drill was on a calm, sunny day, no wind, a millpond of a sea and it took half an hour to get the boat back in. The captain has to man a life raft with men before he can send it out. He has to act as God. When all is said and done the man had jumped." James was quick to correct himself. "That was the information we had at the point until we found out he was washed over." Bob took this in but let him continue. "So, the captain has to risk more men in rough seas where it was very hard to spot the man? And to be frank, life expectancy in those waters was about fifteen minutes. He must have been very fit to have lasted that long, and darkness was not far away."

Bob took a sip of beer then lit a cigarette, then said, "I do understand all of that and see the risk how you have put it, but what does Kim want me to do?"

"I am told the men trust you, and to be fair you are their representative here. Kim would like you to calm down any potential problems."

"What, so when we get to West Cove half of the lads don't jack and stay on the ship?"

"That's putting a very fine point on it, but that's about the size of it."

"Right."

"Can we rely on your support, Bob?" asked James as he stood up and offered his hand.

"Okay," said Bob as he shook the officer's hand.

From the afternoon when Bob and the others lost a workmate in the sea, it was twelve days before the ship would arrive back at the Falkland Islands in mid-August 1984. The atmosphere on the ship in the first few days after the "incident" was very tense with a lot of workers feeling very low about what happened, but as the days went on the atmosphere improved. Bob had been given the use of an office if anyone wanted to talk to him about what had happened and how people were feeling. An announcement was made regarding this, and he was starting to think he had become a counsellor and not a carpenter anymore, but in fact this only lasted a few days and the mood around the ship lifted a bit. Bob was then able to get on with one of the new books he had purchased while at home, *The Hunt for Red October* by Tom Clancy, which he had heard good reports about.

It was a Tuesday when they arrived back at West Cove. Bill and Bob had agreed to share a room, Colin had turned down a room in the staff block, which would have meant him sharing with a new chap, to room with Pete next door to the other two. They had been told to drop their cases off and report to the main canteen to be allocated their new work areas. The workers had been amazed with what progress they had seen since coming back. They had not seen that much but the contractors' camp was now complete as were the main offices and stores compound. The RAF camp was now also well advanced.

Bill had been told he would be on the airfield, Colin and Pete were going to the Tank Farm which meant having to travel the seven miles each day back to West Cove, then an extra mile past the Lay Down storage area. The Tank Farm was near the entrance to West Cove. It was called Pears Harbour and was a large area that would have large round concrete bases built. To these high metal tanks would be fixed and would have fuel pumped into them from tankers out at sea, and in turn shipped to the airfield to fuel the aircrafts and other items. Bob had not been called when the senior welfare manager Joe Benson came over to him with a co-worker.

"Hi, Bob, welcome back." The two shook hands. "This is Ed, he is going to drive you up to the office compound. Kim wants to see you."

"What for?"

"He wants to see you."

"But I have not been given my work area yet."

"Kim will explain. There's a good chap, now pop off as he is waiting for you." Joe turned and walked away.

"Come on," said Ed, the dark-haired, thirty-year-old driver from Newcastle. "I'll get you over there."

*

"Come in, Bob, nice to see you." The project coordinator welcomed Bob as he entered the office from behind his desk. "I have poured you a coffee, old chap." He pointed to the cup on Bob's side of the desk. "Take a chair. Did you have a nice break?"

He's being really nice, Bob thought to himself. What's he after? "Yes, all good thanks, Kim. We had a nice time, nice and hot, bit of a shock coming back here."

"Yes, it is still very cold but not so much snow of late. In fact, I see it's just started raining. I have been home also but I went air bridge and only had two weeks."

"How was it?" Bob asked.

"Yes, very enjoyable, thank you. Now, on with business, and the first thing I must do is thank you for all the help and support you gave when," Kim looked at a piece of paper on his desk, "Mr Douglas Blake was washed overboard."

Bob saw little point in disagreeing with Benjamin how Mr Blake met his end so he just said, "It was fine. I just sat and chatted to a few lads. It was very distressing for everyone, Kim."

"I know," came the reply, "it was very upsetting when we got the news, but as I said you stepped in when you didn't have to, and it helped me make a couple of decisions I had in mind." Bob just let the coordinator continue. "Since you have taken up the role of workers liaison you have helped us to sort some tricky problems, which frankly I don't think welfare could have done. It worked for you because they see you as one of them. Now we want to reward you."

Bob was now really thinking. "Reward me?"

"Yes, in two ways in fact. The first has already been done. We have made you up to chargehand, so your salary has been increased and should you want to you can move into the staff block. Also, we would like your role to become full-time." Kim gave the news time to sink in before continuing. "We have close to

187

two thousand workers here now, and will shortly be up to our full number of personnel. Progress has been good of late and summer here is just around the corner. The point is we don't want any major problems. You would have a full-time driver. I think you've met Ed, a radio, use of an office over at welfare, and of course my full backing. What do you think?"

"Well," said Bob trying to take everything in.

"The truth is we have been a bit lost without you here, sorting out small problems and all. It takes up a lot of time for welfare and section managers. You will have time to get around the whole project and hopefully nip problems in the bud. Welfare will sort all the normal problems, but you will sort any potential…"

"Disputes?" Bob finished the sentence for him.

"Disputes. You're good at it. Small issues you can sort with the section managers and foreman, or if that can't be done I will sort them. We will still have the workers committee meetings, but I really think you can help a lot."

"Kim, I will do it, but I will only be here for another six months or so until the end of my contract. I have promised my wife I would not do another fourteen months."

"Well," came the reply, "there's a couple of things there, and you can make this general knowledge. It has been agreed with London that anyone who has done fourteen months can sign for an extra six months at a time."

"That's better, but I am really not sure at the moment."

"There is plenty of time for that." Kim got up and walked around the desk as if to tell Bob it was time to go. "Pop over and see Joe Benson. He has a list for you and will show you the office etc."

Bob got up and walked to the door, then stopped and looked back towards Kim. "I thought you were going to ask me to repay the favour for not sacking Colin."

"Oh," the project coordinator laughed, "there is plenty of time for that, a minimum of six months, Bob." Kim was still smiling as Bob left the office to go out in the freezing, pouring rain.

*

Bob and his friends didn't really get to have their nightly meeting in their new room until the following evening as Bob had been with Joe Benson until late that first night back, only breaking for a quick meal together which they had in the staff canteen. When he got back to his room Bob was too worn out to answer any of Bill's fifty questions, but promised he would reveal all the next night after dinner.

This was therefore much anticipated by Bill and Colin as they sat in Bill and the committeeman's room who was making tea from his new travel kettle as the other two sat in the two armchairs smoking Bob's duty-free cigarettes, which he had purchased a thousand on South African Airways for the bargain amount total of only ten pounds.

"I don't like being on the airfield," moaned Bill, "just loading one lorry after another. And that new foreman, Larry Harman, just stands by his Land Rover all day just looking at you."

"Is he the one you pointed out tonight?" asked Bob as he put the two cups on the coffee table. "He looks too old to be here."

"Oh," came the reply, "he's a real old git. He must be a hundred and fifty if he's a day." This comment brought a laugh from the others. "I mean," he continued, "he is as deaf as a post if his two earphones are turned off. I was talking to him today when he said stop, he played with his ears then said you will have to start again as I can't hear a thing when these are turned off. It's far too noisy here."

"That's dangerous," reported Bob.

"I think they will bring anyone out here these days," mentioned Colin.

"So, you have a driver now, Bob?" asked Bill.

"Yeah, not sure why."

"Because you killed the last Land Rover you drove."

"Thanks, Bill."

"Think nothing of it. Come on, give us some news. You must have loads now you're mates with Joe Benson."

"Where do you want me to start?" asked Bob as he laid on his bottom bunk facing his friends. "Do you want to hear about Diesel Kev, the diesel tanker driver getting sacked, or the new six-month contracts, or the day trips to Stanley? Well, watch this space – COMING SOON TO A BUS STATION NEAR YOU!" The lads laughed at this. "Or the firebug still being here, or more police moving in, or another death or jacker on a plane?"

"Fucking slow down," said Bill. "Start with Kev, the country yokel. What happened there?"

"It looks like he was flogging diesel to the Bennies."

"You thought that," reported Colin.

"Yeah, but he let on to them it was all above board and he was handing the cash over, which of course he was not. So he has gone on leave and didn't tell them. They turned up at the office complaining that their cans had not been filled up for two weeks. They sacked him while he was at home."

"What an idiot," said Bill.

"Well," said Colin "he must have made some good money while he was at it."

"Yeah," continued Bob, "but he's lost everything. He will not get any money at all that he is owed, and he has got thieving on his record now."

"What's this about trips to Stanley?" asked Bill.

"Well," came the reply from Bob, "the road has almost reached Stanley. It's just over a week away and there's still lots to do, but it will be usable and the lads have a camp halfway now with a bar. So as soon as it's ready they are going to put free buses on each Sunday for the lads to have a day out there."

"That will be good," said his ex-roommate. "We can go and see what talent they have got over there, army girls and all. Only joking before you say anything, Bob."

"Hmm," came the reply from Bob.

"That will make a change from this place," remarked Bill. "In fact I can't wait. It will be a good break."

"The Atlas do a good lunch," said Colin. Bob just looked at him. "Or so I heard."

"Who's dead?" asked Bill.

"Not sure of his name. He was a Welshman. He came out in July, he got on the *Kenya,* we got off in Cape Town. He had only been working two days and he had been out of work for two and a half years before he came here. Had a wife and three kids, all young."

"Bloody hell," said Colin. "Poor sod."

"What happened?" asked Bill.

"I am not a hundred percent certain as I know the new safety officer, Tom Smith, is working on it, but as far as I can make out he was unloading a lorryful of the one-ton canvas bags of cement with a crane, when the straps on the bag snapped and the bag fell on him and crushed him to death. Dead on the spot."

"Fuck me," said Bill, "this place is turning into Death Valley, and I've heard there are more coffins coming on the next cargo ship."

"There are," replied Bob. "That brings me to the firebug. He is still here. They had another incident about three weeks ago, and this time he changed what he has been doing. It was done from outside. He put a load of rags soaked in diesel under a room in our old corridor, C. It was about one in the morning when one the lads in the room had just been for a piss, and when he came back he saw the flames outside the window. He and his roommate managed to put it out."

"That's just really not good," said Colin.

"He's got to be caught," said Bob, "before we all fry one night."

"Yeah," said Bill, "we should set up a vigilante group then hang the bastard when we get him."

"That's not a good idea, Bill. Hanging him that is. But maybe it is up to us to help catch him. I am seeing Karl Davis, head of security, in the next few days. He wants a word with me for some reason, so I will ask him if we can help in any way with the firebug."

"Are you finished, Bob?" asked Bill. "I have some big news."

"Well apart from a jacker who went home with us, nicked a load of duty-free fags in Johannesburg when we changed flights and was trying to flog them to the lads on the plane. He got caught as he was also trying to nick them off the trolley on the plane to Heathrow," finished Bob.

"What a tosser," said Colin.

"Not that big a tosser," remarked Bill.

"Why is that?" came the joint reply.

"I got four hundred cheap fags off him." This brought a laugh from the others.

"So what's your big news then?" Colin asked Bill.

"I heard today that Hack's brother, Del who is here, has taken over from Hack selling drugs."

"Wow!" said Colin.

Bill continued. "It seems that Hack had already asked Del to bring a load of extra English cash out as he was having a problem changing up the Benny money for Chinese John, so he had money, met John in the camp when the ship came in and did the deal."

"Hack kept that to himself," Colin told the others.

191

"He was a smart kid, Hack, he was not going to make that general knowledge. What name is Del going under? Hack 2?" remarked Bob.

"Well," replied Colin, "we will know where to go when we need to get out of here for an hour or so!"

Chapter 11

Don't Worry, It's Only the Wind

Bob was really impressed with the progress that had been made on the project in the two months he had been away. Not only seeing for himself but talking to workmates, foremen and managers, things had really moved on.

The airfield had over three quarters of its length stripped of peat, then crushed stone sub base and a semi-dry aggregate and cement rolled in by large heavy road rollers, and the concrete train was laying PQ (pavement quality) concrete as fast as it could be supplied. The cross runway for the fighter jets was also well underway as were the hangars at the end of this runway that would in time be hidden from the sky and would house fighter jets. At each side of the main runway in the trenches where Dusty had blown everyone up, pipes and cable had been laid in most areas and small blockwork buildings had popped up at intervals. These were electric sub stations which would control the lighting etc.

The main hangar near the end of the runway was now all enclosed with tin sheet cladding. Inside this building the floor was now being laid, again with thick concrete. In front of the hangar a large area of peat was being stripped. This was for a concrete apron on which the aeroplanes would taxi into the hangar. Not far away the control tower could be seen rising up. Also, not a great distance from the airfield, the electric power station was externally complete. This was a very large building that would house the generators that would power the complex when complete. The water pipeline that would supply everywhere with drinking water was also under construction.

*

Bob had been picked up that morning at the camp by Ed in the Land Rover to take him to the office complex for his meeting with Karl Davis before they started going around the rest of the project. Bob ran from the accommodation to his transport as it was pouring with rain, as it had seemed to have been doing since he got back.

While Bob had only known Ed a day or so he had taken a liking to him. They had many things in common. Both had a young family and enjoyed spending time showing each other their family photos. They talked about football and many other things.

"I am not sure why they gave me a driver, but I am not moaning as it is nice to have someone to chat to, and the truth is I don't like driving here very much." Ed gave no answer to why he had been given a driver, nor did Bob expect one. The driver waited in the parking area as Bob went to his meeting.

*

After making their greetings Bob sat at the visitor's side of Karl's desk in his not very big office. The desk was on one side of the office, the rest of the walls were almost completely covered with four-drawer filing cabinets as the office was in the centre of the administration complex. Karl had no windows.

"Cosy in here," Bob observed.

"Yes," came the reply, "very cosy!"

"I see we have still got the firebug here, Karl?"

"Yes, that's my main worry at the moment."

"If they are still happening he must be getting close to his leave."

"Good point, Bob, let's hope we get him soon and he can then go on a long leave."

"If there is anything we can do to help please let me know. None of us want to get burnt alive one night."

"I hate to say this but apart from increasing the fire wardens, which we have done, I am at a loss what to do. Any ideas or plan would be a great help, Bob. Kim is really on my case about this."

"I will think about it and talk to the lads, Karl. Now, what did you want me for?"

"I am hoping you can put your ear to the ground while on your travels around the project to see if you can find something out for me."

"Something? What, Karl?"

"We have got another drug pusher on our hands."

"Oh, right," came the reply.

"I did think it was cleared up with that chap Hack gone, but I have had info that there is now another at it. Not as much as Hack, but at it all the same."

"I didn't hear anything." He got out of his chair. "Was there anything else, Karl?"

"Hmm, no, I don't think so." Bob bid his farewells and turned and left the office.

That ended abruptly, Karl thought to himself. Was it something I said I wonder, or have you just been a copper too long, Karl?

It was still pouring down with rain when Bob came out of the office block and got in the passenger seat of the waiting Land Rover. Ed was about to reverse out when Bob saw George Connors come out of the office and start to walk their way waving to them. "Oh, let me put you right before he gets here. This is George Connors. He comes from your part of the world, Newcastle. We have to go to his new section soon. I think that's what he is coming over to talk about. Watch him, he is a right two-faced, backstabbing bastard, and always going on about when he was in fucking Africa."

Bob wound down his window but he walked straight past him around to the driver's window that Ed had just wound down to greet the outstretched arm of George and to shake his hand. "Hello, bonny lad Ed."

"Hello, Uncle George," came the reply from the driver. When asked by Bill later Bob did think his mouth was wide open at this point. "Thanks for getting me the job here, Uncle."

"Think nothing of it, bonny lad. If you can't help family who can you help? You have met bonny lad Bob then?"

"Yes, Unc. He was just saying he knew you." He turned to Bob and smiled.

"You're coming over to our new site down at Turtle Point I believe?"

"Yes, yes, yes," Bob replied. "I... I was planning... Let's say about two tomorrow afternoon, can we?"

"No problem, bonny lad. Me and David Anthony will be waiting to see you. Oh, by the way, did you know I have been made up to section manager?"

"Oh, that's great, Unc."

"It's about time. I always was when I was in Africa!" He turned and walked away. Bob and Ed sat in silence.

*

"He hadn't told you that bonny lad was his uncle?" Bill asked Bob as the two of them sat with Pete and Colin that evening in the canteen eating dinner.

"No, and I go and call him a backstabbing, two-faced bastard."

"Well that's the truth," said Pete with a mouthful of meat pie.

"Yes, I know," said Bob. "But he is his nephew when all's said and done."

"Am I going around the bend or is this food getting better?" asked Colin as he looked at a new potato on the end of his fork.

"I think you're right," said Bob. "Since we have been back it seems a lot better."

"I heard that Eastham's contract is up for renewal over the next few months and they had been told that unless everything improved they would not get it," reported Bill.

"About time," said Pete as he wiped his mouth with his hand.

"They have sent a new manager out," continued Bill. "She's a woman."

"Most 'she's are women," laughed Bob.

"She came on the ship we got off, and I have been told she has really shaken things up in the two months or so she has been here," Bill continued.

"Going back to your driver, Bob," said Colin, "do you think you have got him so that he can spy on you?"

"Well it did come as a surprise to me, giving me a driver and all," came the reply.

"Not because of your driving skills then, Bob? asked Bill with a smile on his face.

"Piss off, Bill," came the reply. "But it does seem odd. I will keep certain things to myself."

"Maybe it's just jobs for the boys," said Colin.

"Yeah, maybe, but talking about spying..." Bob lowered his voice and the four heads came together across the table. "Karl Davis knows that someone is pushing drugs again and has asked me to keep an eye out."

"What did you say?" asked Bill.

"I said okay. What could I say?"

"Not a lot," came the reply from the others.

"But someone needs to tell Del they are on to him. It's best I keep away from him."

"I am seeing him tonight to get some gear," said Pete. "I will tell him then."

"Okay," came the joint reply as they all pulled their heads back.

"It looks like a secret service meeting here." The four turned to see Wolfie had joined them at the end of the table. Greetings were bid to the newcomer.

"What are you doing here, Wolfie?" asked Bob. "Away from your nice little set up on the Stanley road."

"I am here for the presentation."

"What presentation?" asked a puzzled Bill.

"Get together," he said gesturing with his hands. The four put their heads together again as Wolfie bent over to join them. In a low voice he said, "You see the concrete mixer driver over there, Polly?" The four turned to see the large framed, six-foot, forty-year-old lorry driver from Kent, sat a few tables away with his workmates. "Don't look!" snapped the storyteller. The four quickly turned their heads back. "He is one of the drivers who brings concrete down to us. At the start of this week his lorry had to go in for a service. To be fair he was told it would be finished on Tuesday so on Wednesday he went to the compound to pick it up. It was in a different place from where he left it. He looked in the cab and the keys were there, so he got in and started it. It moved but it had no oil in the engine. The fitters were still working on it! It killed it, ceased the engine up. In fact, nearly blew it up!"

"Wow," said Colin.

"Watch out," said Bill, "the fitters are here."

They came out of their huddle to see the four fitters in their oil stained, navy blue overalls walk past them and stand at the end of Polly's table. Tony, the foreman, was concealing an item behind his back. It was he who spoke to Polly. In a loud voice so everyone could hear what he said, "Would you stand up, Polly, please?" A very surprised Polly got to his feet. "On behalf of the JLB fitters we would like to award you this." From behind his back he produced a six-inch by three-inch piece of three-quarter-inch plywood with an engine oil dipstick mounted on it. Tony handed it over to him. "Polly, we would like to present you with this trophy

197

to confirm you are the dipstick of the month for August 1984. Would you like to say a few words?"

Polly gathered his thoughts for a moment, then after clearing his throat he said, "Gentlemen, as unaccustomed as I am to public speaking, I would like to thank you for this special award that you have bestowed upon me. I would also like to thank my agent, manager and my family who have helped me gain this and supported me over the years it has taken me to get to this position." He put his arms in the air. "And thank you to all of you who turned up tonight. Thank you." The roar, cheers and clapping from the workforce could be heard in the adjoining canteens and outside also.

When the noise had died down Wolfie turned to the four at the table and said, "That was my idea, lads, I saw something like it in Saudi Arabia once!"

*

"I have been thinking, Karl," Bob said as he sat down across the desk from the security manager. "To stop this firebug, what about if I and the three lads in our rooms plus my driver Ed go on nights, undercover, with radios, keeping out of the way but covering the whole camp?"

"Okay," came the reply, "carry on."

"You would have to get it cleared. One person could not do it."

"You have to keep this to yourself, Bob, but there have been fires over the last two nights."

"Then we have to stop this nutter before he kills someone."

"Okay, I can sort everything with Kim. Give me a list of the lads' names and I will get them cleared and have night passes made up for them. By you doing this it would mean we will not have to use security or the fire wardens, so they can carry on with their duties. In fact I will do it with you."

"That's fine," came the reply.

"When will we start?"

"I have things on tomorrow morning I can't get out of, and tomorrow afternoon I have go to Turtle Point for a meeting with George Connors, so it will be tomorrow night or the next. I will firm it up with you."

"Okay," came the reply. "We can meet up first to agree how we are going to do things, but if this is to work no one must say a word about it."

"Okay," said Bob as he got up and walked to the door.

"By the way," said Karl, "it is really good of your friends to volunteer, Bob."

"Oh," Bob looked back at him, "they don't know they have yet!"

*

"You can go and get fucked," said Pete. "There's no way I am going out there to tackle some idiot who's trying to kill us. I didn't come here for that," he told Bob, Bill and Colin in Bob's room. "You must be mad." He pointed at Bob. "You should be locked up, you've been here too long."

"Hold on," said Bill, "it will get us away from work for as long as it takes, and it might just save all of our lives!"

"When we get him," said Colin, "can we kick the shit out of him?"

"Or hang him," said Bill. "I'll bring the rope!"

"We just hand him over to security," said Bob. "Are you in, Pete?"

"Come on," said Bill, "you can tell your grandchildren about it."

"Oh, okay then, but I still think you're mad. But if it gets me away from work for a while, then I am in."

"It's going to take a day or so to sort out, but in the meantime, no one can tell anyone," Bob told the three.

There was a joint, "Okay!"

*

Turtle Point was about four miles north east from the main airfield. The only access by land was from a road that wound down from the high land above, descending about a hundred metres down to sea level. At the bottom of the cliff was a very large open area that runs into the beach and sea. This area had been chosen for a backup Tank Farm able to accommodate tanks that again would be filled from tankers at sea. From there the fuel could be pumped in a pipeline to the airfield.

199

George Connors and David Antony had been chosen by Kim to manage this work, mainly as the start coincided with the work finishing on the main contactors' camp which Kim had to admit that even with the overtime ban which was mainly on at that time, the work had been completed at an impressive rate.

While the distance to Turtle Point was not a long way from the main camp it had been decided to set up a small camp down there, so that the workforce who had been appointed would work long hours seven days a week. The road had been constructed down the side of the cliff, wide enough to carry the heavy traffic that would be needed to carry out the work.

As Bob and Ed approached the work area along the long sloping road that turned to the right at the bottom, Bob looked out of the passenger window of the Land Rover to look at the very rough sea below.

"Bloody hell, Ed, that's a long way down to the sea." The driver made a grunt and nodded his agreement as he concentrated on driving down the slope. While Kim trusted George and David he knew that they would cut corners at times in favour of the company, and as it had been said many times they were, "not in Africa now!" Kim wanted Bob to cast an eye over the camp before the workforce moved in as again this was an important part of the project and the last thing he wanted was a holdup with work if the workforce were unhappy with their living conditions.

"I don't think it has stopped raining since I've been back," remarked the committeeman as the Land Rover arrived at the offices next to the newly constructed camp.

"No," said Ed as turned off the engine. Bob had asked his driver why he had not told him about the section manager being his uncle, and the reply had been, "Things happened so quick I just didn't get around to it. In fact it just slipped my mind." Bob had accepted this but still thought that he would keep some things close to his chest.

It was Antony who met them and showed Bob around the camp while Ed went in the office to talk to his uncle. It was the first chance they'd had since Ed arrived. They sat drinking tea in George's twenty-six by ten-foot site office when the manager asked his nephew, "How are you getting on with him then?" George nodded to Bob outside.

"He's okay, Unc."

"I don't trust him, bonny lad. As I told you on the phone before you came out, any information you may get from him let me know as soon as possible. He's still on the workers' side you know."

"I will, Unc, but he has not told me anything up until now, but I will keep my ears open."

"Well done, lad. Watch out they are coming," said the manager as he saw the two through the office window.

"So, what do you think of our set up, bonny lad Bob?" asked George as the two joined them to sit around the desk.

"Well, George, I must say it's a nice little set up. It has everything the lads will need, plus a little bar for when they are not working, and a video room. It's nice."

"You sound surprised, bonny lad."

"No, no, no," came the reply, "it will be fine. The only thing I will say is that the road coming down the cliff wants some kind of barrier fixed there as it's a bloody long way down into the sea."

"Oh," came the reply from the red-faced man behind the desk, "we used roads that were worse than that when we were in…"

"We will get it sorted," put in David before George could say the "A" word, then continued. "We will get everything started here tomorrow. Please tell Kim how pleased you are with it, Bob."

"Will do," he replied as he got up. "We are off now, still got things to–" Before he could finish his sentence the office shook violently as if it was going to be swallowed by the earth.

"What the fuck was that?" asked Ed when the shaking had stopped.

"Earth tremor, bonny lad, get them all the time in Africa."

"We are not in Africa," snapped Bob.

"That's no tremor," put in David. "I've felt many tremors, and that's not one." The four men hurried out of the office into the still pouring rain, and from their position they could see the bottom of the road was completely blocked with mud and earth. Bob and David ran on to look around the bend at the approach road, which was blocked the complete length with the spoils which had been dug out of the cliff to form the road, and had been stockpiled at the top of the cliff to be removed at a later date. This had been washed onto the road by the constant rain over the last week or so.

"I was going to get that lot moved next week to Long Pond," said David.

"The rain moved it for you," laughed Bob. There was no reply to this comment.

"There's no way out of here," said Ed as he and his uncle joined them. They looked at the totally blocked road. Bob walked away and talked on the radio for a few minutes to Arran Jones to tell him about their problem who said he was on his way over. As he walked back he saw Ed and David around George who was sat on a large rock holding his chest.

"He's had a heart attack," called Ed as Bob got near them.

"Oh, bloody hell," replied Bob as he joined them. He had not been with them long when Arran came on the radio to tell him he was at the top of the road as he was nearby when he received the call. Bob could see him at the top of the cliff. "We have got a man who has had a heart attack, Arran. We need to get him out quick, and as you can see the road is impassable."

"I will get some men and a stretcher to carry him out," came the reply.

"They had better be some very big men, Arran," said Bob. "It's George!"

"Oh shit," the Welshman said.

"Look, Arran, there is no way we could climb out of here, let alone carry him out. The mud is moving all the time with the rain, it would be too dangerous. The only way out is by the sea."

"Bob, it's too rough to set any boat out. They have stopped all work down at the *Adventurer* because of the weather."

"We have to try, Arran, or he could die!"

"Let me talk to them at the ship," came the reply.

"Leave it to me, Arran, I know a man who can help. He is good at being a hero!" It took a little while for the foreman at the ship to find Jimmy by which time it was starting to get dark.

"It's very rough out there, Bob," said the Northern Irish voice on the radio after Bob had explained everything.

"But you are International Rescue, Jimmy, time to save another life."

"Okay, as it is you who is asking, Bob, I will have a go."

"Thanks, Jimmy, you're a real mate."

"I am on my way. Oh, Bob, do I know him?"

Bob looked across at the man sat on the rock who had Jimmy's best mate sacked and said, "No, Jimmy, you don't know him."

*

"Wind fucking wind," said Bill as he, Pete, Colin and Bob sat in his room.

"That's what the little Aussie nurse, Pam, told us," replied Bob as he laid on his bottom bunk for the nightly meeting.

"She's lovely," mumbled Colin as he sat in an armchair next to Pete smoking a cigarette and drinking a cup of tea. "She can examine me any night."

"What happened?" asked Bill from his top bunk.

"Well, after we got George up to the medical centre they were all waiting for him, Dr Death and everyone. They took him in and the three of us were outside waiting, and after a while Pam came out and said, "You can all go, it's indigestion. The little fat fellow is full of wind, that's what gave him the chest pains. We gave him some medicine and stuck a needle in his fat arse and after a few minutes he started bowing and farting like an old warthog." This brought laughter from those in the room. Then she said, "If he was a smaller person he would have lifted off the chair there was so much wind that come out of him." This brought more laughter.

"I would have let the fat twat die!" said Bill from above.

"Well he wouldn't have died of indigestion," replied Bob.

"You didn't know he was full of wind and piss when you called Jimmy out in those seas," put in Pete.

"How did Jimmy take it when he saw who it was?" asked Colin.

"When we were alone at the ship he called me a southern wanker and other names and said he would also have let him die."

"A man after my own heart," said the voice from above Bob.

"Well," said Bob as he got up to answer the knock on the door, "it was the only humane thing to do." He opened the door. "Hello, Ed, come in. This is Ed, GEORGE'S nephew." He turned to the others. "He is going to help us catch this fucking firebug." Bob introduced everyone to the newcomer.

"You had some fun this afternoon then?" asked Pete.

"Oh yeah, I did think Uncle George was going to die at one point. He was in so much pain and had gone bright red in the face."

"That's all the Newcastle Brown Ale he drinks, bonny lad," Bill mocked.

Bob just looked at Bill, then said, "Sit on my bunk, Ed. Karl Davis should be here soon."

"So how are you finding it here, Ed?" Colin asked.

"Oh, not too bad thanks."

"It's a shithole," came the voice from the top bunk.

"That's on a good day," said Pete from the armchair. Everyone laughed at this remark.

"The thing is," continued Ed, "I could have come out here at the start. Uncle George could have fixed me up then, and by the way, I know most of the lads think he is a tosser, but I am not getting into that. No, I didn't want to come out at all, then I found out my wife was having it off. I felt really unwell at work one day and went home early. The kids were at school and I went into the front room to find a racing paper on the floor in front of the telly which had racing on, so that was really odd. I went into the hallway and heard noises."

"Noises?" asked Bob.

"You know, sex, shagging noises!" said Ed.

"Oh," came from the captivated audience.

"Then what happened?" asked Colin.

"Well, I crept up the stairs and at the top I could really hear it as they had left our bedroom door open. I gently pushed the door open more and they were on the bed with their backs to the door, and it was my best mate Robbie shagging the bitch doggy on the bed."

"God, what did you do?" asked a shocked Bob.

"I ran in, punched him in the face and gave her a kick!"

"See," said Bill, "you don't even have to be out here for it to happen!"

"Then what?" asked Colin.

"Oh, it was just a real mess. Robbie and me had a fight, she ran out with him, then a few days later I find out that she'd cleaned all our bank accounts out. And then the bombshell. I find out that a little while before she had taken out a ten-grand loan against the house." He stopped and thought for a moment, then said, "Yes, so she buggered off with him. My grandmother has got my two kids and I am up to my eyes in debt. When Uncle George found out, and because it's his mum who has got my children – my mother is his sister – he moved heaven and earth to get me out here so I can pay the debts off and try and get back to normal, if that is at all possible. So, I know he can be a pain but I can't knock him. He's helped me big time."

There was an almost stunned silence in the room which was broken when Bob said, "I am really sorry to hear that, Ed."

"I know she's your wife, Ed, but I would kill the fucking bitch!" Bill said from the top bunk.

"That wouldn't help," replied Bob.

"You're too kind hearted," said Pete. "I'd kill her and him." There came a joint agreement from Colin and Bill.

"I think I might if I find them, but again I have got the kids to think of and me being locked up would not help. No, being here will be good, tax-free money and all, and I will stay as long as I can to sort it all out."

"Fair play," said Bob. "Why did you not tell me before?"

"I would have in time I suppose, and also Uncle George asked me not to tell people, so don't let on to him please. I don't care who knows but he seems to."

"No way," said Bob, "I won't say anything to him."

"Thanks, Bob." Ed was interrupted by a knock on the door.

Bob got up as Bill called out, "If you're a female leave your knickers at the door!" The door was opened to Karl who came in and was introduced to the others.

There was a bit of chat when Karl explained how he and Bob had planned what they would do. The six of them would be in three teams of two with one radio per team, Karl with Pete as Bob thought Pete would need the most controlling and would behave with Karl, Colin with a radio along with Ed, and Bob with Bill. The radios had been set to a frequency band that no one other than the three teams and Kim Benjamin could listen into.

"Okay, lads," said Karl as they were about to leave the room, "it's important for us to keep a low profile, so whoever is doing this does not catch on to us. I have worked out when the fires started and as no one can stay here more than seven months before going on leave he is due to go on the next ship. We need to get him before he kills people." There was a nod of agreement from the others. "Okay, lads, good luck and good hunting." They all left the room.

*

The plan was mainly to keep out of the way until the bars closed and everyone had gone to bed. Of course, there were fire wardens and security patrolling the corridors, but the firebug must have known them and the ways they would go. Karl and Bob's plan was for one team to be outside all the time and the other two to be inside, hiding in drying rooms or toilets when anyone was around and then moving around the corridors and looking through glass panels in the fire doors.

"I am getting really pissed off with this," moaned Bill as he sat in the drying room smoking while Bob looked out of a slightly open door. "You said we would get him soon. It's been over a week now."

"It's been four nights, Bill."

"It seems like over a week. I am sat in a bloody drying room in the dark at two thirty in the morning when I–" Bob interrupted his roommate.

"Shut up, someone's coming." Bill got up as they had planned to hide behind the full-size lockers in the centre of the room if anyone came in. "He has got a balaclava on and is carrying something," Bob said in a low voice. "Quick, I think he's coming in." The two quickly disappeared behind the cabinets as the person entered the drying room.

As the door was at one end of the drying room the two "secret service agents" hid behind the lockers at the furthest point from the door. As the lockers were made of mesh wire but with clothing in them a person could see through. This is what Bob and Bill were doing as they watched the firebug put a bundle of papers under the wooden bench that ran around the external walls of the drying room, then put his hand in his pocket to take an item out to light them. As Bob was about to rush and grab him, Karl came on the radio and said, "Come in, Bob, come in."

The firebug turned around to look and Bob said, "Let's get him, Bill!" As the two ran towards him Bill clipped Bob's heel with his foot which sent them both falling to the floor which gave the firebug time to make his escape.

While Bob was on the floor with radio in hand he shouted into it, "He's here in corridor F! Quick, he is getting away!"

As Bill told the lads later, "I was the first up." He then gave chase into the corridor just to see a fire door close into corridor G. Bill ran into the corridor as fast as he could only to see the fire door open at the other end of the corridor where Karl and Pete appeared, all looking at an empty area between them.

"Where is he?" asked Karl.

"I don't know," came the reply from Bill as Bob came in behind him, followed by Colin and Ed.

"He can't have got far," said Bill, "he must be in a room at this end."

"Okay," said Karl, "let's get everyone up and start to narrow it down."

"That's fine," said Bob, "let's start knocking." He banged on room G1 while Bill banged on the door opposite, G2.

While this was happing Ed said, "Hold on, what's that smell?" All stopped as the others smelt the air.

"That's Smelly Sid," said Colin. "I sat behind him on the bus yesterday!"

"G5," said Bob. "I had to see him last week." The six agents gathered outside Sid's room.

Karl banged on the door. "Sid, we know you're in there. Please come out." There was no answer.

"I'll kick the door in," said Pete.

"No," said the security manager. "Let me try again." Karl repeated the command twice more, then looked at Pete and said, "Okay, kick it in then." Pete backed up to the door of G6 and ran across the eight-foot corridor and raised his foot when he neared the door. He was about two feet from it when it opened wide. Smelly Sid was stood there fully clothed with the balaclava still on his face. Pete could not stop and went crashing into the room, falling flat on the floor.

"Sid?" asked Bob. "What have you done?"

"I came here to make a statement."

"What?" asked Karl.

"Not washing and setting fire to you lot. It's a statement!" came the reply from the room, as Pete was picking himself up from the floor and the other occupants of corridor G came out of their rooms to see what the commotion was.

"Statement?" asked Bill. "Statement that you're a fucking nutter!" he shouted.

"No, Britain should never have invaded these islands. They belong to Argentina and they should get out of Northern Ireland also!"

"That's it!" snarled Bill, as he rushed into the room followed closely behind by Colin, grabbing hold of Sid and pulling him to the floor along with Pete who was just getting up.

*

"I think it was fair," said Bill, as he sat in Kim's office with Bob, Karl and Kim.

"Beating up a defenceless man then dragging him into a shower block covering him with washing up liquid and hosing him down is hardly fair," said Kim in a loud voice. "I have always said anyone fighting would be sent home."

"It was hardly fighting," smiled Bob, "they just beat the crap out of him."

"Bob, you know what I mean," came the reply.

"Kim, this is a man who was going to burn us all to death," Bob said raising his voice.

"I know," replied the project coordinator, "but we can't have kangaroo courts."

"It was no court," smiled Karl, "they just beat the shit out of him. And don't forget, Kim, the rest of the corridor joined in when they realised it was the chap who was trying to kill them. Some shouted to hang him."

"Just don't say a word to that," Bob quietly said to Bill beside him.

"But it was Bill who threw the first blow," came back Kim.

"Kim," said Bob, "if it wasn't Bill it would have been another. Feelings were running really high over this. That was a man who could have killed us all. Please, Kim, you can't sack Bill. How will the rest of the workforce feel if you got rid of a man who did what any of them would have done in that situation?"

"He could have just brought him to be locked up then removed from the island."

"Kim, you know I don't like violence, but the truth is there are times when we have to turn a blind eye,"
said Karl.

Before Kim could reply, Bob said, "Kim, please, if you have to do anything give him a written warning.

There was a long silence, then the project coordinator said, "Okay, a warning it is, but this must never be repeated. Do you all understand?" There were nods all around as the three made their way to the door. "Oh, Bob," Kim called out as they were about to leave, "have you a second please?" Bob walked back to Kim who waited for the other two to leave, then said, "That's two favours you owe me now, Bob."

*

"I owe you a favour, bonny lad," George told Bob as they sat in Bob's part-time office drinking coffee.

"Why?" came the reply.

"Because of what you did for me down at Turtle Point."

"George, it was really nothing."

"Nothing, bonny lad Bob? You talked the young lad into coming out for me in very rough seas. I know you talked him into it. And I know that lad does not like me, yet you talked him into coming out for me, and while it was only wind you did think you were saving my life, and I know there's plenty here who would have had a beer that night had I dropped dead over there. The thing is that incident has shown me a thing or two."

The two sat in silence for a moment for Bob to take in all that had been said. He decided that he wouldn't mention about lying to Jimmy about who he was picking up that night and how the lads had wished he had died, but he did think of a favour.

*

"You must be fucking mad if you think I am going to work for that backstabbing bastard," snapped Bill as he washed his face in the wash hand basin in their room while Bob sat in an armchair.

"I didn't say you would take it, I just said I would talk to you about it. You don't like being on the airfield. It's a nice little set up down there. He said you wouldn't have to move in there and he would sort transport for you if you wanted to carry on living here. There are Land Rovers going back and forth to there all the time, he knows you're a good machine driver so he would be doing okay out of it as well."

"I just don't know. I do hate where I am, but everything I have said about him and what he did to Eric... I just don't know."

"Bill, you would be doing what's best for you. You can work any number of hours you like down there so that would mount up your tax-free overtime. If you don't want to work late at night you could work Sundays. There are times when you have to be selfish, Bill."

"I don't know." He walked over and lit one of Bob's cigarettes from the coffee table.

"It's up to you. He said he owed me one and I thought of you."

"Thanks, mate, you do look after us all."

"I try to. It's not easy at times. Look, it's up to you, but he needs an answer by the morning as he does need another machine driver. He said that Arran Jones is now overseeing Turtle Point as well as the airfield so a transfer wouldn't be a problem. It's your call, Bill."

Bill sat down in the empty armchair smoking the cigarette and rubbing his bearded ginger chin. "Okay, mate." He leaned across and shook Bob's hand. "I'll take it."

Chapter 12

The Night is Dark

Since Bob had been in his role with the workforce he had also turned into an agony uncle, a counsellor. There was always a call here and there when he turned up on a section from one of the workers saying, "Bob, can I have a word please?" And word had got around that he was a person you could tell anything to and he would not pass any of it on if the person didn't want it talked about.

He had talked to people about Dear John letters, problems at home, lads just being down with being away from family and home. Bob didn't like the term "depression", he had known people who had been depressed and he knew too many people over the years who had taken their own lives. While he was not a doctor he felt he knew the difference between the "D" word and being down.

But there are times when people take their own lives and no one has seen it coming. This had been the case with news they had got from the last *Kenya* that went back to Cape Town. Bob knew the lad. He had been nicknamed "Joey the Indian". He was from Dorset and they called him this because with his shoulder-length, straight, black hair, thin, pointed and slightly dark facial features, and being tall and slim, he looked very much like a Red Indian from the Old West in America.

He had taken his life going home on leave. It seemed that he had jumped overboard one night. It was the next day when no one had seen him that it was reported and a search of the ship came up with nothing. Bob had said, "He kept himself to himself but I didn't see that coming." He didn't seem down or anything like that, in fact the lads had told Bob he had been "really looking forward to his leave."

Bob had been talking to a medic friend of his, Paul the Medic, and he had said, "that a person did not have to be depressed to take their own life, but hit a black hole where they sunk very low and before they could get out of it they did something. This is where you get people jumping in front of a train or a lorry or jump off a bridge, or in this case jump overboard. He may have felt very down and was looking over the side of the ship and then it's all over."

"That sounds like what happened to the lad on our ship," said Bob.

"And also," replied Paul, "Joey would have heard what had happened on the ship before, and if he had been having dark thoughts this may have put it in his mind."

*

Doctor Death had been given this nickname by the lads early on in the project as he always seemed very low and down when people went to see him. One of the lads, Tim, a tall man in his mid-forties from Nottingham, was telling Bob that he went to see him after he came back from leave about being really low and down. "I said to him I was okay leaving the family, I was okay at Heathrow, I was okay on the ship, I was even okay on the bus from the ship. It was when I saw this place, the camp, then before I could say any more Dr Death said, 'This place, I know exactly what you mean, this place would get anyone down.' I felt like putting my arm around him and saying, 'Now, now, Doctor, everything will be fine.' He was more fucking down than I was! He said he would put me on anti-depressants. I am not going to take them as I have been told that in some people they can make it worse. No, I took them off him as there is an Eastham's lady cleaner who will buy them off me."

*

Bob had spent most of the morning over at the power station. There had been a problem about a shift pattern for working nights. As the power station covered such a large area there was a lot of work ongoing. On top of the concrete floors there was to be a thin resin covering, but as it was laid wet it needed time to dry so it had been agreed that this work would be done at night, but this was causing a clash with other work there which was causing dust which had become a problem with the wet flooring. Bob had been asked over to help resolve it. This was completed to everyone's

212

satisfaction, and as he was leaving he saw Tim and asked him, "How are you feeling now, Tim?"

"I would like to say great, Bob, loving every minute, but you would know I was lying. I think I am getting ship fever."

"I know you don't rate him, but is it worth going back to the doctor?"

"He's a tosser, Bob, you know that. Look, I do have good days and I have bad ones. Work does keep my mind off things, being here and all, eight thousand miles and at least two weeks from home. Letters once a week if you're lucky, a phone call once a month as they are so expensive, you know as well as me, Bob, it's not easy being here."

"I know, Tim," came the reply.

"Do you know what I find the worst, Bob? It's the night. I get through most days okay, and the evenings are mostly okay. Even lying in bed reading is okay. It's when the lights are out and you are alone in the dark with your thoughts." Tim paused then said, "The nights can be long and dark, Bob."

Bob stood and looked at Tim in silence trying to think of some words of comfort, but none were coming to mind when his radio came to life. "Come in, Bob English, come in, Bob." This gave both men a start. Bob took the radio out of the pouch on his belt and answered, "Bob here."

"Bob, can you report to Joe Benson's office in the main compound at once. This is urgent, I repeat, this is urgent."

"Okay, will do, I am on my way."

"Sorry, Tim, I have got to go. I will catch up with you in the next day or so."

"Bob, get going, it's urgent." Bob left and got in the Land Rover with the waiting Ed outside.

*

It was less than ten minutes before Bob got back to the main compound and into Joe's office. He was surprised to see Kim Benjamin in the office also.

After their hellos Joe said, "Bob, do you know Jason Hartley? He is working on the power station."

"Yes, he's a Scottish lad, a really nice chap."

"Bob, his wife's new husband, his children's stepfather..." Joe paused as if finding it hard to find the words. He looked sideways

213

at Kim who nodded. "The new husband has just beaten Jason's four year old daughter to death."

Bob thought he was going to pass out. He grabbed the back of a nearby chair to steady himself. "Are you okay, Bob?" asked Kim.

"Shocked."

"I know," said Joe, "we all are."

"Bob," said Kim, "he is being picked up now and is on his way here. He has not been told yet. We want you to be here also."

"Of course."

"Everything has been sorted. There is a chopper on its way here now. This afternoon's plane from Stanley to the UK has been held until he gets there. When he gets back to the UK it has been agreed with Her Majesty's Government that a chopper will fly him to an airbase nearest his home and there will be a police car waiting to take him home. After we have told him, Bob, I want you to take him to get his gear from his room in your Land Rover. Please stay with him at all times until you hand him over to the RAF," asked Kim.

"Is that okay?" asked Joe.

"Yes, of course," said a stunned Bob. There was a knock on the door. The three men looked at each other.

The welfare manager swallowed hard then said, "Come in."

*

"Oh my God," said Colin sat in the armchair next to Pete in Bill and Bob's room that night, as Bob repeated what had happened to his workmates.

From his top bunk Bill said, "I can't imagine a worse thing happening."

"It was some of the worst moments of my life being with him until he got on the chopper," Bob reported as he finished his nightly tea making duties and handed them out.

"How was he when he was told?" asked Pete.

"Joe told us all to take a seat first, cos I nearly fell over when I was told. When he was told he didn't really say anything."

"You wouldn't know what to say," said Colin.

"It was just awful," continued Bob. "They had very little information to give him, the police at home had contacted our office and they passed it on to here. They told him about the arrangements and he was given a room to phone his mum. I went

214

out and told Ed, then Jason came out and got in. I was sat in the middle in the front of the Rover. He was crying when he got in, Ed started crying, then I started, so there were three roughie toughie construction workers sat in the Land Rover bawling our eyes out."

"You would have to kill him," commented Bill from above, "the bloke who done it that is."

"Well he'll be locked up," said Bob.

"He'll be out some day," said Pete. "I would murder him when he got out."

"I would be there the day he got out," said Bill.

"Then you would be inside," said Bob.

"Wouldn't care, he would have to die," came the reply.

"Totally agree," said Colin.

"Jason has also got a five-year-old son. He is with his mum at the moment," said Bob. "I have got to say they have looked after him, getting him back like that. They dropped everything to sort it out."

"So they should," said Bill.

"I just can't believe what Jason must be going through," commented Colin.

"Oh God, I nearly forgot," said Bill. "The deaf airfield foreman, Larry Harman, got run over by a reversing lorry this afternoon. He's dead!"

"No," came the joint reply.

"Our Land Rover driver told us on the way home tonight."

"This is Death Valley," said Colin.

"What happened?" asked Bob.

"I think I told you he always turned his hearing aids off because of the noise."

"Yes."

"It looks like he was having a pee, he was turned away from the runway, he couldn't hear the reversing horn on the lorry, no hearing aids on, lorry driver didn't see him. Bang!"

"Oh my God," said Bob.

"You said that would happen, Bill," said Pete.

"I did."

"This is just not good," said Bob. "I did get a message from Benjamin that the next committee meeting had been brought forward for tomorrow morning. I bet that's what it is. What a day."

"There is good news out of this shit day," said Bill as he jumped down from his top bunk and went over to his wardrobe. He pulled out three packs of two hundred South African cigarettes and threw a pack to each of them. "You owe me two quid each."

"Where did they come from?" asked Bob.

"South Africa," said Bill with a smile.

"I know that," snapped Bob, "but how did you get them?"

"I knew they were coming but I wanted to keep them as a surprise. A little cheer up gift for the three of you."

"It's no gift if we have to pay two quid for them," mumbled Pete.

"Carry on, Bill," put in Colin.

"I was told about it a while ago when I was working on the airfield. Someone, don't know who, has set it up with the coach drivers in Cape Town that takes us to the airport that every time the *Kenya* is there he puts a couple marked suitcases in the boot. Someone on each trip is paid to pick them up at the dock and bring them here, then sold here for a lot cheaper than them robbing bastards Eastham's sell them."

"How does the driver get his money?" asked Bob.

"Don't know and don't care," came the reply from Bill. "What I do know is we get cheap fags."

"I'll smoke to that," smiled Pete waving his packet in the air.

"I saw on the main noticeboard today," said Bill, "that the comedian Jim Davidson is doing a show here in a few weeks when he is on the island. One person can put in for four tickets at a time. Shall we try to get some?"

"Yes," came the joint reply.

"By the way, Bob," said Colin to his friend, "you are the only one who doesn't want to murder the wanker who killed Jason's girl."

"Oh, bloody hell, I just don't want to see harm come to anyone."

"Oh, come on," said Pete, "he's killed his young girl, a four-year-old kid."

"I hate to say it, but how would you feel, Bob?" asked Colin.

"Okay then," came the reply. "The four of us will wait outside the prison and kick the bastard to death when he comes out."

"Cheers!" came the joint reply as the other three raised their tea cups in the air.

*

216

"Kim, when I left school at fifteen in 1968 I saw a safety film a few years after and it started with a man pointing his finger at us saying, 'One of you will die today.' As an industry we were killing over four hundred men a year," Bob told the committee meeting with Reg beside him across the table from the project coordinator, newly promoted contracts manager Arran Jones and safety officer Tom Smith. "We are now in 1984 and I really don't think things have changed that much."

"Bob, you have been in this industry all your working life," Kim replied, "you know how dangerous it is." Bob nodded his agreement. "The thing is this is construction and people get killed doing it, it's a fact, it is part and parcel of what we do. You know that."

"Well it shouldn't be part and parcel," replied Reg.

"Kim, no one knows that better than me, I've had friends die, but as Reg said it shouldn't be. As I said this is 1984, things should have moved on from the 1960s and '70s, but with our accident record here it has not happened." Bob reported this to the meeting with venom in his voice.

"You know how tight the programme is here," put in Arran.

"Oh great," responded Reg with a raised voice. "As long as the plane lands in January it doesn't matter how many of us fucking die!"

Arran was stopped from replying by Kim who said, "Reg, Bob, of course safety is important to us, that's why I have asked Tom to be with us today. We need to work together."

"There is a lot of bad feelings about, aha, dare I say, the lack of safety," Bob said. "We are going through a spell where a lot of men have been here a long time now, and there are a lot of people feeling very low. We have already had two men kill themselves."

"Sorry," said Tom, "I have to correct you there, Bob. One got washed overboard while he was being sick and the other went missing."

"Let's not kid ourselves," snapped Reg. "We all know they both fucking jumped!"

"OKAY!" the project coordinator intervened. "We have two issues here, health and safety and morale. Regarding the first we have another safety officer coming out."

"Sam Crisp," reported Tom.

"When will he be here?" asked Reg.

217

Kim looked at Tom and said, "He's a she. It's Samantha Crisp, she is on the air bridge as we speak and will be working within a day or so."

"A woman?" asked Reg.

"Yes," came the reply from Kim, "she is a young lady in her late twenties. She is fully trained in health and safety and has been working for Johnston's for a while now and is very good at what she does."

"My God," said Reg, "there's no way the lads will listen to a bird telling them what to do. No way."

"They will have to," said Tom.

"This is the future, Reg," said Kim. "There will come a time when there are many women working in our industry."

"No way," replied the man from Derby. "That will never happen. This is an industry for men, always has been and always will be."

"You may see that differently one day, Reg," said Tom.

"I can't ever see it happening, never," came Reg's reply.

"You will be surprised then, Reg. It's going to happen, and remember Britain has a lady Prime Minster at the moment," put in Arran.

"That's what I mean. Look at the miners' strike and unemployment," moaned Reg.

"Anyway, Bob," continued Kim, "I want Sam to spend some time with you to start with."

"WHAT?" came the shocked reply.

"We need to cover the whole project. Tom will continue to move around, but you get around a lot and cover all areas and meet a lot of men. I just want her to get the feel of it for a while, then she can get on with it."

"You'll be in there, Bob," Reg elbowed his committee colleague.

"Piss off, Reg, I am happily married. Look, Kim, I am no safety person. She will be better off with Tom."

"No, Bob, I have made my mind up. I think it will work well. Now, morale, what are we going to do about that?"

"Well," said the safety officer, "I have been thinking about that. What about if we give some sort of reward if a section goes so long without an accident?"

"That's a good idea," said Reg, "what could we give?"

"Well, I was thinking if a section–"

"Tom," put in Kim, "while that is very admirable, and of course a very good incentive, it may just have an adverse effect."

"Sorry, Kim, I don't understand," replied the safety officer. "The thing is..."

"The thing is," Bob interrupted, "if we give the lads rewards for no accidents, the work and output will slow down to make sure there are no accidents. Am I correct, Kim?"

There was silence in the room as all assembled waited for the coordinator's reply, which came after a few seconds thinking time. "I think you have put it very bluntly, Bob. I really do want everyone to come out of this project safely. To give rewards for being safe is just..."

There was a pause, then Arran put in, "It's not a case of slowing the work down. We expect all of the workforce to work safely at all times, no matter what."

"Thank you, Arran," continued Kim. "That is a really good idea, Tom, but let's save it for another time. It may just be difficult to implement at this moment in time and where we are."

"Well if we–" Tom said before being cut off by Kim for a second time.

"Do we have any another morale boosting ideas, gentlemen?"

There was silence in the meeting room for a second time in a short period until Reg said, "What about a fun day?"

"What?" asked Kim.

"We had a day when we first moved up to the camp," continued Reg, "didn't we, Bob? The bowling day when the overtime ban was on." There was no reply from management to this.

"Yes," came back Bob. "We had a good day, a very drunken day I may add, but it was really good."

"So, what are you suggesting?" asked Arran.

"We could have a day," Bob said.

"A Sunday," replied Kim.

"Maybe a Sunday, afternoon," put in Arran, "then if we need, or should people want to work on the Sunday morning, they can do."

"Well done," said Kim. "What are we going to have?"

"It will be games," said Bob.

"It could be like a village fete," said Tom. "We have one in our village every summer."

"We could have stalls and sideshows, we could maybe make some small charges and raise some money," said Arran.

"Oh yeah," growled Reg, "and where is the money going to end up?"

"What if we give it to the Stanley Hospital fire fund?" replied Arran.

"That's a really good idea," said Tom, "and it will look really good on the workforce here."

"Okay," said Kim as he stood up. "I will leave it to you two and Joe Benson," he looked at Bob and Reg, "to organise it. I think this coming Sunday would be good, gents."

"But it's Wednesday today," remarked Bob."

"Okay, next Sunday, but let's make it happen, please?"

"There will be costs," said Bob.

"Talk it over with Joe. Okay, I think that's about it. Let's have a good uplifting day. Thank you, gents," said Kim as he picked up his books and files from the table in front of him and left the room with Bob and Reg left sat looking at each other.

*

As Bob walked along the corridor from the meeting room an office door opened and Karl popped his head out. "Bob, can I have a quick word please?"

"Of course," said the committeeman as he left the others and entered Karl's office and sat at his desk. He took out a packet of the South African cigarettes, lit one and placed the packet and his lighter on the desk. "How can I help, Karl?"

"I haven't really had a chance to say well done on getting Smelly Sid. Kim was really pleased."

"No problem, Karl. The main thing was we didn't want to get burnt to death."

"No, of course not, but well done. Any news on the drug dealer yet?"

"Aha, no, not really," came the reply as the Londoner shifted in his seat.

"Kim is really keen to get him caught and have him out of here."

"I will let you know as soon as I hear anything, Karl." Bob started to get up.

"We have a new problem that Kim wants us to sort out."

"What's that?" came the reply as Bob sat down again.

"Cigarettes."

"What?"

"South African cigarettes. They are being smuggled in here and undercutting Eastham's prices, which they and Kim are very upset about, and of course no tax duty is being paid on them."

Bob stood up and took his cigarettes and lighter off the table in one movement. "No problem, must go, got a lot to do. See you later, Karl." Bob turned and left the small office.

Karl stayed in his chair and smiled and said to himself, "He knows, he knows about both."

*

"It is nice to meet you, Bob," said Sam as she held her hand out to greet him. "I have heard a lot about you."

"All good I hope," smiled Bob as he shook the new safety officer's hand.

"Oh yes, of course. Kim and Tom have told me what a great job you have done keeping the peace around here."

"I am not sure if that's the best term. I represent the lads and help sort as many issues as possible. How was the trip on the air bridge down here? I hear it's a nightmare being shut up in a Hercules transporter plane all day, and the noise is bad as well, isn't it?"

"Yes, it's awful, and a shoebox lunch. No, I don't want to be back on a Herc again for a while."

"Better than two weeks on the old rust bucket of the *Kenya*," put in Ed who was with them along with Tom Smith. The four of them were stood in the camp's large outside open area between the canteens, bars and the accommodation.

"Oh, I wouldn't mind a couple of weeks sailing," said the slim, five-foot-six inches tall with shoulder-length dark hair from Maidstone in Kent.

"You wouldn't say that after bobbing around for two weeks with nothing to do, just reading or walking around all day," said Bob.

"You have been here a while now, haven't you, Bob?" asked Sam.

"Yes, maybe too long."

"How long?"

221

"I came on the first *Kenya* to sail from Cape Town. We got here just before Christmas last year."

"When do you finish?" the new safety officer asked.

"By the time we sail back it will be at the end of next January. Fourteen months done."

"Will you come back?"

"Not if my wife has anything to do with it. She says in every letter don't go back after this. But we have only recently bought our own house and the mortgage is on the large size with all the interest rates going up and up. I have got to say the tax-free money does help a lot."

"You know Kim wants you to come back, Bob, he is very pleased with the job you are doing," put in Tom.

"I know, but I am not married to Kim, thank God." This comment brought laughs from the other three. "So how did you get into safety, Sam? We don't see many women in our industry."

"My Dad was a safety officer. I was very close to him. He died last year."

"Oh, I am sorry," said Bob.

"Oh, it was a relief in the end. He had cancer and suffered for a long time in a lot of pain. No, he always talked to me about safety and I can't ever remember wanting to do anything else. My Mum died giving birth to me, the only child. My grandmother moved in with us so that Dad could carry on working, but apart from my Nan, Dad brought me up on his own."

"Well I have to take my hat off to you," Bob continued. "It can't have been easy, for a woman that is. Not with some of the idiots we employ in this industry."

"Oh, I have heard it all these past years, but my dad always said they are the ones with the problem, and as soon as you react to it you become infected with their problem."

"A wise man your dad," said Bob.

"Yes, he was indeed."

"Look," he continued, "I am not sure why Kim wants you to be with me, and Ed, I should say. You will do more safety things with Tom."

"You know Kim wants Sam with you as you get around so much, and it gives both of us a chance to cover more areas," replied Tom.

"Yes, but over the next week or so I have got this fun day thing to sort out, so I will not be getting around that much."

222

"I will help you," said Sam. "We'll get the fun day sorted out together and we can still get around the site. We can do it all. Many hands make light work."

"Well done," said Tom, "that should work."

*

"Have you told Jane that you have a woman sat in the Land Rover next to you all day long?" asked Bill as they had their nightly meeting in their room along with Pete and Colin.

"No, why should I?" came the reply from Bob as he handed cups of tea out to his workmates. "There is nothing to tell. Sam is another worker like the rest of us."

"There are a few differences from us," put in Colin.

"Have you not noticed?" smiled Pete.

"Oh, piss off," snapped Bob as he sat on his bottom bunk. "It's no big deal. Yes, she is a woman, and a really nice girl, but she is a safety officer here to do a job."

"Yeah," said Pete, "I don't get this woman safety officer thing. How did that happen? I mean she should be a cook or a secretary, this work is for men!"

"It seems times are changing," put in Colin. "Mind you, I don't have a problem with it. The more women the better as far as I am concerned."

"The thing is," said Bill from his top bunk, "can she do the job? It does seem odd a woman and all, you have to see that, Bob. Will she be able to spot things a real safety officer would?"

"Oh, for fuck's sake," snapped Bob as he got up to get a cigarette off the coffee table. "She is a real safety officer, she knows more about safety than the four of us put together. She has more qualifications than the four of us, she has been to university, her dad has been taking her to building sites since she was a little girl, she lives and breathes construction safety. And all of you lads know if a person knows what they are talking about as soon as you start speaking to them, and believe me that young lady knows her stuff. She knows more than a lot of male safety officers I have known. No, I think it's great to have people like her coming into the industry. In the few days I have been with her I have picked up a lot."

"Well, it just doesn't seem right to me, a woman and all," commented Pete.

223

"Oh, for God's sake," said Bob as he sat back on the bunk.

"But how is it with the other lads?" asked Bill. "How are they all taking it?"

"On the whole not too bad, but of course there has been the idiots and embarrassing moments. For me and Ed that is, Sam has taken it all in her stride."

"What's been said?" asked Colin.

"Oh, all sorts. Lads shouting out things like, 'Have you got stockings on, love?' 'Get them off.' Loads of things, childish, just silly, and when she is out of earshot things to me and Ed like, 'Oh, you're in there, lads, I bet you're shagging her,' and loads of things like that."

"You know everyone will think you are giving her one?" said Colin.

"Well I am not, and won't be," came the snapped reply. "She's a co-worker who happens to be female. Now can we change the subject please? This is boring!"

"Hey, Colin," called out Bill from his top bunk. "Bob knows how to keep his dick in his trousers."

"Piss off," came the reply from the armchair. This brought a smile to Bob's face.

"How is the fun day coming on, Bob?" asked Pete.

"Not too bad. Loads of lads have bought into it and are helping out. Don't forget, you lads, I need to know what you are going to do soon. It's not that far away now."

"It's all under control," said Bill.

"What is it?" replied Bob.

"It's a surprise," said Colin. "You will see on Sunday."

"It's not guess the weight of your new best mate George is it, Bill?" smiled Bob.

"There is nothing wrong with him and David Antony when you get to know them."

"You called them backstabbing bastards the other week," put in Colin.

"I know, but they are looking after us lads down at Turtle Point. I think they know they can't treat us lads like they have others in the past."

"In Africa," mocked Colin.

"Well," replied Bill, "when you talk to them that is all they have known for years, having people jump up and down for them

224

all of the time. They say jump and the lads they have had working for them have said, 'How high, boss?' No, they are changing."

"This change of heart with you about them, Bill, wouldn't have anything to do with them taking you in the senior managers' bar as a guest last night, would it?" asked his roommate.

Well, let's just say that a person has to know which side their bread is buttered on."

"Creep," said Colin.

"Well," came the reply from above in a put-on posh accent, "it's very nice in there I'll have you know, old chap!"

*

It was a bright sunny but chilly spring morning in this part of the world as Bob's Land Rover made its way along one of the now many finished roads. The three were playing their new game which was, "how many workers would have their safety helmets on when they got to a work area".

"Just stop the Rover here, Ed," called out Sam from the front where she was sat between the driver and Bob as they passed an area that would be large storage halls like warehouses that would hold supplies coming in from the UK. There was to be eight large sheds in this area. The first one was under construction. The vehicle stopped and they all got out and put their white safety helmets on, as the two lads had now got used to doing since they had Sam with them.

Bob said to Sam, "Be careful, this is Jake Jordan's section. He's a real hothead."

"Thanks, Bob, I am sure everything will be fine."

The lads stood beside the Land Rover and stayed on the road as the safety officer made her way down a small muddy slope to the work area below that had a mobile crane set up lifting large steel beams high in the air, about fifteen-metres, where they were being fitted by two workers. There was a worker to one side on the ground where he was slinging the crane's chains around the steel. Below the workers in the air were six other men working below the steel frame. None of the workers had safety helmets on, and the two men working high not only did not have helmets on but were also not wearing safety harnesses to stop them from falling. The whole area was covered in rubbish and litter and looked a real mess.

225

Sam called out to the two men working high on the steel frame. "Stop work now and come down please." She also called out to the men working below to stop working and to come over to her. All of the workers followed her instruction.

At this point Bob walked away along the road out of earshot from the others and said into his radio, "If there are any senior managers near Section 38, could you please get here ASAP as there is a young lady who may be in need of assistance in the next few minutes!"

Sam was about to talk to the men when out of one of four cabins that made up a small compound that was used for an office along with a canteen, toilets and storage container, a large framed bald-headed north east of England man in his late forties came running over from the far side into the work area.

"What the fuck is going on here? You men get back to work now."

"Hello," Sam put her hand out to shake with the newcomer, "I am Sam Crisp the new safety officer. We haven't met yet."

"I don't give a fuck who you are. How dare you come onto MY site and stop MY men from working. Now fuck off and let us get the work we are here to do DONE!"

"It's Jake, isn't it?" Sam smiled at the section foreman and again offered her hand to him.

Jake looked her up and down. "A fucking woman safety officer," he said turning away. "What the fuck does she know?" He then shouted out, "Right, you lot get back to fucking work. NOW!"

Sam called out, "This work area is unsafe. I am stopping work here until such a time that the area is made fit to work in, and I will make sure that anyone who works before it is safe to do so will get a written warning."

Jake turned back and walked to Sam pointing his finger and almost poking her in the face. At this moment Ed was about to go to her aid, but Bob held him back by the arm. "Just wait a short while," whispered, Bob, "give her a chance. We will go in if we need to or if he touches her."

Shouting at Sam, Jake said, "JUST WHO THE FUCK DO YOU THINK YOU ARE? A FUCKING WOMAN COMING HERE TELLING ME MY FUCKING JOB?"

In a very calm and even tone she replied, "I'll tell you who I am. I am the fucking woman who is going to stop work here until you get a safe means of ladder access for these men to get up to the roof area. I am also the fucking woman who is going to stop work here until those men are working up there with safety harnesses on which I know you have. I am also the fucking woman who is going stop any work happening under where the steel is being fixed. I am also the fucking woman who is going to make you all wear safety helmets in this area, which again I know you have. I am also the fucking woman who is going to stop all work until this whole area is cleaned up and is fit to work in."

"RIGHT," replied Jake in a very angry voice. "You are now going to be told this once more. Get the–"

"I am also the fucking woman," Sam said before Jake could finish his sentence, still in a very calm tone, "who will reserve you a cabin on the next *Kenya* for when you return to the UK dismissed for gross misconduct if what I have asked for is not done in the next two hours."

There was silence all around as everyone waited for Jake's reply. Before he could say a word, a Land Rover pulled up on the road behind Bob's. Arran Jones wound his driver's window down and called out, "Everything okay down there, Sam?"

"I think so. Is everything okay, Jake?" she asked the foreman.

Again, before he could reply, Arran said, "Jake, Sam is here to help us all to get home safely. I want you to take her advice and do everything she tells you to, and do not give her a hard time. Do I make myself clear?"

"The thing is, boss," Jake replied slowly.

"JAKE, do I make myself clear?" Arran repeated in a loud voice.

"Yes, boss."

"And, Jake."

"Yes, boss."

"Get this fucking place cleaned up before someone trips and breaks their neck. It's a shithole!" The Welshman then drove off.

"Okay," said Sam, "we will see you in two hours." She turned and walked away, then stopped and turned back towards Jake and said, "Oh, and one more thing, Jake."

"What?" came the snapped reply from the stunned foreman.

"It's a lovely morning, isn't it?"

*

227

As the three were driving past the power station a group of workers had just come out of the main doors and were making their way to lunch. Bob saw Tim amongst them and asked, "Can you stop please, Ed, and wait one minute. I just want a quick word with one of the lads."

The Land Rover stopped and Bob got out and called Tim over. "How are you feeling, Tim?" Bob asked when they were on their own. "Now the ship has gone and all?"

"Oh, not too bad. Thanks for asking, Bob, but I know it will start again when the ship is on the way back."

"But you go on leave the one after that, don't you?"

"I do, I can't wait."

"Hang in there, mate, I have got to go to a meeting, but I am always here for a chat if you need one."

"Thanks, Bob." The committeeman went to leave. "But there is one thing, Bob."

"What's that, Tim?"

"The nights are still dark!"

*

It was one thirty on a sunny Sunday afternoon when Kim made a short speech to open the first Mount Pleasant fete, "wishing everyone an enjoyable afternoon."

Bob, Sam, Reg and Ed had worked on and off to put it together for the past week or so. They had roped in as many co-workers as they could to put stalls together. Tables had been brought out of the canteen and placed in the large open area outside of the canteens. Joe Benson had talked Eastham's new manager Jenny Walton into donating some prizes out of the shop for the stalls that included, "throw the plastic drainage pipe washers over the concrete filled milk cartons", a bit like hoopla, "guess how many stones are in a bucket", "guess the name of a toy penguin", which had gone down well for the corridor bowls day. There was a, "can you hit a four-inch nail into a piece of wood with two blows from a claw hammer"? and a "throwing the wellie" (Wellington boot) contest. Tom Smith had been to Stanley that week and brought a real set of bowls and skittles and other stalls the lads had set up.

There was a large barrel of water in the middle of the fete's area. This had appeared over the last night and no one seemed to know anything about it.

228

Eastham's had set up a bar outside and were also cooking hot dogs and burgers nearby. Again, red and white bunting protection tape had been used to decorate the area. And with a cassette player playing music, everyone was starting to enjoy themselves. Bob was with Sam, Ed, Reg, Tom and George, when Kim, Joe, Roger and Arran came over to join them.

"Well done, everyone," said Kim. "It all looks very good."

There was a nodded thanks from everyone, when Sam said to Bob, "I thought your mates were doing something, Bob."

"So, did I, and they wouldn't tell me what so I really don't know."

"Look," said Ed pointing at the corner of the staff canteen where Bill had come around carrying a large sack followed behind by Pete and Colin who were carrying a set of stocks that were painted pink and with blue writing across the top of them that said "JLB Entertainment Centre". They walked over to the area that had the full barrel of water waiting for them. Bill tipped out the contents of the sack which was sponges, which when wet would be thrown at the person in the stocks for the cost of fifty pence a go.

"So, who is first in the stocks?" asked Bill when the stocks that Colin had secretly made over the past week had been put in place. "How about you, George?"

"Hell, no, bonny lad, that would kill me."

"Come on," shouted Bill, "we need a volunteer."

He was about to ask Kim when Sam walked forward and put her right hand to the side of her mouth as if to shout, then in a pretend male voice she shouted, "Let's put that fucking bitch of a women safety officer in the stocks, lads!" This was for a few seconds greeted with a stunned silence, then followed by a large roar of approval from the gathered workforce.

Bob grabbed Sam's arm and said, "You don't have to do this."

She looked at him and said in a firm voice, "Oh yes I do!" She then smiled and said, "It will be fun," then she held his hand and shook it and said, "Guess what?"

"What?"

"You're next, after me!"

Chapter 13

A Nice Day Out!

The end of October and the start of November saw a real uplift in the progress of work. As summer was coming in this part of the world, section managers were told to increase the overtime with the longer days if they had the call for it. "We need to take advantage of these long days and better weather, gentlemen," Kim had told a managers' meeting at the end of October. "We have from now until the end of March next year, 1985, and the next winter to make real progress. Any problems you bring them straight to Arran or myself. Do you all understand? No messing about. We have an aeroplane to land in January and troops to move into the new camp before next winter."

The airfield was now working two twelve-hour shifts on the muck shifting and peat stripping, along with rock breaking for drainage. The hammering of the rock breaking machines could be heard faintly at the camp throughout the night.

The concrete train was now working as long as the light would allow and a new consignment of mobile lighting tower sets had arrived on the latest cargo ship which meant more work could be carried out in non-daylight hours.

The water treatment plant near West Cove was well underway and so was the pipeline that would carry the fresh water supply. This would terminate at a smaller pumping station not far from the main camp and in turn water would be pumped to all areas.

*

"That's great news," said Bob. "Do we have tickets for all of us to see Jim Davidson?"

"Yes," replied Pete, "we got picked out of the draw. It's on Sunday night, 11th November."

"Is that not the day we have booked the bus to go to Stanley?" Colin asked the others in the nightly meeting in Bill and Bob's room.

"It is," said Bob as he handed out the tea, "but we can get the five thirty bus back and it will give us plenty of time," he said as he sat on his bottom bunk. Then there was a knock on the door. "Come in," he called out.

"If you are female leave your knickers at the door," Bill called out from his top bunk.

The door opened to reveal Sam stood in the opening. "Well I am female, but I did not intend to leave my knickers at the door mainly because I have been wearing long johns since I have been here and they take an age to get on and off." Bill flew up in the air on his top bunk as this happened and hit his head on the ceiling and Bob nearly fell off his bottom bunk.

"Hi... hi, good evening, Sam," stumbled Bob as he got to his feet to greet the unexpected guest. "Come in, come in. To what do we owe this pleasure?"

"Well, you told me about the nightly meeting and gossip with the boys, and as I would like to be one of the boys I thought I'd join you. If that's okay?"

"No problem," said Bob, "would you like a tea?"

"Oh yes, thank you, Bob." Pete leapt up to grab the girlie magazine he had been reading and had thrown on the coffee table a short time before.

"Have my seat," offered Colin as he went to get up.

"No, that's fine," replied the young lady. "Here will be fine," as she sat where Bob had been sitting on his bunk. "What's the talk tonight, lads? Carry on, don't worry about me."

"Oh," said Pete we were just talking about going to Stanley next Sunday and the Jim Davidson show that night. We have tickets for both."

"Well," replied the newcomer, "I am not worried about seeing the show, but what about me tagging along with you lot to Stanley for the day?"

"That's not a problem," said Colin. "Is it, lads?" They all agreed.

"Sam?" asked Bob. "Did you see the ice dancing on telly, Torvill and Dean winning the gold medals at the Olympics?"

"Oh, it was great. Do you like them?"

"Yes, I follow all sports, and of cause the British ones. It is hard here but I read about it in the paper. I love the music they danced to, 'Bolero', by Maurice Ravel."

"Are you in to all that, Bob?" asked Pete.

"Classical music, yeah. I was false fed on it at school by two teachers to be fair, but I like that, poetry and all the old books."

"Oh, so do I," said Sam.

"That's girl's stuff, ice dancing," put in Bill.

"Go away," replied Bob, "it takes a lot of hard work what they do. And not only are they British, they come from your part of the world, the Midlands."

"Oh, that's good. Whereabouts?"

"Nottingham," Bob replied.

"Oh, just keep it as the Midlands, that's fine," came the reply from the top bunk.

"By the way," put in Sam. "I got something tonight." She put her hand inside her blue jacket pocket and pulled out a brown paper bag. Then out of that she removed five large Kit Kat chocolate bars. "Eastham's just got these in the shop today. I got a tip-off from Jenny Walton, their manager. I share a room with her."

"That's great," cried out Pete. "I can't remember the last time I had one of the them," he said as Sam handed them around.

"As a rule, Eastham's have first dips on anything like that," groaned Bill.

"Well," smiled Sam, "you know someone on the inside now, don't you?"

*

It was another bright but very cold morning with the wind blowing in from Antarctica. There had in fact been some very heavy frosts over the past few nights. It was ten o'clock on Sunday, 11th November, 1984. The four lads along with Sam, Wolfie and Ed waited for the bus at the camp's pick-up points to take them to Port Stanley. Pete had been talking to Del, Hack's brother, who had a large bag with him.

When he re-joined the lads as the first bus pulled up Bill asked, "What was all that about with Del Dobson?"

"He's got a big bag of dope there he is selling to some army lads today. He got loads off the last ship."

232

"He will get caught," said Colin.

"No," Pete replied, "it's all gone quite again."

"Who cares?" said Wolfie. "If it makes everyone chill out it can't be too bad, can it? It was everywhere when I worked in Morocco."

"Well," said Bob, "the point is it's illegal, no matter where we are. We are under British law."

"You smoked it," said Colin.

"Did you?" asked Sam.

"No, well... yes."

"You did," put in Bill, "we all did."

"I know, but only a few puffs. For God's sake it was when we first got here. It was not an easy time, just before Christmas and all, leaving the family at that time of year."

"Here's the bus," put in Ed. The bus with "Port Stanley" spelt out on the front pulled up in front of the now large queue waiting for two buses that would go that morning. The waiting crowd started to file onto the single-deck bus.

"You need to show me your tickets and ID badge before you get on," the driver said. "You must wear your ID at all times in Stanley."

"Hold on, there's Tom Smith. I forgot I had to tell him something about a report. Can you save me a seat please, Bob?" asked Sam.

Before he could answer the bus, driver said, "We can't wait long, love."

"I really won't be long." Sam dashed off towards her colleague who was on his way out of breakfast. They chatted for a short while, then the female safety officer made her way back to the bus whose passengers were now singing "Why are we waiting"? Sam took her seat next to Bob as the bus left for its first stop at Hampton.

*

On 8th June 1982, two Royal Navy ships, the *Sir Galahad* and the *Sir Tristram,* were moored in Bluff Cove, a small inlet of water. The ships mainly had Welsh Guards on board waiting to go ashore.

At approximately two o'clock in the afternoon local time the two ships were attacked by three A-4 Skyhawks from the

Argentine Air Force. The *Sir Galahad* was hit by two or three bombs and set alight. A total of forty-eight soldiers and crewmen were killed and ninety-seven wounded in the explosions and subsequent fires.

Her captain, Philip Roberts, waited until the last minute to abandon ship and was the last to leave. He was awarded the DSO for his leadership and courage.

Chiu Yiu Nam, a seaman on the *Sir Galahad,* was awarded the George Medal for rescuing ten men trapped in the bowels of the ship.

*

This was the second Remembrance Sunday since the conflict ended. Many had gathered for the service around the forty-eight white crosses and the marmoreal that made up the graveyard overlooking the bay. There were many military personnel, along with government officials, the press, locals and some workers from Mount Pleasant. Arran Jones was there with George. Being Welsh, Arran had asked to represent the company and lay a wreath.

Dai Jenkins, a Welsh machine driver from the airfield, had also came with a wreath. This had been paid for by the street he lived in Wales for a young neighbour who had died on the *Sir Galahad.* They paid for it to be made up in Stanley and brought out to him that morning. After the "Last Post" had sounded everyone broke away to go back to their transports. Bob, Colin, Sam, Ed and Bill made their way back to the bus and stopped to talk to Dai on the way.

"Well done," said Bob shaking Dai's hand. "It was really touching."

"Had me crying," said Colin.

"Well you are a southern softy," commented Bill.

"So was I," said Ed.

"We know what you lot from the north east are like," Bill replied.

"Okay" said Bob, "let's continue to Stanley."

"Not us," said Dai, "there's four of us get a Land Rover and come here every Sunday. Have done for months. We take the sheep farmer to the bar, pay to get him pissed out of his head, then one at a time we slip out and over to his house and take turns with his wife. See you later, lads." Dai turned and walked off.

234

"Bob?" asked Sam in a shocked voice. "Is that true?"

"Well," came the reply, "I have heard rumours, but I really don't know if it's true. But saying that, in the months I have been here I don't think there is anything I would disbelieve now!"

*

The lads' bus stopped behind the other JLB bus alongside the water inlet in the capital. It was noticeable that there was a large police and army presence there. When the driver opened the doors an army officer got on and said, "You need to all wait here. We are doing a routine check of all ID cards."

"What's this all about?" asked one of the workers. "I am busting for a pee."

"Won't be long," came the reply. It was just a few minutes before two police officers came on. Three soldiers were stood outside of the bus.

"Okay, lads," said the sergeant, "one at a time show me your pass and you can leave." One by one they started to leave the bus. Del walked along from near the rear of the bus, empty-handed. He showed his pass to the officer who said, "Okay, lad, just sit down there." Del took a seat. When the bus was empty apart from him the police sergeant said, "Where is it, lad?"

"Where's what?" came the reply.

"Don't piss me about, lad," snapped the sergeant. "I've got too much to do. Where's your bag of fucking dope?"

Before Del could say any more the other policeman said, "He was sat back there, sarge."

"Okay, lad, go and take a look." Within a very short space of time the police officer came back holding Del's bag which he had pushed under the seat in front of him.

All of the workers were waiting outside of the bus as Del was taken off in handcuffs by the police.

*

"That is the best dinner I have had since I can't remember," said Bob as he and Sam came out of The Atlas after eating Sunday lunch together. The rest of the lads had gone to the NAAFI where they had been invited by some soldiers who had visited their camp a short time before. They could get cheap food, drink and cigarettes in there. Sam had not wanted to go, so Bob had said he would stay with her. Bob had rung home and was upset when he came out of the red British phone box as he always was after he phoned home. They had eaten late into the afternoon so they started to make their way back to the bus pick-up point.

They walked along the water's edge chatting, mostly about nothing as they had become accustomed to when they were alone when Sam asked, "Have you told Jane about me?"

"What?" Bob stopped and asked.

"Jane, your wife, does she know about me?"

"What's to know?" came the reply.

"You are working almost full-time with a woman, Bob, you should tell her before Colin tells Jean."

"It's no big deal, we are only workmates."

"I know, Bob, but I don't have a dick between my legs like your other workmates."

"Oh, don't talk like that, Sam, you sound like Bill."

"I'm sorry, I don't like swearing and only do it to make a point, but the truth is I think you should tell her in a letter before she finds out. She would be so hurt."

"Nothing is happening between us, is it?"

"No, and that is the whole point. If she finds out another way she will think there is. I know I would!" They walked along in silence for a while in the spring afternoon sunshine, but still with the chilled wind blowing.

They passed the large four whale bones and Government House when Bob said, "Yes, you are right. Again, I might add."

"I am a woman."

"No answer to that one," replied Bob. "Yes, I will do it, and do it soon."

"Well done. Now, what is it you want to tell me?"

"Tell you what?"

"You said in the pub you had something to tell me and you would do so after dinner. What is it?"

"Oh yes. Do you remember the other week you said you loved writing and poetry, the classics and all?"

"I do, Mr English."

"And when I said I wrote poetry, you said could you hear some?"

"I did indeed, kind sir. Please continue."

236

"Well, I have brought two out with me. Do you want to hear them?"

"Oh yes, I do, but this has to be right." She pointed to a bench not far in front of them on some grass near the water's edge in front of the road where the bus pick-up point was. "Let's sit down." They made their way to the seat and sat down, Bob got some papers out of the inside pocket of his jacket.

"Okay, I have been doing some writing here to keep myself sane, to get away from this place for a few hours in my head at night. The first one I will read is just a bit of fun. It's called *The Abduction*."

"Oh my God," said Sam.

"It is really not how you would think. Shall I start?"

The Abduction.

My first day at school was one I will never forget,
For not many four-year olds had to be dragged, I'll bet?

I wasn't hurting anyone by playing all day,
I had made believe friends with whom I would play.

Then the bombshell was dropped, when my mum said to me,
"It's school tomorrow," what a shock, no longer would I be free.

I protested a lot, and said "she was interfering with my human rights,"
Not really, I just cried a lot, and that was out of fright.

I sobbed in bed that night, thinking my world had come to an end,
And what was this rubbish about the best time of my life and meeting new friends?

I ask you, what did my mother know of such things as this?
I would use plan "A" as I was about to resist.

I would refuse to get dressed that very next morn,
Better still, hide my clothes before the dawn.

But that fell through as the shelf I could not reach,
Was I really to be taken away for them to teach?

A uniform was put on me, with much a to-do,
Maybe I was going to prison and not to school?

My mum had her own plan, as I lay stiff, crying on the floor,
She got her heavy, Mrs Field from next door.

They picked me up, as by arms and legs I was caught,
But you'll be pleased to know, every inch of the way I fought.

Oh, the panic that went through me as the big gates got near,
I would never see my home again, that was now the fear.

Into the classroom I kicked and screamed as I was not being coy,
And how dare that teacher to tell me, "you are being a silly little boy!"

When was the last time two ruffians came and took her away?
What did she know of my plight? To her I would like to say.

And as if enough disasters had not befallen me that day,
On top of all that, my mother left me and went away.

And would you believe that the talk was of dolls as next to a girl I was sat,
She didn't want to hear of my abduction, so I told her she was fat!

I tried to escape, but found I could not,
But by me that first day at school will never be forgot.

"I love it," it said Sam. "I can just see you laying stiff on the floor."

"Most of it was true. My dad died when I was three and where we lived didn't have many children about. It was just my mum and me at home, I didn't even know what school was, so it was a big shock when I was told."

"You had no idea about school?"

"She must have told me but I really can't remember. I mean, I wasn't hurting anyone, they could have left me to play all day," Bob laughed. "I just wanted to poke fun at myself because the way I behaved that day was so stupid."

"Bob, you were four, it must have been such a shock. I can understand that."

"Yeah, but I was like that most of my childhood. Looking back, I would have been the naughty boy you just wouldn't have wanted to be around."

"I think you are doing yourself an injustice."

"No, I think I was a nightmare for those who had to put up with me, but hopefully I have grown out of all of that now."

"You have. Now come on, let's hear the next one."

"Well, this is about seeing an Albatross flying behind our ship coming down here. It was lovely, but I will let you make your own mind up."

The Albatross.

It was in southern seas that I first saw him gild,
He followed our ship, never trying to hide.

So graceful he looked, as he flew to and fro,
Always knowing which way, he would go.

He never seemed tired nor in need of a rest,
Just as well, it was far from his nest.

Hardly a flap came from those long slender wings,
He had great ease of doing things.

As the sun went down on his back at night,
What a picture it made, what a beautiful sight.

His wings were black, his plumage white.
So those colours can live together, and be alright!

Soaring so high, he would fly for the sky,
Then dive for the sea as straight as a die.

He never stopped, not even to eat,

239

But some of those fish would be his treat.

Two thousand miles we could be from land,
But that flying wonder never needed a hand.

How could God create such a creature as this?
Then give man a gun, just to kill for his bliss.

In those southern seas he was always there,
I would like to think, he had not a care.

"I actually want to clap," said Sam after a short while when Bob had finished. "I really like it. You made it sound so graceful."

"That's what I wanted to do. It is just a lovely sight to see."

"You like rhyming poetry then?"

"Well, yes. Is that a problem?"

"No, of course not, I like it. I like that it's simple and easy to understand. Do you write much?"

"On and off. I didn't do very well at school when they got me there. I was just the thick kid in the class."

"No!"

"I went to an all-boys school in London and a lot of the teachers hadn't been back from World War Two for long, and if you were a problem in any way they did not have much time for you. So, I left school at fifteen and came into this industry. We take anyone! Doesn't matter what you did at school, can you bend? can you pick things up? can you work? Good, you can have a job then. That's how we end up with so many problem people in the industry, the ones no one else wants."

"Oh, I think that's not fair, Bob. I have met loads of good blokes since I have been doing this."

"You're, dead right, lots are good, lots mature and go on and do well, but I know lots who never seem to grow up."

They were sat on a bench near the road next to the water's edge near where their return bus would pick them up. From the town a crowd of co-workers could be seen walking towards them for the buses. Most of them had been drinking since they had arrived at lunchtime. It was now just gone five pm. As they got nearer they could see what looked like Bill pushing a very large barrow with Pete in it, passed out.

"Oh God, what happened to Pete?" asked Bob as Bill stopped beside them along with Wolfie, Colin and Ed.

"He got into a vodka drinking competition with two Marines," said Bill.

"We tried to stop him," put in Ed.

"He wouldn't have any of it," said Colin.

"What happened," asked Sam.

"Oh, to be fair," said Wolfie, "the lad done well. Too well in fact. He drunk more than them put together, but then just passed out cold."

"Bloody hell," said Bob. "Will he be okay?"

"Nothing a good sleep won't put right," said Bill as he sat on the bench next to Bob.

"He'll get that," said Colin. "He will sleep it off on the trip back. We'll put him on the back seats."

"Oh, watch out," said Bob, "Jake is here." They all looked to see him pushing his way through the crowd, staggering and making a beeline towards Bob and Sam who were still sat on the bench.

"There's the pair of fucking lovebirds!" he shouted as he got near them in a slurred voice and pointed at them. "You pair of fucking wankers got me a written warning."

"No, it was me," said Sam.

Jake pointed at her to say something as Bob said, "No, Jake, it was me."

Jake then turned to Bob to say something and from behind him Ed said, "It was me, Jake."

He turned around towards where the voice had come from, almost falling over this time, then Wolfie said, "No, it was me, Jake lad."

At this point most of the crowd started shouting, "It was me, Jake!" There was also a shout from the rear saying, "I am Spartacus," as the line from the film. This brought great laughter from everyone, apart from Jake that is.

"You're all a bunch of wankers!" he shouted.

Wolfie, who was stood with his back close to the water's edge behind Jake, said, "Jake, lad, just go and have a lay on the grass over there," he pointed beyond the bench, "until the bus comes."

Jake turned around and looked at him and said, "You're just a fucking wanker like the rest of them." He then took a very drunken swing at him, but Wolfie saw it coming and ducked and moved out of the way all at once. The momentum of this sent Jake flying into the water to great roars from the crowd. He went under the water for what seemed an age but did surface coughing and choking. One of the workforce grabbed a life ring on a nearby post and threw it to him holding on to the attached rope, and a few of them helped him out when he was at the side. They got him out on the road just as the first bus was turning up. Once the bus was there Pete was carried onto the rear seat and Jake, soaking wet through, was also helped on, still coughing up water.

Bob and Sam were near the end of the queue when the rest of their friends were on. Bob held Sam by the elbow as she was about to get on, then in her ear said, "Don't get on, I don't want to be on there with Jake. He could start at any time. The next bus will be here soon, let's wait for that."

As they waited on the footpath near the bus Bill came to the door and said, "Are you not getting on?"

"No, we are getting on the next one. Don't want to be with Jake," Bob said in a soft voice.

"Okay. Sam, Pete is not going to make the show tonight, and Colin said he is not going. He's going to have an early night. Do you want to go?"

"Oh, I don't know if I fancy it."

"Come on," said Bob, "it will be good. Make a nice change."

"Okay then. Thanks, Bill," she replied.

"Right," replied Bill as he stepped back into the bus as the doors were closing. "I will see you there." As the bus pulled away the second one pulled up to collect the remaining passengers, as a JLB Land Rover that had been parked nearby for some time overtook it.

*

Bob and Sam ate together in the staff canteen that evening before making their way to meet Bill and the others for the show. They took their seats about halfway back in the large bar which had a stage at one end that had been cleared of tables to make way for rows of chairs. In the front row, centre of the stage, ten seats had been turned upside down so they could not be used with reserved signs on them. It was meant to be first in and get a seat. There was a large roar of jeers and boos as the workforce showed their disapproval as ten Eastham's women were led to these seats. At

242

this point Jim Davidson put his head around the curtain to see what the noise was about. It was about another five minutes before he came out to roars of approval to start the show.

When he came on he asked the audience, "How are you getting on with the cold? I was in Stanley the last time I was here, it was so cold I had to snap a dog off a lamp post." This brought roars of laughter from everyone. "If you look over there," the comedian pointed to a cameraman filming at the side of the hall, "you will see that this is being filmed to be shown on telly at home this Christmas. They have been following my tour of the island, entertaining the forces. I was told that this was a one-off for you lot, loads of blokes who have been here for months on end. So," he pointed at the camera again and said, "you won't be able to use one fucking minute of this one, mate."

Jim continued with the show that lasted almost two and a half hours with one short break. He had dancing girls with him which went down well with the lads. Near the end he said, "At this point I would normally leave the stage and come back on when you all call me back for an encore, but I have been told you lot don't do that here, you just get up and leave. So, I am just going to stay on and do my encore without leaving the stage." And this he did. The evening had gone down very well with everyone who attended.

*

The temperatures plummeted that night at the camp. Pete, who was left on the bus to sleep the drink off, never woke up. He was found on the back seat the next morning by the workers going to the power station. He had frozen to death.

Chapter 14

Another Christmas

"It's just awful. I just can't believe it, and we were all there. In fact we left Pete to die," Bob told the nightly meeting in his room with Bill on the top bunk and Colin and Sam in the armchairs.

"You can't blame us," said Colin from the chair next to Sam.

"No, you're right, you had all been drinking. I hadn't. Well, one pint. I should have made sure he got back," Bob replied as he handed out the cups of tea.

"I think if you were on the bus with him," put in Sam, "you would have done that, so would I, but with that business with Jake you were right for us to go on a different bus. Then the next thing you know we got back and went to the show. We just forgot. We can't be blamed for that, can we?"

"No, you're right, but I feel guilty," said Bob as he sat on his bottom bunk and lit up a South African cigarette.

"How did you get them," asked Sam as she pointed to the cigarettes. "It's a while since you were last in Cape Town."

"Oh, Bill gets them. They get smuggled in. A lot cheaper than the rip-off merchants of Eastham's."

"Blimey," replied the safety officer, "who gets them then?"

"He doesn't know," put in Colin.

"Oh, I do now," came the voice from above. "It's Spalding Walt off the airfield."

"Well, out of everything, at least that tosser Jake got sacked," said Colin.

"It wasn't me," said Sam. "I got him the written warning as I put in a report to Tom Smith about what happened at Section 38 and Tom went to Arran about it, but I didn't report anything about yesterday."

"I heard," said Bill, "that it was Arran Jones. He and George were sat watching from his Land Rover a little way off."

"I didn't see him," said Bob.

"Oh, before I forget," said Sam, as she sat in the chair, "I know that Pete wasn't religious or anything but I had a word with the vicar this afternoon, and now the chapel is finished I thought it would be nice to have a small service for him so that we can say goodbye."

Bob and Bill nodded their approval. Colin lifted his hand up and patted the back of Sam's hand and said, "That is very thoughtful of you." This did not go unnoticed by the two roommates.

"When's Ed moving in with you then, Colin?" asked Bob.

"You have already sorted out a new roommate? Poor old Pete is not cold yet. Sorry, that was a poor choice of words," Sam said.

"You can't hang around here," put in Bill. "They will put some tosser in with you before you know it, love. You have to move fast." Before anyone could answer they were interrupted by a knock on the door. "Come in," Bill continued, "if you're female leave your knickers at the door."

"You got caught out with that one last time," put in Bob.

"I did," came the half laughing reply from above.

The door opened to show Jake stood at the doorway. The room was silent until the newcomer spoke. "Is it possible to have a word, Bob? And you also please, Sam, outside in the corridor?"

Bob and Sam looked at each other, until Sam replied, "Okay," and got up, followed by Bob. They both left the room and returned about five minutes later.

"What the hell was that all about?" asked Bill, when they both sat down again.

"He, Jake, wants me and Sam to have a word with Benjamin to get him his job back."

"You are joking!" said Colin.

"No joke," replied Sam, "he wants us to speak up for him."

"What a waste of space that man is," observed Bill. "I hope you both told him where to get off."

"I would have done," said Bob, "but Sam said we should have a go."

"No, Sam," put in Colin, "not how he has been with you."

"He is up to his eyes in debt," she continued. "This was going to sort it all out for him."

"Well he should have thought of that before he did what he did to you, the arsehole," said Bill.

"As my dad would say, he is the one with the problem, and it is almost Christmas."

"Oh, he's got a problem alright," replied Bill. "He's a bloody tosser."

"When can we get to see Benjamin do you think?" Sam asked Bob.

"It can't be tomorrow as I have to take Del's things over to Stanley for him and see him in jail there before he gets sent back home. He was in court today so I should be able to find out what happened."

"They were just waiting for him," said Colin, "someone must have ratted on him you know."

"Maybe," said Bob.

"He was going to get caught sometime," Bill commented.

"Right, I am off," said Sam. "Early night." As she got up she said, "See you in the morning, lads."

"Oh, I will come with you," said Colin getting up. "I have some things to get from the shop."

"Oh, okay," she replied. The two bid their farewells and left the room.

"Colin is making a play for her, you know that don't you, Bob, trying to get in her knickers?"

"Yes, I think you're right," came the reply. "I just don't want to see her hurt. Colin is only after whatever he can get."

"And you saw her first, Bob!"

"Bill!"

"Little joke, mate."

"Yeah, but I don't think Colin is joking," the committeeman replied in a sad sounding voice.

*

"I am out of here tomorrow, on the plane home. Got £100 fine and dismissed." Bob was in the police station with Del in Stanley, who was telling him what had happened that day in court. "I got ratted on you know."

"How do you know?"

"The police told me. They got a tip-off from our office here."

"Do you know who it was?"

"No, but I think it was your fucking mate, the woman safety officer."

246

"Nooo, Sam wouldn't do that."

"Well, she ran over to talk to Tom Smith."

"She remembered some work stuff when she saw him. No, I don't believe it."

"That's what she told you, and she is one of them."

"One of what?"

"One of them!"

"What, a lesbian?"

"Nooo, a manager."

"Oh, no, I don't believe it."

"Well someone done it, Bob, that's why I am here."

Bob left the police station with the seed planted in his mind. Did Sam inform on Del?

*

Bob and Sam were waiting outside Kim's office for the meeting with him and Arran Jones regarding Jake.

"I heard that Spalding Walt who was selling the smuggled fags got picked up first thing this morning. They raided his room, he had a wardrobe full of fags," said Bob.

"They are no good for you anyway, Bob. Maybe it's a good time to pack them up now you have to go back to Eastham's prices. Mind you, they are still cheaper here than at home, maybe you could pack up for New Year?"

"Maybe. They reckon someone ratted on Walt."

"If you do wrong things there's a good chance you will get caught in the end."

"I suppose you're right. Live by the sword and die by the sword and all that. Del told me he got ratted on as well. The police told him."

"Again, he was doing wrong."

"I suppose so."

"No suppose about it. He was selling drugs to make money, Walt was smuggling cigarettes to make money, I've got no time for them. They both got what they deserved."

There was silence between them for a short while, then Bob said, "Oh, by the way, I think Colin might have eyes for you, Sam."

"No might about it. He asked me out last night."

"Nooo!"

"Yes."

"What happened?"

"He said did I want a drink on the way back. I said no I was going to wash my hair, and he said what about another night, just the two of us going out?"

"Oh God, he's at it again. What did you say?"

"I said no, because you and I are at it!"

"WHAT!"

"Only messing, Bob, I just wanted to see your face. I told him he is married. And, Bob, there is no way Colin is my type, I am not going to be another notch on his belt."

"Well done, Sam, I don't want you to get hurt."

"Thanks, Bob, I do appreciate you looking out for me and all." She kissed him on the cheek. "Thank you, but I can look after myself you know."

Before Bob could reply the office, door opened and George, David Antony and Tom Smith came out. Then Arran Jones appeared at the door and said, "Hello, Sam, Bob, can you come in now."

Bob and Sam sat across the meeting room table from Kim and Arran. "You're here on behalf of Jake Jordan then?" started Arran.

"Sort of," replied Bob.

"How do you mean 'sort of'?" asked Kim.

"It is mainly me, Kim," answered Sam. "He asked to see Bob and I. He has got a lot of debt, his marriage has not long broken up, he has three young children he is supporting, he had a building company that went bust up north, and this was his way back. Being out here and getting some money together to sort his problems out."

"That's all very well, Sam," replied Kim, "but all you have told me is his problems. There are many men out here for the same sort of reasons as that, but they know they have to behave themselves. It is you that he has given the most flack to."

"That's why he came to us. He said he was sorry," replied Sam.

"That's all very well, Sam, but he said sorry after he had been sacked. You are a member of our management team. I can't, and will not, tolerate that sort of behaviour towards one of my staff, how he talked to you out on site and how I was told he behaved in Stanley yesterday."

"Yes, and he got a written warning for the first one."

"Well it didn't teach him a lesson," put in Arran, "did it?"

"No, Arran, you're right," Sam replied. "But I think he knows now, and from a work point of view he does get it done, and he did sort out all of his safety issues when he was told to." Sam paused and then said, "He did take a bit of persuading there to be fair, and with Arran's help."

"You're very quiet, Bob," said Kim. "What do you think?"

"I've got no problem with getting rid of him. He is an awful man, he treats his men like rubbish, and until Sam sorted it out he had his men working very unsafely. We don't need people like him here."

"So why are you here supporting him?" asked Arran.

"I am not supporting him, I am supporting Sam. She wants him reinstated because of her humane side, I would have the twat shot at dawn." They all laughed at this.

"Is this anything to do with you being a woman safety officer out here?" asked Arran. "I mean your role in this industry is not easy at home, but out here... Well?"

"I will have to think about that," came the reply. There was silence for a moment or two, then she continued. "I suppose it is in a way, but this is the future. I am not the first and there will be many after me, and yes, would Jake have talked to Tom Smith like that? I don't think so, but we can't sack everyone who does not like the fact I am a woman. They need to get used to it and treat me and others as co-workers."

"That's the point surely," said Bob. "If he is sacked it will show that people can't be like that with a woman."

"Bob has a good point, Sam," commented Kim.

"Yes, I know, Kim, and what happened both times really upset me, I was shaking, but I know incidents like that will make me a stronger person. They have already, I try to learn from every incident, I look at them when I am on my own and look to see if I could have handled them differently. I am in this industry for the long term, there is change happening all the time and I want to be part of it. I know now I will look back at this in twenty years' time and would not change it for the world. It will be the making of me. Why do you think I went in the stocks first the other week? I don't have a thing about having cold wet sponges thrown at me you know, it was to show I am a co-worker, not a woman co-worker. I am here to do a job the same as the rest of them, and if Jake goes it will look like it's being done because I am a woman." There was silence in the room while Sam's three co-workers took this all in.

249

"What do you think, Arran?" Kim asked after a short while.

"Well, I was with Bob, having him shot and all, but I do understand where Sam is coming from, and I think she is really brave coming into the industry in the first place, let alone coming out here, so I think we should support her in every way possible. I would give him a final warning on the understanding that the next little thing and he is gone, and we also make it clear that he is only keeping his job because Sam didn't want him sacked."

"Right," came the reply from the project coordinator, "that's what we will do then." He stood up. "But the slightest thing and he is gone."

"I will go and tell him now and make it really clear," said Arran.

"Okay, thank you, everyone," replied Kim as he got up and walked towards the door.

As Sam and Bob walked down the corridor Karl put his head out of his office door and said, "Hi, Sam, can I have a quick word please?"

"Of course, Karl. Bob, I will see you in the Land Rover."

They went into Karl's office and they stood up as Karl said, "Thanks for the info on the drug pusher and the cigarette smuggler. I knew Bob knew who they were."

"No problem, Karl, but you must keep this between us. It's hard enough being a woman here, let alone a ratter into the bargain!"

*

The marmoreal service for Pete was held on a Saturday evening after work. All of his mates were there along with Sam. The lads had not seen Andy for some time as he was not working with any of them and had moved in with a friend of his from home who had just come out. This was in an extra section of the camp which had been put up to cope with extra men who had now started to come out for another joint venture contractor who had won a new contract off the British Government.

Kim, Arran, Roger and Tom were there on behalf of the company. It was a simple service and did not last long, but as they all agreed it did the most important thing for them. It let them say goodbye to Pete.

"Do you know what?" asked Sam as she, Bob and Ed drove along after the service. "We haven't been to Turtle Point for a while, let's get over there this morning. If you are okay with it, Bob?"

"No problem. Yes, you are right, we haven't been there for a while. Ed, you can turn off up here and we can go now, we can get a cuppa there and maybe see Bill." Ed carried on driving and missed the turning Bob had pointed to. "Ed, what are you doing? You missed the turning."

"Oh, sorry, you said we were going to the Stanley road. We can pop into Turtle Point on the way back. Anyway, isn't Tom Smith looking after it, safety wise?"

Bob and Sam looked at each other, then Bob said, "No, Ed, please stop now and turn around."

"Oh, we will soon be on our way back."

"Ed, stop the Land Rover. Now!" snapped Sam. They pulled up on the road.

"Right, Ed, what's the problem with going to Turtle Point?" asked Bob.

"Nothing."

"Okay then," said Sam, "let's just turn around and go there now."

"I can't."

"What do you mean you can't?" asked Bob.

"Look, can't we just leave it? Let's just go on to the Stanley road camp."

"Right, Ed, you can tell us what is going on or you can get out here and one of us will drive over there. What's it to be, Ed?" asked Sam in a very firm voice.

"Oh boy, Uncle George told me to make sure you don't go over there until he tells me."

"What the hell is going on over there?" asked Bob.

"I am not really sure, but I have been told to keep you two away."

"Right, Ed, you drive us there or I do. What's it to be?" asked Sam. Ed started the vehicle up, turned around and made for Turtle Point. When they got to the road leading down to the site there was a Land Rover blocking the access road with a worker standing in front of it with a radio.

Bob got out and walked up to the worker. "Hi, Joe, can you let us in please?"

"Sorry, Bob," came the reply, "there's dangerous work going on down there."

"Dangerous?"

"Well, let's say important."

"What work?"

"I have just been told not to let anyone down."

"Anyone? Or just us?" asked Sam as she joined them.

"Look, you can't go down, that's all I know."

"We are going and that's all there is to it. Come on, Bob."

The two passed Joe and headed towards the site down the sloping bending road. As they walked they heard Joe on the radio say, "Come in, David! Come in, David!"

The site had really moved on in recent weeks with the permanent road now in and one-metre high by two-metre long concrete beams had been laid along the edge of the length of the road to stop a vehicle or person going over the side into the sea. Along with the tank bases most of the concrete aprons around them were now complete. As the two neared the bottom of the road David was there to greet them, but from this point they could see why they had not been wanted there. In the water was a floating platform which had the wheelhouse at the rear. It was about twenty foot square and was used for moving small items around. But the sight that greeted them was that the platform was almost sinking under the weight of a large curved section of metal that would go to make up the round fuel tanks. There was a second in the same situation waiting behind the one that was being unloaded by a fifty-ton mobile crane. Water was washing up the sides and onto the deck of the platform, and when the crane lifted the section from the front with two chains all of the weight went on the rear near the wheelhouse and for one minute it looked as if it was going to capsize, but as the section was pulled across the deck it levelled up and the platform rose as the section was lifted into the air.

"Bloody hell," said Bob, "how dangerous was that, and there is another waiting for the same treatment, Sam."

"No way," came the reply. "I am going to have this stopped now. David, what in hell is going on? That nearly tipped over then, and the weight is far too much for them to be carrying," the safety officer asked the section foreman as he approached them.

"Well, Sam, it's all been agreed. We are so short of time we have to get these tanks and pipeline in and filled with fuel for the day the plane lands so it can refuel for the return journey to the UK. They only arrived a few days ago on Cargo 12. We did not have time to bring them by road as it's over twelve miles each way and we don't have the transport to do it in time. As it's only a short trip around the bay it was agreed to do it that way."

"Agreed with whom?" asked Sam. "This is totally unsafe."

"It was agreed with Tom Smith, Arran Jones and Kim Benjamin," said George as he walked towards them holding out a radio. "Kim's on here, he wants to talk to you now."

"Hello, this is Sam," the safety officer talked into the radio.

"Sam," the radio said, "can you and Bob come to the meeting room? NOW please!"

*

Sam and Bob sat across the table from Kim, Arran and Tom. She started by saying, "Bob and I have just witnessed one of the most dangerous acts I think I have ever seen. Not only did two platforms nearly sink, one was almost turned over with three crew on board."

"They all had life jackets on and the Beaver boat was nearby just in case," said Arran.

"And that makes it okay?" asked Bob. "Those men could have drowned."

"They all agreed to the work," put in Kim.

"Well it all seems odd to me," said Bob. "This has been going on and no one has said anything to me or Sam. It sounds like the old JLB way of getting dangerous work done."

"What do you mean?" asked Sam.

"They pay the lads double time, and I would say in this case also to not let me or you know. Am I correct, gentlemen?"

"Please tell me this is not true," said Sam. "And it looks like you knew all about it, Tom?"

"Sam," Kim said, "I believe David explained the situation to you. I am not going to go over it again, but you need to understand that almost everything we have worked for this past year or so hinges on those tanks being ready on time."

"Safety is out of the window, is it, Kim?" asked Sam.

"I didn't say that, Sam."

"What is the point of me being here if you just do as you please? I think," she started to get up, "I have no choice but to–" Bob grabbed her arm and squeezed it as she was about to say "resign". She looked at him and he shook his head gently. Sam took her time and said, "I have no choice but to go away and consider this whole situation." She turned and left the room with everyone still sitting. Bob got up, nodded and went after her. He caught up with her in the car park. "I am so angry," she told Bob when they stopped.

"I know you are, but please don't do anything now. Look, it's Saturday night, me and the lads go to the bar on Saturday. Come and join us tonight and we can chat about it, talk it over. Please?" he pleaded. "It will give you time to think it over as you told me once that's what you do, see the best way to deal with it."

"Oh, okay, but I really feel like going back in there and telling them to poke it."

"I know. How many times do you think I have felt like that over this last year or so? It's nearly knocking off time. Go and have a have a shower, get some food and come to our room at around seven thirty to eight and we will all go and have a drink together."

"Okay, but I am really upset over this."

"I know," said Bob, "but just go and try and relax and then we can talk about it. Believe me, Sam, I am really cheesed off about it also, but what would your dad have said? He would have said it is them who have the problem, so don't get infected with their problem."

Sam thought for a short while then said, "You're never wrong when you're right, Bob English."

*

Bob, Bill, Colin and Ed were all waiting to go when Sam arrived at Bob and Bill's at seven forty that evening.

"Hi, Sam, did you get your shower?" asked Bob.

"Shower?" she replied. "It was bloody freezing."

"Oh," said Bill, "you have been lucky since you have been here. It's not been too bad of late."

"We went through spells where we had no water at all. Freezing water would have been great," said Colin as they started to walk to the bar.

"Nothing at all?" asked Sam.

"There was one point when we were at the beach pioneer camp when I think it was nearly a week we went without water. The water they got had to be used for cooking. We were all chucking up a bit," Colin replied.

"You're joking," replied Sam.

"And you were not here to sort it out for us," remarked Bill. This brought a laugh from everyone. When they arrived at the bar it was fairly busy, but as agreed earlier Wolfie was in there and had saved one of the round tables with enough chairs for all of them, and he also got them all a can of beer each.

"The wife is not talking to me," reported Wolfie when everyone was sat down.

"How do you mean?" asked Ed.

"We have had words, by letter of course. When I am home next she wants us to go to her cousin's and I can't stand her, so I said no. She brought it up in her next letter. At the bottom of the page she said, 'I am not happy about this.' I turned to the next page and it was blank, as were the next two, three in all, then on the fourth page she said, 'That's better, I have given you the silent treatment, I haven't been talking to you!'" This brought laughter from everyone.

"You were told not to tell us then, Ed, and, Bill, for that matter?" asked Bob, "what was going on down at Turtle Point?"

"It wasn't just you. Everyone who was involved in it were told not to tell anyone," reported Ed.

"And you did it, the risk and all for extra money?" asked the female safety officer.

"That's what we are here for, Sam," put in Bill. "We can get sent home at any time for refusing to do what you are told to do and lose a lot of money into the bargain, no bonus, no overtime, pay the fare home!"

"Not for refusing to do an unsafe job," replied Sam.

"What you see as unsafe, Sam, and what Benjamin and co see as unsafe are two different things," Wolfie told everyone.

"Sam, it's upsetting, but the truth is it's JLB law here and that's how it is and has been all the time," Bob told her. "We had an overtime ban months ago because any overtime is paid at flat rate and bearing in mind our hours are sixty hours a week, ten hours a day, six days a week. If we lose any hours because of the weather they take it off any overtime we have." Sam just shook her head to this news.

"They have told us lies all the time we've been here," added Colin. "This thing at Turtle Point really should not be a big surprise to us."

"You know when it's said at the interview the snow does not lay in the Falklands because of the wind?" asked Bill. "I saw it on the back of a toilet door the other day. The snow does not lie in the Falklands, only JLB does." This brought rounds of laughter from everyone.

"I can't believe Tom Smith knew about it and didn't tell me and let them do it," said Sam.

"There's two things there," said Reg who had just joined them. "The first being he knows what happened to the last safety officer who crossed Benjamin, he was sent home, and he knew that if you found out you would want it stopped."

"Evening, Reg," said Bob.

"Evening, all," came the reply.

"Reg is right," said Bob. "Tom would have been pushed into a corner, they would have ganged up on him, all of them."

"Well," said Sam, "I think I should resign over this."

"Nooo," could be heard from everyone.

"Really, don't do that," said Wolfie. "There's an old saying. 'Don't let the bastards grind you down'!"

"Well the truth is, Wolfie, they have. I can't trust any of them anymore. What's the point of me being here?"

"The thing is," said Bob, "before you came everyone would have known about the work at Turtle Point and they wouldn't have given a toss. The fact that they tried to cover it up from you, hide it, just shows you have had an impact on them in the short time you have been here."

"Bob's right, lass," said Wolfie.

As they were talking Jake Jordan came over with an armful of beer cans and put them on the table. "These are for you, lads, and lady of course."

There was a joint, "Thank you."

"I don't do this sort of thing often, but I owe you lot a sorry for last Sunday. And you, Sam, for everything. How I was with you and you got me my job back. You're alright with me. Have a good night, lads." He turned and left them.

There was silence amongst the group for a few moments as Jake walked away, which was then broken by Wolfie who said, "Now I have seen that, I do believe I will see an elephant fly one day." This brought laughter from everyone.

"Well," said Bob, "I think that says it all. Now that you have tamed Jake Jordan you could walk on water!"

A nearby worker, Josh Compton, came over and said, "Can I say something?" pointing at Sam.

As he finished his can Wolfie said, "You pick on her, lad, and you pick on all of us."

"I am not picking on her. In fact I only have good things to say. She is the only safety officer we have had here who has stood up to Benjamin and his cronies."

"I'll drink to that," said Reg as he held his can in the air to cheers of approval from the others.

"You have only been out here five minutes and you're a legend already," said Bob to Sam who was in the next chair to him.

"Oh, I just don't know. I do like being here and everything and doing a job I love doing."

"Just remember, lass," said Wolfie, "this job, project, whatever you call it, will never happen again in the history of the world. This is a one-off, everything about it, the distance, how we live, work, get things out here, and you're an important part of it, helping to keep us safe and all. That will be on your work record forever. You have made your mark here already, just being a woman and standing up to these idiots. Don't throw it away and become another jacker, Sam, because if you leave now that's what it will have on your record, not that you left because you were working for a load of tosser's!"

"That was a nice little speech," Bob told him.

"Well it's true," said Wolfie, "this is never going to happen again and she is part of it."

"And it's Christmas next week," said Colin.

"Can you believe it? Another Christmas here," said Bill.

"I saw on the noticeboard that the chapel is having a Midnight Mass on Christmas Eve. I think I will go," said Bob.

"So what time would that be?" asked Colin.

"Midnight!" they all shouted.

"I am off," said Sam as she finished her beer and got up. "I am going to have an early night and a think."

"You can't walk back on your own with these idiots here. One of us will need to go with you," Colin said and went to get up.

"Okay, it's not really a worry as I am a black belt in judo and a first dan in karate. Come on, Bob, you're walking me home," she told Bob who almost choked on his beer.

"Oh, okay… I will be back shortly."

"Don't call me Shorty," smiled Wolfie.

As the two left the others asked each other, "Do you think she really is that?"

Sam and Bob walked past the video room on the way out. "Oh, let's see what's on?" said Sam as she went to the door.

"Nooo," said Bob, as she opened it and was greeted with a packed room full of male workers watching the Saturday night porn film.

"Oh," she said, as she turned her head sideways to try and work out what was going on. There were cries from the room to, "shut the fucking door!" The two carried on with their walk back.

"I think you should ask to see Kim, but don't tell him you are thinking of going home because I think he is the sort of chap that if you push him in a corner he will say go. Just let him know how upset you are about what happened."

"If I was still going out with Robbie I would give him a ring to see what he thinks. And I don't have my dad anymore."

"Who's Robbie? You have never mentioned anyone."

"Oh, I went out with him for about four years and when my dad died he tried to help, but it was all too hard so I said I needed a break, I just wanted to be alone. Then, the next thing you know, this job was offered to me then bang, I am out here."

"Sam, I will say this again, you have done so well in the short time you have been here. It was because of you that they kept Turtle Point quiet. Please don't do anything you will regret later. Oh, and are you really a black belt and a first what's it in karate?"

"Might be," she smiled. "It's got everyone thinking."

As they walked into Sam's corridor her roommate came walking from the other end. When they got to her door, she said, "I think you are owed another one of these." She kissed him on the cheek. "Thank you, Bob. Night, night." She went into her room.

*

258

Work on the main runway was complete by mid-December leaving the aprons and taxiways to complete so that an aeroplane would be able to move into the hangar when it landed. The cross runway was also well underway.

It was also around this time that the first electricity was generated from the power station. This was a huge turning point in the project, with miles of high voltage cables running from it to smaller substations. Mains electric was now coming on in many areas. none more than the airfield and hangar with landing lights on the runways being seen as they were being tested.

Turtle Point had been pushed forward so that fuel would be in the tanks when the plane landed, as the Tank Farm was many weeks behind programme. While there had been the upset regarding the dangerous work on George's site when Sam and Bob returned, there was very little work to do regarding transporting the tank sections and with the long hours being worked the tanks were complete ahead of time, as was the pipeline to the refuelling area at the hangar.

While there was still work to be carried out at the water treatment plant, one area was producing fresh water and this was being pumped to the airfield by a smaller pipeline that would be used as a backup line. Things were looking good for the January landing date when Kim asked Sam to see him in his office at two thirty in the afternoon on Monday 24th December 1984.

"I know you're upset, Sam, but it was really important for us to hit the dates and the fact is by transporting the sections any other way would have left us wanting," Kim told his safety officer who sat across the desk from him drinking coffee.

"I know how important it was, but why couldn't you have talked to me about it?"

"You wouldn't have wanted it go ahead, would you?"

"I would have looked at it with the people who were going to do the work and worked out the best and safest way to do it and made a plan. There will come a time when that's the first thing we will do before carrying out a job like that. I have been thinking about it. We could have temporarily welded two floating platforms together as this would have carried the weight without the risk of them sinking."

"Well, Sam, we all make mistakes and I am sorry I did not involve you. Were you thinking of resigning over this?"

259

Sam took a sip of her coffee to think about the answer and what Bob had said about not pushing Kim into a corner. She put her cup down and continued. "Well, I was very upset at the time, but on reflection I do know how important it was to you."

"To *us*, Sam, as a team, and of course the project."

"I just want to be part of that team so we can all work together – safely."

"And that is what I want. I promise this will not happen again. You and Tom can meet with the section managers and they will have to discuss any risky work coming up with the two of you."

"Okay, Kim, that's fine with me." They both stood up and shook hands across the desk.

"Sam, I know what everyone thinks I am. 'Just get the job done at all costs.' But I do want everyone to get out of here safely also."

"I know you do, Kim."

"Has Bob mentioned if he will be coming back for a new contract?"

"I think he is leaving things open and will talk it over with his wife when he gets home."

"How are things with you and him?"

"What do you mean, Kim? We are workmates and friends. I will go as far as to say good friends. He has looked out for me when he needed to, but no more than that."

"Oh, okay."

"There is nothing going on between us. He is happily married."

"Well, if there was something he may want to come back."

"NOOO WAY, Kim!" she snapped.

"Of course not. Well, have a nice day tomorrow and I will see you soon."

Sam left the office thinking, I can't believe he said that. Then she thought, is that why he put me to work with him, for him to fall for me? Oh, my good God, I wouldn't put it past him.

*

"Happy Christmas, Sam," Bob welcomed her into his room just before midday on Christmas Day morning. She kissed him on his right cheek.

"Where's Bill," she asked as she sat in an armchair with a carrier bag in her hand.

260

"Don't know. The last I saw of him was in the bar last night as we were going to Midnight Mass. He said he was going to an Eastham's party somewhere. Would you like a cup of tea?"

"Yes please. He was very drunk."

"I know." Bob started to make the tea as the door opened to show Bill, with some of his clothes under his arm. "Oh God," Bob said, "look what the cat dragged in. My good God, you look rough."

"Wow, I feel it," came the answer from Bill as he walked over and plonked himself in the armchair next to Sam.

"Happy Christmas, Bill," she said as she kissed Bill on the cheek, then handed him and Bob a pack of two hundred cigarettes each from out of her carrier bag.

"Oh, we haven't got you anything," said Bob.

"That's fine, really, don't worry about it. In fact, take it as a thank you present for looking after me. Oh, and don't forget, Bob, you are packing up smoking next week at New Year."

"Oh, yes. Anyway, you have looked after yourself," he replied.

"Well let's say you have supported me, and by the way, Bill, what in hell's name has happened to you?" Sam asked the newcomer.

"The truth is," he said as he lit one of Bob's cigarettes from the coffee table, "I really don't know. I went to the Eastham's party and I remember going to the toilet. I came out and had forgot where the party was, then I bumped into this Eastham's woman and she said she would show me where the party was."

"Who was she?" asked Sam,

"I haven't got a clue. She was big, I know she was big. Then the next thing I know it was this morning. I woke up in a room on the floor with just my socks and glasses on. She was asleep in the armchair with just her bra on."

"What happened?" asked Bob.

"I put most of my clothes on and got out of there without waking her up, and the best is I don't know if anything happened, between us that is."

"Oh, Bill," Sam said turning to look at him, "you have got a great big love bite on your neck."

"Oh no!" He held his neck. "I am going home soon."

"Only messing, Bill," Sam laughed.

"Oh, piss off. It's not funny."

"I think it is," said Bob, as he handed the tea out. At this point the door opened to show Colin and Ed at the door who had agreed to come around for pre-Christmas dinner drinks. Everyone got a can of beer and sat to drink. Bill got up to wash and Bob sat next to Sam.

"I told Jane about you in a letter and when I rang home this morning she asked about you."

"What did you say?"

"The truth, just that we were working together. She was fine about it."

"Good, I am glad she knows."

"How was Midnight Mass last night?" Ed asked Sam and Bob.

"Well," said Bob, "I have never seen so many drunk people in church."

"There were people falling all over the place," said Sam.

"It was a mess not a Mass," said Bob. This brought laughter from everyone.

"Let's go to dinner?" said Colin.

"We have got to hear that new song on the radio," put in Sam, "the one you heard about, Bob."

"Yes, you're right, Sam, it's the British Christmas number one. They said they are going to play it at twelve midday." He looked at his watch. "It's almost that time." He turned the radio on which the number two song "Last Christmas" by Wham was just finishing.

"What is it?" asked Colin.

"I don't know much about it. A load of singers has got together to make a song to raise money for charity. I believe it's for Africa."

As Bob finished the DJ on the radio said, "and we have a new number one. It has gone straight into the top of the charts. It's by Band Aid and it is called 'Do they know it's Christmas'?"

You could have heard a pin drop in the room as the five listened to the opening lines.

"It's Christmas time, there's no need to be afraid, at Christmas time, we let in light and we banish shade." While none of them had heard the song before, near the end, apart from Bill, the others could be seen mouthing the words, "feed the world, let them know it's Christmas time."

At the end Ed said, "I think I am going to cry."

Sam put in, "It's lovely, I would like to hear it again."

262

Bill said, "Well, you will hear it every Christmas for the rest of your life. Now come on, you soppy lot, let's get some food. It's me who is starving at the moment, I've had no breakfast."

"Hold on," said Bob. He got up and held his can in the air and was joined by the others and said, "Here's to family, Pete and absent friends."

"Family, Pete and absent friends," came the joint toast.

Chapter 15

The Finish

"Should auld acquaintance be forgot,
And never brought to mind?
Should auld acquaintance be forgot,
And auld lang syne?"

"For auld syne, my dear,
For auld lang syne,
We'll tak a cup o' kindness yet,
For auld lang syne."

The end of the traditional song to welcome in New Year in Great Britain and around the world was greeted by cheers, clapping, handshakes and kissing in the bar. When this was all over the lads, Bob, Bill, Ed, Wolfie, Colin and Sam, returned to the round table they had spent the last few hours of 1984 sitting, chatting and drinking at.

"It is really weird that it hasn't been dark that long," Sam commented to the others.

"I know," said Colin, "it does take a bit of getting used to."

"Is that you off the cigarettes now then, Bob?" asked Sam who was sat next to him.

"Yes, I had the last one just before midnight."

"Think of the money you will save, and you will not smell of old fags anymore," smiled the safety officer. "Mind you, Bill," she continued, "it will cost you a fortune now, having to buy your own fags and all."

"I was thinking that," came the reply as he took one of Colin's.

"You're in your last couple of weeks here now, Bill, Colin and Bob," said Sam. "Who's coming back then?"

"I am," said Bill, "still got lots of debts to pay off."

"And you might have a baby to pay for if you got that woman pregnant on Christmas Eve," laughed Wolfie.

"Oh, piss off," came the reply.

"What about you, Colin?" Sam asked.

"I am going to say no, but I might change my mind."

"How about you, Bob?" she asked.

"I am like Colin. Would like to say no but really don't know."

"It's down to Jane, isn't it, Bob?" asked Bill.

"Yeah, it's a bit like that, but we have got the house to pay off, so who knows?"

"The thing is," said Wolfie, "we are all stuck here now." He stood up and held his can in the air and was joined by the others and said, "Happy New Year, and Happy 1985! Oh, and by the way, this reminds me of one New Year's Eve in Hong Kong!"

*

Early in the New Year troops had started to move into areas of the new camp and a bunker and storage area was now operational to accommodate weapons that may be used in the advent of an attack on the airfield. This was all to be ready before the first plane landed at the end of the month.

*

It was just after seven am and while it was still in the summer month of January, it was a very overcast and misty morning as Bob, Sam and Ed headed in their Land Rover for a meeting Bob had at the hangar regarding a problem that had come up there over the timekeeping of some of the men, who had been turning up late for work and leaving early. Bob was in his usual position at the passenger window with Sam in the middle and Ed was driving.

"Can you believe you have less than two weeks to go, Bob?" asked Ed as they drove along the road adjacent to the airfield.

"No, I can't. It's odd because in some way it has been the longest fourteen or so months of my life, yet in other ways it has gone as quick as a flash with just having my second Christmas here and all."

"You will soon be with your family again," said Sam, "albeit for a short while if you decide to come back."

"Yeah, I just don't know. I miss Jane but not seeing the children has been really hard."

265

"What the hell is happening?" asked Ed as he brought the Land Rover to a halt and pointed to the runway to see appearing from the clouds many parachutes, more than they could count. They were headed for soft ground on the far side of the runway.

"Look," pointed Sam, as from their left-hand side of the road camouflaged soldiers came pouring out of the drainage ditches in which they had been hiding. Buses, Land Rovers and lorries that had been making their way to work had now all come to a halt as everyone got out to see what was going on.

One of the foremen was trying to call the field base to report what was happening but found that all the radios were dead. "Are they ours or the Argie's?" called out one of the workers. No one seemed to know who was who.

"They are ours," Ed said as he, Bob and Sam now stood in front of their Land Rover as the troops from the ditches started running towards the airfield, most of them screaming at the tops of their voices with machines guns pointed at those who had just dropped from the sky. At this point armed vehicles could now be seen coming down the runway towards the paratroopers.

"They must be Argies," called out one of the workers. As this was said gunshots started to ring out from the opposite side of the runway.

"Take cover!" shouted one of the workers. This had everyone on the road running and hiding behind the Land Rovers and buses.

Within a minute of this happening a Land Rover came along and pulled up. George leaned out of the window and said, "What are you lot doing?"

A worker shouted, "We are under attack, George, we are being fired at."

"Get out, you silly buggers, it's a mock attack, they are firing blanks. Now get back to work!" He wound the window up and drove off. The workers came out of their hiding places and were saying things like, "Yeah, I knew it was a mock!"

*

"This is just between us, Father?"

"Of course, it is, Bob." The committeeman sat in the small room at the back of the chapel with Father Vincent, a mid-forties, well-built Irishman with short, greying hair who came from

266

Mitchelstown in County Cork, Ireland. He came in from the capital a few times a week to do a multi-faith service.

"Oh, and thanks for seeing me like this, I just needed to talk to someone. I don't think I want advice, I think I just want to say it out loud."

"That's fine. I am here for this sort of thing as well as the prayers and all, so just tell me what you want to."

"I am in love, Father."

"As a rule, I would say I am pleased for you and congratulations, but I don't think that's the case, is it?"

"No, it's not. I am a married man with two children who I am going home to soon, and this has happened."

"What's happened?"

"This, I have fallen in love."

"Is this with a man or a woman?"

"A woman of course, I am not that way."

"Well, I have to ask, as you never know."

"Nooo! I don't have a problem with people like that, it's just not me."

"Okay, you say you are in love. You're having an affair?"

"No, I have just fallen in love with someone, there is nothing happening between us and she doesn't know. Oh, it's just really odd. If we were having a thing then I would know why I feel like this. It is really so hard to be in love with someone and having to keep it to yourself. I mean I have never felt like this before. I go to bed and think of her, I wake up thinking of her..."

"You didn't feel like this with your wife?"

"No, yes. Oh, I love Jane, and things have been really good most of the time. We have had hard times but overall things have been good, but this is different. I would not have an affair, and I do miss Jane so much, but this... it's hard to explain."

"You feel close to her?"

"Yes, we just seem to have so much in common. Nothing is hard between us. Yes, we have become very good friends, but I have just realised it is more than that for me."

"There are all different kinds of love, my son. We all have love for different things over the years, it could be another person, a football team, a child, a car, many things."

"Yes, but you can talk to people about those things, can't you? This is eating me up."

"Would you want to tell her?"

267

"No, I can't do that. No, I think it could break our friendship, and the truth is I think it is her who has carried me through these last few months. I had some very low points before we worked together."

"The good Lord moves in mysterious ways, my son." Father Vincent let Bob think about it for a short while then said, "Two things. When is your contract over, and are you coming back?"

"I am out of here in less than two weeks from now, and I really don't know if I will be back or not. We could do with the money."

"There's an old saying in the church, my son:
God puts some people in our life for a reason,
Some for a season,
And others for life.

"Well, my son," the priest stood and held his hand out to Bob, "you have to decide which one of those is happening to you. You have got some thinking to do so that no one gets hurt, my son."

*

"Father, this is just between the two of us?"

"Of course, it is, Sam, what is it you want to talk to me about?"

"I am in love with someone and I can't tell them."

"Is it a man or a woman?"

"It's a man, Father, I am not that way."

"Well, I had to ask, as you never know."

"No, it's a man."

"Why can't you tell him?"

"Because he is married with two children and he is going home soon."

"Would that be leave or end of contract?"

"End of contract, and he doesn't know if he is coming back yet. I just needed to talk to someone, Father, it's just driving me mad. I think of him when I go to bed, I think of him when I wake up. I have never known anything like this before. Oh, I have been in love, but not like this, this is just so hard to explain."

"You feel close to him?"

"Yes, very close. We seem to have so many things in common. Nothing is hard between us, everything seems so simple, but not being able to say anything… it's eating me up."

"Have you thought of telling him?"

"Oh, my good God! Oh, sorry, Father."

"That's okay, Sam."

"I have been on the brink many times. Look, I am single which is fine, but he is married and in love with his wife. I can't do or say anything that would put pressure on his marriage, it just wouldn't be right."

"People can love each other and not be in a relationship you know."

"I know, Father, I know, but... oh, I shouldn't say this, but I do in fact want him."

"When does he go home?"

"In less than two weeks on the next ship, and the truth is I may never see him again after that."

"I do feel for you, my dear. Do you think he knows how you feel, or maybe feels the same as you?"

"No, that's the worst. I am not only in love with someone who I can't tell, but it's a one-way thing, it's not returned."

"Well, you never know what's in another person's mind, my child."

"No, he's in love with Jane, that I know for sure. Look, Father," Sam stood up and held her hand out to shake, "thank you for listening to me. I just wanted to say it out loud and get it off my chest, to tell someone."

"Not a problem. Any time you want to talk please come back. But take this old saying from the church with you, my child:

God puts some people in our life for a reason,

Some for a season,

And others for life.

"You have to decide which one of those is happening to you, my child."

"Thank you, Father." Sam turned and left the room.

Father Vincent looked up to the heavens and said, "Oh, Lord, you really do move in mysterious ways, don't you?"

*

While it was still the summer a heavy storm had been blowing for almost three days. Winds had been gusting at over one hundred miles per hour down at West Cove. This had caused a lot of damage across the project. At West Cove unloading of the latest cargo ship had been slow with the cranes being unable to work in the high winds, and with the sea washing up and over the Bailey bridge lorries were finding it hard to cross and pick up the containers. None of the small boats around the *Adventurer* had been able to work as it was deemed too rough for them. Also, many of the roads were flooding with the continued rain.

*

"I heard today," said Bill from his top bunk at the nightly meeting in his and Bob's room whom the latter was making tea for their guests Colin and Sam who were sat in the armchairs, "that the stone from the new quarry has too much clay in it, and the government's agents will not pass it as being fit to use in the concrete."

"That will cause a big problem. That's the second time that has happened," said Bob as he handed the cups of tea out.

"All of the concrete on the runway and aprons are now finished so it won't stop the plane landing," put in Sam.

"No," said Bill, "and I believe that they have another area to start blasting in, but they are waiting on test results on that stone."

"So it should be all go for the plane next week, just a day before we are out of here," said Colin.

"I heard there's another problem," said Bill.

"What is it?" asked Bob as he sat on his bottom bunk with his cup of tea.

"I am not sure, but some very important parts for the landing were meant to be on the last cargo ship that came in and they have just found out that they not here."

"They will air bridge them out, surely?" said Colin.

"I don't know," said Bill, "but I believe it has got that lot, the management idiots that is, sorry Sam," she just made a small smile at this comment, "worried."

"Well I hope they sort it out as it would be nice to see the plane come in before we go, and if it doesn't happen no doubt some heads will roll," said Bob.

"If that happens let's hope it's that tosser Benjamin," announced Bill.

"The thing is with this weather being so bad it is going to be a problem anyway to get things that are needed ashore–"

Bob did not finish his sentence as the door flew open and a breathless Ed said, "Have you heard what's happened?"

"No," replied Sam.

"What is it?" asked Bob.

"The Bailey bridge has collapsed." There was a loud grasp from everyone in the room. The messenger continued. "I have been told to get you two, Bob and Sam, down there ASAP. There are problems that you two are needed to help sort out."

"Collapsed?" asked Bob as he stood up, followed by Sam and Colin.

"I am not a hundred percent certain what has happened, I don't think it has totally collapsed, it sounds as if one of the metal supporting legs has twisted in the storm and has partially collapsed with an articulated lorry on it and the driver is stuck in the cab. He has got his foot trapped and the tide is coming in fast."

"Let's go," said Bob.

"I am coming too," put in Bill from his top bunk.

"And me," said Colin.

"There's never a dull moment here," observed Sam, as the four left the room with Ed.

"I'll bring your wood saw, Bob," said Bill as he grabbed it from behind the bottom bunk.

"What for?" asked a surprised Sam, as the others stopped and looked back at Bill as he picked the saw up.

Bill held the saw in the air and said, "We may have to cut the driver's foot off!"

*

While it was not completely dark when the five arrived at West Cove, it was eight thirty in the evening, which was early in this part of the world for daylight in the summer months. Bob had been told by some night workers that just before Christmas it had been just gone eleven pm when it got dark, and just past three in the morning when they saw the sun start to rise.

But with the heavy clouds that had seemed to be hanging over the project forever, it was now in fact three days and it was starting to get very dark, fast. The lights from the ship were now on and lighting towers had been set up to illuminate the scene that greeted the newcomers from the contractors' camp.

As they arrived there was a small crowd of workers stood at the bottom of the Bailey bridge watching two men making their way

271

down the twisted bridge towards the stricken cab of the lorry which had water lapping around the bottom of its door.

As the newcomers stood looking towards the jetty they could see that on the left-hand side and nearest to the ship that the support leg had buckled and twisted in the storm. In turn the weight of the bridge had caused the bolts and welds fixing it to the ship to snap.

A digger with its long arm had come and had fastened chains to the back of the lorry to pull it out but had been unable to do so. The chains had been taken off in case the lorry went over and took the digger with it.

The two men were now making their way down a rope towards the cab. They were Shaun and David. It had been rumoured that they were both ex-SAS which they had always denied, but the truth was that while they were hired as labourers they had been in the service and had been taken on for just this kind of situation. Reg was already there and had all the information for Bob and co when they arrived.

"Who's the driver, Reg?" asked Bob when they met him.

"It's Henry Patterson," came the reply.

"Oh boy," said Colin, "he's a big one he is."

"It will take more than them two to pull him out," put in Bill.

Bob made no reply to Bill's comment but said, "How is he trapped?"

"It seems his foot got stuck when the lorry jerked forward. It's between the clutch and the brake, and because he is so large he can't bend over to free it. They have taken a saw down there with them."

"Told you," said Bill, "they are going to cut his foot off."

"Oh no!" exclaimed Sam. "They can't do that."

"He'll drown if they don't, Sam," explained Bill.

"No!" said Reg. "It's a hacksaw to cut the brake pedal off."

"Oh," said Bill with an air of disappointment in his voice. "Mind you," he continued, "it would have taken some cutting to get through his leg."

"BILL," cried Sam, "STOP IT!"

"Well, I am just saying," came the reply in a soft sheepish voice.

"Well don't say," snapped Bob.

"Look!" called out one of the onlookers. The lorry which was laid on the left-hand side guardrail had started to give way and it

272

now looked as if the lorry with the three men was about to fall into the sea. If it was possible the rain seemed to be coming down heavier and with the wind blowing it was hard to make out what people were saying. A Range Rover came into sight and pulled up near the crowd. Kim Benjamin, Arran Jones and Roger Clifford came and joined Bob and the others.

"What's happening?" asked Arran.

"The SAS are on the job," remarked Bill. None of the senior managers replied to this comment. Everyone was looking down at the cab. It was very difficult to see or hear what was happening. Then a large cracking sound could be heard as the guardrail snapped under the pressure of the lorry laying on it. As the lorry started to slip over the side of the bridge the three men now waste high in water emerged from the cab. The rope was tied around Henry when Shaun shouted, "Pull!" which was dually done by six workers. As Henry was being pulled up the bridge another rope was thrown down to David and Shaun who grabbed it and started to pull themselves out of the water as the guardrail finally snapped and the lorry crashed over the side into the sea.

Henry was pulled out to the waiting medics who put blankets around him and got him into the waiting ambulance. When David and Shaun got to the top there was much clapping and cheering that greeted the two heroes. Kim held his hand out to thank them then asked, "How did you get him out?"

"We cut it off," replied Shaun, as he took a very large bowie knife out of its sheath which was attached to his belt and held it up in front of him.

"Told you," said Bill.

"You cut his foot off?" asked a very shocked Sam.

"No," said David, "his boot. Shaun cut the laces and his foot just slipped out."

"Oh, you didn't cut his foot off then?" asked Bill.

"No foot cutting tonight, Bill," smiled Colin.

"Well done, you two," said Arran. "We will take you back up to the camp. Wait in the Range Rover, we will be with you in a minute."

The two rescuers walked off with Bill close behind who could be heard to say, "Go on, lads, tell me. I heard you are SAS. You are, aren't you? I won't tell anyone."

Kim said to Bob, Reg and Sam, "We need to talk."

"Okay, first thing in the morning, Kim?" replied Reg.

"No, tonight," came the reply. "In the meeting room in ten minutes please." He turned and walked away, followed by Arran and Roger.

*

Bob and Reg were sat on one side of the table with Kim, Arran and Sam facing them on the other side in the meeting room. Sam was on the management side at Kim's insistence.

"We have got a problem, gentlemen," started Kim.

"I would say," replied Reg.

Kim continued. "We have many items to be unloaded to get the plane landed in just over a week."

"Could it not go back?" asked Bob. "I mean the landing date."

"No," said Arran, "that date is set in stone."

"After what has just happened will there be financial penalties?" asked the committee chairman.

"Well, yes there are, and we have duties to unload the other companies' ships or there are penalties also, and there are many other reasons that we will not be putting that date back," replied Kim. "Our engineers who have already started looking at it have said it is a long job. There is a lot of new steel to go in and to be welded."

"You will just get the lads to work around the clock, won't you?" asked Reg.

"There's the problem," Kim said. "We have already talked to the welders and others we need and they have come back and said they will only work their flat hours, and as it's Sunday the day after tomorrow they will not work unless…"

"Unless what?" asked Bob.

"Unless," Kim looked at Arran and said, "they want the overtime guaranteed."

"I am sure you could do that for them, Kim. They don't lose any time anyway, most of their work can be done inside," replied Bob.

"No, Bob," the project coordinator continued. "They want it for all of you, the whole contract, and also to be paid the overtime the month after it has been worked."

"Fair play to them," said Reg.

"Let's get this clear," said Bob. "The welders who worked overtime when most of the rest of the workforce did not are now refusing to work overtime. I don't believe it."

"Well you'd better believe it," put in Arran, "because that is what they are saying."

"Bob, Reg, I want you both, please, to go and sort this out. We need them to work as many hours as it takes to get the goods coming off the ship again. I cannot stress how important this is. I also want Sam to go with you to agree a safe way to carry out the work. Do I make myself clear?" He got up from his chair followed by the others. "Meet with them in the morning please, then come straight back to me." He walked around the table towards the door. "Thank you for coming, gentlemen. Bob, can we have a word please?" The others left the room, then Kim said to Bob. "You owe me two favours, Bob, deliver on this and they are wiped out."

Bob looked at him for a few seconds and was going to say, "There's an old saying, Kim, something about the boot being on the other foot," but thought better of it and just said, "I will see you tomorrow. Goodnight, Kim."

*

As Sam, Bob and Reg walked from the Land Rover, Bob said to Reg, "I could kill one of them," pointing to the cigarette he had just lit up.

"Oh no you don't," put in Sam, "you have done really well these couple of weeks." Bob just pulled a face.

The three entered the large metal shed in the contractors' compound that was the welders and plant fitters' workshop. There was a large amount of machinery in there which was being worked on. There were ten workers; at the front was Tony, who while being the plant fitters' foreman also oversaw the welders.

"Okay," said Bob in a loud voice, "we have been asked to come and see you to talk about you working overtime to repair the Bailey bridge."

"Well," a voice said from the back, "you can get rid of her before we say anything. SHE's one of them."

"SHE," Bob replied, "has a name, and SHE is here to make sure that you do the work safely and go home in one piece and not in a wooden box. And SHE knows what SHE is on about." There was real anger in his voice.

275

"I'll wait outside, Bob," said Sam.

"No, you won't. SHE goes and we all go. What's it to be, lads?"

"Come on, lads," Tony turned to the workers, "they are here to help us."

"Right," continued Bob, "we are surprised that you are taking this stand as most of you, in fact all of you, did work overtime when we had it banned."

"Some would say blacklegs," mumbled Reg.

"The thing is," said Tony, "yes, we worked, but none of us have ever been treated well here. That's all of us, Bob." There were noises of agreement. "Now we have them over a barrel, they have no choice, pay up or the plane does not land which would be a great embarrassment as the whole world is watching, and all in all it will cost them a fortune." There were nods of approval to Tony's speech.

"If they agree to the overtime payment and paying a month in arrears, you will do it?" asked Reg.

"We want it in writing," came a call from the back.

"And we want it from the UK," shouted another, "not that lying bastard Benjamin."

"Okay," said Bob, "Reg and I will go back and see him now, but you need to work with SHE, better known as Sam," this brought a few smiles and laughs from the crowd, "to tell her how you are going to do the work and Sam will work with you all to make sure it is done safely. Is that agreed?"

There was a joint "yes."

"Okay, then we will leave you in the very capable hands of Miss Crisp while we go to see our leaders!"

*

"That's their answer, is it?" Kim in an angry voice asked Bob and Reg who were back in the meeting room at their usual side of the large table along with Arran Jones.

"Yes," said Bob, "they want overtime paid for everyone the month after it has been worked."

"And you could not talk them out of it?" asked Arran.

"Oh, we tried," said Bob, "we tried really hard, didn't we, Reg?" He gave his fellow workmate a small kick under the table.

276

"Oh, yes, we tried really hard, Arran." The looks on both managers' faces told the committeemen that neither of them believed it.

"I am not being held to ransom," replied Kim.

"Okay," said Bob. He started to get up. "They said that they will finish work tonight after their ten hours, have tomorrow off and be back to work on Monday for the ten-hour day and so on." Bob was now on his feet. "We will go and tell them now."

"Kim," said Arran, "I think we need to have a word. Can you give us a minute outside please, gentlemen?" The two committeemen got up and left the meeting room. "Kim, you know we can't win here, it's either give in to them or the plane does not land, and all in all it will cost a lot of money. I know that you have it in your power to give them the go ahead on the overtime."

"I am not being dictated to by a load of workers who are lucky to be working with all the unemployment in the UK!"

"Kim, what about if we say okay but it starts now. Anyone who has lost any of their overtime before has lost it. What do you think?"

The project coordinator put his hands-on top of his head and looked up to the ceiling for a few seconds, then said, "We have no choice, do we, Arran?"

"No, all the time we do not have them working overtime is really going to put us up against it, the clock that is."

"Okay, get them back in please." Arran went to the door and the two men returned and sat in their seats. "Very reluctantly we will agree to the overtime terms, but it will only start from now. Any overtime that has been lost up until now stays lost."

Reg and Bob looked at each other and nodded their agreement. Then Bob said, "They want it in writing, Kim."

"That's fine, I will do that."

"No, they want it from the London office," Bob replied.

"They don't trust you," put in Reg. Bob looked sideways at his colleague.

"It's Saturday," said Arran, "no one is about."

"We know you have contact at all times. They want a board member to telex here stating everything we have agreed – today. And they will work tonight, tomorrow and carry on until it's complete, but they will stop at knocking off time tonight if they have not got it in writing."

"Okay," said Kim, standing up, "we will get that for you by this evening. Please go and tell the workers."

The two committeemen left the meeting room and walked down the corridor until out of earshot. They stopped and shook hands, and Bob said, "Can you believe what has just happened, Reg? We gave up on the overtime months ago, then out of the blue we get it. I can't believe it, can you?"

"I can only say your nose has grown by a foot, Bob English, with all the lies you told in there."

"Do you know what, Reg, the worrying thing is I really enjoyed putting the boot into Kim. It was long overdue." The two laughed and left the offices.

*

"I heard," said Bill as he and his roommate sat in the two armchairs in their room drinking tea, on their own for once, "that Benjamin had been told months ago that if he had to pay the overtime to keep the work going he could, and that it was really him who wanted to hold out."

"I haven't heard that but it would not surprise me at all. He's a controller, he has to be in charge."

"He lost some control today, didn't he?" replied Bill.

"He did. This time last week we had forgotten about the overtime row, then with the help of the weather and the welders we have come out on top, albeit a bit late for us. Unless we come back, that is," said Bob.

"I think it's great us giving them a bloody nose."

"Can you believe, Bill, we are down to our last few days in this shithole?"

"This time next week we will be on the *Kenya* bobbing up and down on our way home. Will you miss this place? It's been our home for what seems forever now," said Bill.

"I won't miss this place, but I will miss some of the people."

"Sam?" asked Bill.

"She's a workmate, Bill, that's all."

"You called her name out in your sleep the other night."

"WHAT!"

"Only joking, mate, not really."

"Piss off, Bill, it's not funny." Bob took a drink of his tea then continued. "The thing is I have never worked with a woman

278

before, and I didn't know what to think to start with, but the truth is it has been a real breath of fresh air hearing different views and not having big, hairy, smelly blokes next to you all day. She knows her stuff, I think that has impressed me more than anything. She just knows construction safety inside out, there's nothing you can tell her she does not know, and her ideas of where safety should go in our industry are mind-blowing. She is down at the Bailey bridge right now showing them how to do the work safely."

"You're in love, Bob."

"Oh, piss off." Bob got up. "I am off down there now to see how it's going."

"On our last Saturday night? We should be in the bar getting pissed."

"I told Sam I would pick her up."

"You *are* in love!" Bob grabbed his pillow off his bottom bunk and hit his roommate on the head with it.

*

Bob arrived at the Bailey bridge as it was starting to get dark. There were now many lighting towers set up illuminating the whole area. It was very noisy with all the engines running on the tower lights. The storm had started to abate. It had stopped raining about midday but the wind was still on the strong side. A fifty-ton mobile crane that was now standing in front of the bridge was working but stopping at times if the wind was gusting too much.

The nearest left-hand end of the bridge to the *Adventurer* which had collapsed had now been lifted back into position. Welding and bolting were in progress to fix it back to the ship and waiting behind the crane was a new support leg to replace the damaged one. The welders and fitters had been working on this all day. Sam was stood with Kim and Tony watching the work as Bob joined them.

"How's it going?" Bob asked as he walked up behind them. They all turned at once and a big smile came on both Sam and Bob's faces when they saw each other.

"Hi," she said to him. "It's going really well."

"They have done really well," Bob replied. "This time last night you would never have thought it would be back up."

"I must say," said Kim to Tony, "you and your men have really pulled out all the stops to get us where we are now."

"Thanks, Kim. Once the work is finished on fixing the bridge to the ship, and the tide has gone out which is starting now, the lorry will be lifted out then the scaffolders are going to fit a working platform around the damaged supporting leg so our men can work safely down there. They will burn the old section off, lift it out and then lift the new section in with the crane. We will weld it back in place and also weld new steel over the joints as these will be weak points. After that is done we will start on re-fixing the damaged guardrail on the bridge."

"Can that not be done at the same time as the other work is going on under it to save time?" asked Kim.

"Sam will not let us, Kim, and when she explained everything, how dangerous it would be, I totally agree with her. And I will say it to her face while she is here. Her input today regarding how the work should be carried out has been great. She told us which sequence the work should be carried out in, then identified the risks and how to avoid them, such as lads not working under others and falling objects, sparks etc."

"You will not be able to get your safety helmet off in a minute," smiled Bob to Sam.

"I have just done what I am paid for."

"And it sounds as if you have done a really good job, young lady. Well done," said Kim.

"Thank you, Kim."

"Think nothing of it. Now, you two," he pointed to Sam and Bob, "we have some parts which are really important to the plane landing next week. They will land in Stanley on Monday morning. Also, on that flight will be some documents that are really important and have to be signed for by two company representatives. I have given them your two names. Please get across there on Monday morning and get them picked up ASAP. I have to go. Goodnight." He turned and walked away.

Bob and Sam looked at each other with a smile and said at the same time, "A day out in Stanley!"

*

Bob's Land Rover was parked in an area near to the runway control centre. Ed had removed the packages they had picked up in

280

Stanley that morning and had taken them to the control centre. Bob and Sam were outside at the front of the Land Rover with their white safety helmets on. They had gone early to the capital that day, and while they knew the plane would not be there until early afternoon it had given the three of them time to have a walk around, and Sam had wanted to buy them both lunch in The Atlas which had been enjoyed very much before picking up the documents and packages. Sam had a look around the work which was in progress on the structure at the side of the control centre that would be offices for administration and had now returned to Bob.

"Sam?"

"Yes?"

"I go the day after tomorrow. I want to say something."

"Bob, don't say a word, let's get in the Rover." Sam got in her seat followed by Bob. "Continue please."

"Sam, even if this makes me look like a fool I am going to say it. Please forgive me in advance, but I am going to miss you so much."

"Me too, I feel the same."

"You do?"

"Yes, could you not tell?"

"No, I just thought it was me being soft, but you have helped me through these last month's so much."

"Bob, you have helped me so much, you have made things so much easier for me, and, more importantly," she took a deep breath, "been there when I needed help. You have supported me and always been there for me and always backed me up." There was silence as they looked into each other's eyes. It was then broken by Sam who said, "Can I kiss you, Mr English?"

"Yes, you may, Miss Crisp." They put their arms around each other, closed their eyes to kiss, and the peaks of their safety helmets clashed. This brought a laugh from both of them. They took each other's helmet off and dropped them on the floor of the Land Rover's cab then started again. This time their lips did meet.

"Bloody hell, that last box was so heavy." They snapped apart as Ed opened the rear door to the Land Rover. He threw his safety helmet into the back of the vehicle then came around to the driver's seat and got in. "Well they were pleased to get that lot. The top man there said it's all go for the plane to come in this

Thursday." Ed drove off and did not notice while he chatted away that there was not a word spoken between his two co-workers.

*

Work on the repairs to the Bailey bridge had continued throughout Saturday night and into Sunday morning, with workers taking turns to eat and have naps. It was about ten am on the Sunday morning when the first lorry rolled off the bridge with much needed equipment for the control centre. It was also in these areas that the workers were working almost twenty-four hours a day to be ready on time. For the last two days before the landing every available worker had been drafted to the runway and hangar area, mostly on clean-up duties for the areas which would be seen by VIPs. Ed, Sam and Bob could be seen on the last day with brushes in hands sweeping the hangar's apron.

*

"There it is, I can see it!" Ed pointed to a small dot in a clear blue sky.

"I can't see it," said Bob, as he, Ed and Sam stood beside their Land Rover that was parked on the road that ran adjacent to the runway along with many other workers who had come to this point, as only invited guests would be allowed to the hangar area. There was a token number of workers sent there for the world's cameras to see, but these three had not been asked along.

"I see it!" shouted Sam as she also pointed.

"Yes, so can I," said Bob. The workforce watched as the dot became bigger and bigger and the wings could be made out. When the plane passed them all the workers took off their safety helmets and waved them in the air and cheered out loud, but this was drowned out by the roar of the plane's large jet engines.

*

Bob did think he was being taken to the *Kenya* in the Land Rover the next morning by both Ed and Sam, so he was surprised to see just Sam waiting for him as he came out with his cases and bags. As they put his things in the rear door he had a bag which he gave to Sam and said, "This is for you." He held it out to her. "I got one each for my two girls and got an extra one for you."

"Can I look?" Without waiting for an answer Sam pulled out a two-foot high soft toy penguin. "I love it," she said as she grabbed Bob and gave him a big hug and kissed him on the cheek. They drove the seven miles to the waiting ship almost without talking at all with Sam at the wheel.

"Can we pull over before we get to the ship please, Sam, I have something else for you."

"I have something for you also." They drove past the ship and parked out of the way between two containers at the start of the Lay Down Area.

"It's now or never," said Bob as he pulled some paper out of his inside jacket pocket and said, "There's a chance we may never see each other again, Sam. I have written this, it's another poem. Shall I read it?"

"No, no, let me, please." Bob handed it to Sam. She opened it and started to read out loud.

What is Love?

What is love? It can take many forms.
Love as a mother, father, sister or brother.
It can be something we enjoy, playing golf, driving our car, going fishing.
Or even wearing that old hat or coat that we love.
It could be for that favourite place,
It may be for a drink, a wine or food we love to taste.
We mostly think of love for another person, again many forms this may take.
To be in love with a person can be one of the greatest things in our life.
To have that person on your mind all day, to be on another planet when you think of them, talk
to or see them.
You want to do things for them, be with them, care for them, make them feel safe.
If that feeling is returned, it can put you on cloud nine.
But to feel this way and it's not retuned; can make you feel very low.

283

If you have told them expecting great news back and it does not come, no bigger a fool you could only feel.

Is it embarrassment, it seems like one is wearing one's heart on their sleeve.

In some cases, a person can fall in love with another very fast.

For others it has to grow, and that can take years.

The worst kind of love, must be for another whom we cannot tell, never let them know how we feel about them.

Love should be a thing of joy, something for us to behold.

But there again a person who has never made a mistake, is a person who has never done anything.

Love can take many forms; I hope you feel one, at some time or another.

Bob English.

January 1985.

The two sat in the Land Rover looking at each other and Bob said, "There an old saying, Sam,

God puts some people in our lives for a reason."

Sam replied, *"and some for a season."*

Then they both said together, *"and others for life."*

Then, as if instinctively, they threw their arms around each other and started a long, passionate kiss. When they stopped Sam said, "God, I am going to miss you, Mr English." She wiped tears from her eyes. "Come on, you have got to go and check in."

"You said you had something for me, Miss Crisp?" said Bob as he wiped tears from his own eyes.

"Oh yes," Sam took a small white envelope out of her inside jacket pocket and gave it to Bob and said, "Please don't open it until you are on the ship, Bob. And I am going to call the penguin Percy, Percy the Penguin." They kissed once more then Sam drove them towards the ship.

*

Bob stood on the deck of the *Kenya* with the note in his hand that Sam had given him. She stood on the deck of the *Adventurer* facing him as the ship started to move away from the jetty waving

284

to him. Bob waved back. He then opened the small white envelope and took out the folded pink notepaper. It read:

Dear Bob,

I want to thank you for everything you have done for me. You have helped me so much and I know you made things a lot easier for me here. Thank you for being such a good and loyal friend, I have really enjoyed our time together.

Thank you again so much, and please come back.

Lots of love,

Sam,

xxx.

PS. Please, please, please come back!

Bob looked up to see the distance between them growing by the second. Sam put the fingers of her right hand to her lips, kissed them, then blew the kiss across the water. The kiss hit Bob in the heart like Cupid's arrow.

The Finish.

From Start to Finish.

Many a mile we had sailed from land,
With the task ahead, we may have hoped God was at hand.

We had left our family on a tearful day,
All because we wanted to earn some pay.

Long days at sea, no sign of life,
Made one think of family and wife.

We were heading for a southern shore,
Where not long before had seen battle roar.

Men had come and men had died,
Now it was our turn, no time to hide.

Would we make it or would we fail?
That we would find out, as we took to the trail.

The first day that I saw that windswept land,
I thought to myself, this isn't so grand.

Land before that had only seen cattle and sheep,
Now they would have giant tracks running past their feet.

But there was work to be done, no time to spare,
"Let's build roads," the foreman said with a glare.

Virgin soil was turned by day,
Then we sat and drunk some of our pay.

We would laugh and cheer we all looked pleased,
But deep inside we had other needs.

But those thoughts had to be put to one side for now,
As there was an airfield to be built, and they said, "we knew how."

Some days were warm, some very cold,
But that cutting wind was bound to make you look old.

We built a camp so that we could all live together,
But some of those men would bring you to the end of your tether.

And as for some, was it their first time away from home?
Poor things looked like a dog that had just lost its bone.

Then we had the suited men, who said they would make us rich,
Well let's just say, they got up to some dirty tricks.

"Give us all you have got," they would say,
"We will do things for you, you won't forget this day."

But empty promises were soon forgot,
They were just happy to get their lot.

Summer was gone, when the snows they came,
And my word chilled feet can give much pain.

Long cold days and freezing nights,
The end of this job seemed well out of sight.

So, work we did, and time went fast,

We looked to the future and forgot the past.

But the pressure was on, the job had to be done,
There wasn't time to have much fun.

Mental and physical pain was felt by some,
While others looked on as if they were dumb.

As time got nearer we worked day and night,
Things had to be done for that incoming flight.

When toil was done, the plane it landed,
"Let's drink to success," the glass was handed.

"You've done a good job," the boss said with a grin,
But did he expect us to take all that in?

We had done as we had been asked; it was time to go,
Bags were packed, this was the end of our show.

There were many memories none to be forgotten,
Some were good, but others rotten.

The island had seen change, let's even hope gain,
But let's be fair, it will never be the same.

We got our pay, it was time to be jolly,
But would any of this ever have happened, but for one man's folly?

TW.

March 1985.

The End.

Tom Wheeler

The Author was born in London UK in 1952, he now resides in Berkshire. Leaving school at the age of 15 in 1968, he joined the construction industry, where he continued to work for fifty years until retiring on the 1st January 2019. For the last twenty years of his career, Tom worked as a site manager, earning a diploma in construction site management.

Tom's career in the Construction industry was varied and vast, encompassing working overseas in the Falkland Islands after the Falklands war, followed by working in North Africa. In addition to the corporate side of the Construction industry, Tom also volunteered in Namibia South West Africa in 2002 for a charity building two classrooms and a store for a school. He is still heavily involved in multiple charities.

In his spare time, Tom is a travel enthusiast and has a keen interest in history, which includes being a member of the London Historians and the Construction History Society. He is particularly interested in his own family genealogy, which he has been researching for over fifteen years. He is also a sports fan, notably attending twelve advents at the 2012 Olympics in London. But football is his biggest passion and attends as many England Football away games as possible. He also enjoys all genres of music and films.

Tom is married with four grown up children, seven grandchildren and one great granddaughter.